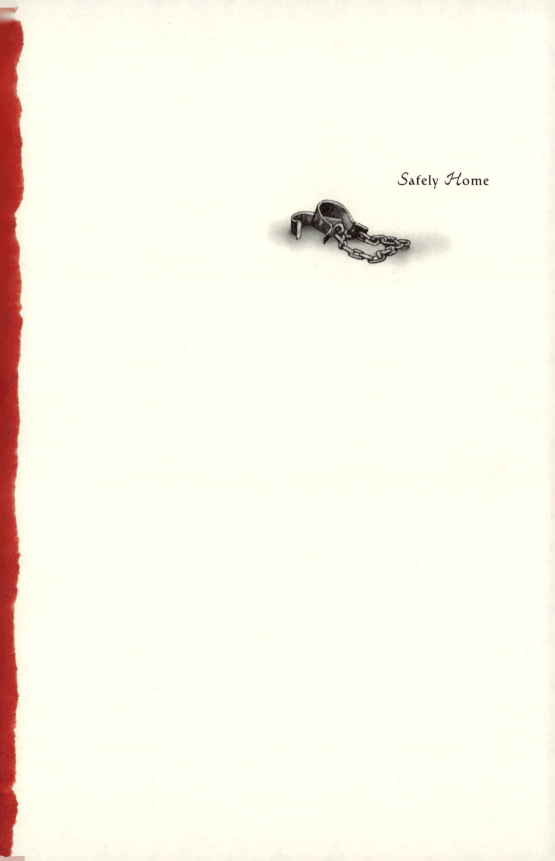

Safely Home

Safely Home

RANDY ALCORN

TYNDALE HOUSE PUBLISHERS, INC., WHEATON, ILLINOIS

Visit Tyndale's exciting Web site at www.tyndale.com

Calligraphy written by John Cheng.

Designed by Jenny Swanson

Edited by Curtis H. C. Lundgren

Library of Congress Cataloging-in-Publication Data

Alcorn, Randy C.
  Safely home / by Randy C. Alcorn.
    p. cm.
  ISBN 0-8423-3791-1
  1. Americans—China—Fiction. 2. Businessmen—Fiction. 3. China—Fiction.   I. Title.
PS3551.L292 S24 2001
813'.54—dc21   2001002235

Printed in the United States of America

06 05 04 03 02 01
9 8 7 6 5 4 3 2 1

Dedication

To Graham Staines,
who left his home in Australia to serve lepers
in India for thirty-four years.

To Philip Staines (age ten) and Timothy Staines (age six),
who at half past midnight on January 23, 1999,
as their father held his arms around them,
were burned to death by a mob in India;
murdered because of Whom they knew and served.

To Gladys Staines,
who continues to minister to lepers and who said to all India,
"I am not bitter or angry. I have one great desire: that each citizen
of this country should establish a personal relationship with
Jesus Christ, who gave His life for their sins."

To Esther Staines,
Graham and Gladys's daughter (then age thirteen),
who said, "I praise the Lord that He found my father
worthy to die for Him."

To the hundreds of men, women,
and children killed for Christ each day,
ignored by the world but watched by the eyes of heaven—
those of whom the world is not worthy.

Acknowledgments

*J*CANNOT name some of the people who have been most helpful in researching and writing this book. If I did, it could jeopardize their safety or opportunity to minister.

Special thanks to Sau-Wing Lam, CH, CCH, JM, MJ, PE, JG, and SEP for their expert advice on Chinese culture, geography, and language. It was a long and tedious process attempting to standardize Chinese spellings in their proper Pinyin forms. This involved wading through various Mandarin, Cantonese, Hong Kongese, Taiwanese, and Americanized spellings of Chinese words. Certainly my own experience of seven days in China didn't begin to qualify me.

Even the experts sometimes disagreed on spellings. Finally, I had to make the call based on the best information I could acquire. My heartfelt thanks to Sau-Wing (who even sent me recordings so I could pronounce the words properly, at least in my head) and MJ for their prompt and exacting replies to my endless e-mail inquiries. They receive credit for the times I got it right, and I take full responsibility for the rest.

Thanks to Doreen Button for her input on an early manuscript. For passing on relevant materials or giving me technical advice, thanks to Tom Dresner, Ted Walker, Barry Arnold, Bob Maddox, Diane Meyer, Jim and Erin Seymour, Doug Gabbert, and Diane Vavra. Thanks to Bonnie Hiestand and Penny Dorsey at Eternal Perspective Ministries. Thanks to Kathy Norquist for reading over every word of the final manuscript and giving valuable input. And thanks to Janet Albers for her excellent proofreading.

Thanks to my wife, Nanci, my best friend, who brings such great joy to my life and patiently put up with me when I was lost in this project. Also, my deepest appreciation for my daughters, Karina and Angie, who are of help in all that I do. I'm thankful for our soon-to-be sons-in-law, Dan Franklin and Dan Stump, two godly men whom God has matched with two godly women. May you honor the King as you love and lead our precious girls. Also, I want to acknowledge Melissa Allen, who asked if she could be named in one of my books.

Thanks to my friend Ron DiCianni for his painting *Safely Home* and to Steve Green for his song "Safely Home," both of which center on a martyr going home to heaven. In a sense, this book, *Safely Home,* is part three of an artistic trilogy. I deeply appreciate Ron DiCianni's heart for the persecuted and his eagerness to join me in dedicating the book's royalties to stand with them. While writing, I listened frequently not only to Steve Green's "Safely Home" but to his song "The Faithful," with its haunting and triumphant expression of the words of Tertullian spoken in the second century: "The blood of the martyrs is the seed of the church."

I'm indebted to C. H. Kang's and Ethel Nelson's *The Discovery of Genesis: How the Truths of Genesis Were Found Hidden in the Chinese Language.* I gleaned from *Understanding China* and various books by Chinese writers, including *Thirty Years in a Red House: A Memoir of Childhood and Youth in Communist China* by Xiao Di Zhu.

I drew from accounts of actual events recorded in *By Their Blood; China: The Hidden Miracle; The Coming Influence of China; Their Blood Cries Out;* and various biographies of Hudson Taylor, as well as *Christian History* magazine. I've also gleaned from the publications of Voice of the Martyrs, The Bible League, Overseas Missionary Fellowship, and Intercessors for China, as well as news accounts in many newspapers and periodicals, including *World* magazine and Chuck Colson's *BreakPoint.*

While doing background research on China, I "happened" (in the providence of God) to read the galleys of my friend Davis Bunn's excellent novel *The Great Divide,* which prompted me to do deeper research into the Laogai. This research contributed to my portrayals of Chinese prisons.

To say the least, there are countless religious and political sensitivities that this book steps into. For any I inadvertently offend, my apologies and also my request for understanding and perhaps openness to another point of view.

Thanks to many at Tyndale House Publishers, who were wonderfully supportive of the vision of this book. These include my editor, Curtis Lundgren, who pored over the manuscript and offered some excellent advice. Also, Jan Stob, Becky Nesbitt, Danielle Crilly, Mavis Sanders, Sue Lerdal, Mary Keeley, Travis Thrasher, Julie Huber, Dan Balow, and many others who have worked on various matters related to the book. Thanks to Ken Petersen, who offered valuable input on the story idea before I started writing.

My biggest thanks goes to Ron Beers, publisher at Tyndale House. His enthusiasm for this book, every step of the way, both encouraged and amazed me. My heartfelt gratitude to Ron and Tyndale House for their passion for Christ, vision for his kingdom, and eagerness to get behind *Safely Home.*

I'm indebted to the faithful prayer warriors who lifted me up in the writing and revision of *Safely Home.* If lives are shaped for eternity through this book, their prayers will have played a central part.

Finally, I acknowledge my constant companion through long and sometimes lonely hours spent on this book. He is persecuted when any one of his followers is persecuted. He takes personally every act of dishonor as well as every act of kindness done to his disciples. Thank you, King Jesus, for your loyalty to us and to every one of our suffering brothers and sisters. Thank you for promising a kingdom where righteousness will reign and joy will be the air we breathe. May that kingdom come quickly—and until it does, may you find us faithful.

Note from the Author

THE CITY I've called Pushan is fictitious. As far as I know, there is no Pushan in the area I've described. If there is, I've never been there and have no knowledge of it. While many things in this book have actually happened in one way or another, I have made up the story. Still, I have attempted to keep it authentic and true to life in as many details as possible. Nearly all my characters are fictitious. Some are composites of several real people. Whenever I was thinking of someone in particular I changed his name and life details so it would be impossible to identify him.

If you, the reader, haven't done so already, I suggest you pull back the dust jacket of this book and look at Ron DiCianni's painting *Safely Home*. This beautiful work of art served as an inspiration for this story.

1

*T*HREE MEN watched intently as peculiar events occurred, one right after the other, on opposite sides of the globe.

"What's happening?" asked the first, tall and dark skinned.

"I don't know," replied the man with long black hair. "But wheels are turning, aren't they?"

"Things appear synchronized," said the third man, compact and broad shouldered. "A pattern is emerging. Something great seems poised to happen. Something else lurks in the shadows. It seeks to devour the greatness before it is born."

"Two destinies are converging. But neither suspects it."

The tall one pointed toward a great palace in the distance. "He searches to find the right man for the right hour. Is this the hour? Is this the man?"

"And if so, *which* man? Or both? We see far more clearly than they do. But still our minds are too small to figure it all out."

"The soil was tilled and the seeds planted twenty years ago," the broad-shouldered man said. "No. A hundred years, at least. Now we will see what fruit the vine produces, or whether it will wither and die."

"Hanging in the balance are not just two men," said the longhaired man, "but two families, perhaps two nations."

"Indeed, two worlds."

"The loss could be immense. Or the gain immeasurable." His voice trembled.

"We must watch closely as the tapestry is woven . . . or as it unravels."

"We must do more than watch." The tall man reached out one hand to the other two, who grasped it firmly, the muscles of their forearms taut. They now looked like warriors.

"The stakes are high."

"Higher than they can possibly imagine. Higher than we ever dreamed when we walked that world."

"Somebody's got to make the tough calls," Ben Fielding muttered. "And I don't see anyone else volunteering."

He picked up the phone from his oversized mahogany desk at the far side of his window office on the thirty-ninth floor of the U.S. Bancorp Tower. It was a bright September morning, and Oregon was the best place in the world to live in the fall, but he had more important things to do than admire the view.

"Doug? We need to talk."

"Sure," said Doug Roberts from his desk in the sales department. "What's up?"

"I have a management team meeting right now. Might take an hour. I'll call you in when it's over. Be sure you're available. I've got a conference call before lunch, and I won't have much time."

"Okay, Ben. But what do you want to talk about?"

"I'll call you when I'm ready." Ben still gripped the phone tightly three seconds after he'd finished talking. Finally he put it down.

Doug was his cousin, his mom's sister's son. They'd grown up on the East Coast, a few hundred miles apart. They'd spent most holidays together, wrestling in the snow or exploring the beach or playing Parcheesi in front of the fire. Those were the days . . . when life was simple, and loyalties easily maintained.

Now they both worked in Portland, Oregon, on the opposite seaboard, for Getz International, a leading-edge multinational corporation. As a department head fifteen years ago, Ben had offered Doug a sales job, and he'd jumped at it. They were both young and hungry back then.

Doug had so much potential. Why had he forced his hand? Once he'd been an asset to Ben. Now he'd become a liability.

That Doug was family made it messy. Ben would probably have to skip the holiday gatherings this year. Doug had backed him into a corner. He had to send a clear message to all the employees—Ben Fielding doesn't tolerate insubordination, and he doesn't play favorites.

"Martin's in the boardroom." His secretary's voice over the intercom yanked Ben back to the moment. "They're ready for you."

"On my way."

Ben stopped in front of the mirror on the back side of his office door, ran a comb through his hair, then straightened his Shanghai silk tie. He went to the door of the conference room, took a deep breath, and calculated his entrance. He walked in briskly but not too hurried. He stood tall and smiled pleasantly without grinning, a smile he'd practiced in the mirror. Dressed in a black Armani with a boxy Italian fit, Ben Fielding was a self-made picture of style, poise, and competence. There were eight men in the room, and every eye was on him.

"Hey, Ben," Martin said, "we're talking about that dream you spelled out for us ten years ago—selling one of everything to a country of 1.2 billion people!" Suddenly Martin's broad smile evaporated. "Travis here and a couple of the team have voiced some concerns."

Ben raised his eyebrows and stared at Travis.

"The situation's not stable," Travis said, looking at his Palm Pilot instead of Ben. "I don't trust that government."

"China won't be bullied by anyone," Ben said. "That's what Hong Kong was all about. And Macao. They won't let 'foreign devils' control their destiny. What's theirs is theirs."

"And what isn't theirs eventually will be," Travis said.

Ben shrugged. "I'll say it again. If one nation dictates everybody's future, it won't be America. It'll be China. The sooner everybody comes to terms with that, the better we can position ourselves."

"One thing's for sure," Martin said; "there's not another semiconductor or microchip company with our access to Beijing and Shanghai. Between Ben and Jeffrey, we've established one major beachhead."

Martin Getz, showing straight white teeth in a smile so big it drew in everyone, was CEO of Getz International. His father had started the company in 1979, just before the computer revolution changed the world.

"Okay, okay, guys. What's the report on the Shanghai factory?"

"All indicators are positive," Jeffrey said. "Production's still going up. With socialism loosening its grip and workers getting more for their labor, there's a new Chinese work ethic. Without all those paranoid safety and antipollution regulations, they get done in a week what takes us a month—and their Q.A. tallies are better."

"I don't want to hear this," Johnny said, his suit lapels flaring as he leaned back, playfully covering his ears. "There are certain things lawyers shouldn't know."

"We can't impose American standards on them," Ben said. It was a mantra he'd repeated at many team meetings. "And even if we could, we don't have the right. But we can demand the highest product standards. And we're getting great results. These people are bright, smart, eager to work. They don't know about unions; they're just grateful to make a living and be able to buy a refrigerator, a TV, maybe even a computer."

Ben's confident voice commanded attention. There was a presence about him. Martin was the boss, but Ben was the brains and energy. Everyone knew it.

"China's still our fastest growing market?" Martin asked.

"In another few years they'll be our biggest customer—period," Ben said. "China has a skyrocketing economy with hundreds of millions of residences that'll add computers and a dozen other electronic devices in the next ten years. Dayton's assembling the network cards in Mexico. They'll ship direct from there to our joint-venture partnerships in-country and bypass China's trade restrictions. It brings the end product cost down and gets it into more hands. Getz benefits inside China; then we score again when it's shipped back here at a fraction of the cost, and we sell it through traditional distribution channels. Our competitors' heads will be spinning. In the next few years they'll be eating our dust."

"They'll never catch up," Martin said, all teeth again.

"I wish I shared your confidence," Travis said. "Seems to me we're walking on a minefield. It's a shaky economy. Human rights issues, over-building in Shanghai . . . not to mention Beijing's ability to pull the plug on anyone for any reason."

"It's capitalists and communists scratching each other's backs," Ben said. "Sure, they've got problems. They know the state-owned enterprises are inefficient, banks are folding, and pollution's terrible. There's still a lot of trial and error, but they're learning fast. I've been saying it since my first trip to Beijing—China's our future, guys. It offers us the most cost-effective partnerships on the planet. And it's a dream market come true."

"Just make sure they keep needing us, Ben," Martin said. "You too, Jeffrey. We don't want them to get any ideas of doing it on their own."

"Oh, they've got the ideas, alright," Ben said. "They're swimming in U.S. and Japanese technology, and they can imitate it like nobody else. Give them a decade, and they'll be improving it. Eventually, they'll be our strongest competitors. We'll be racing to keep up. But meanwhile, we've got the edge. Russia couldn't handle free enterprise, but these people can. Their work ethic gets stronger every day, while ours gets weaker. Another six to eight years, and they'll be putting America to shame."

Martin looked at Ben with undisguised admiration. "Ten years ago when you told us you could bring in millions of dollars if you studied Mandarin on company time, I thought you'd gone crazy. But it worked. Boy, did it work! They trust us—you and Jeffrey, especially. You speak their language, know their culture. That's our edge." Martin stood up. "And I want to shore up that edge. I've been chewing on an idea since that Fortune 500 CEO think tank I attended in Chicago a couple of months ago."

Martin looked around the room the way he always did before announcing an idea he was particularly proud of. Several of the men, including Ben, braced themselves. Nobody ever quite knew what Martin would come up with next.

"I'd like to send Ben or Jeffrey to spend maybe six weeks living among and talking with typical Chinese citizens, the type that might work in our factories and eventually buy our products. Ben, what about that old room-mate of yours from college? He lives in China, right? A teacher, isn't he?"

Ben nodded. Li Quan's youthful face invaded his mind and infused it with bittersweet memories. It was just like Martin to spring this on him with everybody watching. As it began to register, it didn't seem a good idea at all. It had been twenty years since he . . .

"Getting inside the mind of the typical consumer would help our sales strategy and deepen our reservoir for those Chinese advertising cam-paigns that marketing's been talking about. And it would be great PR on both sides of the ocean. We'd be the company that sent a Mandarin-speaking VP to live with Chinese nationals to see what they're like, to learn what they need. It's the 'we care about the common man' angle. It would impress the Chinese, our board, stockholders—everybody. A big image-booster for Getz. The advertising potential is enormous. Ben or Jeffrey could end up in a prime-time commercial sitting next to some Chinese guy grinning at his computer!"

The other members of the management team looked at each other to see which way the wind would blow. Then they all stared at Ben. He hesi-tated. But when Martin felt this strongly about an idea, it nearly always happened. You might as well go with him and look brilliant and loyal. Everyone nodded.

"Anyway, more on that later," Martin said. "Let's hit the agenda. Our third-quarter profits are going to blow them away. When this hits Wall Street, things are going to fly. Hold on to your hats, boys. Your profit shares could increase ten percent overnight."

An hour later Ben walked out of the conference room, glad-handing his associates and feeling the warm rush of competitive adrenaline. As he came out the door, he saw Doug Roberts standing by a photocopy machine. His stomach churned. He looked at his watch.

Conference call in six minutes. "Doug," he called, "meeting'll have to wait until Monday morning. My office, 7:30."

"Sure. But what are we going to—"

"7:30 Monday. My office. I've got a conference call."

Ben strode past his secretary, Jen, and into his office. He shut the door behind him and flopped down on the plush visitors' couch.

Until their lives took different turns, Doug had been not only family, but a close friend. Ben knew he couldn't afford to think of him that way anymore. And if Doug still considered Ben a friend, well . . . he wouldn't much longer.

2

IS THIS the day I die?

Li Quan asked himself the familiar question as he wiped sleep from his eyes. Why couldn't he be courageous, like his father and great-grandfather?

He lit a candle and watched Chan Minghua sleeping, slight and vulnerable. *Minghua* meant "bright flower." She was that and more to Li Quan.

Pulling himself off the thin pad he used for a bed, Quan walked barefoot on the frigid cement floor to the cot four feet away. He knelt down beside eight-year-old Li Shen, resting his forehead against the crown of his only son's head. He reached out to the child's pudgy hands, then touched a finger to his pouty lips. How could this thick, round boy have come from birdlike Ming?

Is this the day I die?

He'd asked himself the question every day since he was Shen's age. Every day the answer had been no. But his father had taught him, "One day the answer will be yes, and on that day you must be ready."

It was on a Sunday his great-grandfather Li Manchu had been beheaded. And it was also on a Sunday his father, Li Tong, lying in a beaten lump, had died in prison. Here in the cold predawn outside Pushan, it was another Sunday.

"It is time?" Minghua whispered, her voice a feather falling upon silk. Candle flame dancing in her brown eyes, she looked as she had ten years ago, at their wedding in Shanghai.

Quan kissed her delicate forehead, ashamed that he, a poor and lowly man, was so unworthy of her. Already in this short night he'd dreamed again that he held her wounded body—Ming's life running red through his fingers in a dark rain.

They moved swiftly, silently, performing their 2:00 A.M. Sunday ritual. Ming awoke Li Shen and gave him a little bowl of sticky rice, holding up his yawning head.

Quan wrapped a gray blanket around his neck, then squeezed into his dark green parka. Stuffing one hundred and forty yuan into his trouser pocket, he stepped outside and strapped a bundle to the back of his bicycle. He knotted the bundle, double-tying and double-checking the knots. Ming and sleepy-eyed Shen followed, coats bulging like overstuffed cushions.

Quan positioned Shen on the seat in front of him. The boy put his hands on the bars and closed his eyes, head nodding. Ming pedaled beside them, a silent shadow. Face stinging, Quan watched the quarter moon cast shadows on the dormant rice fields. He wished there were no moon—its light made the ride easier but more dangerous. He preferred safety over ease.

The road of frozen mud cut between buttresses of naked hills. Even here, ten kilometers outside Pushan, an unnatural silvery dust floated on the wind. He felt the grit on his tongue and spit it out. For a moment the air was God's air, fresh and clean, but then the burning smell of factories assaulted him again.

Quan bounced over hard ruts, pressing tightly against Li Shen. Seeing shadows ahead, he instinctively began the rehearsal. "Our son is sick," he said to the wind. "We are taking him to a friend's for medicine."

Was that a glint of light behind the tangle of boughs and dead leaves? A policeman holding a lantern? He held his breath, the corners of his eyes freezing shut.

No. The shadows were fence posts. Li Quan hung his head, wishing he were a brave man who did not whisper lies into the wind.

The three spoke nothing lest the silence, once pierced, would bleed on them, as it had before.

After four kilometers dark clouds rolled in, as if an artist were suddenly changing his mood on a canvas. The moon hid from the coming storm. They'd have to face a squall on the ride home, Quan thought. That might be better—storms kept curious eyes indoors.

"Slow," Quan said to Ming, as they wobbled blindly onward, the ruts herding them, sky so low now it brushed his face.

At seven kilometers, he saw white wisps of smoke rising from a chimney. A welcome sight. But if he could see it, so could others. He pushed down his fear to that hollow place inside.

They got off their bicycles and quickly walked them behind Ho Lin's house, making no sound. They leaned them against the dark side, hidden in the shadows, by the chicken coop. Quan brushed his hand over other bicycles, counting them. Fourteen.

He walked to the back door, knowing they'd crossed the line of no return. From this moment all excuses for being out in the night were futile.

The door opened. *"Ni hao,"* Quan said. "How are you?"

"Ping an—peace to you," old Ling Ho replied, a childlike smile stretching his tight, dull skin in the candlelight. He gestured toward two large pots of tea, hovered over by his wife, Aunt Mei, whom Quan's mother always called "Fifth Sister." Mei smiled sweetly, reminding him of his mother. She bowed her head. Quan wanted the tea, but since he and his family seemed to be the last to arrive, he ushered Ming and Shen forward.

Quan nodded and returned smiles to the twenty others, especially the three at the rear. He regretted his smiles were forced and nervous. The Li family sat on a backless bench, coats on, leaning into each other's warmth.

The dull luminescence cast an eerie hue over the Spartan one-room house, bare but for a bench, some chairs, a bed, and one hearty bonsai, a dwarfed juniper Mei managed to keep alive. When the church had been smaller, with ten of them, they'd sat in a circle, but now they had four small rows, the last being the bed's edge.

Zhou Jin stood up, eyelids heavy but eyes sharp. His upper teeth protruded in a yellow smile, distinguishing him from most of the wary prune-faced men of Mao's generation. The draft was a wind upon Zhou Jin's wispy hair, a wind that stirred the room, then came out of the old man's lips.

"Zhu, wo men gan xie ni feng fu de zhu fu. Lord, we give you thanks for your abundant blessing."

"Xiexie, thank you," someone murmured.

"Xiexie," Ming said. Whispers of thanks erupted around the room.

Yin Chun, Jin's wife, carefully handed him a treasure wrapped in linen. He unwrapped it gently. He turned pages with a light touch, then read:

It was by faith that Abraham obeyed when God called him to leave home and go to another land that God would give him as his inheritance. He went without knowing where he was going. And even when he reached the land God promised him, he lived there by faith—for he was like a foreigner, living in a tent. And so did Isaac and Jacob, to whom God gave the same promise. Abraham did this because he was confidently looking forward to a city with eternal foundations, a city designed and built by God.

This had been one of the favorite passages of Quan's father, Li Tong. He remembered the old man's face, the look of longing in his eyes as he would recite the verses. Quan also remembered how embarrassed he'd been that his parents were so ignorant, so uneducated and naive. He squirmed in his seat, the joy of the words eclipsed by the memory of his transgressions.

All these came to their end in faith, not having had the heritage; but having seen it with delight far away, they gave witness they were wanderers and strangers, not of this earth. For those who say such things make it clear they are searching for a country of their own. If they had been thinking of the country from which they went out, they would have had chances of turning back. But instead, they were longing for a better country—a heavenly country. And so it is no shame to God to be named as their God; for he has prepared a city for them.

Hearing the ancient words of Shengjing filled Quan's heart with sweetness and sadness.

"This world is not our home," Zhou Jin whispered to his flock. Everyone leaned forward to hear, as thirsty men lean forward to put their lips in a mountain stream. "Yesu says, 'There are many rooms in my Father's home, and I am going to prepare a place for you. If this were not so, I would tell you plainly. When everything is ready, I will come and get you, so you will always be with me where I am.'"

Groans and yearnings, arising from soulish depths, filled the room.

When Jin finished reading, he handed the Bible back to his wife. She covered it in the linen cloth, as if wrapping a body for burial or a treasure for safekeeping.

It was bold to have Shengjing here, Quan thought, and bold that he and three others had brought their Bibles too. He'd been at house churches where people wrote out Scripture portions for the meetings; then the pastor would collect the handwritten copies and put them together to read the complete text. This way, if police interrupted the meeting, no Bible would be lost.

Pastor Zhou Jin gazed at the church, his children. "Remembering where our true home is will help us today as we speak of light and momentary troubles, which achieve in us an eternal weight of glory."

As he said the word *glory,* lightning flashed in the eastern sky. Moments later God's voice shook the earth; then his tears fell from heaven.

Quan felt a hand on his shoulder, chilling him. He turned to see Wu Le, who'd been coming only six weeks. Quan didn't know him. He smiled nervously as Le's palsied fingers, covered with thin white hairs, passed forward a worn hymnal, paper so thin Quan could read the words two pages back. The church sang—too loudly, Quan thought—"Yesu, we praise your name forever. . . ."

Is this the day?

Quan's great-grandfather had been murdered as a young pastor. Quan's grandfather, Li Wen, then eight years old—Shen's age—had witnessed the execution. A vivid image of his decapitation had haunted Quan's dreams all his life. Wen's son, Li Tong, was Quan's father—also a pastor, sentenced to prison during the cultural revolution. One day, after a beating, he didn't get up. Quan's smiling mother became a pastor's weeping widow, and shy, bookish Quan became the object of cruel taunts.

The pastor's voice drew him back. "Sister Wu Xia has tuberculosis. Brother Wang An is in the hospital. They do not know what is wrong. Zhou Jin has many aches and pains," he said of himself. "I know what is wrong with me. I am an old man!" They laughed.

"Some of our people suffer not from illness or age," Zhou Jin said, "but from persecution. Yesu said he was hated for being who he was, and his servants will be too. He said, 'Unless a kernel of wheat falls to the ground and dies, it remains only a single seed. But if it dies, it produces many seeds.'"

After thirty minutes of prayer, craggy-faced Zhou Jin sat down in an old wicker chair, reading verses slowly, leaning forward. Specters from the flickering candles cut across his ancient brow. He spoke each word with the gentle obstinacy of a long obedience. "'Whoever serves me must follow me. . . . My Father will honor the one who serves me.'"

Quan could never look at Zhou Jin without thinking of his own father. The old man raised his arms, exposing red, callous wrists. The sight stabbed Quan. Teachers and students in the communist school had ridiculed him because his father's faith made him a "public enemy." Quan's Baba had been capped a counterrevolutionary, in contrast to the heroic "revolutionaries," who practiced strict conformity to the Chairman's social order. Quan vividly remembered the posters put on their front door. One read "Lover of Foreigners," another "Reeducate these Poisonous Snakes!" In his mind's eye he could still see them clearly, the precise colors and flourishes of the characters.

As a young man Quan had tried to disbelieve in God. He never wanted to stand out or be noticed. He'd tried to embrace the ideals of the Party. He'd longed to blend into the dark green background of modern China. To this day, he wouldn't wear reds and yellows and bright colors. Quan had even joined the student Red Guards to deflect the shame of his parents' stubborn refusal to comply with the demands of the new China. While all the other boys' fathers took them fishing, Quan's father was in jail. His father had said many times, "One day I will take you to the Great Wall." He hadn't. He died. Li Quan had never shaken off the disappointment of his father's unfulfilled promise.

Quan had tried hard not to be a Christian. He had succeeded too, until he went to college in America. But one day his big American roommate, Ben Fielding, had invited him to a meeting of Christians on the Harvard campus. His questions and doubts and resentments fell in the face of truth. The faith that had been his mother's and father's became, for the first time, his own, far away in that foreign land where he had studied to become a college professor. Though they had long since lost touch with one another, Quan thought of Ben often and prayed for him daily.

"Zhu Yesu says, 'No one who puts his hand to the plow and looks back is fit for service in the kingdom of God.'"

It was still coal-black outside, 3:30 A.M. Curtains were drawn. Quan rubbed his earlobe and the rough, spidery five-inch scar on his neck. Church must end before the prying eyes of sunrise.

Old Zhou Jin began singing a hymn Quan had heard and reluctantly sung many times since childhood: "One day I'll die for the Lord."

Is this the day?

As the church sang, Zhou Jin raised his hands again. Li Quan rehearsed every scar on his father's back and arms, the scars he used to run his fingers over, before Father went to prison the last time. His father would be Zhou Jin's age. If only . . .

"Bie dong!"

Li Quan stiffened at the shouted command not to move. The voice behind him rang with the authority of the Gong An Ju, the Public Security Bureau.

Quan swept his left arm over Shen, pulling him close against him and Ming.

With a quick glance Quan said to them both, "Look down. Be still." Quan had learned the drill long ago, hiding in house church under his mother's skirt. Pushing his eyes sideways and glancing through narrow lids, to his left he saw two green uniforms. To his right, two more.

"Do not move," commanded a harsh baritone voice from behind.

At the front right a young policeman held a Type 54 pistol. Quan had seen one close up. It had been waved in his face, then struck against his skull. Mao had said it—government by the barrel of a gun.

Suddenly, Quan's right elbow was banged by the heavy butt of a Type 56 assault rifle, the PSB's version of the Russian AK-47. Not only China's antiforeign politics, but its weapons had come from a foreign power. But police seldom carried weapons, at least not like this.

Quan's head remained bowed, but he peeked up so he could barely see the PSB captain standing three feet in front of him. Narrow-waisted, with oarsman's shoulders, he reminded Quan of a giant wasp. The man stared at the twenty-four believers with the pinched eyes of cold assessment. A three-inch scar, much more prominent than Quan's, rough sewn in his burlap skin, hung over his right eyebrow. Quan didn't recognize him— too many police were transferred in and out. Besides, he never took a close look at PSB, for fear they would look back.

The captain was dressed sharply in a green uniform, straight black necktie, pants neatly creased, cap exactly positioned. The only imperfection was the slight tilt of his shoulder badge. This minor flaw comforted Quan, a reminder the government machinery was not perfect.

Scarbrow raised his hand, fingers pointing inward like gray claws. He grabbed Zhou Jin's shoulder, then pushed him back against Quan. He stood in front of the hushed assembly. His smoked-glass eyes raked the room.

"This is an illegal *jiaotang!*"

His accent reminded Quan of the villages over the mountains.

"This gathering is not registered with the Religious Affairs Bureau," the PSB man said, making this appear the ultimate offense. "You are not part of the Three-Self Patriotic Movement!"

Narrowing his gaze, the captain's mouth fell into a short-fused frown. "You meet in the night like the criminals you are."

He strode across the front of the room, as if making it his own. His gait was arrogant and sure, every movement calculated to intimidate. He looked like he'd walked on the necks of a thousand peasants and enjoyed every step. He was giving a virtuoso performance.

"You have been distributing illegal foreign propaganda."

With dramatic flourish, he waved a thin brown object, gripped tightly by the ends of his gray fingers. Though unmarked, Quan knew what it was—a case containing a compact disc. The movie about Jesus. Last month he and Ming had brought eighteen neighbors into their little house to watch it. "Yesu speaks Mandarin!" the amazed neighbors had said. Five became Christians. Three of those were here this morning. Quan had seen them in the back. Already he'd gotten them into trouble. He longed to turn his head to see them but dared not.

"You are cultists, devious and immoral, no better than the Falun Gong," Scarbrow said. "Do you think you are above the law? If you must worship foreign gods, there is a registered church!"

The nearest registered church was fourteen kilometers away. Just two legal meeting places for a city of a half million. The Li family had only their bicycles. But even if they could get there, they would find infiltrators in the church, people who watched everyone and reported everything. Spies and informants were well rewarded. Even some of the house churches had them.

"Criminals!"

Quan quietly stared down at his twenty-year-old dress shoes. His thoughts turned again to the one who'd given them to him, to the last time they'd seen each other. Ben Fielding, his college roommate. Once, Ben had overheard another Chinese call him *Dabizi*. Ben liked the name and insisted Quan call him that. But Quan was too polite to tell him what it meant—"Big Nose," the slang term for Westerners. When he finally found out, Ben laughed and told Quan he wanted it for his permanent nickname. So Ben became Dabizi, and he always called Quan "Professor." Quan prayed for Ben as he stared at his shoes. They had promised to pray for each other every day. He hoped Ben was praying for him now.

Scarbrow waved his rifle. "We must crack down on all lawbreaking activities to safeguard social stability."

Shen's pudgy face scrunched. The dour-mouthed captain lowered his gaze and stared at the boy. Shen's upper lip quivered. He started to cry. Quan looked at Shen, silently pleading for him.

We never should have come back to China. I was at the top of my class. I was asked to teach at Harvard. We could have immigrated. Ming could have become a U.S. citizen with me. Why did I return to this? Why did I put Ming at risk? And now . . . my son. What kind of a father endangers his only son?

Doubts assailed Li Quan, as they often did.

"Illegal churches are enemies of the state. We must kill the baby while it is still in the manger. You do not deserve to live!"

The giant wasp pointed at Li Shen, who trembled under his gaze.

Slowly, Ming took off her silk scarf, bloodred, and gently pressed it against Li Shen's quivering lips. Quan peered down at his only son's eyes, begging him to be silent, making unspoken promises, knowing he could not keep them.

Protect my son, Yesu. Please.

"It is illegal to teach religion to children under eighteen! How dare you defy the law?" He lifted his hand, poising it in midair two feet away from Li Quan's face.

The father set his jaw in preparation for the impact, grateful it was he who would take the blow, and not his only son.

3

ON MONDAY, September 17, Ben Fielding sat in his lofty West Hills condo, overlooking the Willamette River, admiring his breathtaking view of Mount Hood. The sun was just rising above its peak, the mountain looking like strawberry ice cream. He had just watched Venus, the morning star, surrender its glory to the greater light.

Ben sipped his superstrong Starbucks French Roast, trying to set aside the thoughts about Li Quan that had preoccupied him all weekend. Even now he could hardly shake them from his mind.

Ben looked down at the printout of his career goals. Every Monday morning, ever since he'd set them six years ago at a management seminar in Seattle, he reviewed his goals. It was just after he'd been named the youngest vice president of Getz International, the semiconductor and microchip company that had taken the Asian market by storm. The seminar speaker had instructed them to recite their goals aloud and visualize them before each workweek. Ben had done so every Monday morning as faithfully as the most devout believer went to church each Sunday.

He read them aloud:

> "1. Build Getz's presence into China's business infrastructure, forging strong partnerships that will take GI to the top."

So far so good.

> "2. Become president of Getz International by age forty-eight."

That was just three years away, the year Martin Getz would retire. He was fortunate Martin had no children, no heir apparent to the family business. Everyone knew Ben was on the fast track to CEO. As long as he stayed Teflon, as long as there was no controversy or disastrous decision to stick to him, he'd be sitting in the big chair right on schedule.

"3. Accumulate enough wealth to go anywhere and do anything I want."

Between his salary, his stock options, and his retirement funds, Ben was already worth several million. He'd lost track. Ben felt a twinge of something in his stomach. He barely had time to enjoy what he'd already accumulated. What would he do with more? He wasn't sure. But he had every intention of finding out.

An unwelcome face pressed on Ben's mind. Paul Foley had been at the same seminar. His goals had been similar, if more modest. He'd wanted to be the next vice president of Getz, to become Ben Fielding's right-hand man. They had been tennis partners, first doubles on the 4.5 team at the Mac club. They'd been undefeated. Ben had been certain both their goals would be achieved. Only three years ago Paul, by then bald and feeble from the cancer and chemo treatments, had made a premature exit from the company and, two months later, from the world.

Goal sheet still in hand, Ben went to the bathroom and popped his cholesterol pill and blood-pressure medication.

The goals in front of him were slightly edited from the original, which had said, "Invest wisely. Accumulate enough wealth so we can go wherever and do whatever we want." The "we" had been he and Pam. But a year ago he'd had to replace the "we" with an "I" and print out a clean sheet. Pursuing the first two goals had resulted in the need to make this slight revision of the third. It was just the change of a few letters, the revision of a single pronoun, first-person plural to first-person singular. It was just a divorce.

Melissa's and Kim's names weren't on the page either. His visualization routine didn't include them. What would he visualize—his children hugging him and saying, "We're proud of you, Dad"? Get real. Syrup and sentimentality? Life didn't work like that. Besides, it was too late. He hadn't been there for them, as Pam had often reminded him. Kimmy was always sweet, but he was certain she'd always remember he'd missed her eighth-grade graduation to play golf with clients at Pebble Beach. And Melissa? He'd given her everything, including a classic Mustang for her sixteenth birthday. Yet somehow she'd managed to resent him. Pam had tried to explain it, but Ben never got it. He wasn't sure he wanted to.

Ben looked down at the paper, then tossed it on the coffee table. He dumped the lukewarm coffee into the sink, seeing dark clouds moving in front of Mount Hood. He put on his tie and went down to his red Jaguar, rushing to get back to the real world—or perhaps to escape from it.

Ben sat behind his desk at 7:15, admiring the stunning panorama of the Great Wall of China displayed opposite his redwood barrister's bookcase. He looked through some papers, then read some e-mail, but nothing held his attention. He put on some Mozart, then paced the floor. Finally, he gave in again to what Martin's proposal Friday had so rudely pushed on him. Thoughts about his old roommate.

Quan's dream had been to teach at a university and to write books. A brilliant student and a lucid writer, Li Quan cast no doubts as to whether his dream would come true. Ben called him not only Professor but "Little Grasshopper," from the television program *Kung Fu*.

They'd met as two freshmen who didn't know anyone else at Harvard. It started as an uncomfortable mismatch: soft-spoken, polite, self-effacing Chinese and loud, brash, self-promoting American. Ben tossed footballs out the window, while Quan grew sprouts on the windowsill. Ben was all onion rings and milk shakes; Quan ate bamboo shoots and brewed green tea. It didn't seem a match made in heaven.

They hardly talked first term until one night near Christmas. Quan was lonely. He told Ben his story. Quan's father had died; then his mother perished in an earthquake that destroyed their home near Shanghai. Relief workers came to help, foreigners who otherwise weren't allowed into China. One of the workers took an interest in Quan. When he discovered Quan's dream was to go to university in America, he said he would help get him scholarships and a residency permit. The next thing Quan knew he'd gotten a conditional acceptance from Harvard. But he hadn't even applied. An application was enclosed. In those days only the privileged left China to go to American universities. Everyone told him it would be impossible to get a passport. Yet somehow it happened.

With tuition and room and board magically paid for him, Quan earned a living allowance working at Burger Magic as a short-order cook. He found out later it was illegal to work on a student visa. But he'd needed the money, and somehow it happened. He'd labored day and night, excelled in his studies, and honed his already excellent English.

He and Ben studied Spanish together but, as always, it was Quan who mastered it. Ben smiled, remembering the incongruity of a Chinese man saying, "No problema." It was Americanized Spanish, but it became his catchphrase.

Ben kept telling himself he'd find another roommate, but after that late-night conversation he stopped looking. By the time they graduated—Quan, with high honors—they were fast friends. While Chinese food was hard to get in Cambridge, Massachusetts, in those days, they found a little dive, the Double Dragon, that Quan said was almost authentic. Ben fell in love with the food and hadn't stopped eating it since. Quan taught Ben how to fish. Ben taught Quan how to play tennis. They rode bikes together everywhere.

While Ben got his MBA, Quan stayed on to get advanced degrees and became a teaching fellow in the history department. By then they lived in an apartment off campus. Just after Quan finished his Ph.D. work, the academic vice president took him to lunch and offered him a full history professorship. Meanwhile, letters came from Beijing and Shanghai, offering him prestigious teaching positions. Quan wrestled with the decision and prayed over it for two months. Ben was sure he'd stay in the U.S. Why wouldn't he?

Finally, one evening Quan told Ben, "I must go back to China."

"Why? You're always saying God brought you to America. He rescued you out of that earthquake, did a miracle to get you into Harvard, right? You've got an incredible job opportunity. You've got a great roommate, and you've got the Double Dragon up the street. Why not stay here?"

"God brought me here for a season, to train me, give me credentials. He has given me a platform I can bring back to my country, where it is more needed."

"But didn't you say they frown on people being Christians, that they see it as a foreign devil thing?"

"I first believed in Christ in America, but I come from a long line of Chinese Christians. God will go before me as I return home. I trust him. He will make a way for me to teach. China is my home, not America."

Ben had been hurt by Quan's departure. Had he stayed, Ben was certain they'd still be close. But after he went back to China, they'd written for only a few years before Ben, by then a young businessman, quit writing back. Eventually, Quan stopped too. Each time Ben visited China, twenty-some times in the last twelve years, he'd told himself he should look up his college roommate. But he never had. Now it had been twenty-two years since he'd seen that silly grin on his friend's face when Quan insisted they sing "Fair Harvard" together.

What had kept Ben from making contact with Quan was the same thing that had prompted him to stop writing in the first place. His life had gone down a different path. His faith and his values had changed.

"God will make a way." That was Quan. Simplistic. "China is my home—everything will work out just fine." Ben had no doubt Quan was fulfilling his dreams of teaching at university and writing books and raising a family and enjoying the burgeoning Chinese economy. But Ben's life had taken other turns. Business and finances had gone great. But then there was everything else . . . including Pam and Melissa and Kim.

As for God making a way, well, where had God been when his mother was dying of cancer? And where had God been when his son, Jason . . . ?

He had to stop. He couldn't let himself think about it. Doug was scheduled to arrive in five minutes.

Man. 7:25 on Monday morning and I'm already thinking about getting buzzed on some stiff mao-tais.

4

$\mathcal{S}$CARBROW HELD his hand in the air, poised to strike the flinching Li Quan. He slowly lowered it. His steely eyes stared at Quan, as if probing into his deepest being, searching for what lay hidden beneath his skin. Scarbrow then knelt before little Shen.

Quan prayed. With the regime's one-child policy, Shen was their only future. After Ming had given birth, requiring a C-section, the doctor had sterilized her without consent. It wasn't as bad as what the Zhangs, seated behind them, had undergone—the forced abortion of their second child.

"Brainwashing children! You are a disgrace—traitors to the Republic."

The weapon of *xiuchi*, shame, was as familiar as old shoes and as painful as shoes three sizes too small. When his father had been arrested, a teacher fashioned paper and strings and hung on Quan's neck a sign saying "Li Tong is a criminal." He'd cried uncontrollably. Even now he felt the humiliation.

"China is built on the backbone of hardworking citizens," Scarbrow said, "loyal to the superior socialist system."

As always, propaganda was the seed spread on the ground and tilled by shame. Spoken with passionate seriousness, the words were formulaic. Quan could have recited them in his sleep. Sometimes he did.

With a rigid swagger, the officer took three steps to the side, then turned suddenly, like an owl's head. "You are very bad people!"

In America, Quan thought, such name-calling would seem childish. Yet in China it was routinely used to herd people back into line. Though Quan knew it shouldn't, it worked—his ears burned with shame. Perhaps his father had felt this way when they put on his head that two-foot-high pointed paper hat that labeled him "traitor, spy, and capitalist."

Shen's mouth hung open, disproportionate to his face. Quan longed to protect him not just from the Party's weapons, but also its words.

"Followers of Yesu are traitors. You make me sick." Scarbrow's eyes looked like the points of two ice picks. He reminded Quan of Tai Hong, the deputy chief of police, also powerfully built and cold-eyed, with a passion for persecuting Christians. Quan touched the rough scar on his neck, caught himself, then slowly lowered his arm.

His father had taught Quan to withdraw inside in such confrontations, where men were free. There he could silently resist the accusations, reason against the reeducation.

As a fourteen-year-old, Quan had been taken to his father's jail by a communist worker who made him read a plea—supposedly from his family but written by the communist—to confess his crimes. The memory weighed on Quan's shoulders like an enormous log. Quan had often longed to ask his father's forgiveness for having been ashamed of him. He knew it was his father who should be ashamed of Quan.

One of the young police officers, a smooth-faced lieutenant with faint reddish freckles, approached the captain nervously. They whispered, appearing to disagree. The young man's deep raspy voice seemed to be pleading. Quan prayed for the boy. Atheism had left a huge void. The people's hearts were empty, seeking to be filled by something greater and deeper. Yesu had taught Quan to pray for his enemies.

Wu Le, the recent attendee sitting behind Quan, whispered to his wife.

"Silence!" yelled Scarbrow, drawing up Quan's eyes to his, only for a moment. Pondering what lay behind the smoke in those eyes, Quan heard Lok's wife sob.

Just then Scarbrow spoke again. "For over fifty years we have fought the Western imperialists. We have forged ahead against our enemies and transformed the face of China."

The face, yes. But behind it was something else. Mao had murdered untold millions, far more than Hitler, more than even Stalin. The fatalities included Quan's father, Li Tong. But Mao had not invented suffering. Dreams about his headless great-grandfather reminded Quan that martyrs ran in his family.

Is this the day?

He looked back at the book on the bench, the precious cargo he'd strapped to his bicycle. It had been hand-copied by his mother. Every day, Quan read his Lord's words in his mother's handwriting. It had nearly been confiscated several times. *Is today the last time I'll ever see it?*

"By assembling unlawfully you are subject to imprisonment. But what you deserve is much worse!"

While Scarbrow ranted, Quan remembered visiting his father in his last, long prison term, watching him waste away. Eventually the face that stared back at him was misshapen from beatings, crusted with scabs, puffy with infections. At the beginning of his nine-year imprisonment, his face had looked mottled and leathery, like the sole of an army boot. Eventually it became a chalky mask.

But the eyes peering through the mask's eyeholes, though hollowed and jaundiced, were still his father's. Somehow they were full of determination and joy, welling up from some subterranean reservoir. Quan hated it when his father looked at him and said, "Your day will come." His mother told him his father meant it to encourage him. How, he could never understand.

"Yesu-followers surrender state secrets to foreign devils!"

What secrets do you think we know? And why would we disclose them to foreigners?

His father called policemen who persecuted Christians "fleas on the top of a bald head." They were looking for what wasn't there. To this day, whenever he encountered a dank musty smell, it took him back to visiting his father in prison as a child, before he'd turned hard. Quan had longed to hug his father. But they wouldn't let him. "The prisoner cannot be touched!"

He had no pictures of his father. They'd all been destroyed when the house burned, after the lantern fell in the earthquake. He tried to remember his father's face at the dinner table, before the crackdown, but he couldn't. He could only see that tortured mask. Quan's father wasn't there most of his school years. But he always wanted his father to be proud of him, not ashamed. He never stopped longing to hear his father say to him, "Well done."

"What is that?" Scarbrow pointed at Quan's Bible. The worst had happened—being singled out in a crowd. Would he have to explain why his Shengjing didn't have the government seal?

"What is it?" the captain shouted.

"It is . . . a message from God." Quan heard his own voice, surprised at its steadiness.

Scarbrow pulled from his own pocket a little red volume. *"This* is China's book."

The captain was a Mao-quoter, from the old school. He was a throwback—nowadays the red book was sold mostly to foreigners as a relic of a bygone era. But not long ago everyone had quoted the book.

"Not your Western imperialist Bible!"

How many times had Quan been told Christianity was a Western religion? Didn't they understand Yesu wasn't American? Scarbrow needed to watch that movie so he could understand that the world of Yesu was more like rural China than America.

"Our revered father, Mao Zedong, said, 'The Communist Party is the core of the Chinese people.'"

In school Quan had memorized the sayings of Chairman Mao. *Baihua qifang*—"let a hundred flowers bloom." The church was never considered one of those flowers. Mao was the "Great Savior." And he would tolerate no other saviors. Quan wondered how many thousands of Christians, even today, were trapped in the network of gulags throughout China.

There was much good in China, Quan knew—beauty, history, nobility, decency, hard work, and economic progress. But the chains of prisoners and free alike had choked this great land and had strangled his father and his great-grandfather. One day, Quan sensed, those chains would strangle him.

Is this the day?

"Our revered chairman said, 'A revolution is not a dinner party.' He said, 'If you don't hit it, it won't fall. Like sweeping the floor, where the broom does not reach, the dust will not vanish of itself.'"

He paused, then squared his shoulders, eyes aflame. "Today we come with brooms!"

Every man in uniform lifted his weapon high. Quan stared at the freckle-faced lieutenant, who appeared to be trembling.

What is happening? He pulled Shen against his leg.

"We must kill the baby while it is still in the manger. You do not deserve to live!"

Quan had been threatened, strong-armed, and jailed, and he'd often heard the "kill the baby" line, but never had he sensed such imminent doom. He felt his heart throbbing in the tips of his ears. He'd assumed they'd be given warnings. Marks would be made on their records; perhaps he and the other men would be taken to jail and beaten. This had happened to him before. But these soldiers were different. Something else was happening here.

Ming shook beside him, a tear on her downy cheek. Even Zhou Jin, who had spent over twenty years in prison, trembled.

"With these brooms we will sweep away the dirt and filth that threatens China."

The captain's eloquence frightened Quan. Educated evil was always the worst. Something terrible was coming. Scarbrow stared at every person in the room, one by one, studying them.

"There are two sides to this room. Those loyal to the Party and its people must prove it by moving to the left side and out the door. In doing so, they will declare they do not believe in Yesu. They are free to go and will not be punished. Those who choose Yesu will step to the right side."

Quan looked at Ming, a tempest in her eyes. For a long five seconds no one moved. Then one man stepped to the left, toward the door. Immediately, stoop-shouldered Zhou Jin walked to the right. Quan tried to budge his legs, but they felt wobbly, like rusted rain gutters.

"In three minutes," Scarbrow said matter-of-factly, "we will shoot every man and woman—and child—who does not declare himself loyal to the people rather than the *gweilos,* foreign devils."

Soft groans erupted across the room. Quan turned slightly as Wu Le's wife put her hands over her mouth. No—this couldn't be. Quan had never heard of such a thing. Killings, yes, of course, one or two at a time, but not this!

The captain looked at his watch, stepped aside, leaned against the wall and observed, as if guessing who would be left for him to execute.

Ho Lin and Auntie Mei came forward and joined Zhou Jin on the right side of their home.

"Will they really kill us?" Ming whispered numbly.

"I . . . think so," Quan said.

Wu Le, eyes down, walked to the door, his wife two steps behind. Quan watched him, feeling a moment of envy followed by a long surge of pity and disappointment.

"Two minutes," Scarbrow said, with a machine's voice. Clearly this man knew what he was going to do. The only question was, what would others do?

Quan looked toward the right.

"We must not let Shen die," Ming whispered.

"He is Yesu's gift to us," Quan said. "No, not a gift. A loan. God is his father. He will take care of him."

"We must not lose our only son."

"God lost his only son. He buried him in a foreign land."

"I am willing to die," Ming said, voice cracking, "but I cannot bear to think of their killing Shen. Still . . . perhaps it is the Lord's mercy for us to die together."

"I've always thought I might end like my father and great-grandfather . . . but not you, not Shen." Yes, he'd dreamed a hundred times of holding Ming's bloody body, but he'd always prayed it would not happen. Quan covered his face with his hands. He felt a small, strong grip on his arm.

"Are we not Zhu Yesu's also?" Ming asked. "Are we not his called and chosen? Why should we not walk the way he has chosen for you? Why should you be considered worthy and not us?"

It had always been this way. Whenever she weakened, he was strong for her. Whenever he weakened, she was strong for him. He leaned over Shen and put his arms around Ming. Then Quan got down on one knee in front of his only son.

"Do you understand what the captain is saying, Shen?" The child nodded his head slowly, eyes puffy.

"Will you come with us and follow the Lord, Zhu Yesu?"

Face pinched and wet, Shen nodded again.

Quan started to pick him up, but instead held his hand and let him walk next to him, son beside father, headed to their destiny. Wordlessly, the three turned their backs on the door and took their stand with those on the right.

"Sixty seconds," Scarbrow called.

Three more families, including three children, joined Quan and the others. Five people stood in the middle of the room, starting to move one way and then the other, as if in the center of a tug-of-war. Quan prayed hard for his three neighbors standing there—Fu Gan, Chun, and their teenage daughter, Yun.

"This is your final chance. Leave now or die!"

A woman he didn't recognize headed for the door, followed by a man. Suddenly the three neighbors walked briskly, petite Yun leading the way. They stood close to Quan and Ming. Quan rejoiced and mourned at the same time. When the three had come to Yesu in their home only weeks before, he hadn't dreamed they would die together in church.

He counted. Eighteen people remained. Five had walked out. One last man stood inside the door, glancing back, as if looking for a third alternative. Scarbrow pointed his weapon at the man, who turned and fled out the door into the cold darkness.

One of the police stepped outside, weapon pointed, looking around. Reentering, he shut the door and locked it. Quan, Ming, and Shen clasped each other's hands. Quan breathed deeply and braced himself.

Surely, this is the day.

5

*T*HE MONDAY MORNING knock at the office door yanked Ben up. He ran a comb through his hair, popped in a breath mint, brushed his suit, straightened his tie in the mirror, and opened the door.

"Hey, Ben," Doug said, "do I finally get to hear what's on your mind?"

Ben stretched out his hand toward the small guest chair facing his desk, then walked around to the high-backed chair on the far side. As he sat down, his face took on the aura of the big chair. His desk was clean except for two file folders, top one thick, bottom one thin.

"What's up, Ben? You look a little . . . under the gun."

"I think you've got a good idea what's up. Why did you force me into this?"

"Into what?"

"Into what I have to do."

"What are you talking about?"

"C'mon, Doug. What do you think?"

Doug shrugged. "Okay. I'll play your little game. I think I see my cousin, a high-powered vice president who looks very tired. He's a long way from Ogunquit, Maine, and he looks like he could use a bowl of his mom's lobster chowder. I see a taller, better-dressed version of that scraggly boy we drove up from New York to see every holiday. I think I see that lanky kid and me wandering off from the old folks and having our adventures down on the beach, with his black Lab, Aragorn, running in the surf. That's what I think."

"I won't let you fall back on the family connection."

"Fall back? What do you mean?"

Ben picked up the top file folder. "I've got a half-dozen complaints. They're all right here."

"You're keeping a file on me?"

"We have to keep a file whenever . . . in these kinds of cases."

"As in *legal* cases? What's going on, Ben?"

"I was raised in a family with beliefs like yours, remember? Your mom and mine, they were into that . . . religious stuff. Okay, I can respect that. And frankly, I don't care how narrow or intolerant you are in the privacy of your own home. But why couldn't you put a lid on it in the office? It's been building up for years. Now you've crossed the line. I've tried to warn you. You've become a disruption."

"Come on, Ben. You knew me in the old days. I was outspoken then—radical politics. Protect the ozone, legalize marijuana, you name it. I had an opinion on everything. When I became a Christian twelve years ago, my opinions changed a lot, obviously. I didn't apologize for that. Okay, maybe I was a little in-your-face at first, I admit it. But in the last five years have you ever known me to cram my beliefs down anyone's throat?"

"I'm not the one who filed the complaints! You've been warned before, but you never seem to get it. We schedule diversity seminars. First, you don't want to take them. Then you agree to take them, but you have to tell everyone homosexuality's wrong."

"I took the seminar because I believe in racial equality and gender equality, and I can appreciate the fact that this company's trying to sensitize us to people from different backgrounds. All I said was, I didn't think anyone should expect me to say homosexual behavior is right, because it isn't. I believe the Bible condemns it, and I said so. And I was quick to say it also condemns heterosexual relations outside marriage."

"Oh, well, that really bailed you out," Ben said. "I got a complaint on that one too. You know how many people in this office are living together? Half the marketing staff is sleeping with each other. You've got five or six people within a thirty-foot radius of your desk who are having affairs. God knows how many others!"

"Yes, he does," Doug said.

Ben rolled his eyes. He hadn't mentioned his own affair that had helped end his marriage, but he was certain Doug was thinking about it, and it angered him. "Their lifestyle choices are their own business, Doug. Not mine. And certainly not yours."

"I believe in Christ. I believe the Bible. Even if it isn't popular, I believe what it says about everything, including sexual morality."

"I don't care what you believe, Doug. Nobody does. That's the problem. Listen to yourself, man. You sound like Grandma teaching Sunday school in Ogunquit . . . or Lake Woebegone. I sat on the diversity-in-business committee. We passed the NHSW ordinance—'No hate speech in the workplace'—ring a bell? What message would it send if I looked the other way when it was happening in our own office?"

"Hate speech? Come on, Ben. I don't hate these people. I just disagree, that's all. Hey, I used to sleep around too. But that doesn't make it right."

"Hate speech leads to hate crime. Saying homosexuality is wrong makes you an accomplice whenever someone beats up a homosexual. That's how it works."

"Even if I oppose beating up homosexuals? And if I oppose abortion, does it makes me an accomplice if someone beats up someone who had an abortion?"

"You said it, not me."

"Well, if you say I'm a Christian bigot because I believe the Bible and then someone beats me up, does that make you an accomplice? Is your calling me a bigot a hate crime? Or does it only cut one way?"

"Get serious, will you? The guys tell me that on the sales trips you're too good for them. You can't go out and have some drinks, have some fun. It's called camaraderie, Doug. It's part of teamwork. And what about your clients? I hear you won't meet them at certain places. Who pays for it when you lose a customer? Getz does. Your coworkers and clients don't want to be judged and preached at. You can't bring small-town standards to the city. Times have changed."

"Get real, Ben. You're the one who grew up in Maine. I'm from Brooklyn, for crying out loud! I was a drunk and an adulterer before it was cool. My own sister's a lesbian, and you know I love her. She lived with us when she was suicidal. I'd give my right arm for her. I'm not telling people they can't live that way. But when we're required to be at a diversity seminar and the instructor is insisting there's no such thing as right and wrong, I'm not going to sit there and be quiet. I'll respectfully speak up. That's what I did. I didn't shoot anybody; I just disagreed. It's America, remember?"

Ben pulled a paper from the file. "You attacked Barbara in the copy room because she's pro-choice."

"Attacked? That's ridiculous. Barbara came in wearing a pro-choice button. I asked her—respectfully—if she believed children have the right to choose whether or not someone else should take their life. Ask Denise Edwards. She was standing right there. She'll tell you I was talking in a normal voice. We were just having a civil disagreement, until Barbara went ballistic."

"Denise didn't say you assaulted Barbara, not physically, anyway. But we've gotten three complaints in the last month on your antiabortion slogan posted in your workstation."

"The last month? It's been up there nearly a year. Obviously, somebody stirred up the other two complaints! It's just a little poster that says 'Pro-Woman, Pro-Child, Pro-Life.' Could you tell me what's offensive about that?"

"You're deliberately pushing buttons, Doug. You're creating an antagonistic work environment. It's distracting people. It's bad for camaraderie, and that's bad for business."

"Look at this office, Ben. We have atheists, agnostics, a Buddhist, three New Agers who were Shirley MacLaine in a previous life, and me. I'm the token Christian. Sheila too, I guess. No problem, I'm not complaining. I'm not expecting people to hold back their ideas, and they shouldn't expect me to hold back mine. Did you ask Barbara to take off her pro-choice button? Of course not. I'll bet it never occurred to you. But you asked me to take down that pro-life poster. I told you and Johnny I wouldn't take it down because the law says if other people have the right to express themselves in their work area, so do I. Just because I'm a Christian doesn't mean I throw out my First Amendment rights when I walk into this office."

Ben pointed to another paper. "What about your bumper sticker?"

"That's in your file too? Sheesh, Ben. What else have the thought police reported me for? The bumper sticker just says 'Jesus Is the Only Way.'"

"Don't you realize how condemning and judgmental that sounds? Your way is the *only* way?"

"Jesus said, 'I am the way, the truth, and the life. No one can come to the Father except through me.' The bumper sticker just repeats what he said. I didn't make it up. Your argument's with him, not me. You remember, Ben, the Bible says there's no other name under heaven by which we can be saved and—"

"Stop preaching, Doug. That's what drives people crazy!"

Doug took a deep breath. "I park my car in the garage. I don't drive it into the office. My bumper sticker's not anybody's business."

"Getz International owns your parking permit."

"But Getz doesn't own my car. And it doesn't own me."

Ben stared at Doug, as if by letting his words hang in the air, Doug should feel the weight of their condemnation.

"Look, Ben, last year you said no Bible on my desk. I put it in my drawer, and I only pull it out during a break, when I'm not on company time. I went with that, although I happen to think Getz stepped over the line. I mean, if Stephen King and Danielle Steel can be on a desk, why not God? But come on, bumper stickers? What's next? Are you going to tell me I can't have a manger scene on my front lawn because people know I work for Getz? And what about Hansen's pro-gay bumper sticker? You know the one I mean. I see that in the parking lot every day. What about Bradley's naked women emblems on his truck's mud flaps? I've got a wife and two daughters—you've got daughters too, remember?"

Ben felt his face flush. "What's your point?"

"My point is, those emblems offend me. People wear all kinds of things for various causes, but when Sheila wore her little right-to-life emblem, that little baby, she got a reprimand."

"It wasn't a reprimand. I just advised her not to wear it again. Two women complained."

"Yeah, well, Sheila complained too, remember? Complained about the First Amendment; you may have heard of it. Something about free speech."

"Why do you have to be so narrow, Doug? This attitude of 'I'm right and everybody else is going to hell' just doesn't cut it. Legal says it falls under the category of bigotry, and if we just stand by and let you inflict your bigotry on our employees, Getz can be held liable."

"Doesn't tolerance cut both ways? You require us to go to pantheistic, New Age, mumbo-jumbo workshops so we can all get in sync with cosmic vibrations, and then you tell me I'm inflicting my religion on others because I take a different point of view? I'm sorry, Ben, but I just work for this company. I never sold my soul to it."

Ben stared at Doug, shaking his head. "I've gone to bat for you twice, Doug, but no more. People think I'm protecting you because we're related. They wonder if I'm sympathetic to your beliefs."

"Are you?"

"No, frankly, I'm not. But perception is everything. I heard through the grapevine somebody thinks that because . . . well, you know Pam and I and the kids used to go to church and—"

"Pam and Kim still do, Ben. They're at my church, remember?"

"The bottom line is, the management team met last week. You were on the agenda. I didn't want to do this, but . . . you've forced my hand."

"To do what?"

"It's the no-hate-speech ordinance."

"What about it?"

"Formal complaints have been filed against you under that statute."

"Who filed them?"

"I can't tell you. To prevent retaliation the ordinance says complaints must be kept confidential."

"You're saying I can't face my accusers? Pardon me, but while I slept last night did this cease to be the United States of America? How can I deal with it if I can't even talk to someone about it?"

"Unfortunately, Doug, even what you admit saying to people is enough to incriminate you. You're not going to change, are you?"

"Change my beliefs? No. Refuse to speak up about Jesus? No way."

"Then you've left me no choice." Ben put his palms down on his desk and leaned forward, his tie dangling like a noose. "We're letting you go."

"But . . . I've worked for Getz eighteen years. You called me out here from New York. I've worked hard. I've never taken a day of phony sick leave or cheated on my reimbursements like half the office does. I've done my job well. You know that. And my beliefs have helped me do it honestly." He stared at Ben, hardly able to speak. "You're serious, Ben? You're actually firing me?"

"You've left me no choice. Johnny's worked out a severance package. It's all here." Ben handed Doug the thin file folder, then closed the thick one, stuck it in his desk drawer, and turned the key in the lock. Doug stared at him.

Ben pressed his intercom line and said, "Jen? Call Martin and tell him I'm sorry I'm running late. I'm done. Be there in three minutes."

6

$\mathcal{I}$F YOUR LIFE is more important than your loyalty to this foreign god, leave now!" Scarbrow waved his rifle toward the door. "If you stay in this room, you choose to die."

Quan couldn't bear the thought of Ming and Shen dying like this. Not here, not now.

Please, God.

He pondered the hasty departure of Wu Le and his wife. They'd come to the village five months ago and a few months later had become Christians. At least, he thought they had. And yet, in midnight prayer meetings and Bible studies by candlelight they had been very quiet. Perhaps just reflective. Or perhaps . . . he wondered.

Without a signal, the soldiers each picked their targets. Scarbrow set his steely eyes on Quan. He raised his weapon.

So this will be my executioner.

Quan felt Scarbrow's muzzle press against his temple. He wondered if he would feel pain when the gun fired. He prayed for Shen, for Ming, that God would take care of them. He prayed for Ben Fielding.

Scarbrow lowered the gun. He stepped toward Zhou Jin and put one hand on his shoulder and one on Quan's. His face quivered. He dropped his weapon. It made a dull thud as it hit the floor.

"Forgive us, brothers. I am Fu Chi." The voice was broken. He pointed to the lieutenant. "This is my only son, Fu Liko. We have come from the village of An Ning, across the mountain. We are, like you, followers of Yesu. God is doing mighty things among us. We have much to tell you.

But we dared not put you at risk . . . or our brothers and families at home. Two of our own house churches have been betrayed by spies. We had to drive away your infiltrators. Now you know who they are. But you we salute. For you are the overcomers—more loyal to the King than to your own lives."

Quan stared blankly as his "executioner" embraced him. He felt the man's powerful torso tremble. "We acted like the midwives in Egypt and Rahab in Jericho. They deceived, that lives might be saved. If we were wrong, forgive us."

Scarbrow—Fu Chi—knelt and faced Shen, hands upon his shoulders. He looked into his eyes. "Forgive us, brave one," he whispered. "We knew no other way."

Among the eighteen members of the house church, confusion slowly dissolved into cautious smiles. At Zhou Jin's beckoning, the younger uniformed men, heads hung, joined them. Quan knelt down to Shen, Ming alongside. He pressed his face against theirs and felt their hot tears mingle with his.

Zhou Jin sang, "Zhu Yesu Jidu, we praise your name forever." Fu Chi's strong baritone filled the air. Fu Liko's deep, raspy voice joined, and the other voices followed.

Is this the day?

No. But it would come, Quan knew, whether at gunpoint, at work, or at home in the ease of bed. His day would surely come. If gunfire or knife did not take him, it might be sickness or old age. Or perhaps his Lord's return.

Quan took up Shen into his arms. He gazed into his brown eyes, seeing his reflection in them. But he also saw someone else looking back, eyes he'd last seen behind the holes of a mask.

Quan's insides felt as if hot Longjing tea had been poured down his throat. He thought of the father he longed to embrace, the face behind the mask.

Quan heard a voice. He turned his head to search for it. He saw only Ming and Shen and the followers of Zhu Yesu.

The voice had said, "Well done, my son."

Li Quan thanked Yesu they had remained faithful. But his gratitude did not remove his fear or doubts. Neither did it remove his shame. He knew he was unworthy of both fathers, his Lord in heaven and his baba who'd been on earth. Deep in his soul, Li Quan longed for peace, for assurance, for his father's approval. Pushing those feelings down inside him as he always had, Li Quan placed his hand on the shoulder of Fu Chi, no longer Scarbrow.

"We forgive you, brother," Quan said. "Now, tell us what God has done over the mountains. We have prayed many years for your people. What has happened?"

Fu Chi wiped tears from his eyes. "Something you will not believe. Sit down, brothers. Sit down, sisters. Prepare yourselves for something so wonderful that when you hear it your hearts will leap for joy."

"I am very proud of him," said tall Li Manchu.

"Yes. My boy showed courage," said the short, broad-shouldered Li Tong.

"He is a man now, with his own boy," said longhaired Li Wen, son of the tall man and father of the short one.

"But he will always be my son—as I will always be yours."

"This was not his day."

"But will that day still come for him? The day of martyrdom?"

"There is One who knows. Only One."

"Have you called your old roommate in China?" Martin asked Ben.

"No. I'll get on it."

"Good. I'm telling you, Ben, this strategy's going to pay off. How's this for the advertising campaign: 'Getz knows China—we've lived there!' Don't you love it?"

"Yeah, Martin. It's just great."

Ben returned to the sanctuary of his office. He recalled teasing Quan mercilessly for all his obscure references to Chinese myths. Some of his sayings made sense, like "The more you sweat in peacetime, the less you bleed during war." But Quan would also speak of chasing the sun, asking a fox for its skin, and fishing for the moon in the well. There were sayings about dog hats and bringing painted dragons to life by putting pupils in their eyes. Quan would cite these as if everyone at Harvard should understand what he was talking about.

"The gentleman on the beam," Quan once told Ben, as if that was all the commentary the situation called for. "A wily hare has three burrows," he said—so often Ben started calling him "wily hare." When someone asked them what they'd be doing that night, Ben would say, "The wily hare and I are going fishing for the moon in the well."

The memories warmed him, but just as suddenly he felt a cold, resentful anger. The more Ben had poured himself into his career, the more he'd drifted from his faith, the more Quan became a reminder of something he'd turned from. They'd promised to pray for each other daily. Ben didn't pray for anybody daily. Not for himself, not for his family. In fact, other than that day last year when he had those severe chest pains, he couldn't remember the last time he'd prayed.

Ben contemplated the strange twist of fate—blind fate, no doubt—that he'd ended up doing business in China. He'd been in the fanciest restaurants in Beijing, Shenyang, and Shanghai. He'd often wondered if Professor Li Quan was in the same restaurant and they'd come that close to seeing each other. How would he explain how he'd learned Mandarin and made those many trips to China without bothering to track down his old roommate?

Part of him desperately wanted to see Quan. Another part just as desperately wanted not to. He walked out to his secretary's desk.

"Jen, I need you to try finding a university professor in China. Probably Beijing, though he may have relocated by now. If so, I'm betting it would be a major city—maybe Shanghai, Tianjin, or Shenyang. His name is Li Quan."

"How do I find him?"

Ben laughed. "The term *needle in a haystack* comes to mind, but this haystack has over a billion strands of hay. But you can start with this address." He handed her an old envelope. "I found it in an old book a few years back. But I think he was in temporary housing when he wrote it. He was going to relocate; he was maybe going to teach at a different college. I can't tell you where."

Jen looked at the envelope, pointing at Quan's name. "From this spelling I wouldn't think you'd pronounce it like you do."

"Pinyin is the official standardized form of Chinese words. In Pinyin, *Quan* is pronounced like 'Chuan.'"

"What does it mean?"

"That depends. It could mean 'complete,' 'spring,' 'fist' . . . or 'dog.'"

"One word means all that?"

"Each sound is divided into at least four different intonations. The meaning is different with each intonation. The way Quan pronounced it, it would mean 'spring.' And *Li* means 'plum.'"

"Spring plum. Well, that's better than dog. I hope I can find him."

"Honestly, I doubt you will. Unless they have *Books in Print* in China."

"He's a writer?"

"I'll bet he's written a dozen books by now. But you won't find them on amazon.com, unless they've started carrying Mandarin titles."

"I hope Li Quan isn't a common name."

Ben laughed. "China's full of common names. A phone book would be a bad joke. In a big city you could have a hundred pages of identical names. The bad news is, Li is one of the most common Chinese last names. Maybe second only to Chen."

Jen shook her head. "Thanks for the encouragement."

"This might be a clue. There was a girl he always talked about, exchanged letters with. I wouldn't be surprised if he married her. Her given name was Minghua." He wrote it down for Jen. "Can't tell you her surname. Chinese women keep their family names. And the surname comes first—Li is his family name, Quan is the given name—what we'd call a first name."

Jen rolled her eyes. "I'm not a *complete* China ignoramus, Ben. And if the author or professor angle doesn't work?"

"Call one of our contacts in Beijing or Shanghai. If nothing else, get Won Chi on the phone. Hey, there are only 1.2 billion people. How hard could it be to find one of them? That's why you get paid the big bucks."

He smiled, certain there was no way she could track Quan down. He knew how hard it was to find somebody in China, even when you knew the city. Anyway, he could assure Martin he'd tried, and they could pursue another angle. For some reason he just couldn't admit to Martin he didn't want to reconnect with his old roommate. It was hard enough admitting it to himself.

His smile faded. He looked at his schedule. It was full. Good. He didn't have to think about what he once shared with Li Quan or Pam or Doug. And as long as he kept busy, he wouldn't think about how much he needed a drink.

———

"I traced the last known address, and it went nowhere," Jen said on Friday afternoon. "Everybody I talked to says no way I'd ever find your guy. Lists of university professors? They say you probably couldn't get a list if you worked at the university!"

"So you didn't find him?" Ben tried to look disappointed.

"I've spent three days looking, so I'm entitled to draw out my story. Anyway, there are about as many Li Quans in Beijing as there are pushcarts, but I couldn't get any lists of professors. In Shenyang, I got someone at a university who spoke English. They said they knew a professor named Li Quan."

"No kidding?"

I asked for his description. He's an old man—not that your roommate wouldn't be an old man, but this one's in his seventies. How long ago was it you went to college?"

"Very funny."

"So I called Won Chi. When I told him I was looking for a particular Li Quan you knew twenty years ago, he actually laughed at me. But he has a friend who's a big shot at an Internet company in Shanghai. Based on the name and the name of the woman he *might* have married, they tried different angles and searched through the haystack. They got nothing."

"Is this the end of your story, Jen? Because I do have some phone calls to make before offices close on the East Coast."

She handed him a piece of paper. He looked at it: *liquanminghua @ps.sh.cn.*

"You're kidding me."

"It's registered to a Li Quan, wife Minghua, living a hundred and fifty miles west of Shanghai. Won Chi says it's probably not your guy, but if he's a professor he'd likely be one of the fortunate with an e-mail address. Anyway, better chances than a lottery ticket."

"Thanks."

"That's all? It was ten hours of unremitting toil. You owe me."

"I'll bring you back a silk scarf and some fortune cookies."

"You want me to e-mail and see if it's him?"

"I'll handle it."

Ben walked slowly into his office and sat down in front of his computer, maximizing Microsoft Outlook. He clicked the New Message icon and typed in the e-mail address. Fingers poised on the keyboard, he waited for strokes to flow. They didn't. He slumped back in his swivel chair. Then he started again.

> *Dear Professor Li Quan,*
>
> *I hope I have the right Li Quan. If not, I apologize—but then, you probably can't read English anyway, can you?*
>
> *If this is Harvard's Little Grasshopper, hello from your old room-mate. Have you been fishing for the moon in the well? Are you a bald old scholar now? So, you married Minghua? Do you have children? It's been a long time, friend. I miss throwing the Frisbee with you in Harvard Yard!*
>
> *I know this is out of the blue (if you remember that expression), but I want to come visit you in China. I was wondering if I could stay with you, or if that's inconvenient, in a nearby hotel. (As I recall, a wily hare has three burrows—how many homes do you have?)*

I thought I could see your world, watch you at work, meet some friends and neighbors, interview some locals, maybe show you some of my company's products, and get your feedback. A bit of a working vacation for me, I guess. Kind of a crazy idea, but thought I would ask. If I end up coming, I promise to bring my tennis racket and let you beat me.

Dabizi, otherwise known as Big Nose, Ben Fielding

Ben looked at the letter, spell-checked it, then finally pressed Send and watched it pop up in the Out box. He highlighted it, then rested his finger on the Delete key. He pushed it down. It disappeared. After thirty seconds, he put the mouse on Undo and called it back into existence.

It's probably not him, anyway.

He pressed Send again. Before he could stop it, the message flew beyond his reach.

7

$\mathcal{T}$HE NEXT MORNING, Saturday, sipping coffee and enjoying the view from his living room, Ben checked his e-mail on his laptop. His chest tightened when he saw a message from a Li Quan. He started to open it, then sat back on his recliner. It was probably the wrong Li Quan. But he couldn't bring himself to open it and find out.

What was it about Li Quan that troubled Ben Fielding?

Quan was a gifted pianist who made the instrument come alive when he played classical music. But so what? Ben had no musical interests. He did care about sports, and there he had the edge. Ben had to restrain himself when wrestling with Quan on the dorm-room floor. Pound for pound, Quan was just as strong, but Ben had two hundred pounds to Quan's one hundred and thirty. Quan never caught on to basketball, which is why Ben loved to shoot hoops with him. Their closest match was tennis. Ben would usually win 6-4, 6-3. But Quan was tenacious, chasing down every shot. Even though Ben always won, he walked away feeling he'd been outhustled—outdone somehow.

Academics were the biggest sore point. Quan outworked and outperformed him. They'd had one science class together, and without Quan's help studying, Ben never would have gotten an A. He determined not to take another class with him other than English, where he was sure to show him up. But even working in a second language, Quan managed to beat him. Ben knew he was being a sore loser. He knew Quan wasn't competing like he was. That made it worse.

But this was the clincher—when they'd met, Ben was a Christian, a churchgoer. He was the one who'd invited Quan to a campus ministry event. Then Quan became a Christian. At first, Ben was happy for him. But something happened. Quan was always reading his Bible and Christian books. He asked Ben question after question. By the end of spring semester Quan had surpassed Ben's knowledge level and was asking him fewer questions. He was always going to Ray, the group leader, and Dan, the college pastor at the church.

Quan was his intellectual superior, the one sure to succeed as professor and writer. But worse yet, he'd become Ben's spiritual superior. How could Ben explain to Quan about his failed marriage? And what would he say about what happened to . . . no, he couldn't even tell him about that. He'd lie if he had to, but he wouldn't go there. No way.

Maybe Quan's note would say, "I never went to Harvard; you must be looking for another Li Quan," or "Sorry, Ben, I'm on a writing deadline, and it wouldn't work for you to stay with me. Let's just do lunch."

Ben took one more sip of coffee, leaned forward, and opened the letter.

> *Dear Dabizi,*
>
> *How wonderful to hear from my old friend! Ming and I and our son, Shen, will be most happy to have you stay with us. (I have only one burrow—wily hares have the other two.) You will know you are here when you come to our large ginkgo tree, which is two hundred years old. Of course, there are many other ginkgo trees, so I will send you more specific directions!*
>
> *Will you be renting a car? It is at least a three-hour drive from Shanghai. Four hours or more if it is raining. Please tell us, when will you arrive? We will prepare a bed for you. We have no Frisbee, though I'm sure many Chinese companies have imitated them and sell them much cheaper!*
>
> *Will Pam be coming with you? We hope so. Ming is eager to meet you both. We have pictures of you from college and the wedding photograph you sent in one of your last letters. Twenty years ago now! Do you have children? Shen is our only child.*
>
> *If it is not too much to ask, would you bring a copy of the book we used to study together? I will be glad to pay you what I can. An English version is alright, but if you know where to find a Mandarin book of that kind, it would be appreciated. Thank you.*
>
> *We are eager to have you in our home.*
>
> *Your brother,*
> *Li Quan*

Ben reread each line of the e-mail. "Shanghai."

Well, that part's good. I can meet with PTE and visit the new factory without booking an extra flight.

"Four hours or more if it is raining."

Dirt roads?

"The book we used to read together."

He must mean the Bible. Why didn't he just say so?

"Your brother."

Ben shook his head and sighed. *What have I gotten myself into?*

Nine days later, on Monday, October 1, Ben Fielding was on an airplane headed to Seattle, Tokyo, and Shanghai. His frequent travel wearied him, but he didn't begrudge it. It was his down payment on becoming CEO of Getz International. Besides, he flew first class, and the crews knew him by name. They also knew that nothing pleased him more than to have a few mao-tais to get him off the ground.

He settled into his spacious seat and pulled out the latest best-seller by the Dalai Lama, his smiling face featured on the cover. He read forty minutes, admiring the Lama's homespun wisdom and ancient philosophical insights.

Ben's mind wandered to the adventure ahead. In all his visits, he'd never spent the night outside a major Chinese city. Martin had talked him into making this a six-week trip, with weekly meetings in Shanghai, visits to the new factory, hobnobbing with brass, and establishing strategic business contacts. Realistically, he couldn't imagine staying at Quan's the whole six weeks. Maybe a couple, just enough to say he'd done it, that he'd lived with a Chinese family and seen their world up close. He'd learn things that would give Getz a further edge. And Martin was right—it would be great PR. Back when Ben was a "family man," he wasn't expected to be gone so long. But nowadays, what did it matter? Besides, China had become his second home.

Ben pulled out a familiar sheet from his briefcase. It was Monday morning. Career goals. He closed his eyes and visualized.

Ben got the usual adrenaline rush. But he couldn't just jump in the Jaguar and head to the office. He was stuck in the comfort of first class, wondering if accomplishing these goals would ever make him happy. Was happiness an illusion? Something you strove for and never attained? Maybe the Dalai Lama had the answer. Nobody else seemed to.

Disgusted with himself for the sentimentality, he caught the flight attendant's attention and motioned for a mao-tai. Swishing the liquid comfort in the glass, he buried himself in the *Wall Street Journal.*

8

*B*EN MANEUVERED through Shanghai's Hongqiao Airport, in the din of blustering Chinese and confused foreigners. He was irritated he'd had to fly into this old airport since every flight into the newer Pudong International was booked.

For Ben's body, it was late Monday, but all over China, with its single time zone, it was sixteen hours later, Tuesday afternoon. Ben used a veteran traveler's trick that was the greatest deterrent to jet lag. He simply refused to think about the time back home, fully embracing local time as his own.

As he kept turning his shoulders to avoid being bumped by the press of Chinese businessmen, he remembered the old days when you couldn't rent a car at the airport. He'd made the mistake of taking the 505 city bus to Renmin Square. It wasn't luggage-friendly or even passenger-friendly. He couldn't get out at his stop and overshot it by a mile. Ever since, he'd taken the taxi. Wheeling his suitcase behind him, briefcase securely fastened on top, he walked straight out to the first taxi in line. He nodded at the driver, who hopped up smiling at the sight of a promising American tipper.

As they started the fifteen kilometers east to Shanghai, Ben asked the driver in Mandarin if they were expecting rain. The man immediately turned on the meter, realizing this passenger knew standard procedure and wouldn't let him get away with an overcharge.

Despite his fatigue, Ben looked eagerly out the cab window. He'd been enthralled by Shanghai on his first visit and had never lost his fascination with this swarming metroplex. Once "Paris of the East," it now called itself the "Pearl of the Orient." With its thirteen million people and international character, it was China's New York City.

If it weren't for the few historic places still standing, the city would have been completely unrecognizable from the one he'd first seen just a decade before. He marveled at all the parks, squares, pagodas, museums, palaces, and buildings that made this city one big photo op. Shops were everywhere. Business was booming.

To Ben, the dizzying swirl of Shanghai captured the urgency and excitement of China. From the colonial architecture of the former French Concession to the neon-lit high-rises jutting above the city, it was a strange mixture of beauty and charm. Shanghai sat on the Yangtze River delta, where Asia's longest and most important river completed its 5,500-kilometer journey to the Pacific. Shanghai had been magically transformed from a small fishing village in 1850 to China's great City on the Sea. But pockets of raw poverty and vice erupted in the midst of the unabashed commercialism.

Ben had read a half-dozen books on this city, and he rehearsed what he remembered. When the British named her a treaty port, Shanghai became a center of British, French, and American trade. Each colonial presence brought its own experience, architecture, prejudices, and corruption. Many Chinese chose to live outside the walled Old City, integrating into the foreign settlements. Thus began the mixing of cultures that made Shanghai more reflective of—some claimed, more contaminated by—Western influence than any other Chinese city.

Ben remembered as if it were yesterday the *Wall Street Journal* article he'd read in 1991. Deng Xiaoping had chosen Shanghai as the engine of the country's commercial renaissance, promising it would one day rival Hong Kong. That same week Ben had gone to Martin and boldly proposed he begin intensive Mandarin language study. Some on the management team thought Ben had gone off the deep end, but his understanding of the importance of Shanghai had proven him a visionary. This great city hosted the nation's stock market, housed the most important industrial complex in China, and by itself accounted for one-sixth of the country's gross national product.

On his first visit in 1991, Ben had nurtured a relationship between Getz and the fledgling PTE, Pudong Technical Enterprises. He'd cultivated strategic relationships that firmly established the presence of Getz International in Shanghai and, later, Beijing. From those two base cities, in partnership with PTE, Getz was strategically poised to do business with the one-fifth of the human race who lived in China.

Since Ben's first visit, Shanghai's population had moved out of alley housing in the city center to brand-new apartments in the suburbs. Now he could find the offices of AT&T, DuPont, Merrill Lynch, and Volkswagen in the Shanghai skyline. Ben gazed at another new shopping center, another new mall, another new everything. He couldn't help but smile as they drove by a Starbucks. Fifteen years ago there had been one hundred and fifty high-rise buildings in the city. Now there were more than fifteen hundred—with new ones every week. Ben had read that Shanghai was the home of one-fifth of all the world's construction cranes. He could see a dozen of them from the taxi, and bamboo scaffolding everywhere.

As Ben had counted on, Shanghai's open-door policy had drawn in droves of foreign investors. Tens of thousands of expatriates permeated the place. Ralph Lauren and Christian Dior had seduced the city from the dull blue uniforms of Mao to stylish fashions, turning it into a Milan of the East. Almost all the clothes he saw were Western—not only the suits and ties, but also the coats, jeans, and athletic shoes. He saw only a few throwbacks in the crowd—a little boy in an orange jumpsuit proudly wearing a military cap, and an old man in plain billowy Mao blues and grays.

They stopped suddenly, eight cars back from an accident of car and bicycle. He'd read that one bicycler a day was killed in Shanghai, and Ben hoped this wasn't the one. Still, the statistic struck him as amazingly small as he watched the weaving of thousands of bikes among the cars.

The driver cursed, made a quick right turn onto a curbside, then drove with front and back right tires on the sidewalk to get to a parallel road. Suddenly the main thoroughfare, Nanjing Donglu, was just ahead. The driver threw up his hands, realizing he'd have to turn onto it. Now they were immersed in a teeming sea of humanity.

Ben paid rapt attention like a little boy at a Red Sox game. Nanjing Donglu boasted a higher concentration of people, buses, cars, and bicycles than any other street in the world. The sheer density defied explanation. It reminded Ben of an old *Star Trek* episode he'd seen as a child, in which spaceship windows looked out on people crowded so closely they couldn't move. Yet here they did move, and surprisingly rapidly. Pressed together like slabs of bacon, they still managed to move faster than Westerners with ten times the room.

They pulled up to a stoplight, now just a few kilometers from PTE. On both sides of the street Ben saw brokerage houses, with people pushing their way in to play the market. The sidewalks were unbelievably crowded. He'd never been anywhere in America that was even close. It seemed less like sidewalks and more like a giant rock concert with the fire marshal out of town, and they kept stuffing people in. Ben looked toward the street corner at the pack of a hundred people waiting to cross. Most of the men wore suits and ties. Half the people had pagers and cell phones in hand, many of them in use.

Phones and pagers were practical, but they were also stylish, like designer sunglasses and American sportswear. Shanghai chic. This was America's Eastern mirror—image was everything. Higher salaries, more goods, and way more nightlife venues.

Ironic, Ben thought, that the Communist Party had been born in Shanghai. More than any other city, it was cosmopolitan, international, economically liberated, motivated toward trade—in short, the very contradiction of Communism. The city's fashion, music, and romance—along with large slices of vice, including prostitution—had in 1949 withered under the scalding uniformity and starkness of Mao's Communism. While it conformed on the outside, Ben knew, it had never conformed on the inside. As Communism loosened its grip, the full flower of Shanghai's independence and business energy had exploded. Shanghai was the city that defeated the economics of Mao.

The light changed, and a flood of pedestrian traffic washed through the streets, between cars, hands on hoods and tailgates. Only in Bangkok had he seen traffic even approaching this. If someone fell, Ben wondered, could they get up before being trampled?

A businessman in suit and tie vaulted off the taxi's trunk. Ben felt goose bumps at the giddy entrepreneurial spirit of Shanghai. Of the city's six million bicycle commuters, three million seemed to be on this street. Suddenly rain started to fall. In unison every bike stopped, and a rainbow of colors appeared out of nowhere. Red, yellow, blue, green, and purple rain slickers. It looked choreographed, like synchronized swimmers, wet colors performing a forward dance. The ponchos draped over the handlebars, showing only colors and wheels. Some riders were out of sync, creating gridlock. A million bike bells tinkled. The sensual extravaganza was overwhelming. And hence the saying, "Those who have not seen Shanghai have not seen the world."

As they navigated through one-way traffic behind a Ferrari, Ben looked to the east across the fetid waters of the Huangpu River. There it was—Pudong New Area, a concrete twenty-first–century financial, economic, and commercial center. Rising from former farmland and rice paddies was the magnificent Oriental Pearl TV Tower—a gaudy, flashing, spaceship-like pillar, the tallest in Asia. Shanghai was no longer just a Hong Kong wanna-be. It was the real deal. The aggressive, innovative, never-say-die spirit of Shanghai was the spirit of the new China. And Ben Fielding was in the thick of it.

He spied a flimflam artist fleecing the gullible. They were in a seedy section of town now, one which his grandmother, with her tones of Fundamentalist condemnation, would have called a "den of iniquity." Shanghai's alluring past centered in sepia-lit halls, opium dens, and French villas. The rich took advantage of the dance halls, brothels, glitzy restaurants, international clubs, and even a foreign-run racetrack. Ben felt both desire and discomfort at his memories of his own experiences, most with business acquaintances, in more wealthy and refined dens of iniquity in other parts of Shanghai.

A hoard of bicycles, bells jingling, wove in and out of the paralyzed cars.

"If you're in a hurry, ride a bike," Ben muttered.

He looked out at the JC Mandarin, the magnificent thirty-story, five-star hotel that was his home in Shanghai. He'd be coming back there in just a few hours, before trekking off to Quan's house tomorrow. Ben crooked his neck to see Jin Jiang Tower, the favorite hotel of presidents, prime ministers, and kings. He'd stayed there twice, in the midst of entourages of important-looking dignitaries surrounded by bodyguards and staff.

Part of him longed for the luxury and air of importance of those places, something he knew he wouldn't find in the home of a Chinese university professor. He would miss strolling on the Bund, by the water-front, among the colonial-era buildings at the feet of Shanghai's high-rises, which seemed to reach out to the sky in declaration of the mightiness of man. He'd miss watching the stylish strut by, the dumbstruck tourists, the black marketers buying up foreign currency. But all this was familiar to him. The journey to a semirural China, Quan's China, would be a new adventure.

They pulled up to the skyscraper that housed Pudong Technical Enterprises. The fare came to eighty yuan, about ten dollars. The driver jumped out and removed his luggage a little too eagerly. Ben gave him a hundred yuan, and the driver returned a toothy, capitalist-loving grin.

Ben stored his luggage behind a security desk on the first floor, handing a grateful guard fifty yuan to ensure its safety. He took the elevator to the twenty-eighth floor. When he walked into the office, the secretary rose, bowed her head, and greeted him, then quickly picked up the phone, nodding nonstop. Won Chi, PTE vice president, came bounding out of his office.

"*Ni hao,* Ben Fielding!"

"Ni hao, Won Chi!" Ben said. "How are you?" It was the first phrase he'd learned in Mandarin. He'd come a long way since then. So had Pudong Technical Enterprises. Chi handed him the keys to a company car.

"Not many Americans have license to drive in China." Won Chi liked to practice his English. "Ben Fielding very lucky."

"Ben Fielding is lucky to have a friend like Won Chi. You're the one who cut through the red tape, or I'd still be stuck with a chauffeur! And on this trip that wouldn't work!"

Chi nodded, smiling broadly. "Do not forget. Foreigners cannot stay in Chinese home without registering stay at local PSB and receiving permission. I have called Pushan PSB and explained reason for your visit, but you must still register. Are you sure I cannot take you to dinner?"

"Thank you, but no. I'll just head over to the hotel, settle in, and get a good night's sleep. I'll see you at the ten o'clock meeting. Then I'm off to the Chinese countryside!"

They shook hands warmly. The secretary took him down the elevator to the underground garage and led him to a silver gray Mitsubishi Pajero Mini, a beautiful new four-wheel drive. It had been chosen for Ben when PTE realized how far out of the city he'd be driving. He nodded his approval and drove out into the traffic free-for-all.

Ben checked into the luxury of the JC Mandarin and went down to his favorite hotel restaurant at 6:30 P.M. Though exhausted, he wouldn't let his body force him to go to sleep yet. He would eat, do a light workout in the exercise room, and go to bed on schedule. He prided himself on letting nothing get the best of him, certainly not jet lag.

After a decent sleep for the first night in-country, Ben met Wednesday morning for several hours with the top brass of PTE. They served him a catered lunch brimming with shellfish. Finally, after another round of handshakes, he headed for the car, adrenaline kicking in for the journey he anticipated and dreaded at the same time.

Once Ben drove seventy kilometers out of Shanghai, he realized he'd already gone farther out of the city than he'd ever been. And he still had two hours left to go. He relished his independence. To drive alone was to be in control. But he couldn't help being a bit miffed that Quan hadn't volunteered to pick him up from the Shanghai airport. Couldn't he get time off from the classroom to pick up his roommate, after twenty-two years? Of course, Ben would have insisted on renting the car anyway, since he had meetings and wanted the freedom to come and go between Pushan and Shanghai. But that wasn't the point. Quan couldn't have known Ben was one of few foreigners with the special driving permit. At least he could have *offered* to pick him up.

Why didn't he?

9

FTER THREE AND A HALF HOURS of driving, Ben cut through the eastern hem of Pushan, a city of a quarter million—small by Chinese standards. Nine kilometers outside the city center he found himself negotiating crumbling roads, where the trick was to stay away from the edges. He passed rows of run-down connected houses with brick walls separating tiny enclosures, which gave a faint semblance of ownership and privacy.

Ben stared at tiny women pulling overloaded carts, peasants on rusty bikes, stray sickly dogs, and more chicken coops than he'd ever seen. He wanted to pull out his camera but refused to look like a tourist. Not that most of these people had ever seen a tourist.

Quan must hate city life to live this far out.

Finally Ben passed one of the few marked side roads, Guangxi, mentioned on Quan's directions. He slowed down, then counted the irregularly spaced houses until he came to the seventh. There was no number to identify it. But there was a big old ginkgo tree, with brownish-gray bark and yellow branches pointing every which way. Forty feet back from it sat a tiny house.

This can't be it.

The house was run-down. It was brick, its roof thatched haphazardly with bamboo and plaster. Surely a university professor wouldn't live in a shanty like this. Ben got out of the car tentatively, breathing the smell of sunbaked earth and something else, less pleasant.

Why didn't I insist on a hotel?

Suddenly the front door opened. Out came a middle-aged man with thin gray hair receding from his protruding forehead. The hair was slightly misshapen, suggesting it hadn't been cut by a barber. His clothes were plain, untailored, and apparently homemade.

"Hello, Dabizi!" the man said in English, smiling broadly. He ran to Ben and put his arms around him. The embrace was firm yet polite, not a sloppy European hug. But Ben knew that for a Chinese this was warm affection indeed. In fact, in all his trips to China, this was the first time a Chinese had greeted him with an embrace instead of a handshake. Quan hadn't forgotten everything from America.

"Still calling me Big Nose?" Ben said in English. He tried not to stare at Li Quan's left ear. It looked like a wrestler's cauliflower ear, part of the lobe not just misshapen but missing. Right below, on the left side of his neck, was a five-inch scar, healed over but red and rough. It looked as if surgery had been done without a proper suture.

"Welcome, my friend."

"You look well, Li Quan," Ben lied in Mandarin.

Quan backed up and stared at his old roommate, who twenty years ago hadn't known how to say any Chinese words not on a menu.

"Surprised? I took some classes. And I've gotten practice on trips to China."

"Ben Fielding has been to China before?"

"Yes, but not here. Not nearly this far out."

"Your Mandarin is . . . impressive!"

"Not as good as your English. And it never will be."

"Welcome to Zhongguo, Ben Fielding."

"The Middle Kingdom."

"I was prepared to explain our name for China. Yet this you already know, and much more."

A pudgy little boy bounced out the front door onto a creaky wooden step. Just behind him came a slightly built woman dressed in peasant trousers and a plain, light green Mandarin jacket. Her hair was pulled back in a braided pigtail. Behind her narrow eyelids were large eyes, luminous. Ben stared at her. She looked at his feet.

Quan led him to her. Slight and strong, her beauty was natural and understated. The closer she got, the more striking she appeared. He thought she was the most lovely woman he'd ever seen.

"This is my son, Shen. This is Ming, she who I am honored to call my wife."

She put her hands together, then half bowed her head, reminding Ben of the standard Cambodian greeting he'd seen on his three trips to Phnom Penh.

Ben nodded and smiled at her. "Ni hao."

She looked down sheepishly. She said in English, "We pleased to meet you. Very sorry Pam and children unable to come. Li Quan not say Ben Fielding speak Chinese."

"Because Li Quan did not know!" Quan said, smiling. "If my roommate Ben Fielding has become fluent in Mandarin, I wonder if Burger Magic now sells *bai cai!*"

"Bok choy? I don't think so. And I'm not that fluent, but at least nothing slips by me on the menus anymore. Speaking of which, I want to take you out to the best restaurant in Pushan."

"Restaurant?" Shen said, voice high and cracking. They all laughed, and his broad face reddened.

"Yes, Li Shen," Ben said, reaching down to shake his pudgy hand. "We will have quail eggs if you'd like. And what is your favorite dessert?"

"*Bing xi lin,*" he said, eyes quivering.

"Well, when we go to the restaurant you can have all the ice cream you want!" He looked at Quan. "Where's your favorite place to eat?"

"We seldom go to restaurants."

"No? Well, we'll find a good place to eat—my treat."

"You must be tired," Quan said. "Let me help with your bags. Ming has prepared something for you."

"It is not much," she said. "*Liang cai—huangua, xi hongshi.*"

"A cold dish is fine—tomatoes and cucumbers are perfect," Ben said. Noticing an unpleasant odor, he peered around the back of the house and saw a toolshed and a small wire fence.

"Chicken coop," Ming said, giggling like a schoolgirl. "Quan show me how to fix eggs like in America."

Ben lowered his head as he walked through the doorway. It smelled stale, old, and weathered, as though air and water had worked their way in and taken their toll. He'd told himself that the house couldn't be as small as it looked, that it had to have an extension he couldn't see from the front. But he was wrong. It was tiny, smaller than his office. There was little decoration. The notable exception was a bronze lion, head tilted back in a roar, sitting on the center of the table. The lion's right paw rested on a ball. Ben had seen stone lions outside of buildings and the doglike lions of the Buddhist temples, but this one was different.

A small coal-burning stove sat in one corner and a silver tank in the other. Ben knew of these—"gas bombs," foreigners called them. A propane-like gas cylinder notorious for its sudden explosions.

He and Jeffrey had obviously overestimated a professor's salary. They'd figured Quan's home, especially this far out, wouldn't be as nice as the private homes of their business associates at PTE, the only ones Ben had visited. But he wasn't prepared for how Spartan and tiny this place was. One room. Two beds. No, three beds, all small, with little room to walk around them.

"Not large by American standards," Quan said. "But we have electricity. It works most of the time. We have two lamps. And we have a telephone and . . . new computer!" He pointed proudly at the boxy computer butted up against the small bed Ben assumed to be Shen's. "Saved money for this two years. We got e-mail connection only a few days before you contacted us. Otherwise, you might never have found the right Li Quan. God wanted you to come here, I think!"

Ben saw some books on the desk. He recognized one of them from his college English class—Milton's *Paradise Lost*. There were a dozen books, half of them textbooks from college, at least twenty-five years old.

"Your other books are in your office? And how many books has my old friend written by now? I hope you'll sign one for me. You don't keep any at home? Don't be modest, Professor. Tell me, Ming, how many books has your husband written?"

Ming looked down shyly.

"I will tell you such things soon enough," Quan said. "But do you remember our short-story book from English Literature?" He pulled it off the desk.

"I've tried to forget. You always loved books. What did you used to say? Some proverb about books?"

"A book holds a house of gold."

"Yeah, that was it. You had a proverb for everything."

"I am Chinese. We think in pictures. We invented the proverb. But this you know, for you have studied our language." Quan pointed to a cot and said, "Here is your bed." It was just the right size—for someone six inches shorter than Ben. He wondered who they'd borrowed it from, who'd slept in it last. If it was a child, Ben hoped he wasn't a bed wetter.

"Sheets clean," Ming said. At that moment something came crawling over the far side of the cot, as if it had just ascended a peak and was ready to plant a flag. Ben stiffened. The cockroach seemed to be staring at him, sizing up his new bedmate. Ben felt embarrassed for his hosts, but either they didn't notice or regarded the roach as part of the landscape.

"I hate to put you out," Ben said.

"No problema," Quan said, grinning.

"I'd be happy to stay at a hotel, so I won't be in your way."

"You are not in our way," Quan said. "We have looked forward to having you." He paused. "But we understand if a hotel would be better for you. There is one eight kilometers from here, if you prefer."

"Oh no, this is fine for me. I was just thinking of you. I really appreciate your hospitality."

"Xiexie," Ming said, smiling.

"Buyong xie," Ben said. He looked around the room. "No piano? Remember how we hung out at Warlin Hall? You'd play Bach and Beethoven, and sometimes we'd get you to play rock songs."

"No room for piano," Quan said.

And no way he can afford one, Ben thought, kicking himself for asking the question.

Ben glanced at the pitcher Ming placed on the dinner table and wondered how he could get to one of his bottled waters in his suitcase.

"Please sit down," Quan said, stretching out his hand. There were five chairs, two partially broken, which were quickly taken by Quan and Ming. Shen took another. This left two chairs—one mahogany, large and beautifully handcrafted, with embroidered velvety cushions on the seat, back, and arms. It had an almost regal look, entirely out of place in this modest home. Assuming it was the chair of honor intended for the guest, Ben started to sit in it. Quan quickly stood and pointed to the other chair, the second-best one of the lot.

"Please sit here, my friend." Ben sat next to Quan, directly across the table from the unoccupied fifth chair.

Who else is coming?

"This is *xigua,* correct?" Ben asked.

"Watermelon. Yes!" Quan smiled broadly. "Join hands, please."

Ben swallowed hard and felt Quan's and Shen's hands touch his. He held them lightly but felt them both squeeze. Shen's hand felt like a plump sausage.

"Thank you, Zhu Yesu," Quan said fervently, "that you have brought to us my friend Ben Fielding. We pray he will enjoy this visit with us. And that you would bless his wife, Pam, and their children and comfort them in his absence. Amen."

Ming prayed, then Shen, both in Chinese. Ben fidgeted but kept quiet. He didn't understand some of this unique spiritual vocabulary. Finally Quan prayed again. After his amen and two others, Quan poured water into Ben's glass.

"No need to worry—water boiled," he said. "No Chinese bacteria." Ben shrugged as if the thought hadn't occurred to him.

Ming rose to the stove, only two feet behind her chair, then presented a long metallic plate in the shape of a large fish, with tail and head fashioned on the two ends. On it were four small freshwater fish Ben couldn't identify.

"This was my grandmother's plate," Quan said. "We always serve fish to new guests."

"Did you catch them?" Ben asked. "Still a fisherman?"

"Shen and I caught them together." Shen grinned, proud as his father.

Ming bowed nervously. "I am sorry we do not have . . . " She looked at Quan for the right words.

"Forks and spoons," Quan said.

"*Kuaizi* are fine," Ben said, picking up his chopsticks and wielding them so effortlessly he won another admiring nod from Quan.

Ben considered the bronze lion at the table's center. Whenever he looked at it, he had the sensation the lion was looking back.

He reminded himself to smile as he ate, though the taste was bland compared to what he'd become accustomed to in the nice restaurants.

"Very good, Ming. Xiexie," Ben said when the meal was done. She smiled and bowed her head, then stood, took his plate, and backed away.

After clearing the table, Quan and Ming sat on their bed. Shen crawled onto the center of his, sitting like an American Indian at powwow. Ben sat on the edge of the third bed, two feet from Shen's, pressed against the brick wall. He looked warily for any signs of the roach.

"Minghua's father was Chinese, but her mother was Cambodian," Quan said. Ming told the story of how her parents met and where she grew up. She spoke in rough English, though Ben assured her he could follow Mandarin. All four of them were eager to use their second language.

"Now, please," Ming said, "tell us how Ben Fielding's family is."

"*Tamen hen hao.* They are fine."

"Your Pamela is well?" Quan asked.

"I spoke to her last week. She sends her greetings to both of you." Actually, he hadn't phoned Pam for three weeks or seen her in six. He hadn't even told her he was going to China, though he'd told Kimmy, so Pam presumably knew. There was an awkward silence.

"I don't see Pam much anymore."

Quan and Ming looked at each other blankly, then back at him.

"We've been divorced for a couple of years."

He hadn't been there an hour, and already the unpleasantness kicked in. Quan looked at Ben. "I am sorry." Ming's eyes watered as if she'd just heard a loved one had died.

Ben squirmed, scolding himself for not lying. "I brought you a gift," he said, reaching down and unzipping his larger suitcase. He pulled out a leather jacket and handed it to Quan.

"I have not seen one like it, not even in the marketplace."

"It's a new label, Marpas. Made in Argentina. Their leather has this almost maroon tint to it, very distinctive."

Quan put it on as Ming watched, wide-eyed and giggling, then holding her hands together in girlish delight.

"Thank you, Ben Fielding," Quan said.

"You're most welcome, Little Grasshopper."

Ming's jaw dropped. "Little Grasshopper?" She giggled again. Shen joined her.

Quan blushed crimson. "Nickname is hard to explain. Came from very strange American television program."

Ben pulled out another beautiful leather jacket and held it up. He handed it to Ming, who looked stunned. He'd bought one small enough for a slender seventh-grade girl, but when she put it on, it was still too big.

"I'm sorry about the size. Maybe I could—"

"*Bu*—no, size very good," she said. She ran her hands over it, then held out her arms and stared. Ben looked around the room, searching for a mirror. He didn't see one. Suddenly it dawned on him—there wasn't any mirror. In fact, now that he thought of it, there wasn't any bathroom!

Ben looked at Shen, now on the bed behind his parents, peeking out between them.

"And here's something for Li Shen."

Ben pulled out the box. Shen slid off the bed and walked forward on tiptoe. He held the box, eyes wide, then opened it. He gasped, then smiled broadly and pulled out two brand-new basketball shoes.

"Nike!" Shen exclaimed, as if he'd struck a vein of gold.

Ming covered her mouth with both hands. Quan laughed. "What do you say to Mr. Fielding, Shen?"

"Xiexie. Thank you very much," he added in English.

"You speak fine English. Your father is a good teacher. And you, a good learner."

Quan helped him tie the laces. Shen ran outside. They watched him out the front door, all laughing as his squatty body ran wildly. He touched the corky bark of the ginkgo tree, then ran again aimlessly, skipping and jumping.

"He is perhaps like his father," Ming said. "Little Grasshopper?"

Quan blushed again. Ming couldn't stop giggling.

"Maybe the shoes are a little big," Ben said.

"He will grow into them," Quan said. "My old friend is most generous."

"I almost forgot." Ben went back to his suitcase and pulled out a blue plastic disk, then threw it across the room at Quan, startling Ming.

Quan caught it. "Frisbee!"

He threw it to Ming. It bounced off her shoulder. She laughed delightfully.

Shen ran in the door just as Ben picked up the Frisbee. He tossed it to him. Shen hadn't recovered yet from the shoes, and the sight of the Frisbee was almost too much for him. Ben could see him tremble. They went outside, and for the next twenty minutes all four played catch. As the sky grayed toward nightfall, they settled back indoors, sitting on the beds. Since Quan's English, though a bit rusty, was better than Ben's Mandarin, and since he wanted Ming and Shen to hear more English, Quan insisted English be their language of choice.

"I must know, Ben," Quan said. "Do you have children?"

"Yes. Two daughters. Melissa's twenty. Kim's seventeen." He thought of saying something else but quickly pushed it back.

Ben wanted to sleep off the jet lag and wondered how he could do that when his bed was in the living room—the *only* room. He noticed Quan staring at him, as if waiting for him to say something else. But what?

"Well, how about I unpack?" Ben saw there was only one small dresser, probably shared by his three hosts. "Actually, I think I'd prefer to just keep things in my suitcase. Sure, that's what I usually do." He rummaged through his clothes; then his hand fell on a black box.

"Oh. I forgot," Ben said. "I think this is what you asked for." He handed the box to Quan.

"Shengjing?" he asked, reverently.

Ming quickly moved to the front window and pulled the frayed curtains, then to the back and did the same. Then she locked the front door.

Quan sat on the bed, legs crossed, Ming beside him. He gently placed the box on his lap, slowly taking the lid off, as if it were a box of explosives. He lifted out the black book, hands trembling. He smelled it, then opened it and reverently touched the gilded edges and words on the page.

Ming also touched the book. Then, while Quan examined it closely, like an appraiser judging a diamond, she picked up the box. She carefully ran her fingers over the cardboard. Ming got up and put it under a blanket in the corner of the room, as if she were a dog hiding a bone.

"Did they inventory this?" Quan asked.

"What?"

"At the airport, did they write down that you brought Shengjing with you?"

"No, this was checked luggage. They didn't even open it in customs."

"Forgive me, my friend," Quan said. "You must be tired. We will be quiet now. We will go to bed early, so you may sleep. Tomorrow I am not working. I will show you Pushan. And . . . oh yes, there is a flashlight." He gestured to the yellow plastic object on the desk. "It is nearly dark. There—" he pointed out the window—"by chicken coop, you can see the outhouse."

Ben suddenly realized the toolshed he'd seen wasn't a toolshed.

"We used to share one with five neighbors, like dorm bathroom at college but not so clean." Quan smiled. "But it was a long walk. Now we have our own! You may wish to use it?"

Well, yes and no, Ben thought. He sat on the edge of his bed, trying to figure out his next move. He wished he'd brought pajamas. He'd have had to buy them, since he hadn't worn them since second grade, but . . .

Quan went to his knees in the corner of the room, Bible in his hands, Ming beside him. Since eyes were off Ben a moment, he walked over and picked up the flashlight, trying to look casual. He opened the door and walked out.

After holding his breath longer than he thought possible, Ben raced out of the outhouse and through the chicken coop. Finding no patch of grass to wipe his feet on, he went to the ginkgo tree and used the bark. Shining the flashlight on the tree, he saw someone had carved a heart and in it had engraved "L. Q. + C. M." Li Quan plus Chan Minghua? Ben smiled. The discovery warmed him one moment and struck a blow to him the next. Once he had carved a girl's name on a tree. She had borne him two children. No, three children.

He returned to the house, breathing deeply air that now seemed comparatively fresh. Quan and Ming looked up from their bed and Shen from his, all under their covers. The room was filled with eerie flickering shadows, hinting of an unseen presence. The lion on the table stared at Ben. The Bible was nowhere to be seen. Ben shuffled to his bed and blew out the last candle.

10

$\mathcal{T}$HEY PARKED IN PUSHAN, half on a sidewalk. Ben felt the jet lag, but his five hours of sleep hadn't been so bad, once he stopped wrestling with the short sheets.

Ben and Quan looked both ways before crossing a street that would have terrified a New Yorker. They ran as if their life depended on it, which it did. Drivers seemed not to see them, except some who actually sped up. They stopped halfway across, cars passing within inches on both sides. At the first break they took a mad dash. Quan instinctively stiff-armed a bicycle to avoid being brushed. The cyclist rang his caution bell.

Ben stood on the sidewalk, catching his breath. He laughed. "It's like playing dodgeball . . . but with higher stakes."

They walked by a small park, where at least two dozen village elders stood under the trees doing *tai ji quan* exercises. Their movements were slow and measured, like cats stalking their prey. Several cages hung on branches, containing the exercisers' pet songbirds.

They walked by tiny shops filled with clothing, tobacco, and sundries. It was midmorning, but already the aroma of pork, fish, steamed rice, and vegetables wafted from the hawker stands. Ben bought a few hard candies from one hawker. He was immediately approached by another carrying a rattan basket full of cakes, candies, and drink bottles. Ben handed him a coin and got two cakes in exchange. He gave one to Quan and crunched on the other. On the food chain it fell somewhere between pound cake and Styrofoam.

An orange lion's head towered above the pedestrians. As the crowd parted, two men—only their legs visible—walked by, one in the lion's head, the other supporting its body. Behind them appeared a green dragon's head with perhaps four people inside.

"It's not Chinese New Year," Ben said. "What's going on?"

"A birthday, perhaps? By putting on costumes, it is easier for them to stay together and get through the crowd. When people see a lion and a dragon, they are more likely to move out of the way."

Ben stopped to observe three curbside doctors. One was examining an old woman's goiter; another was dispensing homegrown remedies, herbs, and oils. Next to him stood a street dentist, instruments hanging from a nail on a wall, his foot-powered drill beside him. In a bamboo chair in front of him sat a worried-looking old gentleman. The dentist was preparing to do an extraction. A toothless old woman sat next in line.

"What's she here for?" Ben asked Quan.

"To be fitted for dentures?" Quan suggested. Ben walked quickly ahead, not wanting to hear the patient's appraisal of the doctor's tooth-pulling skills.

Quan handed over a coin to a vendor hawking lice shampoo. Ben cringed, considering the implications of the purchase.

A few shops down, Ben stared at a limp, plucked goose, its neck hanging like a pendulum, swaying in the breeze. Next to it hung a large fish, then what appeared to be strips of pork, crawling with dozens of flies.

Suddenly, a raw fishy smell permeated the air. There was much chatter as two men rolled up a barrel that had just arrived from port. A fifty-year-old eel skinner with short sleeves and powerful forearms—himself the source of much of the fishy smell—squatted on the curb. Another man opened the barrel, dipped in a pail, then handed it to the skinner. It was full of black, shiny eels.

With his right hand he pulled out a boning knife, then with his left grabbed a slithering specimen. Quickly he hung the eel on a board nail, pulled the creature taut, and with a surgeon's precision removed its skin and bones. He did this repeatedly, five eels in a row, splattering blood, so neatly and quickly Ben was still contemplating the skinner's first procedure when he'd finished his fifth. The man's bare arms and old trousers were covered with blood and stray eel parts.

"Want to buy?" the skinner asked Ben.

"*Bu yao,*" Quan said quickly, stepping in and shaking his head. "Xiexie."

When they started to walk away, an itchy mongrel dog eyed Ben suspiciously. The dog was finishing a meal of stringy garbage. He turned his attention toward the more promising spectacle of eel skinning.

"Chinese dogs have reason to be nervous around knives," Quan said.

"So I've heard," Ben replied. They walked by a shoe and clothing store, and Ben pointed and laughed at one clothing label that said "Nixe" and another that said "Adidos." They stepped inside an electronics store the size of a tobacco kiosk. He picked up a faded box labeled Microsoft Office. The box was papered with photocopies. Ben smiled. "Ten yuan? Let's see; what's that, just over a dollar? Microsoft must sell cheap to their Chinese retailers."

"In China," Quan said, "*copyright* means 'right to copy.'"

"Guess I should be grateful it isn't as easy to reproduce semiconductors and computer chips."

"Not yet," Quan said.

It was chillier than he'd expected, so Ben looked at a North Face jacket with a tag of four hundred yuan. He offered two hundred and, when he showed his American dollars, finally got it for two hundred forty, or thirty dollars. Not the real thing, but the jacket was high quality and comfortable. The zipper was on the left side, but he'd bought enough clothes in China that he was used to it. He'd gotten better deals in China but didn't want to barter too much. Why not let the merchants tell their stories about their sales to rich Americans? Besides, Pushan was way off the tourist routes.

He walked by a woman who stuck out a handful of colorful silk scarves. He didn't know when he'd have the next chance, so he bought a dozen scarves, some for Jen and his daughters, and the rest to spread out at Getz. He always got an amazing amount of mileage from six dollars' worth of scarves.

After a few hours they entered a restaurant. Ben insisted Getz International would buy their lunch. He smiled at the quaint meal descriptions on the menu, such as "Beautiful Butterfly Greeting Guest."

Ben ordered bean curd with preserved duck eggs. He insisted they share freshwater crab in wine. At the top of the dessert menu was "Eight Precious Rice." Ben ordered it—steamed sticky rice with red bean paste, topped with eight different candied fruits.

Ben dug into the brothy egg flower soup. When the big bowl came, he poured on the soy sauce, crunched on the snow peas, and drank the jasmine tea. They were far enough south for the best sticky rice. He added celery, bean sprouts, peanuts, and onions. The strong contrasting flavors made his mouth water. The duck eggs and crab were wonderful. Ben's only regret was that some of the candied fruit tasted like . . . well, like nothing he ever wanted to taste again.

"Since you introduced it to me back in Cambridge, I've never stopped eating Chinese food," Ben said.

"When Americans visit China and ask what meat it is, the waiter always answers pork, beef, or chicken. Li Quan's proverb for Americans—always know what you are ordering in Chinese restaurants. Guessing is not a good plan. Ben Fielding knows what he is doing!"

"Do you miss any American food?"

"Hamburgers and french fries at Burger Magic," Quan said. "McDonald's here in China is not so good. Only been one time, in Shanghai."

"You didn't like American food at first, remember?"

"When they first put a big piece of meat and lumpy potatoes in front of me, I thought I would starve. How could they eat such things? But I adapted, as you have."

After lunch, back in the street market, Ben insisted on buying some things for the Li family, including a souvenir fork and spoon. "I don't need them—but just so you can teach Shen in case he gets to visit America."

"I do not think that will happen," Quan said. "But then, I did not think I would go to America either. Yet I was there seven years."

After a while they came to a short, crumbling stone wall and found a space to sit. They drank bottled waters.

"Remember how I used to kid you about your Chinese proverbs?"

"Very well," Quan said.

"One of my favorites was 'Do not use a hatchet to remove a fly from your friend's forehead.'"

"Always wise advice," Quan said. "Very smart, these Chinese. And when you kept telling me there was no way I should expect to get an A in English, since it was my second language, I always said, 'Those who say it cannot be done should not interrupt the person doing it.'"

"That's a great business principle," Ben said.

"Chinese have been doing business for five thousand years. Americans have been at it for . . . three or four hundred? That's a big head start. But Americans have good sayings too. You say, 'Don't bite the hand that feeds you.' We say, 'Do not cook your hunting dog.'"

"You did manage to nail your A in English. You always got what you set your mind to."

"Perhaps not always."

One story led to another, and though they spoke mostly English, they switched at will to Mandarin.

"Li Quan is amazed at the changes in his old roommate."

"What do you mean?"

"When I took you to the Double Dragon in college, you did not know what to do with chopsticks. So when I heard you were coming to China, I went to the neighbors and to the people of my . . . to some other people I know . . . and I asked them for a fork to borrow. No one had any. But now you come and I see you skilled with chopsticks. I listen to your beautiful Mandarin and I wonder if since I saw you last you have become like an egg—white on outside, yellow on inside. Like very large Chinese guy with big nose."

"Large around the stomach, you mean? Last time I saw you I had a thirty-two-inch waist; now it's thirty-eight."

"And last time you saw me, I had hundreds of hairs on my head. Now I have thirty-seven, perhaps."

They walked again. The longer they talked, the more Ben scolded himself for letting all those years slide by. Ben waved his arm at some bamboo scaffolding, where a crew poured concrete, heavy machinery roared, and sparks flew from welders' torches.

"Just look at this place, will you? Everybody's building. Of course, it's even more prosperous in Shanghai."

"You are more impressed with Shanghai than some Chinese," Quan said.

"Not enamored with the Paris of the East, huh?"

"Some call it by another name."

"Whore of the East? Yeah, I've heard that too. The city of quick riches, ill-gotten gains, and fortunes lost on the tumble of dice. The domain of swindlers, drug runners, the idle rich, gangsters, and backstreet pimps."

Quan nodded. "Some say the only good thing Mao did was clean up Shanghai. Unfortunately, he cleaned it up using guns and sticks. He replaced the undisciplined immorality of the body with a darker disciplined immorality of the soul. Shanghai became bleak and gray, my father said, a sad and hard city. But when the world passed Mao by, Shanghai rose quickly from her ashes. Unfortunately, she went back to immoral practices. Proud and arrogant. The poor once more served the rich. Did you know that a businessman's bar bill in Shanghai is easily a month's salary for a Chinese peasant?"

"I've got to go back and forth to Shanghai for meetings while I'm here. I'll be sure to tell them what you think of them."

"Shrewd, glamorous, sophisticated, business-minded . . . driven by money, not principle," Quan said. "The Shanghainese themselves agree with our stereotypes, though they consider us too stupid to care what we think. They imagine outside Shanghai there is nothing but ignorance. They think they can achieve all their goals and lead the way for China."

"You don't sound convinced."

"Look more carefully, Ben. Corruption is everywhere. Bribery is rampant. In Beijing, wealthy parents have given gifts of refrigerators and computers to elementary teachers to get a 'fair' grade for their child. A hundred million peasants have left the countryside to search for quick riches in cities. They float from job to job. They fuel the profits of the drug rings and commit many crimes. People think only about money these days. By some standards that is progress. Not by mine."

"What's the alternative? Do you prefer poverty?"

"I am no friend of poverty. But there is still poverty everywhere—men from good families turn to selling drugs; girls sell themselves. Men desperate to feed their families get middle-of-the-night drug deliveries at their houses. I have seen it happen. In our area last year seven people I knew took their lives, four of them elderly, whose gray heads should have been crowned with honor and respect. You know the meaning of *jiangxi?*"

"No."

"Despair of the elderly. Many commit suicide. With all the changes, the elderly feel out of place. Useless. Helpless. They do not know what their hearts are searching for. There is much depression in China, much hopelessness. Sometimes the poor believe wealth could make them happy. They kill themselves because they are not rich. Sometimes the rich lose everything in the stock market. Then they kill themselves. And sometimes they just keep making more money. And still they kill themselves."

"I haven't heard much about suicides."

"What you hear is chosen carefully. Suicide does not portray a good image to the watching world. Newspapers are controlled by the Party. They talk about bad things in other countries, not in China. Did you know forty thousand Chinese have dedicated their lives to study and teach about UFOs?"

"What?"

"People are looking, searching. They are right to look. But they look in the wrong places."

"I guess I see a different side on my business trips. I see people eager to go to work, happy about their opportunity."

"You see the outside. Do not confuse China's skin with her bones. Yes, many people have a more comfortable life. The main goal is to make more money, to own more things. Posters of the money god are everywhere—on shopwindows, at businesses, in homes. Getting rich is the main topic on television. I'm glad we do not have one. Money-god figures appear on the screen. We still have our old idols, the demons that have plagued China. And now we have your idols also."

"My idols?"

"America's idols. Materialism. Pleasure. Entertainment. Worship of celebrities. Obsession with sex. Food. Fame. All are idols, false gods. A wise pastor said China's problem used to be Maoism, but now it is Me-ism. The problems on the outside are always easier to deal with than the problems inside."

"You sound like a pessimist."

"See those young people?" He pointed to two teenagers, one wearing a T-shirt featuring a blockbuster American movie, the other an English rock band. "They are infatuated with Western movies and music and sports and culture. They have been taught there is no God. They know nothing of right and wrong and cannot discern what is good from what is bad. They have the longing to go somewhere, but no guides to show them the way. Do you see that old woman approaching us?"

Ben looked at her wrinkled, scowling face.

"Do you not see the emptiness in her eyes? She has heard many promises in her life. All of them were broken. She has given up hope. Look around you, Ben. Of a hundred faces, at least ninety-five look like hers."

A cool rain began to fall, washing the dust from the air, so Ben could no longer taste it on his tongue. Quan pulled from his coat pocket two ponchos. "Blue or green?"

Ben chose the green one, and a moment later, they were staying dry and cozy beneath the big hooded slickers. Ben felt a sort of fireside intimacy.

"Quan?"

"Yes?"

"You asked me last night about whether the Bible had been inventoried at the airport. What did you mean?"

Quan hesitated before replying. "You are allowed to bring in a Bible for yourself. But if they inventory it, they can check you when you leave to be sure you take out one Bible for every one you bring in."

"They really do that?"

"Not as often as they once did. My father owned a Shengjing sewn together from four others."

"What do you mean?"

"A visiting English Christian brought in four Bibles. He was inventoried and therefore required to bring out four. My mother came up with the solution. She carefully removed one fourth of each Bible, then resewed them. The man took out four Bibles, each thinner than the original, yet appearing to be a full book. Mother sewed together the four parts; then she and Father had their own Shengjing. Their first one. I will never forget my mother's beaming face. She had big dimples. She smiled bigger than anyone I have ever known."

"Your father was a pastor and he didn't have a Bible?"

"This is common. A famine for the Word of God. Even now, most Christians do not have their own Bible. Preachers have ridden their bicycles a hundred miles to attend meetings, asking for Bibles to take back to their districts, where hundreds of believers share just a few Bibles, sometimes none."

"Is that why you hid the Bible I gave you?"

"It does not have the required government seal showing it came from a registered church. The moment you gave it to me it became an illegal Shengjing. In China, every honest man has hiding places. I still have my old English Bible from college. It looks like a big ordinary book, and most PSB officers do not know English. It has survived many swoops."

"Swoops?"

"Sudden visits from the police."

"Why was Ming so interested in that box the Bible came in?"

"There is a story behind that."

"There usually is."

"Now is not the time." Quan lifted his head and turned it, as if looking at the clouds to check weather patterns. But while his head was tilted upward, his eyes scanned the horizon.

"The leather coats you gave us are beautiful. The shoes for Shen are very nice." Suddenly he lowered his voice, almost to a whisper. "But the best gift you brought was the Word of God, as great as your friendship itself."

"I guess I didn't realize . . ."

Quan moved his mouth close to Ben's ear, uncomfortably close. "When my father was taken to jail, his sewn-together Bible was confiscated and destroyed. Besides his, there was only one other Shengjing in the church. The owner, Lin Chang, tore out all sixty-six books and entrusted a few to each church member. Usually the pastor would have one or two of them bring the needed book so as not to endanger the entire Shengjing. But once a year he would have all of them bring their Scriptures. My mother had been given the book of Romans. One weekend she was very sick. Mother said, 'I must go to church. If I do not go, part of God's Word will be missing.' But she was so sick. Finally she handed me the book of Romans. She said, 'Take it; guard it—nothing is more precious.'"

"You took it to church?"

"Yes. I felt in awe of being entrusted with something so important. Yet in school I was taught that there was no God, that the old Christians were fools. The older I got, the more skeptical I became. As a teenager I was immersed in the Red Guard of Communist youth. I rejected my parents' faith." He swallowed hard. "Now Shengjing is as precious to me as it was to them."

"I need to ask you something, Quan. Okay, I know once there was plenty of persecution. I understand why you don't trust the government. But do you think you're . . . reading into things a bit because of the past? On one of my trips they gave us a tour of the Religious Affairs Bureau. The bureau offered to take us to a church service in Shanghai. I went. They introduced us to the pastor. He talked to us freely. They worship openly. I heard them sing. They had Bibles. They were even selling Bibles at the church!"

"They submit to restrictions many of us cannot accept."

"But I've heard of areas where even the unregistered churches aren't harassed that much."

"I know of villages and cities where no Christians are in jail. But in other cities dozens of Christians are in jail. Often they're beaten and humiliated. If someone says to you, 'Religious freedom in China is like this,' don't believe him. That is like saying, 'The weather in America is like this—always sunny or always snowing.' It depends on what part of the country you are in, and what season. In China the sun is always shining somewhere. Somewhere else the snow is falling. But the government is capable of magic—they can take you to places where it is usually snowing and show you a glimpse of sunlight so that you can go back and say there is no snow in China. You can write your column or say from your pulpit that you saw no persecution, only freedom. You are telling the truth—but a truth that misleads."

"But they actually showed us Bibles printed by the government. I saw them with my own eyes."

"Yes, it is true. Bibles can be bought at such churches. But eighty percent of all Chinese Christians are in house churches. There are not nearly enough Bibles even for those in registered churches, much less house churches."

"I've heard repeatedly that people exaggerate about persecution in China. Aren't things getting better all the time?"

"You, Ben Fielding, are a man of great faith."

"What do you mean?"

"I wish you were as quick to believe Yesu's truth as you are the Party's propaganda."

"I'm not that gullible—and I don't appreciate your implying I am. Remember, I've been around the block a few times here."

"You are a businessman, Ben. Business is extremely important to the new China. Under Deng we moved away from Mao's socialism, but only because it didn't work. To gain trading status with the West, our leaders had to make China appear not to violate human rights. But meanwhile, the government-run newspapers call for stronger control over religious affairs, as if this were the cry of the people, not the Party. Many Christians are arrested. But they do not want the world to believe this. So they take businessmen like you and political leaders and even religious leaders on tours to prove we are free. Then you go back and reassure everyone in your country."

"You're saying they're using us?"

Quan flashed Ben a look of incredulity he didn't appreciate. "*Of course* they are using you. They use anyone to accomplish their purposes. China wants your business. You want China's business. Their job is to make China look attractive. Your job is to accept the picture they paint, not to question it. That way you can sell your semiconductors and computer chips. They are happy. You are happy. They get rich. You get rich. Everyone believes what he wants to."

"No need to get so cynical, Quan. What I'm saying is . . ." Ben stopped when he saw Quan's darting eyes. Though pretending to look elsewhere, Quan repeatedly looked back at a man standing outside a shop looking at miniature lamps on a sidewalk display.

"Time to move," Quan said, walking ahead of Ben. Quan appeared to look across the street, but again Ben saw his eyes look back. Ben turned his head. The man had decided he didn't need an oil lamp. He was moving on behind them, eyes never looking at them.

On the road, mixed among cars and taxis, were noisy motorbikes. A pull cart came by with tree limbs piled impossibly high, at least eight feet. Ben marveled at the little man pulling the cart. They finally stopped at a tiny park, where men sat playing chess.

"It is almost *xiuxi*. The shops will close for two or three hours. Of course, I keep forgetting. My friend Ben knows about our afternoon rest. We can sit on the grass."

The grass was thin and straggly. Quan glanced at the women and children around them.

"Just because people no longer say *tongzhi*, 'comrade,' it does not mean the Party is dead. Nor that it has changed its heart." He looked behind Ben. "Do not stare, but do you see those men?"

Ben turned casually and saw three men on a bench, talking. "Yes."

"They are not talking to each other. They are talking to God."

"What?"

"You cannot close your eyes or look down in public. Even if you could hear them talk you would hear code words."

"Code words?"

"We need to go to your car. We must go to the hotel."

"What hotel?"

Quan moved so quickly Ben had to run ten feet to catch him.

11

*T*HEY WALKED IN THE FRONT DOOR of what a rusty old sign said was the Huaquia Binguan, the Overseas Chinese Hotel. After a few steps on thin, frayed carpet, Ben concluded that this threadbare establishment had probably looked good in its day. But its day was long past.

Quan carried a bulging plastic sack he'd retrieved from the car. Ben glanced at the front desk. The attendant was helping several visitors. Ben walked just behind Quan up the stairs, on carpet in places worn through to the wood. As they passed the second floor, Ben stopped a moment and looked into a big hallway mirror. He saw his droopy eyes and felt his jet lag, then immediately denied it—part of his mental game to stay on top of things. He hurried to catch up. Now that they were at the third floor, Ben gazed at an identical mirror, this time seeing beads of sweat on his face.

"What floor's it on?"

"Fourth."

"Why didn't we take the elevator?"

"You do not know much about Chinese elevators. Or perhaps only at fine hotels? This is not one of those. Besides, Li Quan thought you could use the exercise."

"Okay, okay. I'm a little out of shape. But I can still whip you on the tennis court."

"Sorry, no tennis courts available in our area."

As they walked down the hall, Quan slowed. He appeared to be going to room 419. A maid walked around the corner at the hall's end. Quan immediately started walking again, passing her and pausing outside room 427. When she disappeared, he turned around, went back to 419, and knocked.

"Yes?" The voice was English.

"Family," Quan said.

The man opened the door, looked nervously at Ben, and said, "Hello." He gestured them in and closed the door behind him.

The man went to his television, turned it up loud, then proceeded to ignore it. He came back to Quan and Ben, who were still standing.

"This is my friend from America, Ben Fielding. This is Mister James."

"It is good to see you," Mr. James said. His English had a slight French accent. Ben guessed he was Canadian.

"Here is your bread and meat," Quan said, handing him the sack.

Bread and meat? Ben thought. Quan hadn't bought it at the market. If it was from home, wouldn't meat have been spoiling in the car?

"And here is your music," Mr. James said, handing him a small package wrapped in newspaper and carefully taped. "Classical. Your favorite."

"CDs?" Ben asked.

Quan and Mr. James both nodded.

"I cannot stay," Quan said. "My friend and I have much to do."

"Can you come by Thursday night?"

"Yes, I think so. Late, perhaps."

"Good. I may have more music for you."

Quan said good-bye to the mysterious Mr. James, who hugged him, which made Ben feel distinctly uncomfortable. Quan led the way into the hallway and to the stairwell. Ben followed, with the same uneasy feeling he had when playing a complicated board game for the first time. He hated not knowing what was going on, but he wasn't about to ask.

They walked down the stairs quietly, without talking, passing by two old men in faded blue Mao jackets, hanging loosely. When they walked outside the hotel, Ben noticed two men across the street, one well dressed, with a military posture but no uniform. Though fifty feet away, Ben saw eyes of black steel staring at him. He shuddered.

Quan either did not see them or pretended not to. He smiled and turned to Ben. "What would my old roommate like to do now?"

They had an early dinner with orange beef and stale broccoli, the best they'd found in the Pushan market, but a significant culinary step down from Shanghai. The four of them sat at the table. The unoccupied fifth chair, with an empty plate in front of it, again stared at Ben. If this was some obscure Chinese custom, it was one he'd never heard of.

After dinner, Ben watched Quan and Ming out the back window, tending the chickens. He went to the door and saw Li Shen facing the ginkgo tree. He sneaked up from behind, intending to grab and tickle Shen. He stopped when he saw him holding a stick and drawing in the sandy dirt.

"What are you writing?" Ben asked. Shen quickly brushed his foot over the dirt, erasing the image. He pivoted toward Ben, wide-eyed.

"I didn't mean to scare you. I just wondered if you wanted to play catch."

Shen nodded, still trembling. Ben threw him the Frisbee. For twenty minutes they played catch. Ben tried to remember throwing a Frisbee with his own children. He couldn't.

"I have great stories about Li Quan to tell his colleagues," Ben said, sitting in front of the stove beside Quan.

"My colleagues will not want to hear these stories," Quan assured him, putting on his worn slippers.

"Do you recall our first night in the dorm?" Ben said. "I asked you what kind of school you went to in China. Remember what you said?"

"A Party school." Quan smiled. "You said, 'I didn't think China had party schools.' And I said, 'Oh yes, we have many.'"

Ben laughed. "Then I said, 'America is full of party schools. Even Harvard is a party school.' I'll never forget the look on your face. You said, 'This is a Communist school?'"

Quan bent forward, trembling, his eyes watering, the slightest bit of air coming out his mouth. Ben laughed harder, remembering how his old friend could lose his breath laughing.

"I didn't realize Americans meant something very different when they said 'party school.'" He chuckled some more. "Of course, some of our professors were Communists. The Party would have been pleased with their teaching. Needless to say, none of them had actually lived under Communism!"

A few minutes later, when Quan retrieved a Bible and started reading it to Shen and Ming, Ben excused himself to travel six feet and check his e-mail. He lost his connection through Quan's phone line three times before finally holding it long enough to get mail. He skimmed several messages and moved to the one from Martin Getz.

Ben, I got a disturbing phone call from Won Chi related to your friend Li Quan. It appears he's under suspicion. I'm having second thoughts about your being there. Watch your step. If anything out of the ordinary starts to happen, keep your distance. I'll let you know if we find out more. Sorry I put you in an awkward situation. Maybe you should come up with a reason to relocate. Anyway, keep in touch.

Chi? He's in Shanghai. What does he know about Quan?

Ben disconnected, flipped shut his laptop, and watched Li Quan. When they were done reading and praying, Shen dragged his mother outdoors to teach her how to improve her Frisbee skills. While Ming and Shen laughed and giggled outside, Ben and Quan sat on their beds.

Ben pointed to the tape and CD player on the desk. "Why don't we listen to that classical music Mr. James gave you?"

"I have taken only this day off. I go back to work tomorrow."

"Great, I'll come with you. I want to watch my old roommate handle a class of eager students."

"You are most welcome to come." Quan looked at Ben, as if weighing his words. "You seem to have heard many things about China."

"When we were in college, I knew nothing. I was a cross-cultural ignoramus. I must have offended you with my comments. I made fun of everything from your slippers to your proverbs to your window sprouts."

"I was in your country. I did not expect you to understand mine. But I am honored now, and amazed, by the interest you have taken in China."

Ben shrugged. "Everything changed when I started doing business here. It dawned on me that the people who do good business are always the ones who understand the culture. And the language. That's what motivated me to study. By the way, when you take me to the university tomorrow, you can tell your students you aren't the only professor. The last two years I've lectured on China for a week in an advanced business class at Portland State University."

"Professor Ben Fielding?" Quan bowed his head. "An expert on China."

"No. Just not as ignorant as most Americans. And not nearly as ignorant as I was when we were at Harvard."

"Please tell me what you teach about my country."

"Why?"

"An old friend just wants to know."

"Well, first I give them a little history—how China was the Middle Kingdom, a self-absorbed and xenophobic empire."

"Xenophobic? I do not know this word."

"And I don't know the Mandarin equivalent. It means frightened of outsiders, threatened by foreigners."

"Yes, then we are xenophobic, certainly."

"I tell them that for thousands of years, through dynasties and revolutions, China was mostly indifferent to the outside world. Foreigners forced their way in, but they weren't welcome. Mao typified the attitude, which is what made it such a big deal when he invited Nixon to visit Beijing. I play news videos of that trip."

Quan nodded.

"Then I talk about the turnaround under Deng, when the Beijing communists kicked their Marxist zeal into low gear and set the country on the road to capitalism." He looked at Quan. "How am I doing?"

Quan shrugged.

"Okay," Ben said, "it's my turn to ask a question. A few years ago I visited Mao's memorial, saw his body in Tiananmen. I kept wondering what goes through the mind of the thousands of people waiting in those lines to see his body. So tell me—what do you think of when you remember Mao?"

"I've never been to his memorial," Quan said. "I will never go."

Ben fidgeted. Quan sighed.

"Mao we called the 'Great Savior' and later the 'Venerable Old Man.' But when I came back to China after Harvard, his days were ending. I remember how his face sagged in spite of all the makeup, how he breathed heavily from the tight girdle he wore to hold in his stomach. He became bloated by his eight-course evening meal and glasses of mao-tai. He lived in luxury. People began to realize he was not a god, just a man. By then the horrible damage had been done."

"Which damage are you thinking of?"

"As a history major, I often wondered something, Ben Fielding. Do you ever think it strange when you see the allies of World War II— Roosevelt and Churchill—sitting with Stalin? Do you think it strange that Stalin murdered five times more people than Hitler, and that half of Europe was given to one totalitarian dictator in exchange for his assistance in defeating another? This is what I think when I see the pictures of Nixon and Kissinger laughing with Chairman Mao and his henchmen."

Quan's usually soft voice was uncharacteristically intense. "What I learned of Mao at Harvard," Quan said, "was very different from what I knew of Mao from my own country."

"How?"

"He was a promise breaker. He kept telling us everything was better. There was no more famine. Yet there were many days when all we had to eat was a sliced turnip. Mother stood in line in the freezing winter for three or four hours just to buy one tiny piece of meat. She took it home and prepared it as if it were a feast. She told us she was not hungry and my sister and I must eat her share. I didn't understand then. I do now. There was much more suffering than the government ever admitted."

Ben nodded.

"Honored mother taught us to give. Always with her big smile, she said you must tithe to God first, then buy essential food, then give generously from what was left. We were fortunate my family did not starve. But we were sometimes hungry. Mother often said, 'If you give God everything you have, he will provide everything you need.' Mao's desire was that the people would consider him God. Many did. I remember well when China's millions of teenage students were given red armbands imprinted with the words *Hong Wei Bing.*"

"The Red Guards?"

"With the armbands came authority. They were authorized to be judge, jury, and executioners. I saw it in my own home. I watched them take my father. . . ." Quan's eyes watered; his fists clenched. "And I did nothing to stop them."

"What could you do? You were just a boy."

"What can one person do? That was what everyone said. But my sin was not only cowardice or passivity. It wasn't just that I did not try to save my father—it was that I did not *want* to save him."

"Why?"

"Before they took my father, they made a speech. They said, 'Christians are all traitors; they are parasites. They must be eliminated, like so many fleas on the back of a dog.' I did not want to stand out. For a Chinese there is nothing worse than being noticed when it is unpopular. None of us wants to be a crane standing amid a flock of chickens."

"What did you think when they said that about your father?"

"I felt ashamed my parents were Christians." He paused. "Now I feel ashamed of myself because I was ashamed of them."

"They must have had some reason to drag off your father. What were their charges, besides his being a Christian? When we were in college you'd never tell me the specifics. You always changed the subject."

"Did I?" Quan looked outside. "It is nearly dark. I promised Shen I would throw the Frisbee." Ben watched Quan's back as he walked out the door.

Ben sat up suddenly in bed, thinking his own snore had awakened him. The pale moonlight crept in the window. He stood tentatively, then saw a dark figure through the window, seventy feet away and walking toward the house. He tensed. No, wait, the man was going the other direction. But . . . was he dreaming? The figure appeared to be walking backward. Yes, and he had something in his arms. It was surreal, so dreamlike that Ben kept looking for evidence of reality. Ben moved a few feet toward Quan and Ming's bed, eyes adjusting. He saw a thin birdlike arm sticking out of the covers. Ming. There was no Quan.

Friday morning Ben drove a few hundred meters before tying into the road to Pushan. He negotiated a kaleidoscope of poncho-clad bicyclists commuting to work, not as thick as in Shanghai but surprisingly busy for what seemed a country road. Ben drove cautiously, irritating the driver behind him, who passed him and missed a bicycler by inches.

"Which direction to the university?"

"That way." Quan pointed toward the road to Shanghai. "But first, I have something to show you. It's only six kilometers, on the outskirts of Pushan. I ride my bike to it."

"Just point the way. Listen, Quan, I need to make a quick flight up to Beijing Tuesday. Could you come with me? I've got lots of mileage saved up, and I can get you free airfare, no problem. We could leave early and come back late, so you'd miss just one day of classes."

"We will see."

As they neared Pushan, they saw more sidewalk entrepreneurs who'd set up shop wherever they could find a spot. Suddenly, kiosks and make-shift buildings were all around them.

"Park there, in the mud."

They crossed the street toward a dirty gray building with three doors. The one on the left opened into a tiny market, with fruits and vegetables on the outside. Next to it was a used-bicycle shop. On the right was a closed door and a small window covered with cardboard. The words on a sign were faded and illegible.

Quan walked to the door and opened it. Ben followed him in.

"Ni hao," Quan called.

An old man looked back at him. "Ni hao."

"This is my friend, Ben Fielding," Quan said in Mandarin. "The one I spoke to you about. From America."

The old man bowed his head. "Zhou Jin." The man extended his right hand. Ben noticed red, callous scars on his wrist.

Quan stepped behind the counter, gazed at a row of uncut keys on the wall, and fingered a few of them, matching them up in his line of sight. He chose one, then put it to a milling cutter on a tracing lathe.

A self-serve key-making shop? Okay. . . .

Quan clamped the uncut key in place, then guided a tracing bar over the original. He cut the pattern swiftly, never taking his eyes off it. He brushed away stray bits of metal and held the new key up to the original, examining it for any defect. Finally he smiled.

Ben expected him to pay for the key and leave. Instead, Quan put the new key and the old into an envelope and wrote on it, then stayed behind the counter.

"You may sit down, Ben." Quan pointed to an ugly molded plastic chair that looked like it had been rescued from a dump.

"I don't mind standing."

A few customers came in the door and spoke with Zhou Jin and Quan as if they were old friends. Quan made two more keys and handed them to an old man in worn work clothes.

Ben looked at his watch, wondering what time Quan's first class was. "How many keys are you making?"

"I do not know. It depends on how many customers we have."

Ben stared at him blankly. "Quan, am I missing something?"

"I will make as many keys as our customers order."

"Are you saying you work here?"

"Yes."

"But when do you teach at the university?"

Quan looked first at Ben's shoes, then his belt, then his collar, then his eyes. "I do not teach at a university. I never have."

12

$\mathscr{W}$HAT ARE YOU TELLING ME, Quan? You said you taught at the university!"

"No. I never said that. Not twenty years ago and not since you e-mailed me. You assumed it. Every time you mentioned it I wanted to correct you. But the timing was never good. And perhaps . . . I was ashamed."

"What happened? How did you lose your job?"

"You must first have a job before you can lose it."

A customer came in at that moment, a short man with a too-long cane. He asked Quan a question that Ben didn't understand. Quan pointed to a case with a stainless steel latch and dead bolt.

"This mechanism has only five springs to operate the linkage," he told the customer. "It has a non-handed guard bolt and a one-piece retractor hub. The stopwork is reversible." Quan quickly translated for Ben, as these were not the kinds of words studied in Mandarin class. Apparently Quan had picked up English locksmith terminology from somewhere.

"The latch bolt can be fully retracted with only thirty-five degrees of lever rotation," Quan said to the customer. Zhou Jin uttered an affirming word, as if this baby were the Michael Jordan of locks. "This makes it last very long."

Quan went on about cylinders and cams and latch bolt heads and mortise lock bodies. Finally, Ben suggested he stop translating, since he wasn't understanding half the translation anyway. Ben sat there trying to assimilate his friend's admission.

"Very high quality," Quan said. "The finest workmanship. Far better than anything they make in Shanghai." The customer laughed knowingly. He put out some paper yuan and a coin on the heavily nicked plywood counter, then went out the door, smiling as if he'd won the lottery.

"Quan, what's going on? Talk to me."

Another customer walked in the door, but Ben reached across the counter and grabbed Quan's arm. Zhou Jin stepped forward to greet the customer, and the two embarked on an animated discussion, freeing Ben and Quan to step to the back of the tiny shop.

"When you left Harvard, the job was all lined up in Beijing, right? You could have taught in any university in China, isn't that what you said? What happened?"

Quan sighed. "Before coming to America, I joined the Communist Party. It seemed the only way to get into college. Chinese college, I mean. But I dreamed of going to America to become a great scholar. And you know by a miracle God brought me to Harvard and to my friend Ben Fielding. When I returned to China, I knew the fact I'd become a Christian would make it difficult to advance as a professor. I knew I would never be allowed to be a department head or a college president. But I thought they would be so impressed with my credentials they would overlook my faith and let me teach."

"So what happened at your job interview?"

"They were excited to have me teach history. The interview was just a formality—they said so. Then they backed up and took me through the paperwork. The file was thick. It showed my parents had been Christians, that my father was even a pastor, with a long police record. But it also showed I had denied my parents' faith. They assured me they would not punish me for my parents' views. They asked if I was still an atheist. I told them no, that I had become a Christian. They looked at each other. At that moment I knew it was over. I would not be allowed to teach."

"Just because you were a Christian?"

"For them, that was reason enough. 'The minds of the young must not be poisoned by foreign beliefs.' That is what they think. That is what they have been taught."

"Well, I can see why they want to preserve their culture and not have it westernized by Christianity, but—"

"*Westernized* by Christianity? You sound like them, Ben Fielding! You should know better. Christianity is not Western. Communism is far more foreign to China than Christianity!"

"What do you mean?"

"You do not know Chinese history? The church in China goes back at least thirteen hundred years. We had Christian monasteries in the eighth century. Beijing had a bishop eight hundred years ago. The church is one of the oldest institutions in all China. The real 'foreign influence' is the Communist Party. Only a hundred years ago the philosophy of Marx and Lenin crawled into China like a silent wolf." Quan raised his hands in exasperation. "My great-grandfather Li Manchu and my great-grandmother, also a martyr for Yesu, were Christians before anyone in China was a Communist! Yet they teach the devil's lie that Communism is domestic while Christianity is foreign. And they teach people like you to believe this lie!"

"Quan, look, I didn't mean to offend you."

"I am only explaining why they would not let me teach."

"What happened then?"

"I thought it meant only that I wouldn't be allowed to teach at the best universities. I went to another university, then another. It became obvious that each had been warned. No one would hire me. Several would not even talk with me. I contacted two smaller universities in Shanghai. Finally, one told me I should stop wasting everyone's time with all my applications."

"You were never one to give up. I'll bet you kept looking anyway."

"Yes. I even saved up money and traveled to Tibet, thinking I might get hired at the university there, for low pay, far from the eyes of the Party. I was wrong."

"What did you do?"

"What I had to do. Find a job to feed Ming. I worked a few years in a tool shop. My employer kept a file on me. One day a man was weeping because his son was dying. I put my arm around him and told him about Yesu. The man became a Christian. He came back the next day and thanked me. My boss overheard him. He was very angry, and he wrote notes about me in a file. The file grew larger and larger."

"The file was for PSB?"

"Sometimes police ask employers for files. Some blackmail their employees, telling them they will turn them in if they do not work for lower pay. They say, 'If we report you, no one will let you work at all.' If they hear any complaints from other workers about their being Christians, they write this down. They can fire them. That is what happened to me, even though I was a good worker. Coming from America, I'm sure you cannot imagine that an employer would keep a file on an employee to keep track of words and actions that come from his Christian beliefs.

But in a communist country such things happen. Can you believe such things happen, Ben Fielding?"

"Well, uh," Ben said. "Yeah, I guess that is pretty hard to believe. But . . ."

"When I decided to leave Harvard, I told you China was my home, not America. I was only half right. I was right that America was not my home but wrong in thinking that China was."

"What do you mean?"

"China is my place of service. It is the battlefield where Li Quan has been dispatched as Yesu's soldier. But this is not my home. Heaven is my home, my true country. I know that now. But it was a hard lesson to learn."

"Couldn't you have gotten a job teaching if you'd exercised a little more . . . discretion about your faith?"

"Discretion? Do you mean denial? There is an old proverb, 'He who sacrifices his conscience to ambition burns a picture to obtain the ashes.'"

While Zhou Jin continued his energetic conversation about keys and locks with his customer, Quan stepped behind the counter and opened a drawer. He pulled out a paper and handed it to Ben. "This is a memo that came to the locksmith shop."

Ben struggled with the translation. "'Those who . . . go to unregistered churches are lawbreakers. They are not permitted to work in . . . government-controlled businesses.' What does that mean? Which businesses are government controlled?"

"In one way or another, all of them."

"But your employer didn't turn you in?"

"No. Zhou Jin would not do that."

"Why not?"

"Do you remember the history course we took together?"

"Vaguely. What was that prof's name?"

"Dr. Franklin. For two weeks we studied Martin Luther King Jr. and the civil rights movement."

"Of course. You loved King. Put his picture up in our room. You did a term paper on him, right? Got an A plus, no doubt. Business as usual for the professor . . . oh, sorry."

"You can still call me professor. I do not mind. And I still have that paper. I also have this quote from it, which I keep here." He took Ben over behind a workbench that appeared to double as a lunch table. He pointed at a yellowed piece of paper tacked to the wall. Ben was surprised to see the words in English. He read aloud:

"Dr. Martin Luther King said, 'If a man is called to be a street sweeper, he should sweep streets even as Michelangelo painted, or Beethoven composed music, or Shakespeare composed poetry. He should sweep streets so well that all the hosts of heaven and earth will pause to say, Here lived a great street sweeper, who did his job well.'"

Ben's and Quan's eyes met.

"My dream was to be a college professor and to write books. Yesu, maker of men and God of providence, had different plans. Li Quan is an assistant locksmith. If I am still here when Zhou Jin dies, I will be the master locksmith. Shen shall become my assistant. One day, perhaps, my only son will be the master locksmith of Pushan. I had him memorize what Dr. King said. It is a holy truth. One I had to learn through many tears. Ming helped me. She told me she was proud of me, that she did not care about money. She said if I never wrote a book it was alright. She said all that mattered was that we please Father." Quan's eyes watered.

"Have you ever regretted coming back to China?"

Quan nodded. "First, when I could not become a professor and writer. Then later when they forced Ming to . . . when they made it so she could never have another child." Quan looked away. "Still, I kept believing Father had called me to be something besides an assistant locksmith. I wanted to be a great scholar. I dreamed of teaching at university. I dreamed of writing books. I even dreamed of building for Ming a big beautiful house, like one in America. It is hard to give up your dreams."

Ben gazed at the quivering softness of his friend's face. He remembered his jealousy of Li Quan and hated himself for it. This must be what Quan had felt so often . . . shame.

"For many years I thought God might be punishing me because I was once ashamed of my father, because I was so unworthy of my heritage. Ming said it was not so."

"You said your father was a pastor and he died in jail. That's all you'd ever tell me."

"Yes, he was a pastor. But he was not paid for that. He made his living doing something else. Something I never told you in college, something I did not want you to know."

"What?"

"He was a street sweeper," Quan said. "It was the best job a pastor could get." He smiled widely, nodding toward the words on the wall. He spoke loudly, so that Zhou Jin and his customer turned their heads.

"Li Quan's father, Li Tong, did his job well. He was the greatest street sweeper who ever lived."

―――――――――――

The King nodded, then smiled and said to the short, broad-shouldered man next to him, "Yes, Li Tong. You did your job *very* well."

13

"I WAS AFRAID you'd make me do this," Ben said.

"We *must* do it."

They'd ridden home from the locksmith shop in silence. But dinner talk had turned to old times in college. Now, with Ming watching, the two men stood facing each other. Quan started singing, belting out the school song, "Fair Harvard." Ben, self-consciously, tried to stay with him:

> *Farewell! be thy destinies onward and bright!*
> *To thy children the lesson still give,*
> *With freedom to think, and with patience to bear,*
> *And for right ever bravely to live.*
> *Let not moss-covered error move thee at its side,*
> *As the world on truth's current glides by.*
> *Be the herald of light, and the bearer of love,*
> *Till the stock of the Puritans die.*

Ming laughed and clapped. "What does it mean?"

"Let the history professor tell us," Ben said.

"I think it no longer means what it once did."

"I suppose not. Times change."

"But does truth change? I wonder what those Puritans would think of our alma mater now? Or even when we went there?"

Ben sat back down and sipped his green tea. Shen came in the door, leaning forward and hauling on his shoulders a dirty gunnysack of coal.

"Is that Li Shen beneath the coal?" Ben asked, hoping once again to redirect the conversation.

Shen smiled, set down his load, then proudly began to feed coal into the stove, its once-black exterior now an ashen gray.

"Would you snap beans while I resole Ming's shoe?" Quan asked Ben.

"Sure."

They sat on the floor, hands busy, minds free. A thin throw rug buffered the cold cement, but to Ben it was still uncomfortable.

"Question," Li Quan said. "Do you discuss with your university students Six Four?"

"What?"

"The massacre."

"You mean Tiananmen Square?"

"Our students call it Six Four."

"Why?"

"Sixth month, fourth day, 1989."

"We talk about it, sure. It's still a pretty big issue for some Chinese, isn't it?"

Quan put down his hammer and stared at Ben. "The day is so big it defines our modern history." Thirty seconds of cold silence followed. "When you spoke of Six Four, did you tell them your old roommate was there?"

"You're kidding me."

"I was visiting Beijing, one of only two visits in the last twenty years. Can you believe June 4, 1989, was one of them? There were millions of us watching the pro-democracy demonstrators. My nephew, Li Yue, was one of the protesters. Ming's niece, Chan Bi, was killed. I didn't see her in the crowd, of course. She had been missing three weeks before we found out from another protester. The government never admitted she died there."

"I'm sorry." Ben looked at Ming sympathetically. She bowed her head.

"The Party first said no one was killed, then admitted to a few, then a few dozen. I do not know what they admit to now. But we know there were at least hundreds, maybe thousands, killed."

"It was terrible, of course. But . . . wasn't it a blip on the screen?"

"Blip on the screen?"

"Sorry—I mean . . . an uncharacteristic occurrence. It was a throwback to the old oppression, but it wasn't typical of the new government."

"It is hard to console a mother who loses her child by telling her the killers have not acted typically."

"I'm not trivializing it, Quan. I'm just saying it was an aberration, a jerky phase of adjustment. It wasn't what the new China is about, you have to admit that."

"Or was it exactly what it is about, only it is done each day in private, with small numbers, rather than in public with large numbers where the world can see?"

"You sound so cynical."

"I am not cynical. I am simply saying what many of us know to be true. But forgive me. It grows late. I should not talk politics to an old friend. You say you must travel to Shanghai tomorrow?"

"Just a meeting. No big deal. I'll be back Sunday afternoon. I'll find a hotel."

Though Ben had learned to lie when it was convenient, he felt particularly guilty now. There was no meeting in Shanghai. His plan was to drive only to Pushan, find the best hotel, get a hot shower and a comfortable bed, and talk freely over a dependable phone connection. But the main reason was simple—he didn't want Quan to invite him to church. Quan might not have trusted him enough to invite him anyway. Maybe Ben was doing him a favor by taking off for a night. It would avoid the awkwardness of the family traipsing off Sunday morning to an illegal gathering. Yeah, he was doing Quan a favor.

"Quan, I have to ask—is it really too late for you?"

"What do you mean?"

"You've got your Ph.D. from Harvard. You're still in your forties. You could teach for twenty-five more years. Have you thought about applying again at a university, now that China's opened up?"

"*Opened up?*" Quan stared at him. "Those outside seem to know so much more than those inside. Most citizens are not as frightened now as before, as long as their political and religious persuasions are not a bone in the Party's throat. But Six Four woke up the idealists. It left them shocked and distrustful of China's leaders. They figured out that economic growth does not mean freedom. The progress of capitalism is not the same as the progress of freedom."

"But it's close," Ben said. "Really. I've studied the economics, Quan. Freedom's a seamless garment. If people own property, they're going to use it in ways the government doesn't like. If they have the freedom to own and use a computer, they'll write things their leaders don't approve of. If they can rent and purchase buildings, groups the government doesn't like will meet. Free association. It's inevitable. Free enterprise must lead to religious and political freedom."

"Eventually, perhaps. But 'free association' is selective in China. When disapproved of, it is punished. There are secret places, deep and dark, places most people think do not exist, or pretend they don't. After Six Four it was harder to pretend."

"The Chinese business leaders I've talked with say that if the government hadn't acted decisively to stop the rebellion at Tiananmen Square, China would have collapsed. Many more people would have been hurt. They had to stand up and say they wouldn't let the nation disintegrate into anarchy. People would have starved; the streets would have been filled with violence; homes and businesses would have been looted."

"So the good government saved the bad people from themselves, is that what you believe, Ben Fielding?"

"You're twisting my words." Ben felt the blood in his face.

"Then please untwist them," Quan said. Ming quietly stood and moved away from the men, sitting next to Shen, who was doing homework on the floor in the far corner of the room.

"You asked why I would not try to teach in a university. The answer is simple—the Party would not let me do it now for the same reason they wouldn't let me do it then. They would be even less likely because I am known as a follower of Yesu, and a defender of house churches. And I have a police record."

"Why are you such a threat to them?" Ben's voice was at a lower volume, but it was still intense.

Quan hesitated before responding. "Christianity had a strong role in sparking the freedom surge in Eastern Europe. My mother taught me, 'He who rides the tiger is afraid to dismount.' This much I will say. Six Four was good in some ways. Many students hoped they could change society and find meaning without God. That day, hope was dashed—and, no matter how painful, it is always good when false hopes are dashed. Since then, many have learned to trust not in man but in God. That evening, as he wept in my arms because of what happened, I led my nephew Li Yue to Yesu. He was only eighteen. I hope you will meet him. When men know they cannot hope in a country, in a political belief, or in themselves, they become free to hope in God."

Quan picked his hammer back up, lifted Ming's shoe, and said, "I have talked too much and worked too little. I ask my old roommate a question, and then I fill the air with words. Please tell me more about what you teach students about China in your university class."

"Well, before permanent trade relations, we used to debate favored-nation status. I argued that the less China's isolated, the more transparent to outside observation it becomes, and the easier it will be to monitor human rights. Exposure to the world keeps tyrants in check."

"And what do you say about Deng Xiaoping?"

"I tell them when he was dying Deng joked about 'going to meet Marx.'" Ben smiled, then saw the pained look on Quan's face. "I told them Deng was a realist. Shrewd. Showed them that picture of him at a Texas barbecue, wearing the ten-gallon hat. He was friendly, quotable, somebody Americans could relate to—not scary, like Mao."

"Tell me how they were different."

"You know that. His Four Modernizations rescued the economy. He made the commitment to bring China into leadership in the world marketplace. He nearly succeeded."

"Do you know what Deng told us, Ben Fielding? He said, 'If the Communist Party gives you economic prosperity, you must give up social freedom.' This was the bargain he struck with the Chinese people. Of course, no one asked us if we would agree to the bargain. Six Four happened under Deng's orders—perhaps he was not so different from Mao."

"All I know is, the people I talk with say things are much better, even since Jiang Zemin took over from Deng. He seems pretty reasonable, don't you think? I saw Mike Wallace interview him on *60 Minutes*. The guy memorized the Declaration of Independence, right down to 'all men are created equal.' He quotes Jefferson, Lincoln . . . you name it."

"Was this the interview in which he denied there is persecution of Christians?"

"Well . . . to tell you the truth, I don't remember what he said about that. I was more interested in the . . . you know, economic side of things." The moment he said it, Ben regretted it.

"You seem to get much information about China from television. But ten-gallon hats and big smiles and quoted words do not always mean what you think."

"Hey, I've talked personally with a lot of Chinese businessmen and some government leaders. When I heard his name, I realized I'd even met your mayor of Pushan, at a VIP dinner in Shanghai."

"VIP? Yes, you must be a very important person to have dinner with our mayors. But why do you think they want to have dinner with you? Would it make it easier for you to do business with them if you believe China is free?"

"Yes. Of course, but—"

"Don't you think they know this?" Quan asked. "Or do you think they are stupid?"

"You can't deny the standard of living has gone way up. On the plane I read a feature story about a man who twenty years ago was a young cook in a Shanghai restaurant. Today he's a business tycoon. He wears a diamond-studded Rolex watch and owns two Mercedes-Benz and a red Ferrari. Dreams are coming true."

"Perhaps not all of us have the same dream."

"I'll take money over poverty any day," Ben said.

"Has money brought you happiness, Ben Fielding?"

"It sure as heck beats the alternative."

"Your Deng said, 'It does not matter if the cat is black or white, as long as it catches mice.'"

"He wasn't *my* Deng," Ben said. "And what's with the cat?"

"He referred to a market economy in contrast to state-controlled. But to me it means if one form of dictatorship does not work, then try a more subtle one, disguised as freedom. As long as the Party controls the people—catches the mice—that is all that matters."

———————————

Having checked in at the unusual hour of 10:30 A.M., Ben sat comfortably in Pushan's Zuanshi Hotel. Not a five-star, but at least two stars up from the Huaquia Binguan, where Quan had made his exchange with the Canadian mystery man. Only certain hotels were registered to house foreigners. After some reconnaissance, he had decided this was the best. He got a bucket of ice and positioned into it a bottle of mao-tai, 150 proof. He poured his first drink, which quickly started to take off the edge he was feeling as a result of his first three days with Quan. He picked up the phone.

"Martin? It's Ben. Hi. It's 7:00 Friday for you, isn't it? Well, Friday night's a pain. Take it from somebody who's already lived it. If I were you, I'd just stay home and pop in a *Star Trek: The Next Generation* rerun."

"What's going on over there?" Martin asked. "Didn't you read my e-mail? Won Chi called again. He says your friend's under investigation. He's got a history of illegal activity."

"What kind of activity?"

"Drugs and antigovernment violence and subversion were mentioned. But he wouldn't get specific."

"Drugs? Violence? *Quan?*"

"Look, Ben, Chi recommended several trustworthy families you can meet and interview. Even stay with. Chi offered his own home. I think you need to back away from your old roommate."

"He was your suggestion, Martin. That's why I'm here, remember?"

"I didn't know he was a criminal!"

"They actually say he's a criminal?"

"Look, Ben, if you know anything illegal your friend's doing, you're obligated to report it."

"Obligated by what? Report it to whom?"

"Well, if not the police, I guess you could tell Chi, and he could handle it."

"Handle it?"

"We can't compromise the name of Getz International. We're there doing business with permission of the authorities. We don't want to make any waves, okay?"

"Nobody's making waves."

"When do you go to Beijing?"

"Tuesday."

"Just promise me you'll remember your loyalty to the company. Promise me you won't do anything to jeopardize our relationships in Shanghai or Beijing—okay?"

Ben sighed. "Scout's honor. I promise."

Ben returned to the Li home Sunday afternoon.

"You must be weary after your long drive from Shanghai," Ming said.

"A little," Ben lied. "Traffic wasn't bad." That part was true, but then he'd only come from the hotel in Pushan.

"How were your meetings?" Quan asked.

"Fine. But I still have to go back Tuesday."

"So soon?"

"Mainly to fly to Beijing, remember? Since I'm in-country, they figure why not take advantage? I don't mind. I'm used to moving around a lot, I guess. Have you given any more thought to making the trip with me? Like I said, it's free. I've got frequent-flier miles coming out of my ears, and we've got a special arrangement with Air China."

"Can you get two days off work? We'd only be gone one night. How about it?"

"I mentioned it to my boss. He says I don't take much time off and thinks I should go. Ming and I talked also and she agreed. I can come with you. No problema."

"Great."

"But on the way," Quan said, "would you take me to the Huaquia Binguan Hotel in Pushan again? I need to drop something off."

"Sure." *What are we dropping off?* "Actually, we need to go a few hours early anyway. When we leave the car in Shanghai, I've got a quick meeting before we catch our flight."

Ben determined to watch Quan closely. He hoped it wasn't obvious. He insisted on driving him to work Monday morning, saving him the bike ride. While at the locksmith's shop, Ben listened to conversations. He overheard a few phone calls. He noticed Quan's vague responses and his tendency to withdraw and talk privately with certain visitors. He felt like a spy.

Ben didn't feel like Quan completely trusted him, and he wasn't sure he trusted Quan either. But Ben had good reason. He had to figure out what was going on. Maybe tomorrow when they drove to Shanghai and flew to Beijing, something more would surface.

Before dawn on Tuesday, October 9, Ben drove toward the Huaquia Binguan Hotel.

"Please do not park in front," Quan said. "Park on the side there, and stay in your car. I won't take long."

"Yes, sir." Ben saluted.

Quan stepped onto the sidewalk, duffel bag in hand. As Quan walked around the corner, Ben noticed a sharply dressed man in a car across the street. The man stared at Quan, then stepped outside his car, looking at the hotel's main doors. Ben recognized his military posture. Just as the man's cold gaze turned toward Ben, he looked down. Even at this distance, out of the corner of his eye, Ben saw again eyes of black steel. The man crossed the street toward the hotel.

What is Quan doing? And why is he being watched?

14

*T*HEY MADE THE LONG DRIVE to Shanghai in the rain. As they settled into silence, Ben felt the unspoken tension. Finally he said, "I have to admit, I'm surprised you aren't as excited about the new China as I am."

"Perhaps because I long for the gospel of Yesu to be seen as the solution instead of a problem."

"Are things really that bad?"

"Our government blames Christians for the economic problems in Russia and Eastern Europe. Christianity stirred the thirst for freedom, and those who fear God do not fear the government as they want us to. It's hard for a history major to live in a country where history and every current event is edited. But in China there are more Christians now than Communist Party members, perhaps twice as many. It is no surprise that the Party labors to prevent Christianity from spreading."

"What role do you want the church to have in China's future?"

Quan stared at him as if he didn't understand the question. "The church should spread the message of Yesu. He changes hearts. Changed hearts will make a changed country. I do not think you understand the deterioration of the Chinese family, Ben, the desperation of my countrymen. It is not just suicide. There are tens of thousands of street children, many sold by their own parents to gangs for thirty dollars. You can only disbelieve in God so long before a society is corrupt. America is an example, is it not?"

"Would you prefer Communism to capitalism?"

"*Bu,*" Quan said. "Neither would I prefer to be bitten by a lion than a rabid dog. At least with the dog, you have a chance of survival."

"Capitalism is a rabid dog?"

"Does not Shengjing say the love of money is the root of all kinds of evil? Love for money—and power—was behind communism. My father explained it, 'Capitalism says you scratch my back and I'll scratch yours. Communism says you scratch my back or I'll break yours.' Would I rather have my back scratched or broken? The answer is obvious. But having my back scratched still does not fill the hole in the heart. And even if you do not know it, our hearts still have holes in them—and many backs are still broken in China."

After they were chauffeured to Shanghai's PTE office, Ben left Li Quan to wait in the reception area. Sixty feet away, behind closed doors in a large conference room, Ben and Won Chi finished their hour-long meeting concerning operations at the new factory. They gave each other the customary congratulations on how well business had been conducted.

"Well, got to catch the Beijing flight. I can't wait to see that factory," Ben said. "Call me as soon as you're ready to take me on the tour."

"We want everything smooth before Mr. Ben Fielding visits. Should be no more than week. I will call." Won Chi hesitated. "Is Mitsubishi running well?"

"Yeah. Great."

"How much longer be needing it?"

"Well, you know, we said six weeks or so, give or take. Why? You need it back?"

"We have other cars. Only curious how long you will stay at friend's home."

"Do you know Li Quan? He's out in the waiting area. I'm sorry. I should have brought him in with me."

Chi raised his hand. "No need to meet him, thank you."

"Is something wrong?"

"No, nothing wrong. Only small phone call from government official. Inquiring what you are doing at this person's home near Pushan."

"What did you tell him?"

"Told him Mr. Getz's idea. Get to know Chinese. He asked if I knew your college roommate. Said I had never met him—best to keep it that way."

"How did he know Quan was my roommate?"

"Did not ask."

"What was the point of the call?"

"Routine security, perhaps. But . . ."

"Yes?"

"Your friend has had problems with PSB before. Under suspicion."

"For what?"

"Perhaps . . . drugs?"

"Quan?" Ben laughed. "Look, Martin mentioned this to me, Chi. And I assured him this is unfounded. Quan didn't even smoke pot at Harvard, back when all of us . . . I mean . . . never mind. Quan's a good man. Okay, he and his wife and little boy are Christians, but he's not forcing it on anyone."

"Didn't you say he has a computer in his home?"

"Yeah, he does. You helped find his e-mail address, remember?"

"Where did he get it? How does a locksmith's assistant afford a computer?"

"Well, I don't know, but it's not like he's living high on the hog."

Chi stared blankly.

"I mean, he's not wealthy, not by any stretch of the imagination. Okay, I guess you'd expect a locksmith's assistant to be even poorer, but still . . . I'm sure these accusations aren't true."

"It is rumored he may oppose participation in Three-Self Patriotic Movement."

"Remind me again about this Three-Self thing, would you?"

"I am not an expert, but I will try. China's churches are asked to adhere to three principles: They are to be self-governed, self-supported, and self-sustained. This is not meant to challenge Christian beliefs, but simply to assure that they are not controlled by foreign powers. Many Chinese are good people without Christianity, you know."

"Of course I know that, Chi. I've always thought the world of you, among others."

Chi's head bowed slightly.

"I don't think Quan would disagree with much of this," Ben said, not nearly as sure as he tried to sound.

"Perhaps if you see any problem with your friend you could let me know?" Chi said.

"Why?"

"Chi told PSB I would keep eyes open. They help us out. We try to help them when we can. Good for business."

"Quan's my friend. There's no way I can—"

Chi put up his hand to stop him. "I understand. But for friend's sake, Mr. Ben Fielding may wish to encourage him to stay out of trouble."

"Of course. I'm sure he will."

They sat on Air China, flying toward Beijing. Quan showed all the signs of someone who hadn't flown in many years. The smooth-faced pilot looked like he'd come fresh from the Air Force.

"You should hear me sing China's praises in the home office," Ben said. "I tell them in twenty years it could pass the U.S. in gross national product."

"Chinese say twelve years," Quan said.

"Maybe. Two years ago I went on a tour of the Shanghai Forever Bicycle Company. Ever been there? We should visit together. Did you know they make four million bicycles a year? They have over seven thousand workers. They ship bicycles all over the world. Of course, they go by other names in America."

"Many things go by different names in America."

Ben stared out the window. *I'm not biting this time.*

Li Quan knew how to stop a conversation.

Quan sat in a reception area again, this time in a fancy business office on the twenty-second floor of a Beijing high-rise. Periodically he got up to look out the window toward Tiananmen Square.

At 4:00 P.M., Ben emerged from his meeting. After eating a wonderful dinner, Ben and Quan tried to check into a Beijing international hotel. But when the front desk discovered Li Quan was a national, they wouldn't let him stay. So they tried a different hotel, where it turned out Quan could stay, but not Ben. Finally Ben went to another international hotel, telling Quan to stay out on the sidewalk. He got a room with two beds, telling them his friend would be arriving later. They never asked who the friend was, and Ben didn't volunteer. After getting the key, he took Quan to the room.

"Just talk English all the time and you'll be fine," Ben said as they wandered around the beautiful facility. Quan continuously marveled at everything, even the exercise room. He kept saying he'd never seen anything like it.

Back in the room he looked at the bathroom's huge mirrors and separate tub and shower, with gold-colored fixtures. Quan said, "Not even in America did I see such luxury."

"Well, what living quarters did you ever see besides a dorm?"

As they settled back, each on a separate queen-size bed—over twice the size of the beds in the Li home—Quan stretched out and laughed.

"Ming would be amazed," he said.

––––––––

Wednesday morning, Ben borrowed a company car and drove an hour to his favorite Great Wall viewpoint. They climbed the long walkway, where they could see the wall stretching out across the countryside. Ben marveled at this monument to ancient zeal, built to keep China unstained by the outside world.

"I guess it's ironic," Ben said to Quan, breathing heavily. "I'm standing here on a wall that was made to keep out people like me."

As the climb got steeper, Ben stopped talking. Finally they made it to the highest point and turned to look at the green hillsides.

"Spectacular," Ben said. "Look at it sprawling out across the countryside, winding through the hills and valleys. I've thought about finding some place near here that Getz International could buy. Maybe a retreat center for business getaways."

Quan said nothing. Ben stopped trying to make conversation.

After ten minutes of silently looking off into the distance, Quan asked, "What does Ben Fielding see?"

"I have this panoramic photo of the Great Wall in my office, taken from right about where we're standing. I tell everybody this is what the Chinese can do. You have to visualize your goals to accomplish what you want. The Wall is fifteen hundred miles of hard work and determination. It's an awesome achievement, a tribute to vision, ingenuity, resolve. Nothing else compares to it, except the Pyramids. When it's cloudy, it's still beautiful, but on a day like this you can see forever. It's an incredible perspective."

"A frog was in a well," Quan said. "A bird stopped to drink at the well. They argued about how the sky looked. The frog thought it was very small. The bird thought it was very big."

"O . . . kay."

"The bird could see the sky as it really was. The frog could see only a tiny part of it. We do not always see as clearly as we think we do. Did you watch the fiftieth anniversary celebration in Beijing?"

"Of course. It was awesome."

"Do you know that some people in Beijing were chained in their homes during the celebration? My cousin was among them. His family could not leave their house for three days. The government was afraid they might protest. Those on the streets in Beijing were there only by invitation."

"It was choreographed?"

"Image is everything—that's an American proverb, isn't it? Most of the world saw like the frog sees, not the bird. While the world was applauding the new China, behind cameras it was something else. It was the same when your president visited our streets. Television cameras were permitted only in certain places. Where they were permitted, everything was beautiful. Poverty, ruin, and beggars were all pushed three streets back and not allowed to surface until after the cameras were gone."

"So . . . am I the frog or the bird?" Before Quan could answer, Ben asked, "What do *you* see when you look at the Wall?"

Quan scanned the horizon, unconsciously touching his marred earlobe. "I see a fifteen-hundred-mile-long tombstone marking the graves of tens of thousands of Chinese peasants who died under forced labor."

Ben felt the rush of blood to his cheeks.

"They were stolen from their families. They were slaves who died of overwork, exhaustion, starvation, exposure, and disease. They were covered with dirt and stone where they fell. There were no names, no ceremonies, no grave markers. No notices were sent to families. The work had to go on. Tens of thousands, perhaps hundreds of thousands, died building these walls. For no good reason. You mentioned the Pyramids? It is the same."

"I've visited the Pyramids. They *are* amazing."

"I must ask you, Ben—do you ever think about anyone besides yourself?"

Ben bit his lip.

"Do you think about the families? about those whose loved ones died in slave labor, building the Pyramids and this wall, so that you could come and admire them and put up lovely photographs on your office wall? All for what? To carry out the proud visions of corrupt men. Have you not read what Pharaoh did to God's chosen people, forcing them into slavery to build entire cities? Still, Yesu's hand was upon them, and he multiplied them even when they were oppressed. But forgive me if I do not get so excited about what governments and businesses build, whether cities or pyramids or walls. Look in the tiny backyards all over China, and what do you see? Walls. Walls keep people out and hold people in. Li Quan does not get excited about walls."

"But, by any standards—" Ben waved his hand over the stunning panorama—"this is a great achievement."

"Most Chinese think so. But perhaps it is not so great by the standards of a peasant woman who sacrificed her husband and sons to stones and mortar. We have a saying for this too. 'The beginning of wisdom is to call things by their right names.' That is why I no longer call this the Great Wall. I call it the Wall of Suffering."

Quan turned suddenly and walked briskly down the walkway, Ben two steps behind him. Ben caught up and put a hand on his shoulder. "I offended you again. I guess it's becoming a habit."

"This is a hard place for Li Quan. It is only the second time I have been to the Great Wall. When I was a boy my father promised to take me to it. But he never did."

"Why not?"

"He was arrested. Even when he was released for a few months, he was not allowed to leave town. He was under surveillance. He still spoke of bringing me here someday. But he continued to meet with the illegal church. He was arrested again. And that time he never got out. For many years I would not forgive him for breaking his promise. This place is to me not only the Wall of Suffering but the Wall of Broken Promise and Broken Dreams."

Ben listened to Quan, not knowing what to say.

"I came here the first time after returning from Harvard. I came as a Christian. I spoke into the wind and asked my father's forgiveness. But Baba could not hear me. He had been buried under another wall of oppression. He was gone."

"Not gone, Li Quan. Just out of sight," Li Tong said. "I heard you speak into the wind twenty years ago. And I hear you now, my son. You do not yet understand—some promises made in one world cannot be fulfilled until the next."

15

AFTER A QUIET FLIGHT back from Beijing, Ben and Quan picked up the Mitsubishi at the PTE garage in Shanghai. By the time he'd chatted with PTE managers, it was late enough in the afternoon that Ben offered to put them up in the JC Mandarin, assuring Quan it made the Beijing hotel look like a hovel. But Quan was eager to get home.

"Sorry I didn't suggest it before, but why don't you drive this time?" Ben asked Quan. "It's a great car."

"No problema." Quan raised his hand. "I would like to drive, but I have no license. There is no need, since we have no car. Last time I drove a car was . . . with you, Ben Fielding, to Logan Airport in Boston, the day I flew back to China!"

"That big old Chevy Impala of yours—yeah, then I drove it back and sold it for you and sent you the money. I'd forgotten. That was the last time you drove?"

Quan nodded as they wove through dark, seamy Shanghai streets.

"Another reason you've had second thoughts about your decision to come back to China?"

"Cars do not matter much. But sometimes things happen, and I wonder about my decision. Not long before you came, something happened on a Sunday morning. I was worried about Ming and Shen."

"What happened?"

"I thought perhaps I had been wrong to come back and expose them to the dangers and challenges of life here. I could have lived an easier life in

America. But it was not what Yesu had for me. His way is not always easier. But it is always better."

"You said something happened. . . . Was it at church?"

"First, I have a question of my own for my old friend. What happened to you, Ben Fielding?"

"What do you mean?"

"What happened to make you lose your first love for Yesu?"

Ben felt a surge of tension in his neck and shoulders. "Who appointed you my judge?"

"If Li Quan is wrong, correct him."

Ben clenched the steering wheel and looked straight ahead for five minutes. Finally, he exhaled. "After college Mom got sick. Cancer. She died slowly, painfully."

"Yes. I remember. You wrote me about it. I was very sorry. I still am. Your mother was very kind to me when I stayed at your house that summer."

"I'd forgotten we were still in touch when she died. Anyway, it made me question God. If he really loved me, loved my mom, why would he let that happen?"

"Other people's mothers suffer every day," Quan said. "Strange you did not blame God until it was your own mother."

"Well, sorry, Mr. Perfect, but she was the only mother I had!"

"I did not mean—"

"Who am I *supposed* to blame? If I was all-powerful, I wouldn't let people suffer like that."

"You do not see the end from the beginning. You do not understand God's ability to use suffering for higher purposes."

"All I know is, I trusted God and he let me down. And you don't know the half of it!"

Quan waited silently. Finally he said, "Are you going to tell me the rest that I do not know?"

"Why should I?"

"It is what friends do. We are old friends."

Ben sighed. "I had another child, a son. Jason, our youngest child." The moment he said his name he knew there was no turning back. "One day I was watching him by the pool. The phone rang . . . someone from the office. I stepped inside just for a few seconds. When I looked back, he was underwater. I tried to revive him, but . . ."

"I am so sorry, Ben Fielding."

Ben pulled over to a patch of hard dirt at the roadside. He turned to

Quan and yelled at him, "What kind of God looks the other way when a child drowns?"

The question hung out there for thirty seconds, answered by nothing but silence.

"What makes you believe God looked the other way?" Quan asked softly.

"Weren't you listening? My son died! And this God of yours let it happen."

"Yes, he did. But he loves your son. And you."

"Isn't that a little smug? and naive?"

"I know something of suffering, Ben Fielding. I have learned God is not my servant. Did you think he was like the story of Aladdin? That he was your genie? That he is safe and tame, at your call to do tricks to entertain you? That is an American way to think, perhaps. But it is not true to Shengjing. You cannot rub a magic lamp and command God to do your will. You accepted blessing from his hand, and still you do—yet you reject him because of adversity?"

"He was my only son."

"Yes. And my grandfather lost his only son. Li Quan lost his only father in prison. And my only mother in an earthquake . . . and two cousins, several friends. Some nights I long to see my parents. But I can see Father's eyes and Mother's smile only in my dreams. Yes, your old roommate knows a little of suffering, though far less than many. Are we not the clay, and God the potter? When he refuses to conform to our wills, do we discard him? If you are looking for a religion centered around yourself, Ben, I must agree that Christianity is a poor choice."

"He had no right."

"He has the right to strike us down as we sit. Why do you cling to rights that are not yours? Where did he promise you would not suffer? I can quote many Scriptures where he promised we *would* suffer. Is it God you have rejected? Or have you turned from a false god created in your own image?"

"You always have the answers, don't you? Well, I say you're arrogant to think you can speak for God."

"I do not speak for God. I only repeat what he has said. There is a difference. And there is a great deal I do not understand. But I *believe* God, that he is all-good, all-loving, and all-powerful. He is a God of providence, who works things together for worthy purposes."

"I don't see his providence."

"Then perhaps you should open your eyes. I see his providence in putting me in a room at Harvard with you, Ben Fielding, over twenty years ago. And again in bringing my old roommate to me in China after all these years."

"I say things happen because of hard work or accidents, good luck or bad luck."

"You mentioned arrogance. Is not the real arrogance to disbelieve the Scriptures and trust in yourself?"

"I refuse to believe in a God who sends men to hell."

"And do you think your refusal to believe will convince God to change his nature? He is who he is no matter what you think of him. Despite what Americans believe, the universe is not a democracy. Truth is not determined by the majority. As for hell, if you were as just and holy as God is, you would understand that all men deserve hell. It is no puzzle that men should go to hell. What is a puzzle is that men should go to heaven."

"He killed my only son!"

"He killed *his* only Son so that you and your family might live. So that your son and you would go not to the hell you deserve, but to the heaven you do not deserve. Instead of despising God because he does not follow your instructions, you should fall on your knees and praise him for his grace to you. I am sorry for your suffering, Ben Fielding. I weep for your loss." Ben saw for the first time Quan's wet face. "But do not blame the one who gives you your every breath, who offers you grace beyond measure. He is the Creator; we are but creatures. We are accountable to him—he is not accountable to us."

Ben felt surging anger, defensiveness, and guilt all at once. "I'm no theologian like you are, Professor. I don't know about all this."

"But you do know children need their father?"

"Dead sons don't need fathers."

"It is not the fault of your daughters that your son died. They still need their father."

"It's a little late for that."

"If you are alive and they are, then it is not too late."

After midnight, in Quan's house, a piercing shriek launched Ben out of bed. He instinctively assumed a defensive position, hands in front of him to ward off the attacker.

"It is alright," he heard Ming whisper to Quan. "You are dreaming again." He heard Shen, mumbling incoherently, climb into their little bed. Though it was dark, Ben thought he saw Ming, arms around her husband and her son.

He heard Quan's low moan, followed by sobbing in the darkness. Ming reassured him everything was alright. The unflappable Li Quan seemed to Ben a little boy, afraid in the dark, longing for safety and protection.

Ben sat on his bed, feeling guilty he'd witnessed such a private moment. He hoped Li Quan had forgotten he was there.

Ben spent most of the next three days in Pushan, talking with shopkeepers and people on the streets. He was using compact, state-of-the-art recording equipment to capture answers that could be gleaned for Getz's marketing department and sales team.

On Saturday Ben conveniently left for another "Shanghai meeting," only to stay in Pushan again by himself. He couldn't be there when Quan went to his illegal meetings. He wanted to honestly tell Martin and Won Chi and anyone else that he hadn't seen Quan do anything wrong.

It was now October 14. Ben returned to Quan's that night, feeling guilty about pretending he'd been in Shanghai. As he lay there in his bed, doing an uncomfortable penance for his lies, he heard men speaking softly in the night. He pressed the light on his watch. 2:20 A.M. Prowlers? No. Quan stood near the door, flaming candle in hand. Ben saw a disheveled shadowy figure near Quan. He handed Quan what appeared to be a gunnysack. Quan turned to look at Ben. He shut his eyes immediately. In the silence, Ben turned his head and moaned, pretending to sleep.

The men whispered another minute, while Ben tried to hear. Quan seemed to be trying to convince the man to spend the night. The visitor continuously gazed at Ben, who gazed back through the thin slits of his eyelids. He pointed at Ben several times and asked questions Ben couldn't decipher. This dialect didn't sound close to Mandarin.

Quan took the gunnysack, crossed the room, got on his knees, and seemed to search under his bed with his hands. Ming and Shen were either sound asleep or pretending to be. Ben saw Quan push the sack under the bed, as the stranger glanced back and forth from Quan to Ben. A few more muffled sounds, then Quan stood up. Ben groaned and stretched again, wondering if he was overdoing it.

Quan moved to the door and beckoned the stranger to follow. Both walked lightly. The door closed. Ben heard their muffled voices retreat into the night.

He got up carefully and peeked out the window. The pale moon cast their shadows under the ginkgo tree. Inside, the candle still burned, just two feet from Ming's head.

Who is this man? What's in that sack? Why did Quan hide it? Drugs? Weapons? Money laundering? Surely not Quan.

But hadn't Quan mentioned that good men were being driven to sell drugs, getting deliveries in the middle of the night? Quan had said China was full of corruption. He'd had a decent income withheld from him by not being allowed to teach. He made so little money to care for his family. Could Ben blame him if he was doing something illegal to make some money? He thought of the steely eyes of the man across from the hotel. He thought of the computer an assistant locksmith couldn't afford.

Ben lay down again and closed his eyes completely, in a halfhearted effort to return to sleep. But the sack and its unknown contents held his thoughts hostage. For another two minutes he wrestled, then sat up and swung his legs out of bed. He peeked out at the shadows still under the ginkgo tree, then looked over at Ming's placid face. He was already rehearsing his cover story. "I was just going to the outhouse. I couldn't find the flashlight, so I grabbed the candle."

He picked up the candle and crept across the room. He was finally thankful for the cement floor, knowing he could never coax old wood to be silent under his feet. The light shone on the lion at the table's center, staring at him. Out of the corner of his right eye he saw something moving. He froze. Then he spun suddenly and saw the dark form spin at the same time.

His shadow.

Feeling foolish, he got down on his knees, hoping Ming wouldn't sense his presence.

He put the candle on the floor, just as Quan had when he'd put the sack under the bed. He got down low and reached his hand underneath, searching. His fingers went across the cold cement until they touched something different. It felt like wood. He worked his fingers under the edge. It was a loose board. He pulled on it, sliding it out. He gripped it tightly, soundlessly.

Suddenly he felt something brush his hand. Then he heard it. It ran alongside his arm, coming only inches from his eye, appearing huge in the flickering candlelight. He froze. It skittered near his chin, which was propped up on the floor. All at once it came so close he couldn't see more than a blur. He felt something touching his chin. Antennae? He held his breath, terrified, wishing it would run away. But it stood still, as if trying to decide its next move. Then the cockroach climbed onto his lips. Ben screamed and jerked his head upward, banging into the plywood under the mattress above him.

He groaned, then heard Ming's airy scream above him.

His right hand clinched, he pulled his head out from under the bed as the cockroach skittered into a hole. His left hand knocked over the candle. It went out.

He heard Ming's hoarse, rapid speaking of words in some foreign dialect, nighttime gibberish or perhaps her childhood Cambodian.

"Ming, it's me, Ben. Everything's alright. I came over to get the candle, to go to the outhouse. I dropped something, and it rolled under the bed."

What was the "something"? He rethought his flimsy cover story, while Ming rattled on unintelligibly. He heard Shen's soft crying.

"Ben? That is you?" Ming said in Mandarin. "Where is Li Quan?" she asked.

As if on cue, the front door burst open. It was dark only for a second, and Ben heard the striking of a match, followed by the point of light.

"The candle's here on the floor, Quan." Ben tried to appear as helpful and innocent as he could. "I dropped it. It rolled under the bed." His right wrist ached as if clamped in a vise.

Quan lit the candle. He saw Ming up on her knees on the bed, arms crossed and palms on opposite sides of her neck. Shen had now crawled into bed beside her, eyes big and wet.

"I was just getting up to go to the outhouse," he said to Quan. "I dropped the candle, it rolled under the bed, and there was . . . a cockroach. It startled me, and I woke up Ming. I'm sorry. I . . . "

Ben stood there like a lying child trying to cover his tracks. He heard the stranger say agitated words he didn't fully understand. Then he saw him pointing to Ben's aching right wrist.

Ben looked down at his hand and saw what he'd been squeezing— an eighteen-inch board.

16

I'M SORRY, QUAN," Ben said, "but you were hiding something. I was afraid you were in trouble. It looked suspicious, like it was . . . illegal." He pointed under the bed, trying to get the focus off himself. "It's not drugs, is it?"

"Drugs?" Quan said. "Do you believe I would break the law for *drugs?*" Ben heard the pain in his friend's voice.

"No. But you said yourself times are hard. People do things they normally wouldn't. But not you, Quan. I know that. I feel like a fool."

"He who asks is a fool for five minutes, but he who does not ask remains a fool forever. If you wonder about your old roommate, ask him."

Quan turned on a lamp, then got down on his knees and reached under the bed.

"Bu," the man said, shaking his head. Ming's expression, as she moved from the bedside, also said no.

"It is time," Quan said.

"Are you sure?" she asked.

Quan continued his search, and Ben heard the familiar skittering. Without flinching, Quan pulled out the gunnysack. He stood and handed it to Ben.

"Quan, you don't have to show me. It's none of my business. I mean . . . " Ben saw the confused look on the stranger's face. Obviously he didn't know English.

"Open it, Ben."

Ben slowly opened the sack, bulky and much heavier than he'd imagined. He reached inside nervously, hoping not to find another cockroach. He took hold of something and pulled it out. It was a book with a black vinyl cover, compact but nearly two inches thick, with a fish symbol embossed on the lower front.

"A Bible?" Ben asked.

Quan nodded.

Ben dumped the rest of the sack's contents on the bed. Six Bibles. The stranger, clearly not approving of what had just happened, sat on the floor. Quan sat next to him. Ben pulled up a chair. Still trembling, Ming sat down again on the bed. Shen was in her arms, nearly sleeping again.

"This study Bible is precious," Quan said. "Most house-church leaders have no theological training. They have no Christian books. They call this a 'pocket seminary.' It is the Word of God, with instruction on how to study and use it. Also, it tells how to preach and teach Shengjing."

Quan opened the book, and his voice became impassioned as he flipped from place to place. "It has a topics list, sermon outlines, charts, and maps. Don't you see what this means, Ben Fielding? Even many pastors do not have Bibles. And those who do, have no help in using them. This Bible is Yesu's gift to us."

"What's the meaning of the fish?"

"The Greek word for fish is *ichthus*," Quan said. "The early Christians used it as an acrostic—in English you would say it stood for 'Jesus Christ, God's Son, Savior.' Each Greek letter stands for one of those words. When their faith was illegal in Rome, they drew this symbol on the ground with a stick to identify themselves. When other Christians saw it, they would draw it too. That way they knew they were brothers and sisters. Some of us use the sign. It also reminds us of the fish Yesu created for the multitudes and the fish he cooked and served and ate after his resurrection."

Ben nodded, not sure he was getting it.

"This is why we served you fish on my grandmother's plate the first night. The plate and fish remind us of Yesu, who served himself up on the cross, then three days later served fish to his disciples. We wish to serve Yesu to our family and neighbors. The symbol also links us to our persecuted brothers and sisters two thousand years ago. But the most important thing is not the symbol, but Shengjing itself."

"What will you do with these Bibles?"

"I will take them to a special drop-off place."

"The Huaquia Binguan with the Canadian on the fourth floor. Mr. Rogers, wasn't it?"

"Mr. James."

"The man who turns up the television when guests arrive."

"Many hotel rooms have insects," Quan said.

"What?"

"I am not using correct English word? Bugged? Yes. That is it—many rooms are *bugged*. We must turn up the television to mask conversations. Many go to jail when private conversations are overheard."

"You didn't give Mr. James meat and bread, did you?"

"Oh yes. Meat and bread brought to me from my old American roommate. Shengjing."

"You gave him the Bible I brought?"

"Yes."

"What did he give you? The 'classical music'?"

"Compact discs containing words and images that are music for the soul. Things our government does not want us to have."

"Why did you keep me in the dark about all this?"

"There is much at stake."

"And you don't trust me?"

Quan hesitated but didn't answer.

"Why were you walking backward from the house?"

"You have good eyes. Has nothing escaped your notice? It is an old trick I learned from my father. Footprints may be examined. Sometimes you would rather have others believe someone came to your house than that you left it."

"But why?"

"No need to say. But there was a reason."

"You tell me to ask, but you don't trust me enough to answer? Alright—tell me, who is this man who comes in the middle of the night?" Ben pointed at the stranger.

"I must not say his name, even to you. I would not tell anyone but those who need to know." Quan looked at his hands. "Yet you are right. I have not been sure I can trust you, Ben."

The words stung Ben more than he expected.

"So, as I have told you to ask me, I will ask you. Is your loyalty greater to your company or to your God? Is your business tied to the Chinese government? Are you beholden to the Party? I do not know. Where a man's treasure is, his heart will be also. Where is your treasure, Ben Fielding?"

"I may not agree with what you're doing. But I would never betray you."

"I guessed you would not. But there is a Chinese proverb: 'To guess is cheap. To guess wrong is expensive.' If I guessed wrong about my old roommate, I would put many at risk. I could not do that. But now . . . I believe I should trust you."

"When we went to the hotel, who were the men across the street?"

"One was a PSB agent in plainclothes. The main man was Tai Hong."

Ming shuddered and grasped Quan's arm.

"Who's he?" Ben asked.

"Assistant chief of police. Tai hates believers."

"I saw him at the hotel again, when we were headed to Shanghai for the Beijing flight, when you dropped off your duffel bag."

"Tai Hong was there?"

"Watching you. Where did these Bibles come from?" Ben pointed to the six black books on the bed, one of them now in Shen's hands.

Quan looked at the man and nodded. The stranger, in heavily accented Mandarin, said, "I am Yesu's donkey."

For a moment, Ben thought he'd misunderstood the word.

"A carrier of precious cargo. I have been doing this thirty years. It is my calling." He bowed his head.

"Where are you from?" Ben asked. Ming got up quickly and walked on tiptoe, like a little girl, pulled the curtains on the front window, then went to the back window and did the same. She put on the leather coat Ben had given her. He noticed she was shaking.

"A fall into a ditch makes you wiser," the man said. "I have fallen into enough ditches to know it is best for me not to answer your question. I am ethnically Chinese, but from another country. I know Yesu's donkeys from seven countries, including yours. Sometimes your people bring in Bibles from outside. I take them farther in. I am less suspicious because I have Chinese ancestry and appear to be a poor citizen. I have traveled far into the interior, the least evangelized parts of China—to the Muslim enclaves in the Northwest and Tibet in the Southwest."

"Why do you do this?" Ben asked.

"Forgive me," the stranger said. "Li Quan tells me to trust you, but for you to ask this question shows you do not know the ways of Yesu."

"Perhaps I don't. Instruct me then."

The man held up the Bible. He put it up to his nose and smelled it. "This is the book of God. Nothing is more precious. Last week I delivered twelve of these to a church of one thousand. Until I arrived, they had only five in the whole church. People offer to pay me a month's salary for a single Bible. But I get them free and I give them free. I accept only a bed and meals."

"Is what you do legal?"

"I have gone to jail many times," the visitor said. "But because I am a foreign citizen, I have a passport. I have always been released. I am forbidden to return. So I must come next time under another name. Li Quan of Hangzhou knows one of my old names. But even he does not know my real name."

"Do you have a family?" Ben asked the donkey.

"I live with my wife and children four months of the year. Even donkeys must stop sometimes. Most of the year I transport precious cargo. Yesu rode on a donkey into Jerusalem. His Word brings him to the people. I am a donkey Yesu has ridden to a hundred different cities and villages. It is my calling." He bowed his head.

Quan picked up one of the Bibles, held it close to his nose, and inhaled. "I love the smell of books. But there is no scent like Shengjing's." He put the books back in the sack, then reached under the bed, resituating the boards. "I broke cement to create this sacred hiding place. PSB could look under the bed and see nothing. Because it is cement floor I hope they would not bother moving the bed to look beneath."

"I suppose I can respect what this man has chosen to do," Ben said. "But like he said, he'll just be deported. It would be worse for you."

"Our people are starving for God's Word," Quan said. "What kind of a man would I be if I did not feed the hungry?"

"But you could lose your freedom. Or worse."

"An obedient man is free when in prison," Quan said. "A disobedient man is imprisoned when free." Ben didn't like the way Quan looked at him.

"A disciple's desire is to glorify his Master," said the donkey. "There are things more important than staying alive. Yesu's followers must love him more than their own lives."

Ben returned Quan's gaze. Not knowing what else to do, he nodded.

17

LI TONG SAT in the grass watching two great beings who'd fascinated him since he'd first arrived—the Watchers. They looked nearly identical, but one stood and spoke while the other sat and wrote. As far as Tong could tell neither ever stopped. He had heard their names but could not pronounce them. So one he nicknamed Reader and the other, Writer.

The Watchers gazed through a great portal, observing the earth's continents with the keen eyes of sentries. But what they saw through this particular portal—and what others like Tong saw when they looked through it—was only one specific kind of thing. Never did the portal focus on masses of humanity, but always on individuals, families, and churches.

At this moment, they viewed a man sitting in filth in a dark prison. Next, it was a little girl being beaten by her captor. Then a woman at her son's funeral. A boy with arms around his dead mother. A moment later, and they would see the face of an abuser, a jailer, an executioner. The faces of those inflicting the pain were seen as clearly as the faces of the sufferers themselves.

Writer wrote furiously in the book with a great quill pen that seemed never to run out of ink. He wrote in a perfect script, in a language Tong could not yet read fluently, though he had seen other messengers write in it. One had taught him the meaning of some characters. In some ways it was like Chinese, with characters that pictured people, animals, and events. But it had many more characters and symbols. It was an ancient language, he'd been told, that had once had only a few dozen characters, but it had developed more and more as the drama on earth continued over the millennia.

The other being, Reader, stood, sometimes reading and sometimes reciting words of a great Shengjing, handwritten in the same ancient language. He too watched what was happening on the dark planet. But while Writer wrote, Reader turned from place to place in the Book, reading the words with passion. Tong listened as he spoke, noting that Reader looked in only three directions—sometimes at the Book, sometimes at the people suffering on the dark planet, and sometimes at the King sitting on the throne:

> Those who sow in tears will reap with songs of joy. Blessed are those who mourn, for they will be comforted. The Lord is a refuge for the oppressed, a stronghold in times of trouble. Those who know your name will trust in you, for you, Lord, have never forsaken those who seek you.

Now Reader looked in a fourth direction, this time into the faces of those inflicting the suffering, then again to the King:

> Woe to those who make unjust laws, to those who issue oppressive decrees, to deprive the poor of their rights and withhold justice from the oppressed of my people, making widows their prey and robbing the fatherless. What will you do on the day of reckoning, when disaster comes from afar? To whom will you run for help? Where will you leave your riches?

> I will make justice the measuring line and righteousness the plumb line; hail will sweep away your refuge, the lie, and water will overflow your hiding place. Your covenant with death will be annulled; your agreement with the grave will not stand.

Tong looked at the throne and watched him who sat upon it. His lips moved, appearing to say the same words as Reader. The King spoke them as if the words were his own.

It was late Thursday afternoon, October 18, fifteen days after Ben had arrived in China. He'd spent most of the week on marketing research with folks in the streets and markets. "Do you have a computer?" he would ask. "No," the great majority would say. "When you can afford a computer, do you want to buy one?" "Yes," they would say, smiling and nodding.

Still feeling embarrassed about the middle of the night debacle, he picked out a special gift to bring to Quan. Ben hauled a large package out of the Pushan music store. He walked toward the car past the eel skinner and the street dentist. He noticed a woman in a green dress talking to disinterested passersby. She didn't look like a beggar or a merchant. Suddenly, she turned to Ben and fixed her eyes on him.

"You believe?" she asked Ben in Mandarin.

"Believe . . . what?"

"You believe gospel?"

He hesitated, looking at the people around him, who seemed to take no notice. She pointed, her finger only inches from his nose.

"You two times born again?"

He nodded, just to appease her.

"You covered by blood of Yesu, Holy One?"

He nodded again, trying to look sincere. "Yes," he finally said. His voice had a ring of certainty not felt in his mind.

"Alright. Very good," she said. "Belong to Yesu? Then act like it!" She waved her finger at him, in what seemed half encouragement and half rebuke, and walked down the street in search of her next victim. Ben watched her gesture to a bicycler, then disappear into the crowd. He felt like the casualty of a drive-by shooting.

Unnerved, Ben made one more stop at a store he'd visited twice already. He bought another bottle of mao-tai. He wrapped it in his sack and held it in his left hand, then turned carefully to navigate the long package in his right.

Shen ran to the car to greet him. Ben quickly pushed the sack with the bottle in it under the passenger seat. Then he asked for Shen's help, not that he needed it, to pull out the long box the merchant had wrapped.

"Another gift?" Shen asked. "Mama's gone visiting."

"It's for your father."

"Baba?" With Shen's attentive assistance, Ben took the package into the house and set it down at Quan's feet.

"Open it," Ben said.

Quan, fidgeting, picked at the brown paper. As soon as he saw what was inside he said, "No, Ben Fielding, you have been too generous. We cannot keep accepting gifts."

"You know how rude it is to refuse a gift. Just try it out, okay?"

Ben plugged it into the wall. Quan put his fingers on it. He pressed a few notes to hear how it sounded. He nodded approvingly. Then he started playing Bach. Then Beethoven. Then Mozart. It was awkward at first, but his fingers hadn't forgotten their skill. It was all coming back. Shen watched and listened, wide-eyed. Ben wondered if he'd ever heard his father play.

"Did you know the Red Guards smashed nearly all the pianos during the revolution?" Quan asked. "I was fortunate to have ever learned to play." Suddenly, with a wild smile, Quan broke into "Fair Harvard" and insisted Ben sing with him.

"That's your payback, huh?" Ben said.

An hour later, Quan was still playing. He got up only to pick up the empty high-backed chair, bring it over, and set it down in front of him. Then he resumed playing. The music was something Ben didn't know, but it had a sacred sound.

Ming burst through the door. She stared at the electronic keyboard. Then she looked at Ben as if he were the worker of great miracles. She drew the curtains, and seeing this seemed to bring Quan back to reality.

"Do you know we could be arrested for playing these songs?" Quan asked.

"No way," Ben said.

"There are four of us. I have been playing Christian songs, which makes this a religious gathering. Our house is not a registered meeting place. Shen is under eighteen. It is illegal on two counts, at least. So, Ben, would you have me obey this law or break it?"

The joy that had filled the room for an hour disappeared in an instant. Ben didn't know how to answer, so he changed the subject. "The donkey said you were from Hangzhou."

"Yes."

"I thought you were born in Shanghai."

"I was."

"But you grew up in Hangzhou?"

"No."

"When did you move there?"

"I have never lived in Hangzhou. I have never even been there."

"But . . . you said you were from there."

"I am."

"Quan, what are you talking—"

Quan raised his hand. "I have something to say to you. I am glad we were able to talk about Shengjing. I am glad you met the donkey."

"And I'm glad you finally trusted me enough to tell me what was going on."

"Perhaps I seem overly careful to you, do I not?"

Ben shrugged.

"So many in house churches have been betrayed. We have seen many infiltrators, informants, collaborators. It is easy to dodge a spear in front, but hard to avoid an arrow shot from behind. The government rewards betrayal. Do you know the story of Mr. Nan Guo?"

"No. But I'll bet you're going to tell me."

Ming giggled.

"Yes, and because you value wisdom over ignorance, you will gladly listen." Quan smiled. "In the Warring States period, in the third to fifth centuries before Yesu, there was a state called Qi. The king was fond of listening to music played on the *Yu,* a wind instrument. So he convened a band of three hundred players. Every day at teatime the band was called in to play the Yu for His Majesty. Now, one of the players, Mr. Nan Guo, knew nothing about the instrument. But by pretending to play the Yu he was believed to be part of the orchestra. No one knew the truth."

"Not yet, anyway," Ben said.

"We tell our children, never jump ahead in a story."

"Sorry."

"Finally, the king died, and the prince became king. But the new king did not like to hear the orchestra. He enjoyed solo performances. He called each musician in to play alone for him. This time, Nan Guo could not hide. He was shown to be what he was."

"And the point of this story . . . ?"

"The point is what Yesu said in another story. The tares and wheat grow up together. There are those who appear to be playing the Yu, those who appear to be Christians. Then, when they are put to the test, it shows who they really are." Quan looked at him. "Have you known such Christians in America? Have you known those who appear to be Christians but are not?"

"I suppose."

"Do you have those who say they are believers, but who go along with the world and turn against their Lord and their own brothers? Have you ever known someone to do that, Ben Fielding?"

Ben swallowed hard. "Maybe."

"That is why we must be careful. We are willing to go to jail, willing even to die, but only if necessary. We will not cease speaking about Yesu.

But neither will we unnecessarily put others at risk. This is why I fully trust only those I know."

"Are you still trying to figure out if you trust me?" Ben asked.

"We must be careful in our contacts with any Westerners. They are always suspected to be Christians. However—" he looked down—"you are considered safe."

"What do you mean?"

"I must explain that just as the government has moles, unbelievers within the church, we too have our moles, Christians within the Party and PSB. We have been told by one of ours that no one suspects you to be a Christian."

"Why not?"

"Because, I am told, reliable sources have been with you. They know what you have said and done in your many trips to Shanghai. They make it their business to know where foreigners go and what they do. They have talked with your Chinese businessmen friends, and they have vouched for you. They have said you are certainly not a Christian."

"They said that?" Ben said, swallowing hard.

"So it is ironic," Quan said. "You are safer to us exactly because they are sure you are not one of us. But as for my own trust in you, it is real, yet it has limits. Forgive me, old friend. It is easy for me to love a man who does not trust Yesu. But it is not so easy for me to trust this man."

"Why?"

"Because every man trusts someone. If he does not trust Yesu, he trusts other men or he trusts himself. Neither is trustworthy. Not in China. Not in America." Quan stood and put his hands on the back of the empty chair. "Tell me, Ben Fielding. Why did you stop trusting Yesu?"

"We talked about that. Could we just forget it?"

"I do not think the death of your mother and son are the only reasons."

"Well, maybe Professor Know-It-All is wrong for once; did that ever occur to you? Or maybe my faith was too simple and my world got too complicated. The deeper I got into business, the more I saw how out of touch with my world the church was. The sermons seemed . . . simplistic, naive. My time was better spent reading people who understood my world."

"Your world?" Quan seemed to ponder the expression. "It is God's world, is it not? Does anyone understand it better than he who made it and reigns over it and died for it?"

"There's more to it than that. I live in a world of capital, investments, earnings projections, debt, buildings, leasing, tax issues. It's not a world of superstitious farmers and peasants."

"Have you not read the words of Yesu? He spoke of great treasures. He spoke of investing in jewels and pearls to illustrate investing in what lasts. He spoke of indebtedness and his canceling our debts. He referred to grainfields and harvesters. He talked of farmers leasing property, of property owners' demands on them. He spoke of capital, banking and earning interest, moneylenders, building barns to store grain for retirement income. He talked about counting the cost before undertaking business projects—about dividing up an estate, irresponsible spending, bad financial management, and dishonest business practices."

"How do you remember all that?"

"God has blessed me with an organized mind." Quan smiled. "Yesu spoke of finances and businesses and property to teach us about the greater realities they illustrate. Perhaps it is those greater realities that Ben Fielding needs to give more thought to."

"Religion seems to me to be a lot of wishful thinking."

"That is what the communists say."

"Just because they're communists doesn't mean they can't be right."

"No. But it is not that the communists wish there were a God and have been convinced by the evidence there is none. It is that they fear there is a God and therefore reject the evidence for him. Believers comfort each other in their suffering by the truth that there is a God. Communists comfort each other in their prosperity by the myth that there is no God. So atheism is the real wishful thinking."

"I'm not sure I believe that."

"A true believer may spend a sleepless night doubting God. But what keeps a communist awake at night is his fear there *is* a God. His wishful thinking is that God does not exist. For if there is no God, there is no Judge and, therefore, no judgment for his wickedness. But if there is a God, he knows he will not fare well before him. Or that God will make demands on him he does not wish to fulfill. Perhaps this is what you fear?"

"Who said I was afraid? There's a lot you don't know," Ben said. "Our lives have gone in two different directions. I've spent the last twenty years reading financial reports and investment articles and books by experts in success. And you've . . . well, you've been reading something else. I don't agree with you, Quan. But I admire you. I think it would have broken me to have to give up my dreams like you did."

"Li Quan has given up dreams he could not have held on to anyway. In turn, he has embraced the eternal dreams of the risen Yesu. It was an excellent trade. You see, Ben, your old roommate is not without dreams. He has just replaced the old dreams with dreams that are higher and better."

––––––––––––

Ben spent Friday evening at a dinner meeting with a Pushan business executive. He pulled into Quan's place much later than usual and put his hand on the doorknob. It was locked.

"Who is there?" came the voice from the inside.

"Ben."

"Alone?"

"No—I'm with the Chinese joint chiefs of staff."

Quan opened the door.

"What's going on?" Ben asked.

"We have visitors."

Ben walked in and saw what looked like two families of three. A man, woman, and teenage boy were on Quan's bed. Another man, woman, and teenage girl were on Ben's bed. Ming sat at the desk and Shen on the floor at her feet. All had two open books in front of them, and ballpoint pens in their hands.

"What are you doing?"

"Making copies of Shengjing. Those printed Bibles will soon be picked up by the donkey and passed on to others. But while they are here we can use them, can't we? Shen and I are copying from my mother's Bible."

With a proud smile Shen held up his grandmother's Bible to Ben. Then he picked up his own handwritten copy, handing it to Ben for inspection.

"Shen is a good scribe," Ben said.

"Father checks my work," he said, beaming.

"As we copy," Quan said, "the words of Yesu are written on our hearts."

Is this legal? Ben wondered. He remembered all the reassurances of religious freedom he'd been given over the years. But seeing these people huddled like this, it was obvious they were convinced it was illegal. But he didn't want to hear the words. If something hit the fan, he wanted to maintain deniability with Martin and the Getz board.

Ben was about to go for a walk, anything to get him away from this, when he looked closely at Quan's mother's Bible. "It's beautiful. The characters are so small but clear."

"Mother copied it carefully. She would borrow a Bible whenever she could. She'd work for hours by candlelight, praying the words aloud as she copied. I wish I would have listened more closely. Often she would rest her head on Shengjing. Sometimes she would giggle with delight. It was a labor of love. Months, even a year, went by when she had no Bible to copy. It took her eight years to finish her whole Bible. Six months before she died, Mother finished copying Shengjing's final book. A leather worker in church bound it for her."

"And you kept it all these years?"

"No. She had loaned it to another woman who was copying it at the time. After I returned from Harvard, they heard I had become a Christian. The church gave it to me."

Ben flipped through the pages. "It's been out in the rain."

"No. Always it was carefully covered. Mother bundled it up before going outside. We do the same."

"But the words are smeared in many places," Ben said.

"It was not rain that smeared the words."

18

IT WAS SATURDAY AFTERNOON, Ben's third Saturday in China, and the first he hadn't spent in a Pushan hotel room bingeing on mao-tai, taking hot showers, and watching CNN and soccer matches. He and Quan sat on a patch of grass on the bank of a muddy little river, the Wenrong, fishing poles in hand. It brought back Ben's memories of sitting at their favorite fishing hole fifty minutes from Harvard, dreaming about their future.

Li Quan loved to fish, and back then Ben had too. He'd enjoyed the chance to think and reflect. In recent years, chances to think and reflect had always taken him back to his career goals. Often his idle time ended in depression, his pulling out another bottle or throwing himself back into his work, hoping today or tomorrow would bring what yesterday never had.

This day seemed just right. Sun on his face, yellow flowers swaying in the gentle breeze, butterflies flitting, birds singing, and the soothing sound of water lapping against the rocks. It was glorious. Somehow it awakened desires deep within, yearnings that Ben had long ignored or pressed down or sought to fulfill in ways that never satisfied.

Shen was exploring down by the water, trying to obey his father's regular reminders to stay in clear sight.

"Li Quan has an important question for his old fishing friend Ben Fielding. But first I must ask you to tell me more about your understanding of the Chinese church."

"Well, like I said, I've been told registered churches are free and completely legal, just like the one they took us to, the one where they sold Bibles. I've seen church steeples in the cities. What can I say?"

"Why do you think they make steeples so tall? So visitors can look at them. So they can say, 'See, there is religious freedom in China,' and go home and tell that to everyone they know. But many registered churches are puppets of the government. Yes, some registered churches stay true to God's Word. For that I am grateful. But their pastors must disobey government ban on speaking of Yesu's resurrection and return. They cannot teach the doctrine that evil governments will be overthrown by God. The Party will not tolerate registered churches speaking against the one-child policy or abortion. Who then is the god of most of these churches? Yesu or government?"

"And you think illegal house churches are the only alternative?"

"Third Wave or independent churches try to be a middle way between the Three-Self and house churches. But once they register, either the Three-Self Patriotic Movement or the China Christian Council must approve all pastors. Both are under a government agency, and they can take over congregations by adding or removing pastors of their choice. House churches believe the government should not control what they teach and how they worship."

"It's a shame people don't feel like they can get what they want at the legal churches."

"But even if a registered church was true to Yesu, Pushan has only one, on the far side of the city from here. About thirty kilometers away. Almost none of us have cars, so it would mean the congregation would have to ride bicycles or walk. There is one church for a city of a quarter million. Gathering in our homes is the only realistic option for most of us. You have been to Shenyang, Ben Fielding?"

"Sure. Four or five times."

"Then you know it is a city of over seven million, nearly the size of New York City. Do you know how many registered churches there are in all of Shenyang?"

"A dozen?"

"Last I knew, there was one. Over seven million people with only one legal church! Can you imagine one church in all of New York City? Churches are not allowed to provide for children, because it is illegal to give the Christian message to those under eighteen. Husbands and wives attend separate services so one can stay home with their child. And the messages are censored. The government lets them teach that Yesu was a good man and a wise teacher, just like the great Chinese philosophers. But pastors cannot legally teach him as Savior."

"Why? What's the big deal?"

"The Party insists it alone is the people's savior. When pastors teach about Jesus too much, they can be removed or put in positions where they cannot be effective. So even if every city had hundreds of legal churches, many believers would not think it right to attend those churches."

"But they don't often enforce laws against house churches, do they? Don't they usually just look the other way?"

"Sometimes, in some places. House churches sometimes think of registered churches as compromisers, while registered churches think of house churches as troublemakers, stubborn strong-willed children. Crackdowns on local house churches may begin when a registered church official complains to authorities about underground worship. While the world saw the glorious fiftieth anniversary celebration in Beijing, they did not see my nephew, Li Yue, or my pastor, Zhou Jin, in jail. Then after permanent trade status was granted, the number of persecutions jumped again."

"I didn't know that."

"You know only what others want you to know. Bible studies are illegal. We cannot have pictures with verses or crosses or anything else that says we are believers. Often we are under surveillance; there are cameras everywhere. Christians lose good jobs, and education and travel are restricted. Some of us lose our homes. Church property can be vandalized. Every piece of furniture was broken in Ho Lin's house when an infiltrator told the PSB about the house church meeting there. We are frequently arrested on false charges and made to pay fines. Many of us have been beaten, some even killed."

"But why?"

"We are persecuted not because we do not love China, but because our leaders hate Yesu. When Yesu is everything to you, it is impossible not to speak of him. We say, 'It is hard to keep the Sun in your pocket.'"

"It just doesn't make sense to me."

"Perhaps because you look only for human explanations. There are great powers of darkness who hate Yesu and try to hurt him by hurting his bride. A few years ago Li Quan visited registered church in Shanghai. I went to buy a Bible. There were some true believers there. That morning, a group of visiting Americans sang songs in English. Most of the Chinese could not understand, but I could. The Americans sang about being 'safe and secure from all alarms.' I do not know much about this song. Some of it sounded good. But I think perhaps they did not understand that most Chinese Christians are *not* safe and secure from all alarms."

"Okay. I can appreciate what you're saying, Quan. So tell me. What's it like to be in a house church meeting?"

Quan looked at Ben long and hard. "This leads to my question. Will you come to a house church meeting with us tomorrow? Then you can see for yourself."

"Me? Tomorrow? Wait a minute. You just finished telling me these meetings aren't safe, right? I'm an officer of Getz International. Why would I jeopardize my reputation and my company's? Do you realize the position this could put me in?"

"Yes. I can only say the risk that our families and children take each week is much greater. I have never been in a house church with a foreigner present. But then, I have never had a foreigner live in my house like this. I do not think you can draw your own conclusions about house churches until you see one with your own eyes. I cannot promise you there will be no trouble. But we are careful. The pastor has asked the people if they are willing to take the risk of having you present. They have all agreed."

"They have?"

"Yes. You may not understand this, Ben, but to invite you to gather with us for the holy worship of Yesu is the greatest gift we can offer."

They rose so early Sunday it felt like late Saturday.

Quan put on clothes nicer than any Ben had seen him wear. They were old but very neat. His black dress shoes were carefully shined.

"Do you remember the shoes you gave me?"

"You must be kidding. Those can't be the same shoes."

"They are. I have worn them every week for over twenty years, but only to church. I pray for you whenever I look at them. I have often thought that perhaps you were praying for me at the same moment."

Ben put on an old tattered coat of Quan's—the largest in the house but still too small—and a white smog mask to hide his face. He had volunteered to drive, so they could sleep in until 2:30 A.M. Since there were only two bikes, there was no argument. But Quan insisted Ben park a kilometer away from their destination. They found a quiet little grove of trees and pulled off the road behind some thick bushes. Ben had to stop suddenly to avoid hitting a motor scooter by the bushes. Perhaps another church attender?

As they walked, well off the road, Ben kept hearing his feet slosh, but not anyone else's, not even Shen's.

I must be crazy to have let Quan talk me into this!

They came around the back of an isolated house with a faint glow of candles visible through a narrow crack between the drapes and the edge of the window. They walked past many bicycles. Quan knocked. A quiet man greeted him, and they all came in the door. The room was packed with people, like geese in a bamboo basket on market day. Ben studied the thirty faces—men, women, and children shoulder to shoulder, some on chairs, some on a wooden bench, some on straw mats on the floor. Four sat on a bed, three on top of a desk, two under a table. None of them looked surprised to see Ben. But they couldn't keep their eyes off him.

Quan quietly introduced Ben to person after person. When he met Fu Gan, Chun, and their daughter Yun, Chun and Yun giggled and nodded appreciatively when Ben spoke to them in Mandarin.

Quan and the Li family sat in the front row, in seats obviously reserved for them and their guest. After quiet whispers, the group began singing. Ben gazed at one woman to the front left of the room, sitting on the floor. Her faded black tunic was too big, as were her gray, baggy pants. Her eyes stayed closed most of the time, but her face was perfectly framed by her black bowl-cut hair, laced throughout with lines of silver. Her face actually seemed to shine. Ben looked for a hidden light source. He told himself he must be imagining this. It unnerved him. Suddenly, she opened her eyes. They were pools of fire, like oil ablaze in water.

For an hour they sang songs Ben hadn't heard before, sung with a burning passion so palpable he felt singed by it. Quan stood and prayed, then said, "Our pastor will teach us from the book of Revelation."

An old man with a familiar face walked forward. His tuft of wispy white hair reminded Ben of bleached cotton candy floating above his scalp. His hair moved almost imperceptibly when he turned his head, as if an invisible wind blew upon him.

The locksmith!

"Your boss is the pastor?" Ben whispered to Quan.

"Yes."

"Now I know why he didn't turn you in for being a house church Christian!"

To Ben's right a boy got up from under a table to sit close to a man at a desk. Ben saw that the man had a handwritten Bible. Ben suddenly realized two people were peeking over his shoulder. But when he opened the English Bible Quan had loaned him, one sighed and the other laughed. They repositioned themselves behind Quan. When he looked around,

Ben realized he and Pastor Zhou were the only ones in the room looking at a Bible by themselves.

"This book tells us of Yesu's plan to abolish all other kingdoms and set up his kingdom on earth," Zhou Jin started. "This is why the government says we must not study Revelation. However, since they do not know we are meeting, they will not mind if we study it today."

There was a light nervous laughter.

He read, "'Then I saw a new heaven and a new earth, for the first heaven and the first earth had passed away. . . .'"

Four people without Bibles crowded closer at the feet of Zhou Jin, drinking the words as if they were parched and hadn't had water for a week.

"'I saw the Holy City, the new Jerusalem, coming down out of heaven from God, prepared as a bride beautifully dressed for her husband.'"

Jin looked up. "We are his church. *We* are that bride! We are dressed in the righteousness of Yesu. We wear the spotless wedding gown of his holiness."

Many murmurs sounded as one.

"'And I heard a loud voice from the throne saying, "Now the dwelling of God is with men, and he will live with them. They will be his people, and God himself will be with them and be their God."' As the first man and woman lived with him in the garden, we will live with him in the new garden, the new city, the new earth. We will be in his presence. We will see the Almighty face-to-face!"

"Ahh . . ."

"Yes."

"Amen."

"Xiexie."

"Thank you."

The responses rose like smoke from a fire. Ben felt the fire's warmth.

"The next verse says, 'He will wipe every tear from their eyes.' Our Father, with his own hand, will wipe every tear from our eyes. The tears of the old man who has lost his beloved wife. The tears of the woman forced to be sterilized. The tears of the child whose father was taken from him to prison and death."

Ben saw Zhou Jin look at Quan in the front row. "The tears of the man whose job was taken from him by the wicked, because he stood firm and spoke up for Yesu."

Ben squirmed in his seat. He saw in his mind's eye an unexpected face—Doug Roberts.

Zhou Jin looked back at the book, smoothing the page carefully, as if stroking the head of someone precious. "'There will be no more death or mourning or crying or pain, for the old order of things has passed away.'"

Gasps of wonder spread throughout the room. Ben heard crying and sobbing. But simultaneously he heard sighs of delight and a wave of soft laughter. Somehow the sounds melded together, a diverse but unified expression, full of paradox but without contradiction.

"'For the old order of things has passed away.' He who was seated on the throne—King Yesu—said, 'I am making everything new!'"

Zhou Jin handed the book to his wife, then lifted his hands and put his fingers together, as if holding up something invisible in the air.

"Do you know what this means, little children? It means this world is not our home. We were not made for this world. The bridegroom has gone to prepare a place for us. He promises to come back and get us and take us to a new home in a new world! The true China. Our true country. Our true home."

There was a smattering of light applause, but mostly groans and whispered affirmations.

Eyes closed, Zhou Jin spoke, but the words did not seem his: "'It is done. I am the Alpha and the Omega, the Beginning and the End.'"

Praise erupted. Ben sensed the momentum building.

"'To him who is thirsty I will give to drink without cost from the spring of the water of life.'"

Ben felt that yearning, that longing inside. He realized he'd tasted it yesterday at the fishing hole. It was like a deep yet elusive thirst, suddenly accentuated by seeing and hearing close-up a fresh, cold mountain stream. All his life now seemed like a quest for something he did not know, as if all he had done was to seek the consummation of an unfulfilled promise. As a boy he had felt it in the woods, sensing that around the next bend was something wonderful, the object of his desire. He had been beckoned by an unknown Beauty that called to him in the night, urging him not to find himself in the lesser, but to lose himself in the greater. Something drew him to the hills, onward and upward.

Sitting in this room eight thousand miles from home—no, *millions* of miles from his home—he saw his life with a sudden clarity. From time to time he'd felt he was on the verge of having his soul's thirst quenched. But always what seemed pure had proven to be salt water, not quenching his thirst but deepening it. Something about this room, this gathering, these people made him feel closer to the Stream than he'd ever been. Yet that very closeness multiplied the ache of his thirst.

"'He who overcomes will inherit all this, and I will be his God and he will be my son.'"

Ben heard a soft moan beside him. He saw a tear trickling down Quan's cheek. In the years they were roommates, he never remembered seeing Quan cry.

"Next Lord's day," Zhou Jin said, "we will discuss the martyrs who stand before God's throne. We will read the verses now and teach them next week." His wife unwrapped Shengjing again and handed it to him reverently. He opened and read:

> They called out in a loud voice, "How long, Sovereign Lord, holy and true, until you judge the inhabitants of the earth and avenge our blood?" Then each of them was given a white robe, and they were told to wait a little longer, until the number of their fellow servants and brothers who were to be killed as they had been was completed.

A woman stood and put out her hands. Immediately, Zhou Jin handed her his Bible. She read a large portion aloud, then said, "My son is still in prison. He has been there ten months. I have only been allowed to visit him three times. He has been . . . tortured. Please pray his faith will stay strong."

Zhou Jin lifted his hands and interceded for the boy and his mother. Then the bright-faced woman lifted her voice in prayer. Ben listened to the cries of the woman whose son was in prison. The sound of her weeping would not let him go.

Reader turned to the throne and said,

> How long, O Lord, must I call for help, but you do not listen? Or cry out to you, "Violence!" but you do not save? Why do you tolerate wrong? Destruction and violence are before me; there is strife, and conflict abounds. The wicked hem in the righteous, so that justice is perverted. How long, O Lord? Will you forget me forever? How long will you hide your face from me? How long must I wrestle with my thoughts and every day have sorrow in my heart? How long will my enemy triumph over me?

The King rose to speak. And though he did not shout, he could be heard in every corner of Charis, his great kingdom that reached to the far corners of the cosmos. "I see the misery of my people. I hear your cries.

You are not alone in your suffering. You will weep and mourn while the world rejoices. You will grieve, but your grief will turn to joy. A woman giving birth to a child has pain because her time has come; but when her baby is born she forgets the anguish because of her joy. Now is your time of grief, but I will see you again and you will rejoice, and no one will take away your joy. In that world you will have trouble. But take heart! I have overcome that world."

———————

The prayers were short and long, informal and formal, but all had a passion Ben had never sensed. Many years ago he'd fallen asleep at prayer meetings. No one could fall asleep here. No words seemed nominal. No prayers seemed scripted. More than that, Ben had the unmistakable sense these prayers did not stop at the ceiling. They passed through it, gathering momentum, a cumulative force so explosive it threatened to blow off the roof of the old house.

Several more stood and read or recited words from Shengjing. The words were a gentle wind blowing in the room, life and breath from an unseen presence. The room felt warm and wet and pulsating, as if it were a womb.

Ben heard what seemed a whisper telling him these people were naive, superstitious, gullible, quick to attribute supernatural causes to natural effects. Then another voice inside told him the problem was not them but him. He should stop denying realities just because he could not see or touch or measure them.

They sang, adoring God. A God Ben had once believed in. He too had once read the Bible and sung songs in religious meetings. But never had he sensed the presence of God as in this room now. Why? Never had he been lost in adoration. Why? His "Christian life" had been like every other part of his life. It had always been about Ben Fielding.

What captivated him most were the faces. Joyful faces, smiling faces, wet faces, grieving faces, longing faces, childlike faces. And, especially that woman in the front, shining faces.

"Look at me, Dad," he remembered Melissa saying to him as she first rode a bike on her own. "Do you like my pigtails, Daddy?" Kimmy had asked. Yes, their faces had looked just like these, childish faces delighting in a father's presence, craving a father's approval.

I was like them once, naive and idealistic, but I saw through it; I outgrew it. The wave of cynicism crashed upon him fully formed, as though these thoughts came not from inside but outside.

You were never like these people, something else said to him, a voice without sound. *Never.*

If these people were wrong, Ben considered, they were misguided fools needlessly suffering for an ill-founded faith. If they were right—a big *if*—it meant Ben's life was a washout, and he was guilty of a smug, condescending apostasy.

Some were down on the floor now, on their knees, leaning forward, heads touching the ground. Others looked straight ahead. The man and woman in front of him gazed up at the ceiling. He looked up there too, searching for something loose, ready to fall on him. What were they looking at, and why could he nearly see it, but not quite?

The wind in the house church was blowing, and he sensed his own house of cards was in jeopardy. Ben Fielding felt a gentle inviting breeze that called him to get up and follow it over the horizon. Ben hoped with almost sickening intensity this feeling would not go away. At the same time, he desperately hoped the breeze would not turn into a hurricane.

19

$\mathcal{D}$O YOU SEE Abuk Akec Dhel," Li Tong said, "this woman taken a slave in Sudan? Her husband was slain, her children enslaved. She has been beaten and mutilated. They tried to force her conversion to Islam. Writer records every detail. Watch how her appointed warrior stands by her, even though she does not see him."

"Have you been yet to the great Hall of Reward?" Li Manchu asked Li Tong. "Have you seen the Writer there, the one who recounts not the suffering of saints, but their every act of kindness, every cup of cold water, every financial gift, every prayer uttered on behalf of the suffering?"

"I have heard of this, of course, but have not yet been there. There are so many people to talk with, so many places to go, so many things to see! I have thought that perhaps Li Quan and I might go there together."

Li Manchu nodded. "There are many other Writers, of course, and the King reads all their reports. But I think this Writer before us is the scribe to whom the King gives his closest attention. Every day, every moment, he reviews the accounts of all his suffering children."

"But he sees everything already and cannot forget what he sees. Why does he have them written in books?"

"Perhaps so that we whose minds are finite will also never forget."

Ben felt relieved to have made it safely back to the Li home without encountering any authorities. Ming had brewed green tea, and the coldness of the room made him savor the tea's warmth inside him.

"What did you think of our house church, Ben Fielding?" Quan asked as he pushed in a little wooden cart and shoveled coal into the stove.

"They seemed . . . convinced God was actually in that room."

"This is understandable," Quan said, smiling, "since he was."

"They were so passionate, so excited to be there. I never felt like that in church—or if I ever did, it was a long time ago. Even back in college, and as a kid when I went to church, I don't think most of us had a passion anything like that. It makes me wonder how real my faith was."

"This is a good thing to wonder," Quan said. "Doubts about salvation can be the enemy's attack upon true believers. Yet Shengjing says we should examine ourselves to see whether we are of the faith. We must make sure first we are his followers before we seek assurance. The enemy seeks to accuse us that we are not what we are. But just as surely, he seeks to assure us we are what we are not."

"I can't imagine taking the kinds of risks they take just by meeting. Churches in America would be a lot smaller if the cost was that great."

"Smaller at first. Eventually perhaps larger. Or perhaps like in China, many more small churches, totaling many more believers. A man takes risks only for what he feels deeply about. If someone attends church without risk, he brings no passion."

"I've often spoken on the cost-benefit ratio at seminars. I guess I only saw the application to business."

"Yesu spoke of the treasure hidden in the field," Quan said. "He said that in his joy the man sold all he had to obtain that treasure. It cost him everything he had—but he did not care, for it gained him everything that mattered."

"Their faces were so animated. When some of those people fell to their knees, I almost wanted to do it too."

"Almost? To come near is not yet to arrive."

"I'm not saying I've never prayed. It's just that I've never been a fall-on-your-knees kind of guy."

"Then Li Quan will pray Ben Fielding becomes that kind of guy."

For thirty seconds neither man spoke.

"What do you want, Ben?" It seemed a strange question, but it struck so directly at Ben's thoughts that he decided to answer it.

"Years ago I laid out my life goals. Every Monday I review them. They're business goals, mostly. I want to be CEO of Getz International. Build the company. Strengthen our presence in China. Make a comfortable living."

"That is all you want?"

"Most people would think that's quite a lot, thank you."

"Few men achieve all their goals," Quan said. "But if you achieved all of yours, would it bring you joy?"

"Joy? I guess I'd settle for just a slice of happiness."

"Then you would settle for too little."

"What do you mean?"

"I had goals much like yours. First, to be the best student. Perhaps I accomplished that goal. But my greater goals were to become a great professor and write books. I had to die to those goals. But I was fortunate to die to them. For then I was forced to set other goals, better ones." He reached out his hand and put it on Ben's shoulder. "I do not think your goals are too big, Ben Fielding. I think they are too small."

Ben felt the load of defensiveness land on his chest. He stared silently at Quan, wondering how an assistant key maker got off saying this to the future CEO of Getz International. "So far I've done alright. I've always managed to get what I've wanted."

"Then you have wanted too little." Quan shrugged at him. "Your goals will surely not bring you happiness. But even if they did, how long would the happiness last? A day? A year? Ten years? Twenty? And then what? Your life will be short—all men's lives are short. What will outlast this life? That should be your concern. You are an investor? Alright—why would you invest in what might pay off in ten years when you can invest in what will certainly pay off in ten million years?"

Ben laughed but realized Quan seemed perfectly serious. "That kind of long-range planning is a little out of my league."

"Your deepest desires come from what my father called the hole in the heart. What does it profit a man, Ben Fielding, to gain the whole world and lose his own soul? Or even if a man's soul is saved, what does it profit him to gain the world and lose his eternal reward?"

———————

Their neighbors and house church members Fu Gan, Chun, and their teenage daughter Yun arrived for Sunday evening dinner. Ben sat in the fourth chair, while the fifth sat empty. Quan, Ming, and Shen sat on the cold, hard floor. The families spoke of various neighbors they were seeking to evangelize. After dinner, Quan played on his keyboard some sacred classical music, then a hymn. The others sang along softly. Ming had Quan's Bible in her hands, preparing to read.

Ben excused himself and moved five feet away to sit on his bed, laptop computer hooked to the phone line.

Suddenly, there was urgent pounding on the front door. As smoothly as if she'd practiced it a hundred times, Ming slid under the bed and reemerged an instant later without Shengjing.

Quan went to the front door and opened it. He stepped backward immediately when he saw who it was.

Three men pushed their way in, one holding a pistol. Having seen him twice before from a distance, Ben got his first close-up of Tai Hong's angular face, red and weathered and hard. He looked like he'd spent his youth on the open seas, daring the ocean to drown him. He had a large Mao-like mole on his chin, swollen and discolored. Ben looked, now from just five feet away, into those black steel eyes. Tai Hong shifted uncomfortably, not used to being looked in the eyes for more than a fleeting second. Ben sensed it and forced himself to keep looking. He refused to blink until Hong looked away.

Quan spoke first. "What brings the deputy chief of PSB to visit our humble home?"

"We were in the area. We thought we would pay our respects." His lips seemed not to open even when he spoke. Though the voice was sand-papery, it was highly trained. Ben detected the accent of the Shanghai-bred, with its superior tone. Despite his show at courage, Ben felt prickles on his spine.

"What is going on here?" Hong asked, eyeing each of the seven.

"I was playing my electronic keyboard, a gift from my friend Ben Fielding."

Hong looked straight at Ben, then back at Quan. "Why have you gath-ered?"

"We had dinner. We were discussing the harvest, then playing classical music. Like President Jiang Zemin enjoys."

Hong smirked. "Discussing the harvest? This is what you were doing?" He looked at the Fu family, all three of whom stared at the floor.

"Yes," Quan said quickly. "We anticipate a large harvest."

"You are not farmers."

"Harvest is a subject of interest to us all. We must eat to live, and we must labor to produce food. Tai Hong needs food to eat, does he not?"

"I have plenty of food—I need none of yours," Tai Hong said, moving to the door and gesturing his men to step outside. "I will visit again, Li Quan. Perhaps when your American friend has left. Perhaps before. Next time I may see you at my place." He grinned menacingly.

As he walked out the door, Hong stared one last time at Ben. If he wasn't a prominent businessman with an American passport and a long history in China, Ben realized things would likely have gone much differ-ently. The door shut hard. Ming put her arms around Shen.

"Well, that was a pleasant social call," Ben said.

"Yes," Quan said. "The weasel has come to say hello to the chickens."

Was this Tai Hong's way of telling me he knows I was at the house church, and I'd better watch out?

As he'd done his whole life, Ben kept his fears to himself.

20

WHILE MING HELPED Shen prepare for bed Sunday evening, Quan sat on his bed, Ben on his.

"How many people in house churches have Bibles?" Ben asked.

"Often there are some Bibles, usually not many. Some say there are five or ten thousand more new Christians in China every day. There are more new Christians than new Bibles. No matter how many Bibles come in, it is never enough."

"I probably have three on my bookshelf at home," Ben said. What he didn't say was he couldn't remember the last time he'd read any of them.

"Chinese proverb: 'Distant water no help to put out fire close at hand.' There are those here who would gladly go without food for weeks in exchange for the spiritual food sitting on your shelf. In a country of more than a billion, even ten million Bibles would be only a drop in the bucket."

"It would take a lot of money to provide that many Bibles."

"Hudson Taylor said: 'God's work done in God's way never lacks God's supply.'"

"Who's Hudson Taylor?"

"You have never heard of Hudson Taylor?" Quan looked dismayed.

"Was he one of Elizabeth Taylor's husbands?"

"Who is Elizabeth Taylor?"

"You've never heard of Elizabeth Taylor?"

"Hudson Taylor was the founder of China Inland Mission. He led to Yesu my great-grandfather Manchu when he was a boy. Hudson Taylor performed eye surgery on him. Did you know that on some days he did two hundred eye surgeries? I suppose you did not know, since you have never heard of him! But I am also ignorant—I do not know this Elizabeth Taylor. Was she also a great missionary?"

"Not exactly."

"Li Manchu lived in Hangzhou, first headquarters for China Inland Mission."

"Hangzhou? Is that why you say you're from Hangzhou, even though you've never been there?"

"Where our ancestors are from, we are from. Li Quan's life did not begin with Li Quan."

"But it didn't begin with your great-grandfather either."

"We choose someone in our family history who sets a direction for the family line. Li Manchu was the first Li to follow Yesu. That is why I am from Hangzhou, and so is Li Shen."

"He's never been there either, right?"

"No. Why is that important?"

Ben laughed. "It just seems strange."

"To me, America is strange. Each person acts as if his life begins and ends with himself."

"I can't tell you where my great-grandfather lived," Ben said, "or what he did, or even what his name was."

Ben squirmed at what he saw in Quan's eyes—pity.

"After I became a Christian," Quan said, "I researched the Boxer martyrs in the Harvard library. I found the names of all the two hundred and thirty missionaries who were killed. But the history books record few of the names of the thirty-five thousand Han Chinese Christians murdered by the Boxers. My great-grandfather's name, and my great-grandmother's, were not there."

Ben looked at his friend's eyes. They were dark pools of sadness.

Li Tong, standing beside Li Wen and Li Manchu, pointed to the names inscribed on the Wall of Martyrs. A Reader was speaking aloud each of hundreds of thousands of names. He never stopped reading.

"When he finishes," Li Manchu explained to a new arrival, "he starts reading the names again, beginning with Stephen. And whenever new martyrs arrive, as they do throughout every day, he pauses and says their name."

The new arrival walked up to the wall and placed his hand on it, running his fingers over one of the names.

"Let us stay and hear the name of the next martyr," Li Wen said.

"Someday," Li Manchu said, "the next martyr will be the last."

The Li men nodded, trembling with anticipation. They joined their hands together.

"Tell me about your father's imprisonment," Ben said. "I mean, if you feel up to it."

"I am honored you would ask," Quan said. "My father first went to jail in the early days of People's Republic. He was imprisoned again in the sixties during the cultural revolution. I was eight when Li Tong went to jail for the last time. I was permitted to visit him a few times a year, though they would not let me touch him. But by the time I was twelve my heart had turned away from him. I was a proud little Communist, and I refused to visit my shameful father anymore." Quan winced at the memory. "Then when I was fifteen, my mother forced me to visit him in prison."

"What was it like?"

"The man I saw did not look like my father. His face was like a pale, twisted mask. But I could recognize his eyes. The last thing he said to me that day was 'Zhen jin bu ba huo lian.'"

"Real gold fears no fire," Ben said.

Quan nodded. "And he added, 'One day you will die. You must spend your life preparing for that day.' I have often asked myself, 'Is this the day?'"

"What did your mother do after he died?"

"She had already taken over my father's job. They called her 'the smiling pastor.' She was a good preacher. She preached at me many times! I regret I did not listen. Not even the night I came home and she'd been beaten. They knocked out two of her teeth." Quan trembled. "Even in her pain she managed to smile, but it hurt me to see the missing teeth."

"Who beat her?"

"PSB."

"Why?"

"Because she was a Christian. Even worse, a pastor. God's enemies need no more reason."

"How old were you when she died?"

"Eighteen. I was off with my friends when the earthquake happened.

When I ran through the rubble to my house, I saw smoke rising. It had collapsed and was burning. In it I found my mother's body. She had done everything for me. No son had a mother so kind, so filled with the joy of Yesu. But I did not appreciate her as I should have. Yes, I wept for her, but more for myself, because I had no home."

"Where did you go?"

"To my mother's parents. They were Christians. They did not know what to do with all my arguments against Christianity, which I got from school. I was even angry I wasn't allowed to sit in our beautiful chair, made by my grandfather. When we had company, I sat on the hard floor many times while that chair sat empty." He pointed to the large mahogany chair at the table. "I saw no point in having a beautiful chair no one was allowed to sit in."

"What *was* the point?"

"Do you not know?"

"I'm not sure."

"Then it is best for you to learn for yourself."

"I do not deserve to have my name on this wall, with you and the other martyrs."

"Yet here is the name of Li Wen, the carpenter," said Li Manchu. "Does not the Builder of the wall, who inscribes the names, know who belongs upon it?"

"I did not die for my Lord like the two of you."

"There are different ways of dying," said Li Manchu. "You died to a normal life. You died daily in the service of Yesu. You witnessed the deaths of your father and mother. What could be harder?"

"And many years later, when your son died," Li Tong said, "you cared for his wife and children. When my work was done, yours continued. Martyrs are not only those who die, but all faithful witnesses who suffer for the Name."

"Was it easier for you to see mother and father and son die than to die yourself?" Li Manchu asked. "No. It was much harder. Zhu Yesu knows sometimes the families of martyrs deserve as much reward as the martyrs themselves. And that is why names of wives and husbands and fathers and mothers and sons and daughters and sisters and brothers of martyrs are often written on this wall as well."

"Besides my mother, I respected my father more than anyone I ever knew," Li Tong said to Li Wen, putting his hand on his father's shoulder.

"And I respected my son more than any man." Li Manchu put his hand on his son Li Wen's other shoulder.

"Besides, Li Wen," Li Manchu said, "you were the builder of the chair."

"I wonder," Li Wen said to Li Tong, "if our line of martyrs ends with you, or if Li Quan will follow."

"And if not Li Quan, then Li Shen?"

"We shall see."

"Perhaps one of them," Li Manchu whispered, "will be the last martyr."

The men looked at each other, hardly daring to speak of an honor so great.

On Tuesday evening Ben opened an e-mail from Martin.

> *Ben,*
>
> *I've been worried about you since our last phone call. Won Chi called this morning and told Jeffrey that you were present at a suspicious exchange at some hotel called the Huaquia Binguan. Somehow he got wind of dinner guests at Li Quan's home and a visit from the deputy chief of police, a Tai Hong? Chi says they don't appear to have specific accusations against you, but they're building a case against your friend, and they don't trust you.*
>
> *Ben, if you ever listened to me, listen now—I can't emphasize how important it is that you do nothing illegal. You can't even be a party to anything illegal. Do you understand me? I'm counting on you. A single incident could ruin the company rep. Don't let it happen.*

The letter disturbed Ben but relieved him on one count. *They know nothing about my going to a house church!*

The next morning Ben drove Quan to work. He walked around the city, continuing to conduct interviews. Most people were friendly and eager to talk. Ben was amazed at how much more he was learning about the thoughts and dreams of commoners. He realized he didn't know China as well as he'd thought. And knowing people was the key to selling them anything. The material he was getting would blow their socks off back in the office.

At lunchtime Ben made his way to the locksmith's shop. When he entered, Quan handed Ben a piece of paper.

"What's this?"

"It's a circular from the Party forbidding the use of a word. They hand-delivered several copies to our shop. It is an official declaration of a Party ban on the word *qianxinian*, 'the thousand-year happiness.' They say it is a Christian expression, and antigovernment, since it is used of Christ ruling over the earth, defeating all human governments. They claim such a word has no place in China. They know that Zhou Jin and Li Quan are Christians, so they made sure we received the circular. Still—" he smiled—"they do business with us because we do the best work."

"Will the churches obey this?"

"Most registered churches will, but not all. None of the house churches will obey. Can you imagine, Ben, American Christians being told words they cannot use in public? Can you conceive of a society in which Christians are told that if they say certain things in the workplace, if they say what is politically unpopular, they could actually lose their jobs? To you it is unthinkable, I know. But here, it happens."

Ben sighed, not having the heart to tell Quan it was actually not at all unthinkable.

"What do you know about the leader of our Religious Affairs Bureau?" Quan asked.

"Not much."

"Did you know he is an atheist?"

"What?"

"My father, Li Tong, used to say, 'Church leader who does not believe in God is like barefoot shoe salesman.' We call our bureau leader the Caiaphas of China."

"What does that mean?"

"You remember Caiaphas from the Bible?"

"No."

"Did someone take your Bible from you?"

"No. It's on my shelf. Remember? I've got three of them."

"Perhaps Ben Fielding should give two away and then start reading the other one."

"Sorry to disappoint you."

"Caiaphas was a high priest who plotted Yesu's crucifixion. Sometimes those in the most significant positions of religious leadership are the greatest enemies of Christ and the church. How else can you explain that the most prominent church leader in China is an atheist?"

"At my meeting in Shanghai, I was talking with my friend Won Chi about the Three-Self Church."

"Why?"

"We were just talking, that's all."

"Did you tell him you were having discussions with me? Did you mention my name?"

"I might have. Why?"

Li Quan's eyes darted across the room.

"Look, I didn't say anything bad about you, Quan! Chi assured me what I've heard a hundred times. There's room for everybody in the registered church. They just don't want the subversive stuff. They've had a lot of problems with cults."

Quan waved the piece of paper like an attorney presenting evidence. "Circulars like this are passed out to remind people what they cannot say. The Party is frightened of Christianity, because it is the revolution of the heart. They cannot control it."

"Come on, Quan. I went to your church, and I respect the people there. Really. But you have to understand that every government has rules. They have to. You don't get any more free than the United States. But in Portland we had a church that was having vagrants in for services and serving meals to the poor. It was causing parking problems and upsetting a nice quiet neighborhood. So the city limited the times they could meet and the number of people that could come."

"The church agreed to this?"

"Well, they didn't like it. But it's a question of zoning ordinances. Some of these churches think they can just bring in more and more people and meet whenever they feel like it. But what about the neighbors who have to put up with the traffic and noise? Don't they have rights?"

Quan stared at him.

"Look, in our old neighborhood every Thursday night there were twenty cars or more, some of them double-parked. Doors were always shutting, teenagers coming in and out of the house across the street. It was a big Bible study. Well, several of us talked to them and they were polite, but they kept right on doing it. Finally, we called the police. They said take it to the county. We got a ruling that stopped them from meeting there. Period. If they want big meetings, that's what church buildings are for, isn't it?"

"Except they limit the number of people at church buildings too, you said."

"Well . . . not usually."

"Were these teenagers using drugs?"

"No."

"Were they damaging your property?"

"No, but they were taking up all the parking spaces."

"Were they stealing from you?"

"What's your point, Quan?"

"I am wondering why you would oppose young people studying the Bible so they will become better people. If they cannot meet to study Shengjing, perhaps they will meet to break into houses or get drunk or sell drugs or fight or vandalize. Is not a high price paid when you take away the church's freedom to meet?"

"You're not getting it, Quan. You don't understand how it works in America. It's nothing like China."

Quan's face registered confusion. "Isn't it?"

"We pray for Sister Wu Xia, who suffers with tuberculosis."

It was October 28, Ben's second Sunday in house church. That same bright-faced woman prayed for person after person. The electricity flickered three times, then went out, but only a single lamp had been turned on anyway.

Li Quan stood. Ming took out his mother's Bible from a wrapped bundle. She handed it to him. He stepped close to a flickering candle, then turned to a marked page and read. Ben struggled to understand. Chinese Christian vocabulary was unfamiliar to him, as it was even to most Chinese, since it had been banned so long from public life.

> So be truly glad! There is wonderful joy ahead, even though it is necessary for you to endure many trials for a while. These trials are only to test your faith, to show that it is strong and pure. It is being tested as fire tests and purifies gold—and your faith is far more precious to God than mere gold. So if your faith remains strong after being tried by fiery trials, it will bring you much praise and glory and honor on the day when Jesus Christ is revealed to the whole world. You love him even though you have never seen him. Though you do not see him, you trust him; and even now you are happy with a glorious, inexpressible joy.

Quan turned a page and looked at several smeared words.

> Of course, you get no credit for being patient if you are beaten for doing wrong. But if you suffer for doing right and are patient beneath the blows, God is pleased with you. This suffering is all part of what God has called you to. Christ, who suffered for you, is your example. Follow in his steps.

154

A ringing noise startled Ben. Zhou Jin pulled a cell phone out of his pocket. He opened it, then listened.

A pastor's answering the phone during church?

Zhou Jin jumped to his feet. "You must leave now," he said to the congregation, voice urgent. "God be with you. Pray as you go. Will send word about next gathering."

Jin handed the cell phone to Quan. "Go now. I will try to detain them."

"I cannot leave you."

"You must. We have discussed this. It is my decision—I am pastor. Take care of them. Remember the horse that ran away."

Quan embraced the old man, then quickly herded his family out the back door. All the bicycles were gone, and people were scattering in every direction. Quan led his family and Ben running through the woods.

"Shouldn't we go to the car?" Ben asked.

"Yes. But we cannot be seen near the road."

They had gotten only fifty yards away, barely into the trees, when they heard car doors slam and loud voices behind them.

Quan stopped and grabbed the hands of Ming and Shen. Shen grabbed Ben's. "Be with Zhou Jin, Yesu."

They ran through the sparse woods, tramping loudly on fallen leaves, Shen's little legs moving furiously. He cried, and his father picked him up and carried him in his arms. After a half mile, Ben took Shen from Quan and lifted him up on his shoulders. Ben grasped Shen's pudgy, muddy legs. Finally they emerged on a side road and came to Ben's Mitsubishi. They got in, and he drove toward Quan's. Everyone breathed heavily. Ben rolled down the windows.

"What's going on?" Ben asked.

"A swoop," Quan said.

"You mean PSB?"

"Unless police were stationed in the outlying areas, most probably got away. Zhou Jin stayed so they would not leave again and chase people into the woods and capture them. In their anger, they sometimes hurt the people. Zhou Jin would rather be arrested than see his sheep hurt."

"They're arresting him?"

"They usually do."

"How often has this happened?"

Quan shrugged.

"What's with the cell phone?"

"Technology can be used for good also. We have a friend at the police station. He is one of few special people with this phone number. He called to warn us of the swoop."

"This is outrageous," Ben said, as he drove slowly toward Quan's house.

"This is life," Quan said.

"What did Zhou Jin mean by the horse that ran away?"

"This is an old story that all Chinese know. Long ago, near a frontier lived an old man. One day his horse was gone. He was told the horse ran far away. His neighbors came to comfort him for his loss, but the old man was calm. He said, 'This may not prove so bad. It could even turn out good.' One night the old man heard a great deal of noise, and he got up to see what was happening. To his surprise, he saw not only his old horse, but another more beautiful than he. His horse had brought home a companion. The neighbors all came to congratulate him."

"And the moral is . . . ?"

"Zhou Jin was saying that what appears to be a loss may actually be a gain, when we understand it fully. Chinese wisdom tells us this, and it is usually right. God's Word tells us this, and it is always right. After being sold into slavery and being in prison for years, Joseph stood before his brothers and said, 'You intended it for evil, but God intended it for good.'"

"There's no way what just happened was good."

"Not from our perspective. Not here and now. But perhaps from another viewpoint? Besides, what you just witnessed was the carrying out of laws you once thought reasonable. Are you starting to change your mind about this wonderful religious freedom in China?"

Ben ignored the question. "Why did Zhou Jin give you the cell phone?"

"Because," Quan said, "I am now the pastor."

21

$\mathcal{I}$ STILL CAN'T BELIEVE IT," Ben said, pacing.

Quan sat on the floor, a bowl of water and old rags in front of him. He'd cleaned the mud off Ben's shoes first, then Ming's and Shen's, and now was working on his own.

"Seeing it with your eyes makes it more real to you? But to us it has been real all along."

"But why do they do this?"

"Mogui hates the church. His home in heaven was taken from him, and given to the church."

"What's *Mogui*? I don't remember the word."

"Satan."

"The devil?"

"One of our brothers from Canada says that the Chinese church is the fastest-growing church in the world. He claims there are more Christians here than in America and Europe combined. Mogui is the dragon. I mean, in the biblical sense. The dragon is good in Chinese history, but bad in the book of Revelation. Mogui is this bad dragon wishing to devour the church." Suddenly Quan's eyes lit up, and his hand with the rag stopped moving. "But Yesu is the great Lion, powerful and wise, who slays the dragon. The dragon is already defeated. He will be crushed under our feet. The One in us is greater than he. But as his time grows short, Mogui thrashes about in desperate death throes, inflicting on us what punishment he can."

It wasn't the explanation Ben was looking for.

"They are in this room, you know," Quan said.

"Who?"

"Righteous and evil warriors. Engaged in mortal combat."

"You really believe that?"

"Of course. God does not lie. And can you not see all the evidence around you?"

Ben looked around the room. "In a word . . . no."

"Did you not feel the forces today when we gathered and when we scattered? Are you so blind that you do not realize earth is the battlefield where two kingdoms wage a savage war for the souls of men?"

Ben felt his defenses rise but let them fall in favor of giving this some thought. Finally he asked, "Have you ever . . . actually seen an angel?"

"I'm not sure, but I think so."

"When?"

"Some of this you know—I told you at Harvard. But some I never told you because I knew it would sound too strange. After the earthquake, when my mother died, I was all alone. I was an atheist. I had turned my back on my parents' faith. I had denied my father and rejected Yesu." He hung his head. "But I did pray—something very selfish. I prayed I could go to college in America. I knew it was impossible. Just a few hundred Chinese students from privileged families were permitted to come to America in those days. My grades were good, but still it was impossible. I was sitting in the rubble of our house, angry at God, when someone tapped me on my shoulder."

"Who was it?"

"Someone who said he was there to help the earthquake victims. There were Europeans there with a relief organization, and one American with them. But he did not wear the standard clothes. This man asked if he could help me. I said I had hoped to go to college in America, but now I knew I could not. He told me he would help. I gave him my grandparents' address. He said I would hear from him. Though the other workers stayed two weeks, I never saw him again, though I looked for him. A month later I received an invitation from Harvard, saying I had a full scholarship. All I had to do was fill out the application form and send it back. It also seemed impossible to get a passport, but somehow I did. Someone gave me the exact amount of money for airfare to Massachusetts. I had only the clothes on my back. That is why I had to wear your baggy shirts until I earned money at Burger Magic. Even that was a miracle, to be able to work on a student visa. We do not always recognize miracles at the time they happen—back then I just felt very lucky. Now I know it can only be explained by the hand of God."

"What about the man? The relief worker?"

"I never saw him again. But I do not think he was a man."

"You think he was an angel?"

"I think even when I was bitter against Yesu, even when I rejected him, Yesu was faithful to me. In his providence, and out of love for my faithful ancestors and my father and mother, God sent an angel to make a way for me to go to Harvard University so on that foreign soil I could become a follower of Yesu Jidu. And so I could meet Ben Fielding."

Sunday afternoon Li Quan prayed for Zhou Jin. They'd still heard nothing. Quan opened his Bible and read portions to Shen. Ming listened as she mended clothes. Still shaken by what had happened, Ben opened his briefcase, hoping to find something to read to settle his mind. He set out on his bed two books and a *Fortune* magazine.

Quan glanced over at Ben's reading material and stood up, a look of horror on his face. "Remove that from this house!" He was pointing.

"You don't like *Fortune*?"

"I'm talking about that book." He pointed at the book with the Dalai Lama on the cover.

"What's wrong? Okay, he's not a Christian, but he's a decent guy. Religious. Compassionate. Thoughtful. More than a lot of Christians, that's for sure. He has a very positive message."

"To you, perhaps, this is just a book." Quan's voice trembled. "You have not seen the darkness of Mogui's stronghold."

"What are you talking about? The Dalai Lama? He's kind and generous and well respected—not to mention he's been on the *New York Times* best-seller list!"

"I do not know the Dalai Lama. But I do know about his religion. I live here, and I have been to Tibet. I could tell you stories, but you would not believe me."

"This is what I mean, Quan. You're so narrow and unreasonable. There probably isn't a more benevolent and wise man alive. Did you see *Seven Years in Tibet*, with Brad Pitt?"

Quan looked at him blankly.

"It's a movie. Anyway, the Dalai Lama was this cute kid, really gifted, who grew up to be a wise leader. It shows how China conquered Tibet and—"

"Two hours before dinner?" Quan asked Ming, switching suddenly to crisp Mandarin. Then looking back at Ben, he said, "First I am going to change my clothes. Then we will go in your car to Pushan."

"Go where?"

"You will see. But please—" Quan pointed to the book on the bed— "remove this book now from the house of Li."

When Quan wasn't looking, Ben stuffed the book under the driver's seat. Ten minutes later they pulled on to the street.

"Really, Quan, I think you're overreacting."

"Have you been to Tibet?"

"No. I've always wanted to, but not yet."

"So you have read a book and seen a movie? This is what makes you a great expert on Lamaistic Buddhism?"

"I never claimed to be an expert. When were you in Tibet?"

"When I was turned down for teaching positions, remember? I saved money and went to apply at a university. I stood before Jokhang Temple, one of Lamaistic Buddhism's holiest shrines. China is very guilty of taking away Tibet's political freedom. But do not let your sympathy for these oppressed people become sympathy for a religion that also oppresses them."

"Where are we going?"

"Take the main street into Pushan. I'll tell you when to turn. It's another ten minutes."

"You're not going to like this, Quan, but I have to say, I've really bene-fited from Buddhist philosophy. There's a lot of good in it. It has a seren-ity, a focus that's appealing. It's being used now in business contexts—everything from success seminars to employee mental health enhance-ment. It helps people be at peace with themselves."

"Who tells you such things, Ben Fielding?"

"Articles. Television. Books. Some experience too."

"Then these things are the voice of Mogui. Yesu said the devil is the father of lies. If you believe peace is found in the dark religions that deny Yesu, you also have been deceived by Mogui."

"Could we have a little tolerance, a hint of open-mindedness, please? Where do you get off telling me I'm deceived? Somebody needs to teach you to back off."

"Li Quan means no offense. I know Mogui well. I once served him. One must know his enemy to win the battle. I think you do not under-stand the strategy of Satan. He is a master of disguise."

"Are you seriously saying all those hundreds of millions of Buddhists are lost?"

"Yesu said, 'No man comes to the Father except through me.' I did not make up those words. I simply believe them."

"Isn't that arrogant and judgmental?"

"God is entitled to pass judgment—he is the Judge. You think him judgmental? I do not think he cowers in fear of your opinion. He will not stand before you in judgment. You will stand before him."

"There's a lot of truth in different religions, including Buddhism."

"You do not know what you are talking about."

"Of course not. Professor Li Quan is the one who knows *everything.*"

"Buddhism calls for dependence on one's heart or inner nature. But Shengjing says the heart is deceitful and wicked. It says there is a way that seems right to a man, but that way ends in death. People cannot find truth on their own, but only by revelation of God. Shengjing is that revelation. Religions do not reveal God's truth; they hide it." He pointed ahead. "We're coming closer to the Lama's den."

"Tibetans here in Pushan?"

"Yes. Most have stayed in Tibet, but some have moved across China. They have small communities in many cities. Over there, park by that building."

"This is a temple?"

"They are not allowed to build true temples. But this building is called a temple and is used for worship. It's open to visitors during the day."

They got out of the car and crossed the street, walking toward the entrance. Quan turned and looked Ben in the eyes. "Follow me, but do not speak. I do not know what will happen. But you must see for yourself. Be careful."

Quan bowed his head and mumbled something Ben couldn't hear.

They walked up to the building. Standing by the door frames, half inside, were two men with shaved heads, wearing long saffron robes, almost the orange of an overripe pumpkin.

As Ben neared, one of them looked at him curiously, the other with transparent hostility. The unfriendly one then looked at Quan. Ben could sense two emotions on the monk's face—hatred and fear. Rather than seeing these feelings, it was more like smelling or tasting them. Something was in the air, he knew, but it was a knowing for which there was no explanation.

This is weird. The Dalai Lama is always so friendly in his interviews. Why—

Quan spoke to the priests in a strong but shaky voice. "The one true

God says in his holy Book, 'Before me no god was formed, nor will there be one after me. I, even I, am the Lord, and apart from me there is no savior.'"

It seemed to take a moment for the words to be absorbed into the vacant-eyed monk. "Begone," an otherworldly voice cried, hissing like butter on a hot skillet. The voice was deep, deeper than Darth Vader's, deeper than any Ben had ever heard. The sound of it made Ben nauseous with foreboding.

Suddenly the voice began speaking in an eerie dialect, totally foreign to Ben. He stepped back, all at once hardly able to breathe, as if some foreign power had sucked the oxygen out of the air.

Quan spoke again. "Yesu said, 'I am the way and the truth and the life. No one comes to the Father except through me.' The Buddha is not the way. The Lama is not the way. Yesu is the only way. The holy Book says, 'There is no other name under heaven given to men by which we must be saved.' Yesu is the only name, the only Savior."

The first priest disappeared into the darkness, but the second's eyes clouded, his jaw dropped, and the horrid voice spoke again. "Leave! Go or we will kill you!" The contortions on his face made it look like a rubbery mask with some living thing pulsating inside. "This place is ours," he hissed.

"This place is Yesu's," Quan said. "All places are Yesu's!"

"Do *not* say that name," the monk screamed with such explosive rage that Ben was sure he could be heard blocks away. The priest leaned near Quan but seemed unable to go forward. Abruptly the priest took one step toward Ben, reached out his arm, and touched him on the chest. Ben flew backward onto the ground. He lay in the street seven feet from where he'd been standing a moment earlier.

Quan raised his voice. "I *will* say the name of Yesu. You cannot stop me. It is the name above every name, the name to which you shall one day bow. It is he who shed his blood to purchase our way to heaven!"

The priest let out a bloodcurdling howl, sounding like a wounded animal. He retreated into the darkness of the doorway's jaws.

Quan leaned down and reached out his hand to Ben. "Are you alright?"

"I . . . don't know," he said. "I still can hardly breathe." Quan led him back to the car. They sat in it a few minutes. Ben glanced back at the doorway and thought he saw eyes looking out at them.

Still gasping, Ben asked, "Quan—what just happened?"

They drove out of Pushan in complete silence, Ben shaking. Finally,

Ben pulled over by a mango grove, its trees bare. He wiped his shirtsleeve across his face. It was wet and sticky.

"I'm sorry, Ben. I have been very foolish. I should have warned you. I shouldn't have taken you there. I was angry. . . . I didn't know it would happen that way. It was different last time."

"That man's voice was . . . otherworldly."

"Yes. The one inhabiting the priest lives in another world."

"Are you telling me that was . . . the voice of Satan?"

"No."

"No?" Ben felt relieved and confused.

"It was the voice of one of Satan's warriors. A demon."

"What language was he speaking? I mean, I heard a few words in Mandarin, of course. I assumed the other language must be Tibetan, but it sounded different from anything I've ever heard."

"Perhaps it was a language from a world you have never been to."

"This was your way of showing me Lamaistic Buddhism?"

"It was even more overtly demonic than before. But several times I have seen things that were oppressive. Always I can sense the darkness. The Tibetans are in bondage to the Lamaistic monks. Years ago forty percent of Tibetan men had become monks. The population had to feed all of them plus take care of all the women who were left unmarried. While the clergy was in control, the population was kept in poverty and ignorance. The people still live in fear of their gods. Their spiritual bondage is deepened by chants, rituals, sacrifices. Demonic possession is an accepted part of their lives."

"I had no idea. Why isn't that talked about in the books and movies?"

"Because it would make poor strategy in America, would it not? Mogui is evil, but he is not stupid. As for Tibet, it needs more than political deliverance. It is one of Mogui's greatest strongholds. There are perhaps but fifty Christians in the entire country. Our church often prays that the Dalai Lama would be saved and lead his people to freedom in Yesu. But even if he remains the servant of Mogui, we pray the Lama's prisoners would be liberated to become children of God."

"He barely touched me, but it felt like my chest was hit by a baseball bat."

"I had not anticipated this. It is a hard lesson, more dangerous than I realized. Forgive me. I was angry, and in turn I enraged them. But perhaps you will remember not to be deceived by a smiling face and wise words. Pray for the man on your book cover. Weep for his people. But do *not* embrace his message. For his voice, like many voices that seem wise and kind and generous, is the tool of another, one who spreads his darkness masquerading as an angel of light."

"He was so strong."

"Compared to Yesu, he is weak. The evil one is but a *gou*, a dog on a leash."

"I've . . . never heard a demon's voice before."

"You are wrong."

"What do you mean?"

"It is not that you have never heard the voices of demons, but that you haven't known you were hearing them." Quan put his hand on Ben's trembling arm. "In America, the voices of demons sound more pleasant."

22

SUNDAY NIGHT after dinner, three hours after their visit to the temple, Ben was still on edge. When the phone rang, he jumped. Quan listened, then explained to Ming, Ben, and Shen what had happened. Zhou Jin and Ho Lin, whose house the church met in, had both been arrested and put in jail.

Quan, Ming, and Shen gathered to pray, inviting Ben. But he decided to take a walk, feeling he wanted to do something more than pray.

Monday morning, October 29, Ben dropped Quan off at the locksmith's shop and spent the day in Pushan, talking to some of the strategic contacts he'd been making. He discussed Getz International's business plans, asking what products they would like to see in China, and what the price would have to be to afford them. He also brought up Zhou Jin and Ho Lin in a couple of strategic conversations, expressing how concerned Americans were about the perception that human rights might be violated. When he picked up Quan at day's end, he told him what he'd done.

"Exactly who did Ben Fielding talk to?"

"A couple of prominent businessmen gave me some ideas. I ended up meeting with one of the mayor's assistants."

"You went to the mayor's office?"

"Yeah, it was a guy I met with last week. You know, I took him through the survey I'm using to compile input for my report. The mayor's son is sick, so he wasn't available, but I've requested to see him. His assistant thinks he can get me a meeting soon."

"Did you tell these people anything about our meetings?" Quan asked, pronouncing each syllable, his face extra close to Ben's. "Did you mention any names at all?"

"I . . . don't think so." Ben took a step backward. "I was just saying I hoped these men wouldn't be in jail long. See, when they know an American business executive is watching what's going on, it puts pressure on them to make sure things are done right. Actually, I found the mayor's office sympathetic."

"Did you know it was the mayor's office that directed PSB to invade the church and arrest Zhou Jin?"

"No! Who told you that?"

"Better not to say. No need for you to know more names."

"What? I was just trying to help. You think I'd turn people in or something?"

"I think, Ben Fielding, you believed you were doing what was best."

"I told them I thought house churches weren't hurting anyone. I never mentioned you or anyone else."

"They keep track of all foreigners. You act like they don't know where you are staying. Do you think Tai Hong has kept it secret? If they know you were at any house church, they know that I took you there. I am already on their list. I have been arrested before at house churches. It is easy to figure out. Did you tell him about the Bibles?"

"Absolutely not!"

"Did you mention Shengjing at all?"

"Only to clarify whether it's true some Bibles are legal and some aren't. I never mentioned your name, of course, and they seemed understanding, but . . . I suppose the fact that I was asking about Bibles might have cast some suspicion on you. I'm sorry. I didn't think of that."

"It is alright, Ben Fielding. It is hard for free people to learn to think like the enslaved."

For three days Ben saw little of Quan. Ben continued to interview people on the street and in shops and offices. He was compiling information that to him was fascinating, and he was also taking plenty of pictures. He wondered about the possibility of writing a book about an inside look at China, seen through American eyes. A book with lots of photos in it.

Meanwhile, Quan was working extra hours because his boss was in jail. Ben figured they both needed the space. For reasons unexplained, the PSB ordered the locksmith's shop closed on Wednesday.

"They didn't tell you why?" Ben asked.

"No. They don't have to."

"An American business wouldn't put up with that."

"Not in America. But in China they would have to."

After Thursday dinner, one month to the day after Ben's arrival, Quan announced the evening's plans. Ming and Shen quickly got ready.

"Let me get this straight," Ben said. "The church is meeting at the home of a woman who has tuberculosis? Isn't that, you know, a contagious disease?"

"Yes. That is why Wu Xia's house is safe."

"Doesn't TB stay in the air for hours? Generally, in America we try to stay away from coughing and sneezing when it spreads serious diseases."

"Infiltrators and police will not come into the home of a woman with tuberculosis," Quan said. "They will not put themselves at risk. Those who follow Yesu willingly take risks that those who oppose us will not. They believe in luck or chance. We believe in a God of providence. That is our advantage—we trust God to protect us. But if he gives us tuberculosis, then good, we will serve him with tuberculosis."

Ming looked at Ben. "Are you coming, Ben Fielding?"

"Uh . . . no, thanks. I need to make some phone calls tonight. Check e-mail. Work on my report. You know."

Saturday morning Ben and Quan worked repairing the chicken coop. It was unseasonably warm for early November. Ben wasn't a skilled laborer, but he was actually enjoying learning some skills that didn't involve high finances, budget projections, and long-term strategies. The men spoke of old classmates, dorm buddies, and campus escapades, uncovering a flood of pleasant memories that had long lain dormant.

Ming brought out a tray with water and biscuits for the men. While seated under the ginkgo, they talked and laughed a half hour.

"Li Quan is not a professor. But I wish to teach something to Ben Fielding."

"Sure. What do you have in mind?"

"Language studies," Quan said. He jumped up, picked out a long, firm stick, and drew a character in the sandy dirt. Ben was amazed at how quickly Quan's hand moved and how perfect the character appeared. It consisted of eight different strokes and would have taken Ben five times longer to draw.

"You know this word—it means 'to create, to begin, to come from.' This part means 'dust.' This is 'breath of mouth.' It's followed by the radical *p'ieh,* which is 'life.' The final two characters are a mouth and walking. It means 'from the dust, by the mouth was breathed life, and it walked.'"

Quan looked at Ben as if expecting a light to turn on. It didn't. "Do you know what Genesis 2:7 says, Ben?"

"Not offhand."

"'The Lord God formed the man from the dust of the ground and breathed into his nostrils the breath of life, and the man became a living being.'" He drew in the sand again. "Here is another." Quan was animated, his spirit soaring. "Do you see this?"

"Yes. It means 'spirit.'"

"Very good. Look at the six components: heaven, cover, water, rain, three persons, and magic-worker. Genesis 1 speaks of the Spirit of God, who is the third person of the Trinity, hovering over the waters as the miracle of creation is worked."

"But you can't seriously believe that—"

"And here is our character for desire." He drew quickly again. "What is it?"

"A woman with two trees."

"Correct. Student gets an A."

Ben smiled. "So what—"

"Genesis 3:6 says the woman saw the tree was good for food, and she desired it to make her wise. Look at this." He drew again. "The character for tempter is also part of the word *devil.* You see the two trees and garden? It literally means 'in secret, the man in the cover of the garden, by the two trees, was tempted by the devil.' Do you recognize that?"

"I'm not completely ignorant of the Bible."

Quan wrote a new character next to it. "Now, the word *chuan* means 'boat,' or 'ship.' The radical 'mouth' can be translated 'people' or 'dependents,' like 'mouths to feed.' The breakdown of the character is this: 'Eight mouths, meaning eight people, were in the ship.' What does that mean?"

"I don't know."

"Think, Ben Fielding."

"I don't get it."

"Genesis says Noah and his wife and his three sons and their wives entered the ark. Eight people."

"You're saying this Chinese character is about Noah and the ark?"

"That is what many of us believe. We do not think it's a coincidence. China is the most ancient culture. All ancient men knew about the Flood and the ark. All families told stories, passing them on for thousands of years. Every ancient culture has its story of the Flood. When China's language developed, would it not make sense to see our central stories reflected in our characters and words? It also means our ancient people may once have served the true God. In our language, God's history was preserved for all to see. All who have eyes to see, that is."

Quan drew quickly in the sand, then pointed. "What does this mean?" he asked.

"Hate."

"And what is this symbol that is part of it?" He pointed.

"Isn't that the older brother?"

"Yes. The older brother is hating, striking out at the younger brother. Does this sound familiar?"

"Cain and Abel?"

"There are many more examples, but I will give you one, the most important." He drew frantically with the stick. "'Righteousness.' This character is a combination of two smaller ones: 'I' or 'me,' and 'lamb.' Compare to Genesis 4—Abel brought a sheep to sacrifice. God said if he would bring forth the best of his flock, he would forgive him and consider him righteous. Notice the lamb is positioned over the pronoun. The 'lamb' over 'me' means righteousness." Quan was speaking quickly, at a fever pitch. "Do you not see?"

"Well . . . I'm not sure."

"Let yourself see, Ben Fielding! The character for righteousness presents the story of a lamb from above changing men below. Righteousness comes only from what has been done in the sacrifice of the lamb over me. This is more than the story of Abel's sacrifice. This is the death of Yesu! This is the gospel! It is right there in the characters of our language."

"You really think so?"

"Yes, Dabizi, I do! If I were a history professor at a university, this is what I would teach my students. I would also point out that the lion and dragon are among our most ancient symbols. The banned book of Revelation calls Yesu the 'Lion of Judah' and Mogui the 'dragon.' Confucius recorded in *ShuJing* how the emperor would sacrifice to Shang Di, but they had lost the reason and significance for the act. They used a large oven to sacrifice sheep and cattle. This mirrors the Jewish sacrifice. Chinese can trace this sacrifice back to 3000 B.C., before other nations' history began. Noah and his sons and their descendants migrated to each continent. As the most ancient of languages, Chinese takes us back closer to Genesis than anything else."

"My friend Quan is a gifted teacher."

"Do not think about my teaching, Ben. Think about *what* I am teaching! The tragedy is, ancient men did not stay true to God. Other religions developed. Buddhism, Hinduism—all of them. Nations began to forget why they once offered sacrifices to God. Still, God was faithful to the Chinese in allowing his truth to be preserved in over a hundred and twenty-five characters for thousands of years. That is why when Chinese come to God today, we say they are returning to the true God our ancestors once knew."

"I've never heard any of this. We never talked about it in my Mandarin class."

"And certainly not in mine," Quan said, laughing. "I am not surprised. How can those without eyes be expected to see? But perhaps the church grows so fast in China because God tilled the soil of our myths and proverbs. The greatest truths are hidden in myths, and perhaps Chinese myth is not so far from God's truth. Then when we see Yesu, the great truth, for us the lesser truths fall naturally into orbit around him. The emptiness of atheism and communism have tilled the soil further. We long for the sun and rain—even that hidden inside the words we use every day—to fall upon us and give us life."

"You really think God is behind all this?"

"Only the blind would not see this. It is not important whether China is most favored nation to America or Europeans. What is important is China's favor in sight of God."

Quan beckoned Ben over to the chicken coop. "We will finish our work, and I will finish teaching. You have been to Tian Tang, have you not?"

"The Temple of Heaven? Of course. Fascinating place. I've visited it probably three times on trips to Beijing. It covers far more ground than the Forbidden City itself."

"Did they explain to you why there are no idols there?"

"No. I guess I didn't notice there weren't."

"It is striking that a place of that sort would have no idols. Some of us believe there are no idols because the emperor had become a Christian and worshiped the true God. They say it is a temple of worship of the heavens. But we think it may have been a temple of the worship of the God who made the heavens. We cannot prove it. But we do know Christianity had already come to China. And we know the temple has no idols even though most worshiped idols in those days, and all the other temples have idols. We believe Tian Tang may be a national symbol of Christian heritage in China, a symbol of the one true God, Zhu Yesu Jidu."

"That's an amazing claim. Incredible."

"I have discussed this often with my nephew, Li Yue, whom I hope for you to meet soon. I hear that many Christians throughout China dream and pray that one day Tian Tang may become the nation's largest gathering place of the bride of Christ."

"A church building?"

"A legal church building that will symbolize China's transformation by Yesu." Quan sounded more excited than his old roommate had ever seen him.

"Would that not be *glorious*, Ben Fielding?"

That evening, after an early Saturday dinner, Ben took Shen for a long walk, as he did several times a week, giving Quan and Ming some privacy they never asked for but which he knew they appreciated. Ben enjoyed the walks, but he was ashamed that he couldn't remember going on a long walk with even one of his children. He hoped he was just forgetting.

After they returned, Quan sat at his desk for three hours, preparing his Sunday morning message. First Shen, then Ming, then finally Ben stopped reading and put out the lamps and candles by their beds.

Suddenly, a mechanical ring erupted. Ming jumped out of bed. Ben sat up.

Quan picked up the cell phone. "They are coming," a voice said. Before he could ask who, loud fists fell upon the door. Quan immediately turned off the phone.

Ming looked out the window. "It is PSB," she said weakly. She went to Shen's bed, put her arms around him, pulled off his blanket, and led him to the far corner of the room, then squatted on the floor.

While Ben put on his pants, Quan opened the door. A young officer stepped into the room, scanning it. "Police chief asks to speak with you," he said firmly.

Ben stepped forward in front of Quan. "Do you have written authority to take him? What is your name, Officer?"

Quan raised his hand to silence Ben. "You are not here on behalf of the deputy chief, Tai Hong?"

"No. Chief Lin Shan has sent this request."

"The chief of police does not ask, he commands. What do you mean he requests me to come speak with him?"

"He sent me himself. He is my uncle. He said to ask you, but not to force you. The decision is yours."

"What does he want?" Ben asked.

"I will come to him," Quan said. "Now?"

"That is his request."

"Then I'm coming too," Ben said.

"No," the officer insisted.

"I wish my friend to accompany us," Quan said. The officer looked at Ben, then back at Quan. He nodded, then turned on his heel and marched out the front door.

"Wait," Quan said. Ming was holding a small duffel bag, stuffing it with a few clothes and some fruit. Quan looked out at the officer by the vehicle, then quickly ducked under the bed, grabbing a few items and stuffing them into the bag.

Quan kissed Shen good-bye and whispered in his ear. He then kissed and hugged Ming, who clung to him tightly. Finally, Quan walked out the door to the PSB vehicle, Ben right behind him. Quan and Ben crowded into the backseat. Quan turned around to see Ming and Shen standing at the door, watching them drive away. He knew the question on their minds, for he had asked it about his own father a half-dozen times in similar situations: *Will we ever see him again?*

23

 $\mathcal{A}$FTER DRIVING SIX KILOMETERS, the officer turned left, away from Pushan.

"Why are we not going to the police station?" Quan asked.

No answer.

"He asked you a question," Ben said. "I demand an answer."

Quan put his hand on Ben's arm, squeezing it gently and shaking his head.

"Where is your uncle?" Quan asked.

"At his house."

Quan sat quietly, bowing his head. Ben bowed his head too, feeling as awkward *not* praying as he would have praying.

They drove into an exclusive neighborhood, passing through a security gate. They pulled up in front of a boxy two-story house, huge by Chinese standards.

A guard stood posted outside the home. He nodded to the officer leading Quan, then stared at Ben, looking like he'd never seen a foreigner on this property. Likely, he hadn't.

Think I'm a security risk? Well, maybe I am!

Ben took mental notes of everything, envisioning an affidavit swearing to what happened—while still wondering what that would be. He tried to appear confident, unafraid. It was a false front.

A maid greeted them at the door and pointed to the stairs, then led the way. Ben looked at the family photographs and artwork on the walls. The kitchen he saw off to his right was small and primitive by American standards, but the hallways and wall hangings were impressive, as were the oak dining-room table and hand-carved chairs. The living room was meticulous. Ben wondered if the house was really so beautiful, or if it only seemed that way because of the stark contrast to the Li home.

The maid led them to an upstairs room. Even in the hallway he could feel the room's hot, stuffy air. Quan stepped in, Ben right behind him. He saw a sagging-faced man of about fifty, who looked as if he hadn't slept for days. A watery-eyed woman, presumably his wife, sat still beside him. Only her eyes moved, examining the faces at the door. She stared at Quan, as if she'd seen him before and was surprised to see him again.

In the bed, covered with thick downy blankets, lay a girl the size of a ten-year-old. But Ben thought her face looked older, perhaps fourteen.

The escorting officer looked at the sagging-faced man. "He insisted this American come with him."

The man nodded. "Leave us." Chief of Police Lin Shan stood and walked toward Quan and Ben. He brushed past them, then shut the door. He returned silently to his chair. Ben heard his joints creak as he walked.

"My daughter, Lin Bo." To Ben's surprise, he spoke English. "She very sick. In hospital two months. Worse and worse. Asked to come home. Many doctors visit. Say she is dying. Say there is . . . no hope."

The mother's head fell, her face hitting her hands so wildly the slapping sound startled Ben. She breathed shallow panicky sobs.

The girl's eyes were barely open. She didn't seem comatose, but Ben wasn't sure if she was conscious. If there was something between dead and alive, Lin Bo appeared to be it.

"I am very sorry for you," Quan said. "But why have you asked me here?"

The chief looked out the window, then at the closed door. He cleared his throat. "For many years, my men have arrested house church Christians. I have been given instructions by high-ranking Party members, and in turn I have given orders to my men. You have been arrested by my PSB, I am told. Three times?"

"Five," Quan said. "I have been beaten while in three of your jails, tortured twice." He didn't say it accusingly, but as a matter of fact.

"We understand each other, I think," Lin Shan said. "We are enemies, perhaps. We both do what we think necessary. Do you remember when I visited your cell and saw you inside?"

"Yes. I remember. Two years ago."

"I asked why you, an educated man, believed this nonsense, these things about a foreign God."

Quan nodded.

"You said you believed in a Christ who came from heaven, who died and rose from the dead. You said he defeated death. You said he brought people back from the dead and healed the sick. Then you said to me what I have not forgotten. You said you have seen miracles. You have seen the dying healed. Do you remember saying this?"

"Yes. I remember."

"I am an old man, older than my years. I have believed in nothing but the Party and the Republic. I do not know if I believe any longer even in them. I act on the outside as if I still believe. But inside, my faith is dead. I asked you here because there is no more hope for this father who loves his little Bo. She has not had strength even to raise her head from pillow." His fleshy cheeks shook. His voice cracked. "She has no will to eat. We are out of hope. If you know a God who heals, please, I beg you, tell him to heal her."

He slumped backward, after saying what Ben imagined might have been the hardest words he'd ever spoken.

Quan looked at Lin Shan, then stared at the floor. When he looked back up he said, "I do not tell my God to do anything. He is the one who tells. He is the master; I am but the servant. Li Quan is not a healer. I have seen healings; I have laid hands on the sick with others in my church. I am not a pastor, except when our pastor is . . . absent. I am not a seminary graduate. I am a lowly locksmith's assistant. But this much I know—my God, Yesu Jidu, has the power to heal, and should he will it, he can heal without difficulty. I do not know his desire. But I will ask him to heal Lin Bo."

The man nodded, resting his head against his wife's. At Quan's words her dull stare showed a slight stir, as if there was one last flicker of fire.

Ben stiffened. It smelled like a setup. Quan was being called on to do the impossible. When he failed, when the girl died, he would be blamed. An angry chief of police would have another reason to put him in jail. Ben wanted to intervene, to speak up and stop the charade. But when he looked into the eyes of the girl and her mother, he could say nothing.

Quan stood and placed his hands on the girl's head. Ben squirmed. Quan prayed, "Yesu, I am your lowly servant, nothing more than a locksmith's assistant. My father was a street sweeper; my grandfather, a carpenter; my great-grandfather, a farmer and a digger of ditches. We are nothing in the world's eyes. I am but your errand boy, nothing more. Yet nothing less."

Ben stepped back a foot, giving room to . . . he didn't know what.

"You created Lin Bo and her mother and father. I know you love her and them. I know they need salvation from their sin. That they may see your power and your grace, that they may know Yesu is the only true God—I ask that you touch her now, raise her up, heal her. Do this for your glory above all, but also for their good. I ask this in the name of Yesu. Amen."

"Amen," Ben heard the parents say aloud. He wondered if they'd ever said the word until now. He almost wished he'd said it too. Ben looked at Bo. For a moment he thought he saw a light in her eyes. He thought her shoulders flexed and her neck moved ever so slightly. No. She lay still.

"It is all I can do," Li Quan said. "But I ask you to talk to your daughter about Yesu, even if you are not sure she can hear you. And I have brought you a gift." He reached into his little duffel bag and pulled out a black book.

Ben's heart raced. He put out his hand to stop Quan.

"No," Quan said in a quiet but commanding voice. Ben dropped his hand. "It is Shengjing, Word of the Almighty. It is he who came to be one of us. It is he who died that we might live forever with him."

Lin Shan leaned forward and reached out a trembling hand, taking the Bible.

Quan searched the bag and took out a movie on disc. He handed it to Lin Shan's wife. "This is the story of Yesu. He speaks Chinese." He pointed to the player and television at the foot of the bed. "Perhaps you can watch it. Your daughter might also hear the words."

They both stared at the gifts. Ben saw Shan look at the Bible's spine and turn to the inside cover. He knew what Shan was looking for. There was no red seal—this was an illegal Shengjing. For a moment, with his daughter not healed, Ben wondered if the chief would call in his nephew to arrest Quan.

"Xiexie," the mother whispered.

"Xiexie," the chief said quietly.

"Our church will pray for your daughter," Quan said. He turned to the girl. "We will pray for you, Lin Bo." He put his hand on her forehead again.

Quan and Ben left the room, escorted by the servant and the officer. Lin Shan's nephew drove them back to Quan's house.

"Do you think that was smart?" Ben whispered. "Talking about your house church? Giving an illegal Bible to the chief of police?"

"He knows about our church. They need the Bible. And the story of Yesu."

"But . . . aren't you just asking for trouble?"

"I am already in trouble. I have been in trouble many years. I was in trouble before you came and will be in trouble after you leave. If I chose

176

the path of least trouble, I would not follow Yesu. I asked him if I should give Shengjing to them. I believe he led me to do so. He will do whatever is best."

"And when the girl dies?"

"Life and death are not in our power."

"But will the chief blame you for her death?"

"Perhaps."

24

$\mathcal{D}$ID YOU FILL out an absentee ballot?" Martin Getz asked Ben.

"What?"

"Election's day after tomorrow."

"Guess I forgot about it."

"You're a political junkie, Ben. That's not like you. You don't forget stuff like that. You're just visiting China, remember? You're still an American. And you've got a job back here in Portland, Oregon."

"I know. And I've been doing my job. The interviews are going great. You're going to love what I'm coming up with. I've just . . . had a lot on my mind."

"Look, Ben," Martin said, "I don't want to hear another one of these reports from Won Chi. He tells me your friend is causing trouble and you aren't distancing yourself from him."

"Chi's four hours away in Shanghai. How would he know what Quan and I are doing in Pushan?"

"He says you were called in by the chief of police!"

"How could he know that?"

"Is it true?"

"Well, yes, but did he tell you why?"

"No. Just a nice social call? Asked you to play a hand of bridge?"

"No. He wanted to ask Quan a favor. He had us personally chauffeured to his private home. And Quan wasn't in trouble!"

"What kind of favor can a locksmith's assistant do for the chief of police?"

"Well, he . . . it's hard to explain."

"I'm not a complete idiot. Say it slowly, in words without many sylla-bles."

"He asked Quan to . . . heal his daughter."

"What?"

"I mean, to pray for her to be healed."

"Are you okay, Ben?"

"Yeah, sure."

"I'll say it again—Getz International has a huge amount at stake over there. I don't want us tainted by your friend. Am I clear on that?"

"Perfectly clear."

Ben and Quan bundled up in the early November chill, taking a walk down the dark road, tree branches moving ominously in the slight wind. Quan had invited Ben on a long walk over the rolling countryside.

"All I'm saying, Quan, is you don't have to be so outspoken. I think you need to use more discretion, that's all."

"Some say nearly ten percent of Party members quietly attend churches. Others say there may be several million Party members, intel-lectuals, and professionals who keep their faith secret and rarely, if ever, attend meetings. They use what Ben Fielding calls 'discretion.' Joseph of Arimathea was a secret follower for a time. But we do not believe secret followers should stay secret for too long. A man who is a follower of Yesu inside must be one on the outside too. At the right time those in his family and his workplace—at least those who might be open to the truth—must learn that he belongs to Yesu. Zhou Jin was released from jail yesterday, and today he came to work and told each of his customers about Yesu."

"You have become . . . very bold, Quan."

Quan laughed. "I trembled with fear as I spoke to the chief. I will never be bold. But I do seek to be obedient."

"You were so quiet back in college," Ben said. "You hardly said anything the whole first term."

"I came to Harvard afraid people would find out about my father. Their fathers were all important men and respected. I was ashamed because my father had been a street sweeper and the pastor of a Little Flock church."

"Little Flock?"

"The churches of Ni Tuosheng."

"Never heard of him."

"You know the names of many celebrities, but not the name of one so cherished among us? His Western name was Watchman Nee. Ni Tuosheng died June 1, 1972, in a labor camp in Anhui Province. He had spent twenty years in prison. We remember him every June 1. Father loved his sermons and writings."

Quan's eyes looked off in the distance, as if the road were calling him farther than they could walk together.

"Baba's favorite hymn was 'Heaven Is My Home.' He used to sing it over and over again. When I got older, sometimes I would cover my ears because I did not want to hear it."

Quan sang softly in Mandarin:

> Heaven is my home.
>   Earth is a desert drear.
> Heaven is my home.
>   Danger and sorrow stand
> Round me on every hand.
>   Heaven is my fatherland.
> Heaven is my home.

"It's beautiful," Ben said.

"But my father's foolish son would not sing it with him. And now it is too late."

Another voice, in another place, said, "Even now I sing it with you, my son. And we will sing it together again. Mogui lies to you. It is not too late."

"How long was your father in prison?" Ben asked.

"Nine years in 'reeducation.' A good name for a bad thing."

"How was he arrested?"

"One day without warning the PSB invaded our house. They took all Mother's pictures and Father's books. He had twelve of them—a large library. They carried the confiscated articles into the courtyard and piled them up. They took off my father's shirt. A young girl, perhaps fifteen, walked up to my father. Without a word, she slapped Father across the face. My mother rose to defend him. I did nothing. A young man pushed Mama down. Still I did nothing. She wept as she saw the blood coming from the side of my father's mouth. I did not weep. I was angry at him."

"What happened?"

"I do not remember what I saw, perhaps because my eyes looked at the ground. What I remember is the smell of our few family photographs burning. And the sound of my father's flesh being hit by heavy shoes and sticks. I remember them shouting and swearing. I remember silence when Father was unconscious and Mother so frightened, shaking on the ground. What I remember most is that I did nothing."

"You were only a child. It must have been hard on you."

"Yes, that is what I always thought about. But I never thought about how hard it was on Baba and Mama. Only on me. I was a very selfish son. Someone from the Party would tell us they offered to let Father out of jail or give his family food if he would only say a few words: 'The chairman is greater than the Christ.' That is all he had to say. I was angry he would not say it. They told us he must hate his family not to do this small thing for us. They said it was terrible for him to put us at risk. I believed them."

Quan looked at Ben. "And now it is Li Quan putting his own son at risk. But there is no other way. I cannot deny my Lord, who died for me. I will not. I will not leave a legacy to Li Shen of one who turned his back on Yesu. Many times I have asked my father's forgiveness."

Quan stopped walking and sat on the roadside. Ben watched helplessly as Li Quan put his wet, swollen face in his hands. "I wish he would have been able to hear me."

"I have heard you, my son," said one Father.

"I also have heard you, my son," said the other.

The sounds of the voices rode on the gentle wind, but Li Quan and Ben Fielding could not hear them.

Two hours after nightfall, while Ben answered e-mail, Quan and Ming told Bible stories to Shen. Headlights flashed in the front window.

"Someone coming," Ming said, voice shaking. She hid Shengjing and turned a perfect circle, scanning the house methodically for anything else that could incriminate.

Ben looked out at the long, shiny black car as it came to a stop by the

Mitsubishi. Shen, who'd been at the outhouse, came running inside, shutting the door behind him, flashlight still on.

"Who is it?" Ming asked.

"A driver opened door for man and woman," Shen said, out of breath.

"Who?"

"Someone very rich."

Quan went to the door. There was no porch light, and the indoor candlelight did not penetrate the outer darkness. In the dark shadows he could not see who it was.

"Li Quan," the voice said, "we have come for you." Ben recognized it but couldn't identify it. Then the man stepped forward, and Ben saw his face. Lin Shan, chief of police.

Standing behind Quan, Ben deduced what had happened. Lin's daughter had died, and he had come to point his finger at Quan. Arresting officers were likely in place.

"Why?" Quan asked.

Lin Shan did not answer. Beside him walked his wife, who passed her husband and came in the door. She looked around and saw Ming, then nodded to her.

Why does the chief's wife accompany him on an arrest?

As Ben tried to figure out what was happening, Lin Shan stepped all the way inside. Then from behind him came someone else.

Ben stared into the shining eyes of a beautiful young woman. She smiled broadly at Quan. "I greet you," she said. "And I thank you."

It was a voice Ben had never heard before.

"Welcome, Lin Bo," Li Quan said.

The name hit Ben like a slap. "Lin Bo? You're alive?" he blurted. Every eye in the room turned to him. Lin Bo laughed. Everyone else laughed with her.

The woman looked at Ming and extended her hand. "I am Chaoxing."

"Minghua," she said, bowing her head.

They sat and told the story. A few hours after Quan and Ben had left, when Lin Bo's parents had given up and gone to bed, she suddenly awoke, got up, threw open the window, then walked downstairs and asked for something to eat.

"Maid came running to our bedroom—very frightened," Chaoxing said. After they talked and laughed and cried for another half hour, Ming sang a song of praise and taught them the words. Quan got out his keyboard and plugged it in, and they sang together. Ben kept staring at Bo.

"You have chauffeur in car?" Ming asked, looking out the window. "He must come in. It is cold."

"No," the chief said. "He keeps blanket in car. He is fine."

Quan read from Shengjing. "'Praise the Lord. Praise God in his sanctuary; praise him in his mighty heavens. Praise him for his acts of power; praise him for his surpassing greatness.'"

He then read from the book of Romans: "'All have sinned and fall short of the glory of God.'" He turned to another passage. "'The wages of sin is death, but the gift of God is eternal life in Christ Jesus our Lord.'"

He turned to another and read words written in his mother's hand: "'If you confess with your mouth "Jesus is Lord" and believe in your heart that God raised him from the dead, you will be saved.'"

Chaoxing said, "I confess Yesu is Zhu."

Ming prayed with Chaoxing, then with Lin Bo, who eagerly declared her loyalty to Yesu. "I saw Zhu Yesu in the movie you gave us."

"Chaoxing and I watched it downstairs right after you left," Lin Shan said. "We had just gone to bed when we heard the maid scream and saw Bo was healed. Then we watched it twice more with Bo." He looked at Quan, eyes pleading. "I, too, wish to follow Yesu."

Quan led him in confessing his sins, then prayed, "Yesu, worker of miracles, do the greatest miracle of all in these hearts—do in them a miracle of your grace."

They wept and laughed and embraced and told stories for another hour. Ming insisted on taking tea and bread cake out to the chauffeur.

"We must tell you something," Lin Shan said. "Perhaps I should have told you when you were in my home. Before I called you, my wife had a dream. She said she saw a man lay hands upon our daughter and pray for her. I had seen you once in jail, but she never had. When you came into Bo's room, she whispered to me, 'That is the man in my dream.'"

Chaoxing nodded. "The moment you walked in, I knew it was you. The American was not in my dream, but you were. When I saw you, I believed my daughter would be healed. You were the messenger of a God I did not know. But now I know him. And I will gladly serve the God who has given me back my daughter."

"The path you choose is not an easy one," Quan said. "Shengjing says that those who live godly in Jidu Yesu will suffer persecution. Other things change also. For example, when one is a Christian, he does not leave the chauffeur sitting in the cold."

"Alright," Lin Shan said, springing to his feet. "I will invite him in. I will tell him we have become followers of Yesu. He will do the same."

"That must be his decision," Quan said.

A few minutes later the chauffeur followed Lin Shan through the door, looking jittery. Quan insisted he sit in his chair. The man listened quietly as the chief of police explained how they had become Christians. The man, eating more bread cake and drinking tea, listened wide-eyed to their story.

"My cousin is a believer in Yesu," he said meekly. "He told me he once kept Shengjing in his house for nearly a week."

"I am sorry to say," Lin Shan said to Quan, "but we no longer have the Shengjing you gave us."

"Why?"

"Somehow it disappeared. Perhaps a servant or a visitor. I do not know. But not my chauffeur, I am sure." The man nodded.

"This happens," Quan said, smiling. "But we do not feel too bad when a Bible is taken. It is because people are so hungry for God. When bread is taken by the starving, it is no surprise and no tragedy."

"But we must have this bread too," Chaoxing said.

Carefully and reverently, Quan handed her his mother's Bible. "We will get you another. But until then, please borrow this one. It was hand-copied by my mother, Lu Lan."

Bo's mother reached out trembling hands and moaned softly. "I tell you now of another dream I have often had since I was a little girl, growing up in the home of vice chairman of Communist Party. I dreamed of a peasant woman with a great smile, who sat under candlelight with an empty chair beside her. She wrote out words in a big black book. I dreamed that she gave me that book, and in it I would discover great secrets, including the secret of her smile. I have wondered sometimes if that book would be Shengjing."

"My mother had just such a smile," Quan said. "The biggest smile I have ever known."

"We are honored, Li Quan," Lin Shan said. "And we will take your mother's book tonight. But I have thought of something. I *do* have access to Shengjing—perhaps many of them."

"How?"

"Whenever Christians are arrested, all their belongings are stored at prison. We do not return Shengjing. We put them in room to be destroyed. But some time ago I decided to put them under lock and key in storage cabinet. I do not know why. One day when Lin Bo very sick, I was angry and decided to burn Shengjing. I ordered one of the officers to do it. But he came back and said the key had broken in lock. No one could get in. He could not even saw it open. The blade broke. The books have been sitting there ever since. There are dozens of them, I think. Of course, I will not destroy them now. I will give them to you . . . perhaps Li Quan can return them to their owners? And if owners cannot be found, perhaps we can keep one of them ourselves and you can give away the others?"

"Yes," Quan said.

"But first we must get them out of the storage cabinet," Lin Shan said.

"This will not be a problem," Li Quan said.

"Why do you say that?"

"Because," Ben said, "my friend Li Quan is the best locksmith in China."

"Can you come tomorrow to open the cabinet?" Lin Shan asked. "Will your employer let you come?"

"Yes," Quan said. "For this, I am certain my employer will let me leave work for however long it takes."

"We will pay you, of course. Yes, the PSB will pay the locksmith to open the vault. I will be sure no one is in the room but us. You will take all the Shengjing with you. I will pay you to take them away and do with them as you will. But you will need something to carry them in. Do you have such a thing?"

"I can find such a thing," Quan said. He pulled out the faded green burlap duffel bag from under the bed and held it up. "Perhaps this bag."

"Yes, that would be very good. That is perfect."

They rose to leave. Ming hugged Bo. Bo nodded to Quan and shook his hand. She then looked at Ben. He reached out his hand and felt her gentle warmth. The delicate yet strong grip confirmed the reality of what he'd been telling himself must be a dream.

"Tomorrow night," Chaoxing said, "I hope for the first time to have my own Shengjing." She paused and stared hard at the high-backed empty chair. She ran her fingers over it, as if somehow held by it.

Quan stood there, gripping the back of the big chair. When the visitors drove off, Ming closed the door and walked over to her son. She said, "Do you know what you have witnessed, Shen? The chief of police and his wife and daughter are part of our family now. Tonight, in the house of Li Quan of Hangzhou, they have become followers of Yesu."

The great party was filled with joy and singing and laughter. The celebration was unrestrained.

Li Manchu raised a glass. "Three more sinners have repented. The Lin family of Pushan, in the home of Li Quan the locksmith of Hangzhou, have become part of the King's family!" A great cheer erupted, followed by backslapping and infectious smiles. Even the angels, not so quick to smile as the children of Adam, became caught up in the contagious spirit of joy.

But no one smiled broader than one small woman with big dimples and a shy, cheery face. She stood on the edge of the celebration, looking down at a family of three rescued from darkness. She marveled to hear she had appeared in a seeker's dreams. She remembered the long hours copying the words of Shengjing, reading it, weeping over it with pangs of sorrow and joy. To see her eight-year labor of love in the hands of her son, Li Quan, and now this family of Lin Shan, filled her heart with joy.

Lu Lan put her arms around the one next to her and buried her slight frame in his warm embrace. It felt like being lost in the mane of a lion. He ran his fingers through her hair and kissed her head gently. She reached up and drew his hand to her lips. Lu Lan kissed his great scar and gazed into the eyes of the One who was the secret of her smile.

25

𝒜FTER BEN had tossed and turned for an hour, Quan got up at 2:00 A.M. and sat on Ben's bed.

"I cannot sleep either," he whispered. "Sorry we have no bunk bed like at Harvard." He got under the covers next to Ben, who scooted as far away from the center as he could, hanging precariously on the edge. But after a few minutes he took his cues from Quan, and his horror of being in a small bed with a man subsided.

"I guess I never believed in healing," Ben said in the darkness.

"No one can believe in God and not in healing," Quan said.

"I think most miracles are phony. Or at least exaggerated."

"Some money is counterfeit. Does that mean that you no longer believe in money?"

"I've never seen a miracle until now."

"Have you looked for one? Have you asked for one? Or have you assumed that because some miracles are imagined, all are?"

"But things have natural explanations."

"Yes, and if you try hard enough you could find one for Lin Bo getting better. What miracle is greater than creation itself? Yet men have invented a natural explanation for that. Why? Because they wanted to. Atheists are naturalists. Christians are supernaturalists. One who does not believe in miracles cannot be a Christian."

"But . . . in America this doesn't happen. I mean, not real miracles like this one."

"How would you know? Are you always and everywhere present? How are you qualified to say such things? If you lived in a cave and did not see the sun rise, would it mean the sun did not rise?"

"Well, when you were at Harvard did *you* see any miracles?"

"Not like I have seen in China. But I did not see demons in America like I have seen here either. Yet I know they were there. I could not see their feet, but everywhere I saw their footprints. Yet I am wrong to say I did not see miracles in America—for the greatest miracle of my life happened there. I was born again."

"But I'm talking about physical miracles. The kind that can be discerned with the five senses. You've really seen those?"

"Last year we borrowed a television and showed the movie about Yesu in this room. At one point a blind man cries out to the Lord, 'I want to see again.' Just two feet from the foot of this bed sat a woman, Sun Fen. She had been totally blind since an accident as a child. Her eyes had shriveled. At the moment the blind man was healed, in her spirit she pleaded, 'I also want to see again.' Yesu healed her."

"Just like that?"

"I saw her eyes, clear and shining. She touched Ming's face and said how beautiful she was. That was when I knew she could truly see."

They heard a giggle.

"Minghua is pretending to be asleep," Quan said. "But she is eaves-dropping on old roommates!"

The giggles came again. "Old roommates very big men sleeping together in very small bed!" They all laughed, especially Ming.

"Tell me the rest of the story," Ben said, no longer whispering, since Shen could sleep through anything.

"We had to turn off the video and wait an hour before watching the rest. Sun Fen's sister was there. She could not control her happiness. We were all amazed, for such things do not happen often. We celebrated. But I said they must see the rest of the movie. When Yesu, the healer of the blind, was crucified, they all wept, none more than Sun Fen. She and every member of her family and most of the thirty others became follow-ers of Yesu that night."

"You had thirty people in this house?"

"Yes."

"And you knew this woman well enough that it couldn't have been a fake healing?"

"Of course. We knew Sun Fen the blind woman for many years. Every-one knew her. She is a member in our church. You have surely seen her."

After ten seconds of silence, Quan said, "Do you think we are gullible, Ben Fielding? That we are quick to believe because we are superstitious peasants? Many Americans think this of us. But we were taught to be atheists, remember? It is Americans who are gullible."

"What do you mean?"

"I remember the newspapers in supermarkets. People believe things in your country no Chinese would ever believe. That President Kennedy is still alive on some island? That Elvis is seen by witnesses everywhere? That fifty-pound, two-headed babies are born?"

"Most people don't believe those things," Ben said.

"Then what about your science? Don't they say first there was nothing and then the nothing exploded and turned into everything? Do not tell me people don't believe that—I was taught it at Harvard. So do not think Chinese are foolish and gullible until you look in own mirror."

"Sorry."

"So do not believe I don't know when a woman is blind and when she can see. We are not stupid." Quan breathed deeper and relaxed. "I also know when an evil spirit has been cast out."

"You've seen that?"

"Perhaps since our visit to the Lama's den you are not so skeptical?"

"Why didn't you tell me about these miracles before?"

"Because you did not ask. Besides, would you have believed me?"

"Probably not. But explain this to me, would you? God saved the daughter of Lin Shan, a man who persecuted Christians, because he asked for a miracle. But when I found my son in the water and asked God to save him, he was silent. He did nothing to help Jason. Where was a miracle when I needed one?"

"I cannot speak for God. Nor does he need me to. Miracles are unusual or they would not be miracles. A dying girl is suddenly healed. That is a miracle. I have seen miracles of deliverance in prison. I have also seen men suffer terribly. I have seen children healed, and I have seen them die in their mother's arms. I suppose my grandfather, Li Wen, prayed for a miracle when the Boxers were about to cut off the heads of his parents. But they were still beheaded—though God answered the prayers of his parents by delivering their son. Never believe a man who says God no longer does miracles, Ben. But never believe a man who says God must do a miracle the way a man wants him to. God is God."

"I'll never forgive him for taking Jason."

"God does not need your forgiveness. It is you who need his."

"I'm still angry at him."

"You do not have reason to be angry at him. He has reason to be angry at you."

Ben resisted the urge to kick Quan out of bed. "You still have Shen. I don't have Jason."

"But you do have Melissa and Kim. Li Quan and Ming would give everything we own for the opportunity to have another child. Do not take your children lightly, Ben Fielding."

"Who says I take them lightly?"

"A path is made by people walking the ground. My father walked the path before me and his father before him and his before him. I pray my son will walk it after me. So I ask my old roommate a question—what path are you walking for your children to follow?"

"Kimmy's a sweetheart, sharp as a tack. Melissa's a business major. I think she got her interest in business from me."

"And did she get from you an interest in God?"

"I provided a beautiful house for the kids, nice clothes, bought them each a car. I'll pay their way through college. And one day I guess I'll leave them a big inheritance."

"In China we have different words for inheritance and heritage. Even a bad father can leave an inheritance. Only a good father can leave a heritage."

"I have no room for a God who lets children die."

"The innkeeper had no room, but it did not thwart God's plan. Who is Ben Fielding to have no room for God? Shall the dog decide whether there is room in the house for the Master? Shall the cricket decide whether there is room in the forest for the Lion?"

"That doesn't justify the suffering."

"Does my old roommate imagine that Yesu is a stranger to suffering? He wept for the sisters of Lazarus. He sweat great drops of blood in the garden. On that hill he took upon himself the anguish of all men. He was despised by men, a man of sorrows and familiar with grief. Even now when his people are persecuted, he feels their suffering. Ben Fielding has not suffered first, nor has he suffered most. As for the God you have no room for, who knows better than he what it is like to lose his only Son?"

"In the last two weeks, there have been no raids of churches anywhere near Pushan, right?" Ben asked. "With the conversion of the PSB chief, perhaps a new era of freedom has come for your churches."

"I am not so sure," Quan said. "But I am sorry my old friend must leave tomorrow."

"It's been six weeks. I've taken advantage of your hospitality too long.

The time went by so quickly. But next time I'm in Shanghai, I'll come out for a visit. I promise."

After dinner, Ben packed, trying in vain to fit everything in. He was already bringing back two extra bags, one filled with handcrafted gifts from Ming and women in the house church. Many of the gifts were for Pam and the girls.

Without a knock, the door suddenly opened. Ben recognized the young man from church. He was out of breath.

"What is it, Zhang Shilin?" Quan asked.

"Message from Zhou Jin. Bad news. Lin Shan, police chief, no longer there. He has moved away."

"Why?"

"Sudden transfer. So they say."

"So they say."

"The deputy has been promoted to chief."

Ming covered her mouth. Ben pictured the steely-eyed man who'd followed Quan and paid him that intimidating visit.

"Tai Hong is loyal Party member," Quan said. "His head is filled with passionate, empty words. Mogui's words."

Ming's cheeks were wet. She put one arm around Quan and drew him near. She put her finger to the five-inch scar on his neck and then to his marred ear lobe.

"I've never asked you how that happened," Ben said. He'd wanted to, but he kept hoping Quan would offer an explanation.

"It happened in jail."

Ming cried out, "Tai Hong's knife did this!" She spoke with fear and fury. It was the first time Ben had seen her angry.

"We have prayed often for Tai in our house church," Quan said. "Perhaps I will have opportunity again to speak to him of Yesu."

Two hours later Ming and Shen slept soundly. Quan sat on Ben's bed beside him, covered with a blanket.

"There's something I want to know before I leave," Ben said to Quan. "This is probably my last chance to ask."

"Yes?"

"I want to know more about what happened to your father and grandfather and great-grandfather. If you feel up to telling me."

"It honors me that you would ask this." Quan gathered his thoughts. "Perhaps I told you Father taught me to ask myself, 'Is this the day I die?'

He would quote a verse, 'Man is destined to die once, and after that to face judgment.'"

"That's a scary message to send to your child."

"Does not a loving father tell his children the truth? He also taught me, 'Show me, O Lord, my life's end and the number of my days; let me know how fleeting is my life. You have made my days a mere handbreadth; the span of my years is as nothing before you. Each man's life is but a breath.' He taught me that our lives 'quickly pass, and we fly away.'"

"Sounds morbid."

"No, because our life does not end here. We do not cease to exist at death; we relocate to another place. How can we prepare for death if we deny it? One of Baba's favorite sayings was 'Real gold fears no fire.' I tell Minghua and Shen, we must go through times of testing, but the fire of our trials proves what we are made of."

"Fire seems a high price to pay."

"Purity is worth the highest cost, is it not? God is with us in the fire. Shengjing says our works done on earth can be either wood or hay or straw that will burn in the fire of God's holiness. Or they can be works of gold and silver and precious stones that will be purified in the fire. The choice is ours. If we are faithful, we will come out purer than when we went into the fire. This is why real gold does not fear the fire."

"But does a father who loves his children put them through such fire?"

"Suffering was not new to my father. I have told you his own father— my grandfather—was only eight years old when the Boxers killed his parents."

"Your grandmother was killed too?"

"Yes."

"Who were the Boxers?"

"Beware—you have asked a history major. Alright. The Opium Wars left China humiliated and helpless before Western imperialists. Our rulers wanted to rid China of all foreigners. The empress dowager claimed the spirits were angry because of the foreign religion—Christianity—and the disloyalty of Chinese Christians who did not pay temple taxes or worship ancestors. There were mystics who looked back to China's golden days and believed that martial arts—Chinese boxing— could ward off Western bullets. Under the influence of drugs and under the spell of Mogui, young peasant boys set out to rid China of Christians. What happened was the largest martyrdom in all history. More than thirty-two thousand Chinese and two hundred missionaries were murdered."

"It sounds horrible."

"I have always wanted to write a book on the Boxer martyrs and dedicate it to my great-grandparents. That will never be, I fear. But I do not regret my research. Did you know that whole families were beheaded? A seventeen-year-old had his body cut into pieces and parts nailed to a wall in Tangshan. One missionary in Shanxi Province was stoned, stripped, and run over with a cart until her spine was broken. A teacher at the Zunhua Girls School, Hebei Province, was shot, stabbed, sliced, and burned to death. Over three hundred Christians were beheaded in the northeastern provinces. Others were strangled, burned, put in stocks, and beaten severely, then left to die. One student at Beijing University refused to renounce his faith in Christ, and burn incense to idols. They cut off his lips, arms, and legs. Another had his heart cut out and placed on a stone in Yongping."

Ben cringed. "But what happened to your great-grandparents?"

"My grandfather Li Wen told me this story when I was young, and my father repeated it to me many times. My great-grandfather was Li Manchu. My grandfather, when he was Shen's age, watched the swordsman cut his father's head off. He saw it fall to the ground. My great-grandmother tried to stop the Boxers, but they beat and kicked her. She lay in the dirt ten feet away from his severed head. She kept saying to them what they did not wish to hear. Finally, as she lay in the dirt, they cut off her head too. My grandfather's aunt held him in her arms while it happened. It was a miracle they escaped. The Boxers often murdered children along with the adults."

"Why did they let your grandfather and his aunt live?"

"The first reason is because God was not finished with house of Li. He had a purpose for us to continue. He had reasons for Li Wen and Li Tong to be born, and for Li Quan to be talking today with Ben Fielding. He had, I hope, his highest plan for the life of Li Shen. But a second reason was related to me by my elderly grandfather. He said his aunt told him it was because his mother frightened them."

"What do you mean?"

"As she lay in the dirt, she quoted Shengjing. The verses she spoke were copied by my father's aunt, and she passed them down. My father taught me what she said to them, as his father taught him."

"What did she say?" Ben leaned forward.

"She pointed at her children and said to the executioner, 'If anyone causes one of these little ones who trusts in me to lose faith, it would be better for that person to be thrown into the sea with a large millstone tied around the neck.' The man trembled as he raised his sword. He killed her."

"And then?"

"Two men came toward my eight-year-old grandfather and his aunt, to behead them. But the leader, the one who had killed my grandparents, ordered them to stop. 'Leave the children alone,' he told them. The other man yelled at him, and soon they were fighting. The one who killed my great-grandparents protected their child. At the same instant, the men struck each other with swords. They fell to the ground and bled to death in front of my aunt. My grandmother's killer stared up into the sky and whispered something. Grandfather's aunt didn't know what to think of it at the time, but later she thought it might have been a prayer."

"A prayer?"

"Yes. She thought the Boxer warrior had whispered the name of Zhu Yesu. She wondered if he might be like the thief on the cross—perhaps he repented just before he died."

———

"It was almost as Li Quan recounted, was it not?"

"Except his great-grandfather was not so brave as he appeared. But Quan was right about his great-grandmother. Nan Hu was the most courageous woman I have ever known."

"Thank you," Nan Hu said to Li Manchu. She looked through the portal at earth and spoke to one who could not hear her words.

"It *was* a prayer, Li Quan, a prayer of repentance. Recently I shared another meal with Song Ding, the Boxer warrior who became a child of Elyon that day. We prayed for you! You should have heard him. He has great passion for the King. You will enjoy meeting him."

"A true servant of Yesu," Li Manchu said to Quan. "We entered Charis minutes apart. Of course, he earned no reward except for saving Li Wen's life—but the King treasures that single act of obedience for which he died. Now Song Ding has grown great in knowledge and insight. He who is forgiven much loves much." He smiled at Nan Hu. "We could not have been killed by a finer man."

———

Quan had put on his leather jacket to go out and look at the stars. As he stepped toward the door, it flew open. Three PSB officers stormed in, one with a rifle couched tensely in his arms. Ben stood up, knocking his laptop computer to the floor. The man with the rifle pointed it at Ben. He stuck his hands in the air.

The armed man watched Quan and Ben, while Ming huddled in the corner with Shen. One of the police pulled drawers out and dumped them on the floor, rummaging through the contents. The other flipped each bed over and found nothing under Ben's or Shen's. But under Quan and Ming's, he found some boards painted gray, level with the floor. He yanked off one of the boards, reached in, and pulled out a gunnysack. He turned it upside down. Three Bibles came out. He checked for the red seal of a legal Bible. There was none.

"Li Quan is under arrest," the officer shouted.

"What are the charges?" Ben asked.

The man pulled a piece of paper from his shirt pocket and read: "'Possession of illegal literature. Distribution of illegal propaganda. Participation in illegal religious meetings. Leading illegal religious meetings. Illegal religious instruction to a child under eighteen. Undue association with foreign influences.' Tai Hong says there may be other charges too."

The cell phone rang. Ming reached for it, but the officer grabbed it out of her hand and flipped it open. "What do you want?"

The phone went dead. He threw it against the wall, and it shattered into a half-dozen pieces.

"Tai Hong says to tell Li Quan he is eager to see him at his place. He instructed me to give you this greeting from him." He pulled a two-foot baton from his belt and whipped it into Quan's knee. With the sound of the crack still in the air, Quan fell to the ground, groaning.

Ming screamed. Shen wailed. The men dragged Quan to the door.

"No! No!" Ming cried. "Yesu, help him!"

One of the soldiers turned around and tumbled over the mahogany chair. He swore and kicked it, then cried out because he'd hurt his foot. The chair did not turn over.

Ming grabbed a prepacked duffel bag. She tried to hand it to Quan. The officer yanked it away, rummaged through it, then dumped it on the floor. Tan trousers, a blue long-sleeved shirt, underwear, an old coat, and a blanket. He motioned to the other men. One of them pushed Quan toward the door.

"I go peacefully," Quan said. The man who'd injured his foot on the chair, now limping, pushed Quan out the door and onto the dirt.

"Get up!"

The other two officers dragged him to the police car, while Ming stuffed the clothes back into the duffel bag and ran behind. Crying, now on her knees in the mud, she pleaded, "Please take this for Li Quan."

The man kicked it out of her hand. Ben rushed toward him, saw him raise his stick over Ming, and suddenly froze.

"If big-shot American takes one more step, he will find out his passport will do no good."

They shoved Quan into the car. He looked out at Ming and nodded to her, then spotted Shen standing inside the doorway by the lamp, watching helplessly. Quan thought he saw a discoloration of his son's trousers. He remembered that once when his father had been dragged away, he'd wet his pants. He hoped Ming and Ben would say nothing to Shen. "Please, Yesu," Quan whispered, "do not let him feel ashamed."

The car drove off, spitting mud on Ben's shirt and all over Ming. Ben went to her, still on her knees in the mud, next to the duffel bag. He drew her up to her feet and put his arm around her. She pressed her face into his chest, trembling.

After a few minutes they slowly walked inside. Shen had changed his clothes and was straightening the room. He examined the empty high-backed chair to see if there was any damage where the man had kicked it. He couldn't see any.

As his mother came in the door with Ben, Shen's face shook, then pinched up. Ming dropped the duffel bag and put her arms around her son. Together they wept.

Ming said she should phone Zhou Jin. Ben looked at the pieces of the shattered phone on the floor and handed her his. While she spoke with him, Ben helped Shen pick up the dresser. He started putting the sparse selection of clothes back in the drawers, not knowing what went where. One old shirt felt like it had something inside. He reached in and took out a dozen photos.

Who was this? They were pictures of him! In one he held a Frisbee. The background buildings showed it was Harvard Yard. In another he stood beside Quan, both with big smiles. Where was it? Of course. Barstow Hall, where the campus Christian group had met. Two pictures on the tennis court, four in their dorm room. Everything on the dorm wall, their clothes, their hair length, all brought back a flood of memories. Especially the last one—a photo of him and Pam pushing wedding cake into each other's smiling face. He must have sent it to Quan. He stared at the picture long and hard until Ming got off the phone.

"Why was he hiding these photos?" he asked her.

"Sometimes not good to have pictures of Americans." She pointed to the picture of the Christian group. "Here you and Quan are holding

Bibles. Picture is risky." He looked at the Bible in his hand in the photo. He wasn't even sure if he still had that one.

Ming took the photographs, then went over to a pillow on the floor and pulled the Bible box out of the middle of it. She placed the photo of Ben and Pam, along with the others, carefully inside it.

Ben sat down. "Is it worth all this?" he asked.

"Minghua does not understand question."

"I mean the hurt it brings to your family. Is it worth it?"

"Family very important. Yesu more important. Quan must put Yesu before Ming and Shen. Ming must put Yesu before Quan. Must put him even before our only son." As she pulled Li Shen to her side, her lips quivered.

26

LI MANCHU, Li Wen, and Li Tong held hands, watched, and prayed. Then they turned to Reader and listened:

> Weeping may remain for a night, but rejoicing comes in the morning. I will be glad and rejoice in your love, for you saw my affliction and knew the anguish of my soul. You have not handed me over to the enemy but have set my feet in a spacious place. Cast your cares on the Lord and he will sustain you; he will never let the righteous fall. The Lord hears the needy and does not despise his captive people.

"Perhaps now it begins," Li Tong said.

"The threads are being woven together," said Li Manchu. "The tapestry takes shape. Yet what the Weaver's final product will be, we cannot yet know."

"But at least now we can see the top side of the tapestry," Li Wen said. "They can only see its underside."

Ben looked at Ming. "I can't believe this happened."

She wiped her tears. "It has happened before."

"He told the police chief he'd been in jail five times."

"In Pushan. Two other times also. Or three. Zhou Jin in jail many more times. He calls it 'seminary.' Once there twelve years."

"How long will they hold him?"

"Do not know. Few days, sometimes weeks. Longest time for Quan eight months."

"Quan was in jail *eight months?* Why didn't he tell me?"

"Not easy to talk about. Does not wish to . . . draw attention to self."

"That may be the Chinese way, but I'm from America." Ben looked at her. "I'm canceling my flight. I won't leave until Quan's out of jail."

Ming looked surprised, started to object, then nodded slowly.

"Maybe I should move out of here, with Quan gone? I mean, if that would be more appropriate, you know."

She looked up at him, confused.

"Or I could stay and help. I mean, Shen's here with us, of course. I can shovel coal, do some repairs. Maybe I can help with Shen. Most of all, I can stir up dust, talk to the right people, and get Quan out of there as soon as possible."

Ming smiled faintly, then said, "Xiexie, Ben Fielding. Chan Minghua most grateful."

———

"You sound groggy, Johnny."

"Ben? It's 4:07 A.M. What's going on?"

"Sorry. Guess I miscalculated the time difference."

"Where are you?"

"China."

"Weren't you flying in yesterday?"

"My friend Li Quan was arrested. The PSB barged in, pushed him around, and dragged him off. The new chief of police is harassing him."

"What are the charges?"

"Several, but they all relate to illegal religious activities."

"Is it true?"

"Well, yeah, some of it."

"You break the law in China and you'd better be prepared to face the consequences. The jails there don't have ESPN, either."

"Look, Johnny, there hasn't been a hearing. I've made calls all over. They won't even tell his family where he is. I need some legal help here. I've got to get Quan out. I've already put a call in to Liao's. You know them?"

"Of course," Johnny said. "They're the top law firm in Shanghai. Getz has used them a half-dozen times."

"I dropped Getz's name and went right to a senior partner. I told him we need help with someone accused of a crime and, as far as we could tell, being held without due process or bail or anything. I called yesterday, and I still haven't heard back."

"I'm not surprised."

"Why?"

"Look, Ben, we need to talk. You flying home tomorrow?"

"No way. I told Martin it was a crisis. These people have put me up six weeks. I can't bail out on them until this situation's under control."

"Okay. Let me know what Liao's has to say. Meanwhile, I'll check around on this end, see what I can figure out. I know some Chinese business law, such as it is, but criminal law's out of my league. I have to find out what their due process is, prisoner's status and rights, all that."

"Thanks, Johnny."

"Sure. But next time, could you wait just a couple more hours to call?"

They sat quietly at Thursday dinner, with two empty chairs and two empty plates. After Ben played with Shen, it turned dark.

Ming said, "It is time."

They went out to the car, drove three miles, parked behind thick trees, then walked the rest of the way.

Ben sat in a front seat at the home of Wu Xia, the woman with tuberculosis. To his surprise, Ming stood up. Shen, sitting in front of her, unwrapped his grandmother's Bible, then stood and handed it to his mother. She opened and read.

> Don't ever forget those early days when you first learned about Christ. Remember how you remained faithful even though it meant terrible suffering. Sometimes you were exposed to public ridicule and were beaten, and sometimes you helped others who were suffering the same things. You suffered along with those who were thrown into jail. When all you owned was taken from you, you accepted it with joy. You knew you had better things waiting for you in eternity.
>
> Do not throw away this confident trust in the Lord, no matter what happens. Remember the great reward it brings you! Patient

endurance is what you need now, so you will continue to do God's will. Then you will receive all that he has promised.

For in just a little while, the Coming One will come and not delay. And a righteous person will live by faith.

On Friday, November 15, Ben placed another call to Liao's Law Service. The receptionist put him through to the partner he'd spoken with before.

"This is Ben Fielding, vice president of Getz International. I called you three days ago."

"Yes. I remember."

"Well, were you planning on calling me back? I was told Liao's was the top law firm in Shanghai. I've told people that myself. My company's done business with you before. We hope to do business again. But first I need help with this prisoner, Li Quan. I've gone to the jail in Pushan, Facility Six, and they won't talk to me. They won't even confirm Quan's there. His family needs to locate him. We need to see him. We need legal counsel."

"Yes, Mr. Fielding. I spoke with several of my associates after your call."

"And?"

"We regret . . . we cannot help you."

"Why not?"

"It is a difficult situation."

"Yes. That's why I went to the top law firm in Shanghai. Are you saying it's too difficult for you?"

"We are not suited for such cases."

"Such cases as what?"

"Liao's specializes in business law."

"Yes, but you're a full-service firm, aren't you? Are you telling me you never deal with criminal law?"

"Mr. Fielding, because we have a working relationship with your company I will say this much—Liao's does not take cases involving PSB or Party."

"Why not?"

"We have found this is not profitable. The government handles these matters."

"Right. That's the problem."

"We regret we cannot help you."

"I regret it too. Attorneys afraid to hold the police and government accountable? This would never fly where I come from."

"This is not America, Mr. Fielding."

"You can say that again." Ben slammed down the phone.

He sat down at Quan's desktop computer, opened the e-mail program, and typed in an address.

Hey, Johnny. Ben here. It's the middle of the night for you. I almost called, but I'll have mercy and send you a flaming e-mail you can read over morning coffee. My laptop's having problems, virus or something, so I'm using Quan's computer. You're lucky he's got a toggle switch so you can read this in English.

Here's the scoop: Liao's is afraid of the government. You knew that, didn't you? They call themselves a law firm but won't do anything to help us find an innocent man, let alone get him out of jail. Back home I'd call a newspaper, get an investigative reporter on it, and we'd be on top of this thing by tomorrow. But here the media's under tighter control than this lousy law firm.

Well, I'm shooting off some e-mails to our associates in Hong Kong, Taiwan, and Singapore to see what I can stir up. Any help would be appreciated. If you can't reach me by phone, just reply to this address. I'll be checking Li Quan's e-mail.

Shen sat in the corner reading his father's Shengjing, in the handwriting of the smiling grandmother he'd never known. The police chief had returned the Bible the day before he disappeared.

Quan had reminded his family it had nearly been lost, yet once again it had somehow returned to its family. Shen wondered whether his father also would be returned.

"Quan told me something on the plane from Beijing," Ben said to Minghua, as they sat thawing near the coal stove. "Schoolchildren near here were punished for attending Sunday school at an unregistered church. He said the students were slapped and threatened. They were warned never to go to church again."

Ming nodded. "The way of the Cross comes early to our children. Even now Shen reads his father's Bible and wonders what is being done to him."

Ben nodded, seeing the pain in her eyes. "There's something I've been wanting to ask you. The first day I was here I gave Quan the Bible he requested. But while he was looking it over, you kept looking at the box. Then you hid it. I see now you're keeping it inside your pillow. Why?"

"Minghua's mother had such a box. She never owned Shengjing. But once four boxed Shengjing were given to her pastor. He took them to his church of three hundred, and they cast lots. Bibles were passed out to winners. They took them home, knowing if discovered they would be imprisoned, yet nothing could rob them of joy. But when pastor gave away last Bible, Mother noticed someone had taken Bible but left box behind. She ask pastor for box. He say, 'I am sorry, there are no Bibles left.' She say, 'I know—I am asking to have the box, for it is holy—it once contained the Words of God.' We kept our most valuable possessions, including family photographs, in that box. Ming will do same."

"Not only is my laptop fouled up, I can't send and receive from Quan's e-mail," Ben told Johnny. "This morning I find a note from the service provider that says Li Quan's e-mail privileges have been revoked. No explanation. What does that mean?"

"It means somebody didn't like the e-mails he's been sending," Johnny said.

"He hasn't been sending any—he's in jail."

"But you've been using his account, right? The e-mail you sent me was probably enough. But you said you were sending some unflattering notes off to Hong Kong or Singapore, right? This is their subtle way of saying, 'Knock it off.'"

"They've been reading my e-mails? You're kidding."

"Wake up and smell the green tea, Ben. Even *we* do that, or at least we can. The FBI has equipment that can scan every incoming and outgoing e-mail message on a server, looking for telltale words or names. If the ISP lets them in on the grounds they're tracking for criminal activity, it can automatically save those messages for retrieval by law enforcement. They can track instant messages, who's visiting what Web site, you name it. So if the FBI can do it, do you think Beijing can't?"

"But . . . they shouldn't be able to do that!"

"No newspaper's going to take them on—they own them. There won't be a public outcry like you'd get in the U.S. And what's ISP going to say to the government—'You can't have access to our data'? Yeah, right. When hell freezes over. So they've got the equivalent of this gigantic wiretap on e-mail. They can screen anybody's. If they don't like it, they can arrest them or remove their e-mail privileges. They already arrested your friend. Now they take away his e-mail because they don't like what you're doing."

"Big Brother is watching," Ben said.

"And Beijing's the ultimate big brother. About eight feet tall and five hundred pounds."

27

I PULLED SOME STRINGS with a supplier that doesn't want to lose our business," Johnny said. "Of course, we don't want to lose theirs either, so I'm walking a tightrope. Tighter than Martin would like. Anyway, they managed to get some info from PSB."

"How?"

"I'm not asking, but I'd bet they paid a few thousand yuan for it, anyway. We'll get the bill in one form or another. Guess we'll have to put it under 'Bribes' on the annual report."

"What did they tell you?"

"The police chief, Tai Hong, was notified that your friend had Bibles in his home. Brought by late-night visitors. Then there was the matter of an American who's been staying there six weeks."

"Thanks to the arrest, it's been seven," Ben said.

"Li Quan's got a prior record. He's a known associate of someone with a long criminal record. He's named . . . here it is. Zhou Jin."

Ben laughed.

"That strikes you funny?"

"He's an old man who runs a locksmith shop. And he's a pastor."

"Unregistered church?"

"Yes, but—"

"Like I said, he's a criminal. Anyway, after getting the tip, they started tailing Quan. He showed up on a hotel video. Apparently they have them set up behind mirrors on each of the floors. Your friend carried something into the hotel he didn't carry out. And later pictures show him carrying nothing into the hotel, but leaving with a heavy duffel bag."

"I need the name and address of the jail where they're holding Quan."

"I don't have it. It's in Pushan, but they have several facilities. You're not going to go there, are you?"

"I'll start with the same jail I went to before, Facility Six. If necessary, I'll try the others."

"Watch yourself, Ben. We don't want an incident."

"We already have an incident."

———

"First you told me he wasn't here at all," Ben said to the woman behind the front desk of Facility Six. "Now you tell me he's *no longer* here?"

"Perhaps he has been released."

"No, he hasn't. I'd know. I'm staying at his house."

"Then he must have been transferred to another facility."

"Fine. Tell me where."

The clerk whispered to a supervisor, then returned. "We do not have this information."

"You mean you're refusing to tell me."

"It is against policy. You must go through legal channels."

"I tried that. No law firm wants to get on the bad side of the PSB."

"I am sorry, Mr. Fielding."

"No you're not. But you're going to be."

———

"What's going on, Johnny? It's been six days since Quan was arrested."

"It's like walking through a maze. You think you're almost there and then you're back where you started. I've got nothing new for you."

"Chi's giving me a tour of the PTE factory outside Shanghai tomorrow. It'll take most of the day. I'll get back to you Friday. We've got to find him. It's like he's disappeared. I don't know what to do, Johnny. I should be back home."

"Yeah, Martin mentions that about three times a day."

"But I can't leave Quan's family," Ben whispered. "Doesn't he understand that?"

"He understands we're trying to run a multinational corporation and his point man is tied up on the other side of the planet in some godforsaken village nobody's ever heard of because it turns out his old college buddy is a member of an illegal cult."

"I've got to find him," Ben said. "I'm starting to wonder if he's . . ."

"Dead?"

"Thanks for your sensitivity, Johnny. I appreciate it."

Ben hung up, then tried to think of what else he could do, who else he could call, what other wheels he could turn. He couldn't think of anything he hadn't tried. His helplessness was punctuated by a gnawing emptiness. He went out to his car, poured a couple of stiff drinks of mao-tai into his teacup, then returned to the house. He sat in the corner, staring at the empty chair. Ming was on the floor in front of it, looking through the pictures in the Bible box. Ben saw pictures of her and Quan and Shen. Then he saw the wedding picture of him and Pam.

Ming looked up at him. "It does not help much, does it?"

"What?"

"Mao-tai."

Ben stared at her.

There are times when it's too hard to be sober.

Ben drove toward Shanghai on November 18. It was Monday, but he couldn't bring himself to review his career goals. If he was going to visualize anything, it was finding Li Quan and getting him out.

Won Chi had given him directions to the PTE factory twenty minutes west of Shanghai. The last thing he wanted to do was tour the plant. He'd seen it six months ago. How much could it have changed? But at least he could tell Martin he'd done it—to prove he wasn't being totally irresponsible by extending his time in China. He strolled into the plant manager's office to meet Chi, greeted respectfully by every worker he saw.

Ben walked with the plant manager and Won Chi over the factory floor on a rope bridge, twenty feet above the workers. Seeing people from above like this gave him a strange sensation. The workers seemed oblivious to their watching eyes. He felt like he stood above the world. It was a completely different perspective.

All the workers in the main factory appeared to be men. There was a separate smaller section with women, but there didn't seem to be access between the sections. The workers were focused and efficient. But their poverty was striking. Though they wore factory uniforms, they were ragged, as were their faces. Like most Chinese, they no doubt put in long hours and were grateful to have this job.

Chi led Ben over to another separated area, where a few dozen men labored over semiconductors. Ben admired their workmanship. While Chi and the plant manager spoke with a supervisor, Ben watched one man assembling a component, his hands moving as quickly as a surgeon's. Ben saw the scalp beneath his thin hair. He wondered about the man's family, who he was, what kind of house he lived in, what his life was like. He wished he could interview him. China had 1.2 billion people, but each was a person, each with his own story. Ben wondered what this man's story was.

"Over here," Won Chi called to Ben. He was about to follow Chi when the man below turned his head to the side to take a closer look at the component he was assembling. The man's ear seemed slightly misshapen. Even from twenty feet Ben noticed his tattered earlobe and underneath it a reddish scar. . . .

"Li Quan?" Ben shouted.

The worker looked up at him, cringing at the sudden sound of a voice from above. He said in a stunned voice, "Ben Fielding?"

28

"OKAY," Johnny said. "Once I told him you made a positive ID on your friend at the factory, my source was on it. He found out Li Quan was transferred a week ago from Pushan to a prison thirty kilometers west of Shanghai."

"Near the factory."

"They probably shuttle them there every morning, then back to prison at night. My source dried up, wouldn't tell me how many other prisoners work in the factory. He sounded nervous. Didn't want to lose his job."

"No one does. Chi claimed he knew nothing about it. I believe him, because otherwise he wouldn't have taken me on the tour in the first place—especially not right where Quan was working. But he wouldn't let me go down and talk to Quan. He and the plant manager escorted me into an office, and the next thing you know they're railroading me out of there. I insisted on going back to where Quan was. By then he was gone. I was ready to knock some heads together. What's going on, Johnny? Why's Quan working at any factory, much less one of ours? Something's rotten in Shanghai."

"Ben, listen, I . . . this isn't the best way to discuss this."

"What do you mean?"

"I mean, I think we should talk face-to-face. I've got two more days in Singapore. I fly into Hong Kong Thursday. Saturday I'll catch a flight to Shanghai. I'll e-mail the specifics—no, wait, I'll fax them to the number you gave me at the locksmith's. Okay? You can pick me up or I'll take a shuttle or taxi."

"No shuttle or taxi's going to get you where I am. I'll meet you at the airport. Can't you give me a hint what this is about?"

"Actually . . . that wouldn't be a good idea."

Ben and Johnny sat in an exclusive Shanghai restaurant, in a far corner with no one dining nearby, at Johnny's request. They looked at the menu and chose quickly, waiting to order.

"I head out Tuesday," Johnny said. "Got to be home for Thanksgiving, you know."

"Thanksgiving?"

"Yeah. It's an American holiday. Pilgrims. Indians. Turkey. Family. You may have heard of it. Guess you're not going to be back, huh?"

Ben shrugged. "Even if I were, I don't know where I'd go. After firing Doug I wouldn't be welcome in that family gathering."

"What about Pam and your girls?"

"Holiday with my ex-wife? We get along fine, but . . . I can always feel the strain, the regret. Maybe I'm better off here."

"You can't mean that."

The waiter came and they ordered, but Ben's mind wasn't on food. As soon as the waiter headed for the kitchen, Ben said, "Okay, Johnny, spill it. What couldn't you talk to me about on the phone?"

"It's the *Laogai*," Johnny whispered.

"The what?"

"Laogai. It's a part of the Chinese economy. Kind of a dirty little secret."

"Sure, I've heard of it, but I've always been assured it's an urban myth. You're saying it's real?"

"Yeah. Forced labor operations. Political and religious dissidents are arrested. Some go to trial; some don't. The government figures, why should we pay to house and feed prisoners? Why not use them productively? Maybe not a bad idea if they were serious criminals and treated decently."

"Who told you all this?"

"Nobody in Pudong Technical Enterprises, that's for sure. They plead ignorance. Let's just say my primary source is three guys in a prestigious Singapore law firm, one of whom worked in Hong Kong until the assimilation. They all know China inside out. They gave me reams of documentation. Took me most of a day to cull through it."

Johnny reached for his big leather briefcase and pulled a thick file labeled *Vacation*.

"Vacation?"

"Yeah. The guys told me this is highly sensitive stuff to bring in-country. So I chose a benign label."

"You're acting like a secret agent, Johnny."

"Tell me about it. One of our Singapore guys had his briefcase rifled in Beijing security. They held him half a day for questioning. Missed his flight to Shenyang. And he wasn't carrying stuff as serious as this." He pushed the file to Ben, right past the soy sauce.

"I appreciate you going the extra mile on this."

Johnny shrugged. "Hey, you're the VP. They say eventually you'll run the show. When you do, give me a nice raise and a new car, and we'll call it even."

"What's this?"

"A page from a book published by China Railways. It's called *Laogai Economics*. You could probably read the Mandarin, but I couldn't, so the next page is the translation."

Ben read it aloud. "'Laogai production serves as a means for reforming prisoners and bears the political obligation of punishing and reforming prisoners. It serves as an economic unit producing goods for society. These dual obligations and dual accomplishments (the reforming of prisoners into new men and the production of material goods) must be advanced and practiced through the entire process of Laogai production.'"

Ben stared at the page, then looked at Johnny.

"That's just page 31 of a whole book," Johnny said. "Up until the early nineties there were lots of books like that. But with international pressure for China to clean up their human rights record, publications like this were suddenly restricted. They're still used internally but they're not supposed to cross the Great Wall, so to speak. What you've got in front of us is officially classified as 'state secrets,'" he whispered. Seeing the waiter coming, he covered it with the file folder.

The waiter poured water and coffee. When he left, Ben uncovered the paper and flipped a few pages while Johnny scooted his chair around to where he could see over Ben's shoulder.

"That one's from the *Criminal Reform Handbook*," Johnny said. "Check out the title page—it's an official state publication, put out by the Ministry of Justice Laogai Bureau. What you're reading isn't a dissident's claims about the Laogai. It's an actual government document."

Ben read aloud, just above a whisper: "'The fundamental task of our Laogai facilities is punishing and reforming criminals. To define their function concretely, they fulfill tasks in the following three ways: (1) punishing criminals and putting them under surveillance; (2) reforming criminals; (3) organizing criminals in labor and production, thus creating wealth for society. Our Laogai units are both facilities of dictatorship and special enterprises.'"

"That's their own wording," Johnny said. "Can you believe it?"

"How many prisoners are we talking about?" Ben asked.

"Nobody knows. At least tens of thousands. Maybe millions. I have it on good authority that one-third of China's tea is produced in Laogai camps." Johnny looked at some handwritten notes. "Sixty percent of China's rubber-vulcanizing chemicals are produced in a single Laogai camp in Shenyang. One of the largest steel pipe works in the country is a Laogai camp. It goes on and on. 'Forced labor is the means; thought reform is the aim.' That's from their own material. The Laogai isn't just a prison system; it's a source of free labor."

"That's a double incentive to put people away," Ben said. "First, to nullify resistance to the Party. Second, to put them to work for the same government that imprisons them."

"Sort of a perverse blend of capitalism and communism," Johnny said.

"So what does this have to do with PTE?"

"It appears they've made some arrangement with the government to employ prisoners. Except they don't pay them. Somebody gets paid—somebody *always* gets paid. But it's not the workers. Maybe they pay wardens or guards or the Party, I don't know."

"So . . . you're telling me Quan is in a prison that daily transports its workers to PTE's factory to do forced labor for our closest business partner in China?"

"Those workers with green shirts you saw on the factory floor, all in that same contained area? Those are probably all prisoners. Political or religious. The attorney in Singapore called it the Chinese gulag. He said no one talks about it—everybody looks the other way."

"And Getz International is partnering in this?"

"Ignorantly, yes. In a funny sort of way, your friend Quan is working for us."

"*Funny* isn't the word that comes to mind. But we're no longer ignorant, are we? Quan works for the Chinese government and for us, but nobody pays him. No salary, no retirement program, no benefits for his family. What it means for Ming and Shen is losing their husband and father and their household income. What it means for Getz is, we're in bed with tyrants. We're a party to slave labor, Johnny. I can hardly believe it."

"The boys in Singapore told me there's a Chinese law allowing sentencing of up to three years with no formal hearing. And the Laogai facilities operate under multiple enterprise names to interact in the commercial arena and avoid detection by international observers. They might be called—" he paused, looking at his notes—"the Hedra Saltworks or the Nampo Metalworks."

"Or the Pudong Technical Enterprises production factory."

"But, Ben," Johnny said, "ultimately, this is China's internal affair. The rest of the world doesn't know about it, and those who do know don't care. And those who do care can't do anything to change it. You're the one who always tells us we can't bully China. We can try to help your friend, but we can't change a corrupt system."

"Really?" Ben said. "Just watch." He punched his cell phone so hard it hurt his fingers.

"How long, O Lord, how long will the wicked be jubilant? They pour out arrogant words, full of boasting. They crush your people; they oppress your inheritance. They slay the widow and the alien; they murder the fatherless. They say, 'The Lord does not see; he pays no heed.'"

The entire gathering of martyrs, Li Manchu and Li Tong included, called out in a loud voice, "How long, Sovereign Lord, holy and true, until you judge the inhabitants of the earth and avenge our blood?"

The King looked from the throne and said to the gathering, "My righteousness draws near. But you must wait a little longer . . . until the last of your brothers is killed for his faith."

"Hi, this is the Fieldings', Kim speaking. Mom and I aren't home now, so please leave a message and we'll get right back to you. Thanks."

"Uh, hi, Kimmy, this is your dad. I hope you got my e-mail a few weeks ago. I was going to be coming home, you know, but there've been some problems. I'm fine, but I had to stay longer. I wanted to see you around Thanksgiving but since I'm still in China, obviously that's not going to happen. Just wanted to tell you I love you. And listen, I don't seem to have Melissa's new number, so could you pass on the message that I said hi to her too? With the phone situation and the time difference here it's probably best not to call, but you can e-mail if you need anything, and I can call you. And, Pam, if you hear this, I hope you're doing okay too. Have a good

Thanksgiving. Hello from the Lis in Pushan. And please say hi to everybody at the family—" Before he could say "get-together," the message cut him off, leaving the word *family* hanging.

Ben leaned back against the headboard in the Zuanshi hotel room where he'd come to get a hot shower and a good night's sleep. He couldn't remember feeling more lonely.

"I read all the stuff you gave me on the Laogai," Ben said to Johnny, who was in Shanghai, ready to fly home the next morning. "I saw a reference to Harry Wu and the Laogai Research Foundation. He's a former Chinese political prisoner. I went on-line and found some info that referred to Wu's site, even gave its address, but I can't get into the site itself. So I called Han in Singapore, and he said the regime regulates the content of all China's Web sites, and even which outside sites you can access."

"Doesn't surprise me."

"Han says the government requires every company using encryption technology to register, and they monitor them. Not only can they watch e-mails, they can censor Web content! Fortunately, he says the Party's finding out they can't control the Web like they control newspapers and television. It's borderless; it's outside the lines. Anyway, about Harry Wu—since I couldn't access the Web site, Han printed out about fifty pages and faxed them to me."

"What do they say?"

"Harry Wu spent nineteen years in the Laogai. He claims the Business Coalition for U.S.–China Trade has totally glossed over the Laogai. I checked them out, and I'm afraid he's right. They spent twelve million dollars lobbying to grant China permanent trade status. They talk about international groups being allowed to visit Chinese prisons but don't mention the State Department's report that says—and I'm quoting this printout—'In all cases of forced labor identified by U.S. Customs, the Chinese Ministry of Justice refused the request for inspection, ignored it, or simply denied the allegations without further elaboration.'"

"Listen, Ben, I need to tell you—"

"There's more, Johnny. Singapore gave me five other Web site addresses on Chinese civil rights violations. I went to a hotel and got a connection, and I couldn't call up a single one. They're blocked out, not just to Quan but to everyone in China, for all I know. Can you imagine? They censor sites that accuse them of censorship. And Han says if the source is in China, they may not just shut the operators down. They can arrest them!"

"Can you prove that?"

"Who knows? Anyway, the Laogai Research Foundation has documented one hundred forced labor camps, which produce eight hundred million dollars in sales. They're listed under pseudonyms in international business directories. They claim there are a thousand more of these camps they're trying to get documentation on. It's unbelievable, Johnny. No due process, no compensation for work, terrible conditions, physical punishment rampant. It's like a horror movie. And Quan's in the thick of it!"

"Ben, listen, you really have to—"

"I'm telling you, Getz is sending the message to the Chinese government: Go ahead and do what you want to these people as long as we make a profit. It's appeasement. It's hypocrisy. We boycotted South Africa for a lot less than this. We're pumping money into China while we look the other way. Free trade is one thing. But partnership? We need to send them a message: If you want our money and technology and partnership, you can't do this."

"Ben, hold on, okay? We had this conversation years ago. We knew what we were getting into. We sat in a management team meeting and went over that poll of five hundred international businesses that named China the most corrupt country in Asia. Remember? We can't change that overnight. The best thing we can do for human rights is what we're doing. Prosperity will bring social reform with it; how many times have you preached that sermon? By doing business with them we pull China into the world community, and that's going to further human rights."

"Or is that doublespeak, Johnny? We further human rights by participating in a business partnership with religious and political prisoners working without pay? Human rights is being furthered by the violation of human rights? We think we can bribe dictators into being nice to people?"

"Look, Ben. Stop right there."

"No, you look. This report talks about the same thing in Iran, Iraq, Myanmar, Sudan. U.S. companies are in bed with governments that are persecuting people! And Getz is right there with them!"

"Ben! Calm down, would you? I've been trying to tell you, but you haven't stopped to take a breath. I met with legal this morning."

"Yeah?"

"Everybody sympathizes with your friend."

"But . . . ?"

"But we can't just pull the plug. What you've done hasn't worked, and we've already jeopardized our partnership with PTE. Won Chi is really upset. We met with the executive committee, and they voted. We're telling you to take no further action. Everybody agreed, including Martin."

Five seconds of silence.

"Ben, are you there? Did you hear what I said?"

"Yeah. I only wish I hadn't."

"Come on, it's just that—"

"It's just that we care more about making money than about human rights."

29

$\mathcal{A}$S GRANDFATHER, father, and son stood shoulder to shoulder, Reader, standing before the portal to the earth, read the ancient words:

> Why do the nations conspire and the peoples plot in vain? The kings of the earth take their stand and the rulers gather together against the Lord and against his Anointed One. "Let us break their chains," they say, "and throw off their fetters."
>
> The one enthroned in heaven laughs; the Lord scoffs at them. Then he rebukes them in his anger and terrifies them in his wrath, saying, "I have installed my King on Zion, my holy hill." I will proclaim the decree of the Lord. He said to me, "You are my Son; today I have become your Father. Ask of me, and I will make the nations your inheritance, the ends of the earth your possession. You will rule them with an iron scepter; you will dash them to pieces like pottery."

Watcher looked down at several hundred faces spread across the earth. These were men, mostly, who resided in palaces and mansions and white houses and royal residences, most of them living in opulence, under the illusion of unbridled power. He raised his voice:

> Therefore, you kings, be wise; be warned, you rulers of the earth. Serve the Lord with fear and rejoice with trembling. Kiss the Son,

lest he be angry and you be destroyed in your way, for his wrath can flare up in a moment. Blessed are all who take refuge in him.

"I believe you didn't know anything about this, Chi," Ben said. "But this man's in jail. As of today, he's been in jail two weeks. Getz is part owner of this factory—we can't be involved in forced labor of political or religious prisoners."

"It is Chinese factory."

"Yes, but we're in partnership. We put up a large part of the money."

"Contract says it is Chinese ownership."

"I'm not arguing with that. I'm just saying . . . this is a very sensitive issue."

"Has the Getz board said this, or is it thinking of Ben Fielding?"

"Well, I've talked with Martin, and he's concerned."

"Mr. Getz called yesterday to assure PTE he doesn't want anything to upset our partnership."

"That's why I'm hoping you'll do what you can to be sure my friend is released."

"I am not a warden. I am a businessman."

"Look, you don't have to agree with these Christians, but they're decent people. They're good citizens."

"Do good citizens break the law?"

"Well, not usually, but—"

"Here, good citizens do not break the law. I have been told Bible says to obey government. Then why does your friend not obey Bible's command?"

"Well, I—"

"Perhaps instead of trying to get business partners to reform Chinese society, Mr. Ben Fielding should ask his good citizen friend to obey what he claims to believe."

"Let it go, Ben," Martin said.

"We were duped into participating in slave labor. How can I let it go?"

"*Slave labor's* pretty extreme, don't you think? So is *participating*. We never agreed to this. We never knew about it."

"Well, we know now."

"Right. And they've assured us this won't happen again, haven't they?

Chi says it's all taken care of." Martin sighed. "Besides, it's a different culture."

"This is wrong in any culture."

"Prisoners in America work, don't they?"

"But they have a choice. And they're compensated, even if it's not much. At least they're taken through due process and convicted and sentenced. And the conditions are decent. It's not the same thing."

"Would you think that if it wasn't your friend?"

"Of course."

"Really? When we first started doing business in China, weren't you Mr. Culturally Sensitive, the one who told us about the Emerging Giant and how we could have this mutually beneficial relationship? *Symbiosis,* you called it, remember? We all laughed at Johnny because he didn't know what it meant—flunked science, I guess. And wasn't it Jack and Doug and some of the sales guys who brought out this whole history of China jailing dissidents, violating human rights, bribery—the whole nine yards? Do you remember what you said when people got cold feet?"

One of the most annoying things about Martin was his memory.

"I said, 'Sure, there are some human rights issues, but they're blown out of proportion. Some of those people are lawbreakers. That's why they're in jail, and we can't assume everything the amnesty groups say is true.' But this is different, Martin. We *do* know it's true. Quan isn't a lawbreaker."

"Not in your eyes. But then, it's not *your* country, is it?"

"I knew these people weren't paid much. But not paid at all? Forced labor?"

"They're criminals. Why not let them be productive?"

"You're telling me this doesn't nag at your conscience?"

"Look, Ben, I feel sorry for your friend and his family. But if we try to force human rights issues, England and France and Germany—not to mention a dozen U.S. companies—are right there to take our business. You said free trade's a human right, and the people will suffer if we try to punish their government. 'Business trumps politics.' You said that. Remember?"

"I still agree with some of that. But maybe I was partly . . . wrong."

There was a long pause as both men considered words Ben had never spoken before.

"Well," Martin said, voice barely restrained, "don't you think it's a little late to have a conscience attack? I mean, first you reassure all of us there aren't any moral reasons to stay out of China and that we'd actually be helping their huddled masses yearning to breathe free. Now you've gotten Getz so dependent on our China trade, if we fall through in Shanghai or Beijing, our stock will drop like a pheasant at a shotgun range. What do you expect me to do? Go to the board and tell them Getz International is going to pull the plug on China because Ben Fielding's college roommate got arrested for breaking Chinese laws?"

"We don't have to pull the plug. But we can't stand by and let them persecute Quan just because he's a Christian."

"Maybe your friend's the problem; did that ever occur to you?"

"What do you mean?"

"Well, you're the one who fired Doug Roberts, aren't you? Wasn't it because his religion made him so obnoxious, people didn't want to work with him?"

"That's not the same thing. Quan's been put in jail. And he's doing slave labor."

"Is that a difference in kind or degree? Okay, we all know Beijing goes overboard, but just like we have to stay on top of our personnel at Getz, they have to stay on top of their citizens. If what somebody thinks is the exercise of his faith interferes with the smooth operation of a business—or in their case, a society—the people in charge have to be able to take action. Of all people, I'd think you'd respect that."

"I can't believe this conversation."

"I can't believe you're willing to hang my company out to dry."

"That's not what this is about."

Martin sighed. "I've got a business to run in the absence of my top VP. What is it you want from me, Ben?"

"Won Chi is stonewalling me. He's covering up. Give me the okay to take this straight to Dexing or someone else in PTE upper management. Anybody but Chi. Clear the way to get me to the PTE factory manager. Send me on behalf of Getz to the PSB chief, the Pushan warden, the mayor, the deputy mayor, the dogcatcher, anybody, everybody."

"Stay away from the mayor's office! I don't want a scene." Martin sighed again. "Okay, go to Dexing. I'll e-mail him and tell him you're just checking things out, trying to help your friend, but we have full confidence in PTE's operation. We know it was an honest mistake. Okay? Tread lightly. Maybe it was just a misunderstanding. Maybe there's only a few prisoners brought in, and maybe it's no big deal. But listen to me, Ben, and listen well. I don't want you to do anything that jeopardizes Getz. You hear me?"

"I hear you."

"I don't want to have to yank you and give the PTE partnership to Jeffrey. I don't want you off the fast track to getting my job when I retire.

But make no mistake—if you take advantage of your position to exploit our partners for your own agenda, your credibility will be gone, and the reputation of Getz International will go down the toilet with it. I'm not going to let that happen, Ben. Bank on it. Our friendship can only take you so far. And, trust me, you're getting near the edge."

Ben chopped down a rotten tree, taking big swings and enjoying the opportunity to smash something hard. He replenished the coal supply, black dust sticking to his sweaty skin. He wiped off what he could, then went to the sink and took a spot bath. He missed his weekly jaunts to the hotel—and missed showers more than anything. In four more days it would be December, two months since he'd left home. He pictured Pam, Melissa, and Kim, probably all at Pam's mom's for Thanksgiving. He wondered . . . were any of them thinking of him?

Ming sat on the floor looking at family pictures again. He saw her put her finger on a picture of Quan at the locksmith's shop.

Ben poured a glass of water and sat on the floor. "You and Quan seem very much in love."

Her face flushed red. Her eyes flickered, but before she looked down Ben saw the unmistakable tugging of the smile on the edges of her lips.

"Yes," she said with a girlish voice. "Very much."

"Pam and I were in love too, once. It seems like a long time ago." The moment he said it, he regretted it. Ming looked at him. He saw the pity in her eyes and squirmed.

"Quan knew you both in college," Ming said slowly. "He does not understand why you would divorce."

Ben shrugged. "Things happen. People change. We stopped loving each other."

"What does this mean?"

"We lived our own lives. I had my career, golf, tennis. She had her writing, aerobics, the kids. You know how it is."

Ming gazed at him, face blank. Clearly she didn't know how it was.

"Did not your children bring you together?"

"For a time, I guess."

"And do you not face difficulty together, hostility from the world, persecution that makes you stand together?"

"We had hard times. Real hard. But hostility, persecution? No. Those aren't that common in America."

Ming nodded. "Perhaps that was problem."

"I've never thought of lack of hostility and persecution as a problem."

"Wife and husband must be more than lovers. Must be comrades, soldiers fighting side by side for same great cause. Ming's mother say, 'Wife and husband should not only lie down face-to-face, but stand up shoulder to shoulder.' They must face together the worst Mogui can do to them. And when they draw strength of Yesu, he bind them together."

"That's what happened to you and Quan?"

"We depend on each other, need each other. Quan tell me couples in America speak very openly of love. But also that they lose love and move from person to person. This I do not understand. Ming miss Quan as lover," she said, voice quivering. "But especially as friend and comrade."

Ben thought about his poor unsuccessful roommate, whose professional dreams had been dashed, who made a hundredth of Ben's income and now sat in some godforsaken jail. What shocked Ben was the particular feeling he had toward Quan at this moment. He felt envy.

"Good news," Johnny said. "As a result of shining the light on this thing, my source tells me they've transferred Li Quan back to Pushan Facility Six."

"Transferred? Not released?"

"It's a step in the right direction, isn't it?"

"The Pushan police chief has it in for him. I don't know how much influence he has at the jail, but . . ."

"If you're telling me he'd be better off working in the factory, you're a little late!"

"Sorry, Johnny. I really appreciate everything you've done. At least Getz is in the clear. With Quan, anyway. Who knows how many other prisoners still work there."

"I don't think I want to know," Johnny said.

"Now that he's back in Pushan, I'll be there at Facility Six tomorrow. They'll have to let me visit him."

"I don't think they *have* to let you do anything. But while you knock on doors at your end, I'll check with my source. I hope we can get you access to your friend." Johnny cleared his throat. "There's one more thing, Ben. I'm not sure how to say this."

"What?"

"My source got a photocopy of the charges against Li Quan. I had someone translate it for me. Not much new, except one thing. According to this report, there was someone else who relayed the information that

Li Quan is illegally teaching Christianity to his underage son. That's one of the most serious charges against him. It's a major criminal offense."

"Who made the accusation?"

"Well, the report was filed by our own PTE partner Won Chi. But it lists as his source of information . . . Ben Fielding."

30

FTER AN HOUR at the front desk of Facility Six, citing his business credentials and demonstrating his fluency in Mandarin, Ben was escorted by an armed guard to the edge of an eight-foot cyclone fence with a line of barbed wire woven through each diamond-shaped opening. The guard outside spoke to one inside, who disappeared through a shadowy door into the cell block.

Ben knew his ticket to see Quan was that he was a prominent American working in a business producing profits for China. If not for his Getz connection, he'd have never gotten this far. He needed to play his cards right and give them a reason to let him visit Quan until he could get him out.

Even here, forty feet from the nearest building, the cell blocks smelled like a skid-row mattress. After ten minutes, the guard reappeared, escorting a pale, bent-over man. Li Quan! The moment he saw him, Ben felt simultaneous relief and shock. His meticulous roommate, who'd parted with Chinese custom by showering regularly in college, still wore the same clothes he'd been arrested in two and a half weeks ago. Only now they were smeared and crusted with dirt. Other than the work shirt in the factory, Ben wondered if this was all he'd had to wear.

Quan poked his index finger through the fence.

Ben squeezed it. "How are you doing?"

Quan smiled and nodded. "Zhu Yesu is faithful."

"I brought you clothes from Ming." Ben held up the duffel bag, then opened it and pulled out a long-sleeved light blue shirt, tan pants, socks, and brown leather casual shoes. Quan's eyes lit up when he saw a blanket left inside the bag.

"I hope they let me keep them. It is cold."

"I'll figure out a way," Ben said. "There's a big water bottle in here, too."

"Fresh water would be good. My cell mates would be grateful." He looked Ben in the eyes. "Why are you still in China?"

"Did you think I'd leave you in jail without doing something to get you out?"

"Ben Fielding is even more powerful than I thought if he can get me out of a Chinese jail."

Ben looked at the guard, standing only six feet behind Quan. He switched from Mandarin to English. "You?"

Quan shrugged. "Not much food. Less since I've stopped working at the factory."

"I guess it's my fault you're not there."

"Here, we only sit in a cell. We don't need much food. But we were each given an egg yesterday. My cell mates taught me to crush the eggshell into powder and drink it down in water, for the calcium."

Ben choked. "It must be hard not to have good . . . cleaning facilities. The Quan I knew used to wash his hands after petting a dog."

"Perhaps I am no longer the Quan you knew."

"Ming had your bag packed the night they arrested you. She said you knew they were coming."

"One of our . . . friends at PSB saw my name on an arrest list. The word was passed to me."

"Did you think of running?"

"Only for a moment. But I do not want them to harass Shen and Ming. It will be hard enough for Shen at school. I know how hard."

"Why did they arrest you?"

"When you go up to the mountain too often, you eventually encounter the tiger. It was only a matter of time before I was caught. But I have been arrested before. Each time, they have let me out."

"Ming said once it was eight months?"

"Less this time, I hope. How is my family?"

"They're doing well. They miss you."

"Tell them I miss them, please. And tell them . . . it is not all bad here. There are many Christians. I can speak the gospel and have brothers to worship with. Some guards are very cruel. Some are not so bad. We pray for them."

"It must be awful."

"No, not awful. Difficult. It is not worst for me. A guard told one of the brothers there is a pastor in a lower cell block here who has been imprisoned alone in darkness. He has not seen the sun for six months."

"Six months?"

"I have heard many stories from my new friends. In some villages Christians are unharmed. In others, they are beaten and their houses destroyed. In one village, a brother was crucified. In another, a sister was doused with gasoline and burned. One told of Christians being buried alive, but that is worse than anything I have ever seen. This prison is not so bad. Compared to the winter of persecution in my father's day, this is the spring."

"I still can't believe they have prisoners doing forced commercial labor," Ben said.

"I have heard of the Laogai factories, but this is the first time I have been transported to one. Yet I have done commercial labor in jail before. Two years ago I was arrested at an orchard seminary. The other prisoners and I were put to work gluing boxes. We each had to complete two hundred boxes a day or be beaten. Five years ago I was in another prison. Every day I assembled Christmas lights."

"Christmas lights?"

"My quota was three thousand lights per day. When I went over quota two days in a row, they increased it to four thousand. I had difficulty seeing clearly and failed to meet my quota. I was beaten. The next day I started at sunrise and worked by candle until 11:00 P.M. That's how long it took to make quota. I did it every day for seventeen hours."

"This is the time of year Christmas lights go up back home. But I didn't even know Chinese used them—obviously not for Christmas?"

"I was told these were sent to America, to be sold there. Do you use Christmas lights, Ben?"

"I haven't celebrated Christmas the last few years. But when Pam and I and the kids were still together, yeah, we put up Christmas lights."

"Then perhaps you put up lights assembled by your old roommate."
Ben stared at him, weighing the words.

"Did some of the bulbs fail to work?" Quan asked.

"Yeah. Every year we had a few problems."

"Ah, then they were not the ones I put together," he said, grinning. "For Li Quan was the finest assembler of Christmas lights in all China."

"I'll bet you were," Ben said.

The guard grabbed Quan's shoulder and yanked him back, then herded him toward the brick doorway.

"I'll get you out," Ben called. "I promise."

Quan disappeared into the doorway's darkness. Ben approached an outside guard six feet away. He asked him if he would take the duffel bag to Li Quan's cell. The man shook his head. Ben pulled out of his pocket three American twenty-dollar bills and handed them to him. The guard nodded and took the bag.

———————

Ben leaned against the ginkgo tree while a group of women prayed with Ming in the house. Shen was at school.

Finally the women exited the house like a swarm of giggling bees; three got on bicycles, while four more walked down the road toward the main highway. Ben entered.

"I'm glad you have women to pray with. But I feel like I need to do more."

"What could you do that is more than prayer?" Ming asked.

"I need to rattle some cages."

She cocked her head at the senseless words. "It is not so cold today. Would Ben Fielding like to have tea by the ginkgo tree?"

Minghua made the green tea, poured it, and took two cups on a little tray out to the tree. They sat right beneath the carved heart with Ming's and Quan's initials. Ming seemed comfortable with the silence. Ben was not.

"What's it like here for women?" Ben asked. "Is it true what they say?"

"What do they say?"

"Well, when the international conference on women was held in Beijing, there was a lot of controversy. Some delegates from Western countries said women here are oppressed. I'm sure you heard about all the protests at the conference."

"I heard nothing of the conference at all."

"Nothing?"

"There is much happening in China that Chinese do not know about! And much that we know about, perhaps, that does not happen." She laughed. "But please tell Chan Minghua more about this conference."

"Well, to be honest—I hope this doesn't offend you—one of the big themes was how religion, especially Christianity, has held women down."

"I do not understand."

"The presenters said Christianity teaches that men are superior and women are inferior."

Ming stared at Ben incredulously, like someone who would call him an idiot on the spot if she weren't so kindhearted.

"Perhaps they speak of Confucianism? Old proverb say when son born he should be given a piece of jade to play with. But when daughter is born she should be given only broken piece of pottery. Buddhism and Communism have same view of women. Mao Zedong said, 'Women hold up half the sky.' But these were only words—everyone knows men are always considered more important."

"It must have been hard growing up with that view of women."

She tilted her head. "I did not grow up with that view of women."

"You grew up in China, didn't you?"

"I grew up in Christian home. I grew up in church." She smiled broadly. "Minghua's father and mother gave her jade." She laughed. "Of course, we could not afford jade. But my brother and I were equal. I never felt parents loved me less. Does Ben Fielding not know that for years pregnant Chinese got a test? The tests are illegal now, but bribes still get them done. When test shows baby is a girl, parents kill her because they want boys. Believers in Yesu will not kill their daughters. They did not mention this at conference in Beijing?"

"No, I don't think so."

"Did they talk about how missionaries taught Chinese to respect women?"

"Uh, actually, I think those conferences tend to see missionaries as . . . a big part of the problem."

She shook her head. "Quan could say better, because his great-grandparents came to Yesu under missionaries. But with the gospel came first teaching that men and women equal in God's sight. The missionaries insisted as much medical care be given women as men. They made sure girls were given education as good as boys. The missionaries opened first school for girls. Later, they started women's colleges. Quan's aunt went to one before it was shut down by the Communists."

"But I thought the Chinese government built the first women's schools."

"Oh, no. They made schools only after missionaries."

"Tell me about the one-child policy."

"Very hard. Very cruel." She looked down. "After give birth to Shen they sterilize Chan Minghua."

"I'm sorry."

"Ming's sister is Yaomei. Her only child—a little girl—died, but she had been sterilized too. Can never have another."

"It must be hard for her."

"Ben and Pam Fielding have had three children?"

"Two still living."

"Great blessing. Shengjing say so."

"I've heard about enforced abortions for second or third children. Is it true?"

"In village of Caidian, central Hubei province, fourth baby drown by family planners in paddy field outside home, in front of parents. Waiting for them in their home after return from hospital. People angry so officials were punished. But if they had done it quietly, nothing would be said. Yes, many forced abortions. In some villages, posses formed to round up pregnant women in trucks and drag them to clinics to kill children. Very horrible."

Ben remembered several occasions when he'd defended China's one-child policy. He was glad Ming couldn't hear what he'd said.

"Not easy to raise one child. Do not want him to be a spoiled 'Little Emperor,' like so many boys. Minghua worry whether Shen ever have wife."

"Why?"

"Sex-selection abortions. Many more boys now than girls, many millions more. Very sad. Make God very angry. Zhou Jin say China must be judged. Shengjing say God judge all nations who kill their children. Did they speak of this at Beijing conference?"

"I'm pretty sure they didn't."

"Did they tell about foot binding? I remember Grandmother's bound feet. I saw her wash them. Very small and pointed. All her toes bent over to one side. Girls had feet bound when they were only a few years old. It was believed that the smaller a woman's feet, the more beautiful she was. Those who failed to bind feet had hard time finding husband. Very cruel. But missionaries taught people not to bind feet."

"Strange. All I've heard about the missionaries is that they didn't respect Chinese culture."

"They did not respect foot binding. Did not respect teaching that women inferior and should not be educated. Did not respect child brides and prostitution. The missionaries were mostly women, you know."

"I didn't know. I guess there's a lot I don't know about China— especially about Christians."

"Because missionaries taught women as well as men, when most male pastors sent to prison and labor camps, women took their places. Government thought if they arrest men, church will die. Very wrong. Wish we had more men pastors. But when men are in prison, women must step forward. Most Christians in China are women. Church is only place men and women truly equal." Ming smiled broadly. "In China, government has given women broken pottery. Yesu has given us jade."

31

Q UAN, YOU LOOK AWFUL."

"Many thanks to Ben Fielding for his encouraging opinion of old roommate's appearance."

"I'm not joking. This is taking a toll on you and your family. It's December now—and getting colder all the time."

"Yes, I have noticed."

"I have to ask—is it really worth it?"

"To do right is always worth it. Not always today. But always tomorrow. Does Ben Fielding think it would be worth it?"

Ben felt the weight of the question and pushed it off. "Pastor Zhou Jin told me there was no way I'd be allowed to see you again."

"I am also surprised. It is rare enough that families are allowed to visit. But a foreigner? I've never seen it. Someone with power in Facility Six must believe it is to their advantage. Or perhaps it is a miracle."

"Well, as long as they let me, I'm coming back." Ben felt guilty not mentioning the bribes, but he knew Quan would disapprove. "Can I ask you something, Quan?"

"As you can see, I am a very busy man with many demands on my time." Quan smiled. "But yes, you can ask me."

"Is it right to disobey the government?" Ben peeked below the strand of barbed wire at eye level.

"I disobey my government every time I pray with my family before a meal."

"But doesn't the Bible tell us to obey the government?"

"My old roommate remembers so little of the Bible, but this

admonition he remembers? Or perhaps someone has reminded him?
What you fail to remember are the many examples where godly men
and women broke the law. Daniel's three friends would not worship the
emperor instead of their God. Hebrew midwives, Moses' parents, Rahab,
courageous Obadiah who rescued the prophets from Queen Jezebel,
Esther who trespassed in the king's court to rescue the Jews, the Magi
who disobeyed King Herod to protect the baby Jesus. I have studied these
Scriptures and taught them in our orchard seminary."

"I'm not familiar with all that. But civil disobedience seems pretty
extreme. Not to mention costly for you and your family."

"What is legal is not always right," Quan said. "What is illegal is not
always wrong. We obey government because Paul and Peter say government is an instrument of God. But when it acts in violation of God's law,
that is different. The apostles said, 'We must obey God rather than men!'
Jesus, Peter, and Paul all went to jail. They were all executed as criminals,
breakers of the law. When laws are unjust, just men must break them.
When caught, they will go to jail." Quan stared at him. "Ben Fielding
asked question of me. Now I will ask question of him."

"Okay."

"Why does my old friend care what the Bible says about disobeying
government, when he cares so little what it says about other things?"

"What do you mean?"

"Marriage. Church. Obedience to Yesu. These things and others."

Ben pulled away from the wire. "Who appointed you my judge?"

"God is your judge. I am your friend. Friends warn each other when
they walk wrong paths."

A loud scream erupted, and both men turned toward the outside of the
main gate. A young woman was waving her arms at a prison guard,
speaking so fast that Ben couldn't understand her.

"What's going on?" Ben asked.

"Her husband, Wen Zhiyuan, never came home. She's screaming,
'Where is he? Where is he?'"

The guards tried to subdue her, but she was inconsolable.

"I know her husband, Zhiyuan," Quan said. "He was in the cell across
from mine. Last week they took him to the hospital for a checkup—he
never returned. We hoped he was released."

"What was his medical problem?"

"He had no medical problem. He was tired and had been beaten, like
many of us. Perhaps a little malnourished. But otherwise, he seemed
healthy. In any event, they do not take us to the hospital for treatment—
for anything."

"But why . . . ?"

"I do not know, Ben. But there is talk."

"What kind of talk?"

"I cannot say if it is true."

"Tell me what you've heard."

"One day they chose six of us and took us to the prison medical office. They gave all of us blood tests."

"Why?"

"I, too, asked why it was the six of us and not the other prisoners."

"What's the answer?"

"The only thing I could think is that of all the prisoners, we appeared to be among the most healthy."

"That doesn't make sense."

"Perhaps."

"Quan, tell me what you're thinking!"

"It has been reported that authorities sell organs of executed prisoners to meet the demand for transplants."

"They're not planning to execute you!"

"No. But it is also common knowledge that some prisoners die suddenly and mysteriously."

Just then the guard stepped over and put his hand on Quan. While Ben watched helplessly, he pulled him away.

The King looked down through the transparent floor of the throne room, eyes on the earth's Far East. "I will call them 'my people' who are not my people; and I will call her 'my loved one' who is not my loved one. It will happen that in the very place where it was said to them, 'You are not my people,' they will be called 'sons of the living God.'

"Turn to me, people of that great and ancient nation. Remember what you knew long ago. Listen to those I have sent with my message. Come through this open door before I forever close it."

While Minghua was with Shen at a school ceremony, Ben took advantage of the opportunity to type out his latest interview insights. His next trip to the hotel he'd try to e-mail them to Martin and the board. Though he was taking accrued vacation time now, he was doing everything he could think of to justify to Getz his still being in China. He kept reminding them he hadn't taken full vacation time for years.

He'd had the door open for hours to clear out the stuffiness. Every once in a while he would look out at the ginkgo tree, the breeze blowing its great boughs. They seemed to beckon him somewhere. But where? He looked up now. A man stood in the doorway.

Ben jumped up and stared at his visitor. A moment ago, he hadn't been there. The tiny old man's tuft of white hair blew to the side. His furrowed face suggested a life of hardship. Yet he had an almost childlike look.

"I seek Li Quan," said the light, airy voice.

"Li Quan is not here. I am his friend, Ben Fielding."

"I am Wang Shaoming."

His stooped shoulders and crooked knees sent one message, his fiery eyes another. Skin almost translucent, his veins bulged, looking like they could spill blood any moment. Wang Shaoming reached his hand out to Ben. It felt like a cowhide glove, rough and weathered. In comparison, Ben's own hand seemed as smooth as a little girl's.

Shaoming's fossilized body couldn't move across the room without a continuous sequence of starts and stops. Finally he sat down, relieving Ben more than himself. As he sat, Ben heard the creaks. Ben got him a glass of water. Shaoming's hair moved almost imperceptibly when he turned his head, as if an invisible wind blew upon him. This reminded Ben of Pastor Zhou Jin.

"Quan told me about you, I think," Ben said. "Are you the evangelist to the mountain villages?"

He looked at Ben, then slowly smiled, showing two front teeth surrounded by gaps. "I take gospels and literature, but most of the mountain people cannot read. So I read Shengjing to them, or recite it." He stared at Ben. "You are wondering, how does this breathing corpse travel hundreds of kilometers a year without an automobile or even a bicycle?"

"The mountains are rugged, aren't they?"

"The mountains are not so rugged when the Father's bidding draws you forward, the Son walks beside you, and the Spirit empowers you to put one foot in front of the other."

"Why do you go?"

"Because I am alive. When Yesu wants me to take his message no more, he will let me know. When I die, that will be a sign he wishes me to do something else." He smiled, barely visible because his head was hanging. "I will likely die in those mountains. But Yesu may yet have other mountains for me to climb." Ben slouched down in time to see Shaoming's eyes gleam.

"Why not send younger men?"

He slowly raised his head, fighting gravity and barely winning. "Romans tells us persecution and hardship cannot separate us from Yesu's love. But Revelation warns us wealth and comfort can cause us to lose our love for him. I cannot get the younger men to go with me. They want to travel on buses and trains. They think even thirty kilometers is a long walk. They are soft. Most have spent no more than a few weeks in jail. They know nothing of suffering."

"Do you have to walk?"

"Buses and trains do not go there. No roads. Too steep and rocky for bicycle. Messenger must walk. Young church leaders want power and fame and wealth. They want to meet with rich foreigners, be invited overseas, send their children to your colleges."

"Does anyone else go to the mountains?"

"From Pushan, only Wang Shaoming. Four from other towns. Old women or men like me. I see them sometimes. We have tea and tell stories of God's great works." He smiled again, the gaps in his teeth somehow accentuating the expression of joy. He looked like a delighted child wandering around Disneyland. "I wish others would come with me. For many times I have witnessed the hand of God."

"What do you mean?"

He closed his eyes, as if trying to choose which story to tell. The eyes opened. "There is a village, An Ning, on the other side of the mountain. The pastor there is Fu Chi, he with the long scar. Pastor Fu came to Yesu when I visited there two years ago. He knew how to read. I left him a Bible. When I returned two months ago, I came to share the gospel with those living in darkness. But I could not."

"Why?"

"Because there was no one left walking in darkness. All had come to the light." He smiled. "This makes it difficult to evangelize. Now they are breaking up their village, spreading out to make converts. Pastor Fu Chi has left to seek Bible training wherever he can."

"How big is the village?"

"No more than two thousand."

"Two thousand people? And they all became Christians?"

"Only God knows the heart. But they all claim now to follow Yesu."

"How long have you been going to the mountains?"

"Guan Mei and I were married fifty-five years ago. After our wedding, we were given a week away from the factory. That is when we made our first trip to the mountains, carrying gospel booklets. Few could read, but all could listen. We found ways to speak to the deaf as well. Most of the villages are small. Before leaving we made sure everyone had heard about Yesu. Then we moved on. We had gone to only four villages before we had to return to the factory. We walked straight to work without sleeping, but though we hurried, we were one hour late for our shift. We were docked the whole day's pay. But it did not matter." Shaoming's eyes glowed. "In the mountains twelve people had become followers of Yesu."

"That was your honeymoon?"

"It was glorious," he said. "We kept each other warm under the face of God. And now I speak to the children and grandchildren of those I first went to with my Guan Mei."

He bowed his head low.

"How often have you gone on these trips?"

"When we were young it was hard to leave work for more than a few days at a time, and we could reach only the lower villages. Of course, we could walk much faster then. Sometimes we ran, to cover more ground before having to return to the factory. We laughed as we ran, Guan Mei trying to outrun me and I pretending she could. But—" he sucked in air—"I was not always pretending." His eyes watered as he laughed silently. Ben laughed with him.

"Guan Mei got out of prison first. She traveled alone to the mountains, living on whatever people could feed her."

"How long were you in prison?"

"Sixteen years. Guan Mei only nine. Her sister raised our children. They were able to visit Guan Mei a few times a year. Never me. But they prayed for us. And they became great soldiers of Yesu. Our son is home now. Our daughter is an evangelist in Hunan province. Far better evangelist than Wang Shaoming. More dedicated. Also, walks much faster! Very proud to be her father."

"Li Quan is in prison. We hope he'll be home soon."

He sighed, then lifted his eyes and said, "Zhu Yesu, we lift up to you brother Li Quan. Give him ministry. Give him congregation." He paused.

Ben squirmed, hoping he wasn't expecting him to pray. "I've been thinking a lot about Quan in prison. What was it like for you?"

"Place of great learning. One of the prisoners had Shengjing. He taught us from it and somehow hid it from guards. We memorized portions. I memorized the New Testament."

"The whole thing?"

Shaoming smiled. "I had sixteen years in that seminary. During the days when I dug trenches and moved rocks I recited the words until I could remember them."

"Prison labor must have been hard."

Shaoming shrugged, appearing to weigh his words. "I do not speak often of it. We rejoiced that we were counted worthy to suffer for the sake of Yesu. By the time Shaoming released, children had grown up. Returned with Guan Mei to mountains. In the seven years she was out of prison before I returned, three hundred mountain people came to Yesu. Because I had been trained in God's Word while in prison, I could teach the many mountain churches, help them memorize the book. God graciously trained me so I could teach those Guan Mei had evangelized."

"Did you go back to work at the factory?"

"No. Mountain people and house church supported our work. We needed only food and shoes and one set of clothes each. We lost house when we went to jail. This freed us to travel."

"Where do you live?"

"When here, I live with house church families. In mountains, I stay with whoever offers. When traveling in between, I stay in the houses of believers. Or sleep by road."

"By the road?"

"More comfortable than prison . . . and I can see the stars, the face of God. If too cold to sleep, spend night worshiping."

Ben had never seen such a clear division between a man's body and spirit. Old Wang Shaoming struck him as a great warrior undercover, disguised in an old man's body. He felt drawn to him in a way he'd never have expected and couldn't explain.

"Where is your wife?"

His eyes brightened. "She is at home with our son."

"Where is your home?"

"Very far from here. Very far. Yet sometimes very near."

"How long does it take you to get home?"

"Will take but a moment."

"I don't understand."

"Wang Shaoming's home is somewhere he has never been. It is very far away, but when it is time, he will go there and meet his Master and see his beloved Guan Mei."

"Are you . . . talking about heaven?"

He laughed. "What else would I talk about? It is the only home I have. My wife is there. My son is there. My daughter will one day be there."

"Your son is dead?"

"Died in prison. They could not keep him quiet. He was like his mother. Wang Shaoming is unworthy of them—and of his daughter, the great evangelist. He is honored to be named with them."

Ben brushed his fingers across his cheek. "Where will you stay tonight?"

"Wherever Yesu provides."

"Would you spend the night here?" Ben asked. "My cot is comfortable. I can sleep on the floor. I know Ming won't mind."

"Wang Shaoming can sleep anywhere. The floor is fine." He smiled. "Perhaps I will sleep better if I bring in a few rocks to lie on."

"Please—sleep in my cot."

The old man nodded and stared into Ben's eyes. "You are most kind, servant of Yesu."

Ben squirmed. "You're welcome to stay as long as you like."

"One night only. Tomorrow I go back to the mountain people, to train them in Shengjing. Ben Fielding speaks good Mandarin. Perhaps he would like to come with Wang Shaoming and see for himself what Yesu is doing. I would welcome a strong companion. You could be a son to me, and I a father to you. Yes, yes, I think Yesu wants Ben Fielding to come with me."

"I can't. I'm busy with . . . other things. But I have a car. Can I drive you somewhere in the morning?"

"Can drive me to road's end, where cannot go farther but on foot. Will save two days' walking. This means I will be able to begin teaching Yesu's Word two days earlier. If you do this, Wang Shaoming will be in Ben Fielding's debt. Zhu Yesu will reward you. He repays all the debts of his servants."

32

THOUGH COLD OUTSIDE, Quan's cell was near the boiler. When it was on, the cell jumped quickly from frigid to hot. Sweat poured from Quan, stinging his eyes.

The loud coughing a few cells down yanked him awake. It sounded like tuberculosis. Yet that could be a blessing for a prisoner, Quan knew. The guards were not eager to interrogate or beat prisoners with contagious diseases. He prayed for Eli, his name for the coughing man.

Quan listened to Tai Hong and flinched. His voice had an unnerving ring to it, a fierce, grating sound with an ice-cold, otherworldly resonance. Now Quan heard a scream, then a low moan. As always, this triggered his prayers. At first the screams and moans had been indistinguishable, but after a while he'd begun to recognize the voices, and even the moans. He gave names to the voices, guessed how many cells away each might be. He prayed for them by the names he'd given them.

But this was a new voice. And yet . . . it sounded familiar. It was baritone, with a distinctive rasp. Where had he heard the voice of Silas?

He heard the dull thud of a stick being beaten across flesh, followed by Silas's moans. Quan prayed for him. But he could not bear to think the man might die without having heard of Yesu. Suddenly, Quan stepped to the opening and cried out, "Believe in Zhu Yesu Jidu and you will be saved."

He did not stop. He yelled Scripture after Scripture until his voice was hoarse.

He heard the guard moving down the smelly corridor. He sat down. Someone fumbled at the door, swearing at him. Quan coughed hard, spitting just as the man rushed in. He stared into the eyes of Tai Hong. Quan's bones turned to water.

"You do not fool me with coughing, Li Quan. You do not have a disease . . . except your diseased religion!"

Tai Hong calmly removed his shiny Rolex watch—a bribe that had purchased someone's freedom or torture, Quan did not know which. Tai carefully put it in his front pants pocket.

He moved his face an inch from Quan's and screamed, lips barely quivering. Quan could not believe the voice was Hong's own. It sounded more like the voice of the Lamaistic priest who'd thrown Ben to the ground, but higher pitched. Hong raised up a thick oak stick, then turned it and swung his arm underhanded, punching Quan in his stomach so hard that he could not breathe. While Quan was still gasping, Tai Hong kicked him in the groin. Then he stripped off Quan's pants and beat him below the waist, again and again and again.

Tai Hong's face was smooth, flawless—the perfect, placid face of evil.

When Quan looked at that face, he saw a black yawning hole, like the mouth of a railroad tunnel that disappears into the darkness. Li Quan was afraid of death and ashamed of his fear. The scream he heard now was his own.

Only two dozen men on earth could hear his scream. Five of them prayed for Li Quan, including the one with the deep, raspy voice, though none knew his name. They knew him only as "the singing man"—called Silas by Quan—at the far end of the cell block.

"They do not know the one they are praying for," said Li Tong.

"But they know the One they are praying to. That is what matters," said Li Manchu.

"This PSB chief is infuriated by the word of King Elyon," said Li Wen.

"Yes. Because it has the power to set men free, even within their cells. Those who live by power cannot stand to have their power taken."

"But soon all their power will be gone anyway. And all the suffering of Elyon's family, forever gone. He promises to wipe away the tears from every eye."

"He always keeps his promises."

Li Tong looked at the Carpenter, a hundred feet from them, scarred hands lifted out toward the portal, tears streaming down his face. "But who will wipe away his own tears?"

"When his children's tears are gone, his will be too."

Li Manchu whispered, "How long, O Lord? How long?"

"The longer the night lasts," said Li Wen, "the more men dream of the dawn."

"*Zhen jin bu ba huo lian,*" said Li Tong. "Real gold fears no fire. My son is real gold."

They fell to their knees, facing the Man of Sorrows who was their King. They spoke on behalf of his servant, Li Quan.

Tai Hong hovered over Li Quan's broken body. "Do you think I am afraid of your God? If you will not stop talking about your religion, I will see that you are put in the lower cell blocks, in solitary confinement, where you can talk to yourself!"

Hong put his Rolex back on. Before leaving the cell, he drew back his heavy boot and kicked Li Quan in the ribs one last time.

One question repeated itself within the aching mind of Li Quan: *Is this the day I die?*

Reader gazed through the portal and spoke passionately:

> Arise, O Lord, in your anger; rise up against the rage of my enemies. Awake, my God; decree justice. O righteous God Most High, who searches minds and hearts, bring to an end the violence of the wicked and make the righteous secure. In his arrogance the wicked man hunts down the weak, who are caught in the schemes he devises. In his pride the wicked does not seek you. In all his thoughts there is no room for God. His ways are always prosperous; he is haughty. He sneers at all his enemies. He says to himself, "Nothing will shake me." He lies in wait near the villages; from ambush he murders the innocent, watching in secret for his victims. He lies in wait like a lion in cover; he lies in wait to catch the helpless; he catches the helpless and drags them off in his net. His victims are crushed, they collapse; they fall under his strength. He says to himself, "God has forgotten; he covers his face and never sees."

Arise, Lord! Lift up your hand, O God. Do not forget the helpless. Why does the wicked man revile God? Why does he say to himself, "He won't call me to account." But you, O God, do see trouble and grief; you consider it to take it in hand. The victim commits himself to you; you are the helper of the fatherless.

Li Tong looked at Li Manchu. "Day and night the watchers cry out to our King, but still he has not moved his hand."

"He has moved his hand every moment of every day and in the darkest passes of the night," Li Manchu said. "But not as we always wish, nor in ways clearly visible to us—and certainly not visible to them."

"But his is a throne of justice. How can justice be so long postponed?"

"His is also a throne of grace. The grace is not only to the persecuted, but to the persecutors. If the postponement of justice for one more day brings more image-bearers—whether persecuted or persecutors—to grace, so be it."

"You are right, of course. Even here, the waiting is not easy. But it is far harder for those still trapped in the Shadowlands."

"Yes. But with the King a thousand years is as a day. Ask the earth-dwellers a million years from now if their momentary suffering was an acceptable exchange for eternal glory."

Li Tong nodded. "As inhabitants of the true country, it is our privilege to already know the answer to that question."

"Okay, Won Chi. Since it seems so important, I'll get the car back by Saturday. I don't suppose you have another one I can use?"

"All other cars needed by PTE."

"There were plenty before, and suddenly they're all needed, huh?"

There was no answer.

"Look, Chi, I don't know what people are telling you, but my friend should be released from jail. I'm not going to back off on this. I've talked to the mayor's office, and I've made dozens of other phone calls. If I have to call the garbage collectors, I'll do that. So, yes, you can have your car back. I'll rent my own. But you can tell whoever you've been talking to that I'm not giving up on Li Quan. I've got a new set of life goals—number one is getting my friend out of jail. This isn't about Getz anymore. This is personal."

33

*A*FTER TWO DAYS of phone calls and visits to government offices in Pushan, Ben drove toward Facility Six. It was Friday morning, December 7. He tried to review his life goals, but once again he couldn't stay focused. How could he center himself on becoming CEO of Getz in three years when he didn't even know if Quan would be out of jail by then? Though he'd said it to Won Chi in anger, it was true. His compelling goal now—the thing that fueled his thoughts and actions and overshadowed his life—was Li Quan's freedom.

Ben drove to a back area, out of sight, as a prison official had instructed him over the telephone. He located three broken bricks near a wire gate, lifted them, and put underneath an envelope with the money. Then he went through the gate and past two guards, who nodded slightly as if to say, "We were told you were coming." He walked around back toward the high fence through which he'd spoken twice with Quan. Ben watched a prisoner picking up garbage with a pointed stick on the inside grounds. The man came near the fence, looked at Ben, then used the stick to draw in the sandy dirt. He drew the sign of a fish.

Ben looked around and saw a thin, broken branch. He picked it up, then drew his own fish on the ground, not as distinct as the prisoner's. The man smiled at him approvingly. But behind him came a tall, thin guard, looking over the man's shoulder onto the ground. Ben pointed to warn the man, hoping he would wipe out the sign with his foot. He didn't. The guard took the man's stick and held it. Then he, too, looked both ways, put the stick to the ground, and drew his own fish.

The guard went to the cell block building, bent his head, and disappeared. Within five minutes Quan emerged, this time with manacles on his wrists.

"Why did they put those on you?"

"Tai Hong ordered this to cause discomfort or humiliate. But I take them off at night when sleeping."

"You have a key?"

"No. But I found a firm wire. Li Quan is very good with locks." He smiled.

"But you're still trapped in a cell."

"Zhu Yesu will free me in his time."

Quan and Ben both looked at the tall, thin guard pacing ten feet behind him.

"That guard is a Christian?" Ben asked.

"Yes. How did you know?"

"He drew the fish in the sand."

"Very good."

"How can he justify being a guard in a place like this?"

"He serves us from within. He brought an extra bowl of rice last night. Besides, he is a young Christian."

"How young?"

"He bowed his knee to Yesu in a cell . . . just seven days ago. Or perhaps six or eight. It is hard to keep track. I have not been outside since you last visited me. Was that seven days ago?"

"Four. I was here Monday. This is Friday. You say he became a Christian in a cell?"

"Yes."

"What cell?"

"The cell of Li Quan, assistant locksmith."

The fat guard pushed Quan down the dark steps, then threw his crumpled body into an underground room in the lower cell blocks. There was no light. The floor was wet, the smell nauseating. Quan vomited into the dark refuse around him, not seeing but only hearing and smelling. He heard something on the ground. A small rat or a large cockroach, he guessed. As his eyes adjusted, he felt around in the darkness. There was no bed or toilet. If he were to sleep, it would be lying or sitting in the waste of others who'd been here before. He felt something warm running down his neck and back. He reached for it and realized he was still bleeding from Tai Hong's beating.

His eardrums rang, feeling like they were about to burst.

Please, Yesu, give me silence.

It was quiet now. In the darkness all he could hear was the thumping of his heart. He felt his face throbbing and swelling. Silently, squatting so as little of his body as possible would rest on the floor, he spoke.

"Zhu Yesu, *ganxie ni.* I thank you for your mercies. I pray for the church. I pray for my prison mates, whom I may not see again. Please help them. For that far-off voice moaning in the dark, I pray your comfort. I lift up Minghua and Shen to you. Be their husband and father in my absence. Protect and provide. Help them to feel no bitterness. Help them not . . . to be ashamed of me." He wept into the darkness that covered his face.

"You teach us, 'Love your enemies and pray for those who persecute you.' So I pray for the guards. I pray for Tai Hong. Perhaps you will yet make him China's apostle Paul. I pray for Ben Fielding. Put your hand on my friend. Make him a warrior for your kingdom. Use him for something greater than you use me. Help him give up his lesser goals for your greater ones. Teach him that his soul's deepest longings can only be met in you."

Longings—even the word stirred up in Li Quan the reality itself. It was more than a yearning for pain relief. It was a longing for the filling up of his insides, the quenching of his deepest thirsts. Yet somehow there was a sweetness to the thirst itself. It was a reminder he was made for more than this, that his destiny was not throbbing pain in the darkness of a filthy jail cell. His destiny was something far greater—a place of deliverance from fear and shame, an entrance to the perfect peace and joy he had caught glimpses of as a child and again since first surrendering his life to Yesu.

At first he thought he would never see anything in this darkness, but Li Quan's eyes adjusted. He faintly saw something written on the wall. The elusive characters he could see, then not see. The words appeared to have been written with soap. They stretched across the wall. To read it, he had to move close in front of every character. He read aloud in Mandarin:

"Wait for the Lord. My soul waits, and in his word I put my hope. My soul waits for the Lord more than watchmen wait for the morning."

Underneath, he saw another few sentences.

> Blessed is the man who does not walk in the counsel of the wicked or stand in the way of sinners or sit in the seat of mockers. But his delight is in the law of the Lord, and on his law he meditates day and night. He is like a tree planted by streams of water, which yields its fruit in season and whose leaf does not wither. Whatever he does prospers.

"Help me to prosper here, Yesu."

Li Quan began to recite the Word of God. It was as if he were inflating inner tubes to buoy himself up on water. His cell had no window. He did not know whether it was day or night. But he thanked Yesu that even after just a few hours, his stomach was no longer retching at the smell. He thanked him that he no longer feared the sounds of invisible creatures in his cell.

Above all, he thanked him that he was not in solitary confinement after all. He could hear prisoners in the distance. More importantly, he sensed someone else was in the room. More than one person. He felt one great presence inside him and another lesser presence outside him. He did not understand, but he knew he was not alone in the darkness, that someone else shared it with him. Somehow he felt transported to another place, beyond the cell. He felt safely beyond the reach of Tai Hong, enemy of his body, and the fallen prince of many names, enemy of his soul. Li Quan's longing was for a better country, an inheritance forever his. Not yet. But soon.

In the far corner of his cell, where he had feared to go, Li Quan now discovered two old buckets: one for waste, the other apparently—judging by the soapy smell—for washing, though there was no water or soap with which to wash. He turned the wash bucket upside down and set it a few feet from him. He turned the other bucket upside down to use it as a chair, then sat gazing at the first bucket, barely visible.

Though the walls were thicker and it was harder to hear, he heard a raspy, baritone voice in the darkness. Apparently Silas had also just been demoted to the lower blocks.

Li Quan spoke quietly to the friend sitting on the empty pail, then sang to him. He sang louder, and soon others joined in, faint and distant at first but growing in strength. Perhaps a half-dozen voices sang now, their deepest longings being expressed and not quite satisfied, lifting their souls above the darkness and filth of the Shadowlands.

Just as Zhou Jin finished reading his passage from Revelation, the cell phone rang. Ben sensed the tension in the small room as the pastor answered, every eye on him. Zhou listened quietly.

"Stay where you are," Zhou Jin said to the people, hands raised. "They are not coming."

"What is it?" his wife asked.

"They claim Li Quan has admitted his treason. He has signed a confession."

Ben stared at Ming.

"Let us pray for him," Zhou Jin said.

"Give Li Quan strength, Yesu," Aunt Mei said.

"Have mercy on those who would harm him," prayed Ho Lin. "And on those who have invented this false report."

"Protect Li Quan from Mogui's lies to slander him," Zhou Jin said.

After three more people prayed, Ben began to squirm. He was starting to wonder if he was the only one in the room who believed Quan might have signed that confession.

"It was not easy for me to talk the mayor into meeting with you. His son is very sick in the hospital, and he is extremely busy. He has only five minutes."

The mayor's assistant escorted Ben into the office. They both sat in guest chairs, while the mayor sat in a big chair behind an imposing desk.

"Thank you for agreeing to see me, Mr. Mayor," Ben began. "As I told your assistant, we met at a business luncheon in Shanghai a year ago."

"I attend many luncheons."

"I hear your son is in the hospital. I'm very sorry. I hope he gets better."

The mayor didn't even nod.

"As I said when I called, I'm here to ask about my friend Li Quan, a locksmith's assistant being held in Facility Six."

"What about him?" he asked, looking at a few papers in a file in front of him.

"I'm asking that he be let out."

Locking his powerful eyes onto Ben's, the mayor picked up the file, tapped it on the desk, then let it drop. "If I came to your city in America asking your mayor to let my friend out of prison, what do you think he would say?"

"But there's not even a hearing scheduled, is there?"

"Do you expect us to change our system to be like America's?"

"No. But Li Quan's innocent."

"Innocent? He has confessed to his crimes."

"Alright. If he confessed, why not let him out?"

"And when men confess to murder in America, why not let them out?"

"This isn't murder."

"It is illegal."

"When is his trial?"

"I do not know. I am the mayor. I am not a judge. I do not set trials."

"I found out the law permits certain accused to be held up to three years without trial. That may be legal, but it isn't right."

The mayor's look chilled Ben. It was not a look of anger or defiance. It was a look of sleepy indifference. The mayor simply did not care.

"Mr. Mayor, if you would let this man go it would be an act of good-will between our countries." He knew if Martin heard what he was about to say that he'd be outraged, but he decided to say it anyway. "And it would increase the likelihood that Getz International could do business directly in Pushan. We might be able to build a factory here—it could mean many jobs, boost your economy."

The mayor stood, nodded to Ben, and extended his hand. "It was good to see you again, Mr. Ben Fielding. I hope your business prospers."

The mayor's assistant escorted Ben out. A young man stood outside, wearing a fine leather jacket with a distinctive maroon tint. Ben stared at it.

"Where did you get that jacket?" Ben asked him.

"It was a gift from my uncle," the boy said.

"Let me see the label."

The boy backed away. The mayor stepped out. "What is the problem?" he asked.

"That coat belonged to my friend who's in jail."

"There are many leather jackets in Pushan," the mayor said.

"Not like that one. Check the label—it says Marpas. I bought it myself and gave it to Li Quan. It doesn't belong to this boy."

"This boy is my son. His twin brother is in the hospital. Leave my office, Mr. Fielding, or I will make phone calls to see to it you also leave my country." The mayor escorted his son into his office and closed the door, hard.

Ben put his hand on the doorknob, but the mayor's assistant grabbed him from behind. He whispered in his ear, "Mayor's younger brother is assistant warden, Facility Six." He walked out with Ben, then led him to the far corner of the hallway. He spoke in a whisper. "I process most of the mayor's papers. I sign for him when he is out of the office."

"Yes?"

"I might be able to arrange a directive to release your friend from prison."

"How?"

"Does it matter?"

"How much would it cost?"

"You seem a reasonable man."

"I am. What remains to be seen is whether you are."

"Two thousand American dollars."

"That is most unreasonable."

"What would be reasonable?"

"Five hundred."

"One thousand."

"Seven hundred fifty is the highest I will go."

"You are a good negotiator, Mr. Fielding. Seven hundred fifty American dollars, cash."

"I don't have it on me."

"When it is ready, call this number." He handed Ben a business card and pointed to the cell phone number. "Please do not call at this office. I will meet you. Then I will try to have the release order signed within a few days. The mayor does not always read what he signs. But you must forget about the jacket. Do nothing to antagonize the mayor. That would only hurt your friend."

34

$\mathcal{T}$HERE WAS A KNOCK, then a pause, then three knocks in close succession. They breathed easily. Whoever was at the door had signaled there was one God in three persons.

Ming opened the door to a rain-soaked teenage boy.

"Huang—what has happened?"

"An inside friend at Facility Six made a copy of the signature on Li Quan's confession. Zhou Jin asks you to say whether or not it is his signature."

He opened the paper and held it out.

Ben pointed to the bottom and asked Ming what he was sure he knew the answer to: "Is that Quan's signature?"

She nodded, then drew Shen next to her.

"Where is the confession itself?" Ben asked the boy.

"They do not have yet. Only sent signature. Zhou Jin has asked to see whole confession."

"I don't understand how they can keep denying you rights to see Quan."

"They can do as they wish," Minghua said, her voice indicating not resentment but resignation.

"I think I can get him out of jail," Ben said.

"But how?"

"A little tip to someone at the mayor's office."

"You mean bribe?"

"That's one word for it."

Her shoulders slumped. "You cannot do this, Ben Fielding."

"Sure I can. It's not that much money."

"If Christians are bought out of jail with bribes, encourages more arrests. Becomes way of making money. Sometimes same man is arrested every week to get bribe money from family or church or foreigners trying to help. You cannot pay money. Might help Li Quan. But would hurt others."

"But Quan needs to get out of there. He's obviously having it rough. He doesn't look good, and now . . . there's the confession."

"What does Ben Fielding mean by this?"

"I mean . . . they're mistreating him, putting pressure on him. That's all."

Ming put down the phone. "Zhou Jin wants us to come to his house. He has copy of Li Quan's confession."

"Maybe Shen should stay home?" Ben whispered to Ming, as he grabbed his jacket.

"Why?" Ming asked.

"Never mind," Ben said, helping Shen zip up his jacket and lifting him up on his shoulders—no small task. He ducked through the doorway and walked briskly toward the car in the cold rain. They drove silently, parked abruptly, then hurried to the door. Yin Chun sat them down and served them tea. Only then could Zhou Jin get to the point of the meeting.

"I will read the confession of Li Quan," he said. "It has been typed. His signature is at the bottom."

Ben looked uncomfortably at Ming, then nodded toward Shen, wondering if he should be in the room. She seemed not to understand his concern.

Zhou Jin read in Mandarin, but Ben still thought in English, so he made the translation:

"I confessing that Li Quan terrible criminal, puppet of foreign devil gweilos and distributing illegal literature not approved by government. I guilty of terrible crimes against people and Party. Not deserving freedom, my crimes I confess."

After a moment's pause, Ben laughed.

"Either Quan's Chinese grammar has really gone downhill, or he didn't write this."

"Right above signature," Zhou Jin said, "statement reads, 'I withdraw my faith in Yesu and say that the Party is right and the state is right and the illegal house churches are wrong forever.'"

"Now I know he didn't write it," Ben said.

"Of course he did not write it," Ming said. The tone of disappointment and anger was unmistakable. And it was directed right at Ben.

"But you said it's his signature. What was I supposed to . . . ?"

"They had him sign something else," Zhou Jin said. "See how low on the page his signature is. They may have written something in pencil, had him sign in ink, then erased and typed over it. Quan knows not to sign bottom of blank page."

"They did to his father," Ming said. "For a while Quan believe he had recanted faith. It was only later he discover truth." She looked at Shen. "But Li Shen has known all along his father would never deny Zhu Yesu."

Everyone else talked while Ben sat in silent misery. When it was time to leave, Ben helped Ming on with her leather jacket.

"I'm sorry, Ming," he whispered.

"Chan Minghua has been Li Quan's roommate much longer than Ben Fielding," she whispered back. "She must know him much better."

35

*L*YING AGAINST THE STONE WALL in the darkness, Li Quan tried to repeat the words written in his mind. At the same moment, a great Watcher said the same words, and with him Li Manchu, Li Wen, and Li Tong.

> How long, O Lord, until you restore me? Return, O Lord, and rescue me. Save me because of your unfailing love. I am worn out from sobbing. Every night tears drench my bed; my pillow is wet from weeping. My vision is blurred by grief; my eyes are worn out because of all my enemies. Go away, all you who do evil, for the Lord has heard my crying. The Lord has heard my plea; the Lord will answer my prayer.

Ben drove to the jail the next Friday, December 14, but this time it was different. In his car were Ming and Shen. When he approached the gates, they ducked low. He parked the car as close as he could to the wire gate leading to the metal fence.

As he walked from the car Ben knelt down, blocking the view from the car with his back. He quickly stuck the envelope under the broken bricks. At least this time it was three for the price of one. He passed the same two guards as before. He wondered if they were getting a share of the payoff.

He stood at the part of the fence that allowed the best view from the car. A short, heavy guard brought Li Quan out. Quan's body was bulky from the blanket stuck under his coat. His face was drawn. He'd lost weight. He walked slowly, blinking hard. Ben wondered what Ming and Shen were thinking and was grateful they could see him only from a distance.

As they touched fingers through the fence, Ben whispered to Quan, "Move over to your left a little. Ming and Shen are in the car. They want to see you."

Quan pretended he was looking at Ben but instead looked over at the car, searching. Suddenly he saw a pudgy hand move. "Shen is waving to me!" he whispered in English.

The guard walked over by the fence and stared at the car.

"I see nothing now," Quan whispered. "Ming is probably holding down his arm."

"I'm doing everything I can to get you out."

"And what of the others who are here because they are followers of Yesu? Will you get them out too?"

"I'm afraid not. Just you."

"Then I am privileged, and the others are not." Ben saw the same sadness in Quan's eyes he heard in his voice.

"I've met with the mayor, asked for an appointment with the warden, and I'm trying to find the equivalent of a district attorney. I've been in touch with one of the amnesty groups and a human rights watchdog organization. We've talked about petitions, letter writing, going to the State Department, applying political pressure, the whole deal."

"I have done something more, I think."

"What do you mean?"

"I have talked with the person in charge."

"The warden?"

Quan shook his head.

"The mayor?"

"I speak to this person every day. He is always the One I go to first."

Ben's face fell. "You're talking about God, aren't you? Well, no offense, but I think we need to talk to some people with skin on."

"God put skin on. His name is Yesu."

"Okay, but I'm talking about someone who's actually here. I mean—"

"Yesu says he is here with us always and—"

"I'd think you'd be grateful I've been contacting all these people to try to help you."

"I am grateful. I thank God every day for my friend Ben Fielding, and all he has done for my family, and what he is trying to do for me. I do not wish to stay in prison. I am not a revolutionary. I am not a brave man. I am a simple locksmith who wants to be home with his wife and child. All I am asking Ben Fielding to do is to take his concerns first to the One who has all power, who reigns above all mayors and police chiefs and wardens and judges, who holds their hearts in his hand and can turn them as if they were droplets of water."

"It's hard to get them to listen to me."

"God can help you."

"I can't get through to them."

"God spoke through Balaam's donkey. He can speak through Ben Fielding."

"Thanks."

"The similarity to the donkey was unintentional," Quan said. "I only meant that prayer is far more powerful than civil petitions and phone calls to human rights groups and state departments. Those are good, but prayers are much better."

"Whatever."

"You have spent long hours each day in many efforts on behalf of your unworthy friend. Are you willing to spend one hour in prayer each day? If so, you might accomplish far more. In prayer we learn that the power resides in Yesu, not in us."

"I'm a hands-on guy. I need to actually do something."

"Do you imagine prayer is not doing something?"

The guard moved toward them. Quan stared at the car. He saw a quick movement and smiled. The guard pulled on his shoulder.

"Wait, Quan," Ben said. "I asked Ming about the chair. She said you should explain it to me."

As the guard shoved Li Quan back toward the darkness, Quan began to sing.

―――――――――

Once they'd gotten over the shock of Quan's haggard appearance—it turns out they could see him more clearly than Ben supposed—Ming and Shen were elated to have seen Li Quan. As they drove off, Ben asked, "How about we stop for bing xi lin?"

Shen's eyes grew large and he clapped his hands. Ten minutes later he was enjoying his ice cream. They told stories and laughed. But suddenly, tears streamed down his face.

"What's wrong, Shen?" Ben asked.

"They don't give Baba ice cream, do they?"

"I don't think so," Ben said.

"But Baba wants Shen to enjoy bing xi lin," Ming said. "He always wants very best for his only son." Shen wiped his face and finished his ice cream.

As they got back in the car to head home, the dark sky pressed down on them, bleeding a gray, heavy rain. Ming and Shen sang songs. Ben drove down muddy roads, grateful he'd managed to rent a four-wheel drive. As they approached the house, still a hundred feet away, Ben slowed down. Something wasn't right. The house appeared fine but . . . what was it? Of course. The ginkgo tree.

Ming and Shen were oblivious, singing and giggling in the back. As they turned the corner, Ben could see the ground where the tree had stood. There it was, lying flat. It had fallen over the chicken coop, destroying the wire fence.

Ben pulled in. As the car stopped, the backseat was silent. He jumped out and ran to the tree. Standing in the pounding rain, he looked at the yellow wood of the ginkgo where it had been cut by a chain saw. The broad, leathery leaves were already starting to wilt. Soon they would shrivel, and nothing, not even this rain, could bring them back to life. A two-hundred-year-old tree cut to the ground. By whom? Why?

Ming and Shen stood beside Ben now, speechless. Ming bent her knee by the tree and touched the stump; then she got up and looked for something farther up on the tree. She found the engraving and ran her finger over it.

Ben took Shen's hand, then led him to the house. The door was open. The furniture had been turned over, clothes dumped on the floor. Ben picked up the high-backed chair, then looked around the room, wondering what to do next. He stared out the open door at little Ming, rain gushing off her leather coat, knees buried in the slushy mud, head resting on a fallen tree that would no longer bring her the relief of shade, the assurance of love, or the soft whispers of a far-off beauty.

36

*T*HE FAT GUARD entered the prisoner's cell. Quan instinctively cringed.
"Your visitor is here."

Quan stumbled past a bare lightbulb hanging from the ceiling by a
frayed wire. He turned the corner to the stairs. Seeing daylight above, he
eagerly ascended, yearning not only to see his friend but to behold the sky
and breathe fresh air. On stepping outside he discovered, to his delight,
that it was raining. The moment the cold, wet air hit him, he sucked it in
and smiled broadly.

"Hello, old friend," Ben said from the other side of the fence.

"Your face is pained," Quan said.

"I can't stand to see you suffer like this."

Quan ran his fingers over his wet face. "You speak as if suffering is
unusual. It is not. Shengjing tells us, 'Dear friends, don't be surprised
at the fiery trials you are going through, as if something strange were
happening to you. Instead, be very glad—because these trials will make
you partners with Christ in his suffering, and afterward you will have the
wonderful joy of sharing his glory when it is displayed to all the world.' I
have recited those words often. I try to set my mind on the *afterward*."

While Quan's words hung there Ben sensed two warring voices inside
himself. One claimed that Quan was right, that he had a perspective Ben
lacked and desperately needed. The other voice argued that Quan was a
well-meaning but ignorant fool for believing something so outrageous.
Right now, the second voice spoke louder.

Ben told the story of the fallen ginkgo tree. Meanwhile, Quan tilted his bruised face up to the sky, eyes closed and mouth open, trying to catch the falling rain.

"Tai Hong ordered the tree cut down," Quan surmised.

"Why?"

"To send a message."

"What message?"

"Chinese think in pictures. It is meant to say that no matter how old is my family's heritage of faith, it can be destroyed. My family will be cut down. Li Quan's life will end. My wife's and son's lives may end too. There will be no shade, no relief from the sun of suffering. None for me, none for them."

"Do you believe that?"

"I believe that is Mogui's message. He almost succeeded in destroying my faith when I was young. I pray he will not take hold of Shen as he did me."

Ben pulled a bottle of water from his jacket pocket, opened it, and stuck it through the fence, propping up the bottom. Quan eagerly put his mouth to it. Ben held it steady, tilting it gradually. Quan choked a few times but didn't stop suckling the bottle. Ben tried to position it differently and, when he did, Quan pursued it with his mouth. Ben had a strange sensation that he was nursing a child. When the water was gone, Quan wiped his mouth and sighed. Ben put the empty bottle back in his coat, wishing he had more to offer his friend.

Li Quan recited from memory, "'My soul is in anguish. How long, O Lord, how long? Turn, O Lord, and deliver me; save me because of your unfailing love.'"

He could not hear the voices of angels and saints asking the same question: "How long, O Lord, how long?"

Nor could he hear the words of the One gathering his servant's prayers into a bottle and treasuring them. From the throne came a still small voice, which for a fleeting moment Li Quan heard: "Not much longer, my son. Not much longer."

Li Quan began singing to the chair in the center of his cell.

Heaven is my home.
Earth is a desert drear.

Heaven is my home.
Danger and sorrow stand
Round me on every hand.
Heaven is my fatherland.
Heaven is my home.

Li Manchu, Li Wen, and Li Tong sang the same words, in perfect harmony.

"You have comforted me, Lord," Li Quan said, "but I burn to serve you. How can I minister without people to reach out to? I can sometimes hear their voices, but I cannot see and touch and talk with these men. Make a way for me, Lord. Give me a ministry; use me as a vessel of your grace. Help me also to know what to say to Ben Fielding."

"You are testing them both. Will they pass?"

"That is not yet for you to know. Experience is a hard teacher because she gives the test first, the lesson afterward. But properly learned, the lesson forever changes the man."

"My grandson is a good friend, is he not?"

"The best of friends. In a man's life the multitudes pass him by. What changes the man is one friend, one family, one church, one teacher, one roommate, one coworker. Then the man can change the church, and the church, the nation. Ben Fielding must yet choose his path. The path I have already chosen for him."

A guard rushed into Quan's cell, with Tai Hong on his heels. Quan clicked his manacles closed just in time. They dragged him up, unlocked the manacles, then stretched his hands behind his back and locked them together. They leaned him forward, placing his head against the wall so it bore his entire weight. Tai Hong moved Quan's feet back farther to increase the strain.

"You must keep your head against the wall, or you will be beaten and not fed," Tai Hong said. "We will see what your God does for Li Quan! Should you decide to deny your God, call upon the mercy of Tai Hong. Perhaps he will deliver you. For surely you are in his hands."

"You have no power except what I grant you, son of dust."
The One on the throne turned to listen to the words of Reader:

> Break the arm of the wicked and evil man; call him to account for
> his wickedness that would not be found out. The Lord is King for
> ever and ever; the nations will perish from his land. You hear,
> O Lord, the desire of the afflicted; you encourage them, and you
> listen to their cry, defending the fatherless and the oppressed, in
> order that man, who is of the earth, may terrify no more.

Eighteen hours later, Quan fell to the ground, unconscious. A guard
kicked him, beat him, and propped him back up. He fell again.

"He can no longer stand," the guard reported to Tai Hong.

"Then sit him in a chair and lean his head against the wall!"

"We've already circulated a confession from him, haven't we?"

"He did not really confess. I will make sure he does! I will not let him
say he has defeated me."

When the guard returned to the cell, bringing a chair with him, Quan
still lay in a heap in the corner. He pretended to be unconscious. The
soldier left the chair behind, slipped off his manacles, and shut the door,
giving the prisoner time to regain strength before the next round of
torture.

In the darkness Li Quan sat up. He stared at the wooden high-backed
chair for several minutes, then reached out to touch it, as one reaches out
toward what might be a mirage. When he felt its substance, he fell upon
the chair, embracing it, washing it with his tears.

37

LI QUAN CAME OUT, a gopher from his hole. He squinted in the brightness, searching for a face. When he saw Ben, he nodded and walked quickly to him. He wobbled, picked up a stick from the ground, then leaned one shoulder against the fence.

"What happened?" Ben said.

"It is nothing."

"*Nothing* is when your face looks normal. Yours is badly bruised. What happened?"

"Tai Hong paid another visit."

"If I could get my hands on that guy, I'd kill him."

"Then I hope you do not get your hands on him. I would not want you to become like Tai Hong. An old saying goes, 'He who seeks revenge should remember to dig two graves.'"

"It might be worth it if he was in one of them."

Quan shook his head. "Is it almost Christmas?"

"Two days away," Ben said.

"Do you remember the market next to the fish store where we saw the eel skinner?"

"How could I forget?"

"The market owner is a friend. Sometimes he is able to get an orange for me around Christmas. Very hard to find here. I give it to Shen and Ming on Christmas morning. They split it. They insist that I have some, but my joy is not in eating it but in watching them eat it. Please, could you try to get them an orange?"

Ben swallowed hard. "Of course." He didn't mention that he'd already bought a beautiful sweater for Ming and a sweat suit for Shen.

"Now, please tell me about Ming and Shen."

Ben had learned to tell Quan carefully chosen stories. It was the Chinese way of selecting just the right anecdotes that revealed the person. Ben told of taking Shen on a cold fishing trip on the Wenrong River, and how they saw a badger, which Shen followed. Ben spoke of interesting conversations with Ming. Quan smiled appreciatively and pressed him for details.

Ben decided not to tell him of the several times he'd taken them out to dinner. But he did mention going to one nice restaurant. When he did, Quan's eyes lit up. He showed no jealousy, no depression, but pure delight and gratitude. Ben was relieved, but disturbed. He knew he wouldn't have reacted the same way. That reminded him how different he was from his old friend. He didn't like the difference.

"And how is my friend Ben Fielding? Tell me a story about him."

"Still making phone calls, having meetings. Trying to get you out and get Getz untangled from this Laogai mess."

"No, no. Tell Li Quan a story that captures the heart of Ben Fielding."

The request took Ben off guard. Nothing came to mind but . . . "I could tell you a story. But you wouldn't want to hear it."

"I will not know until you tell me, will I?"

"It's too cold for you to stand and listen to this."

"I will stand here until the guard takes me away. The longer you delay, the colder it will get. Please warm a cold prisoner with your story."

Ben sighed, then plunged in. "A few weeks before I came here I was teaching a business success seminar. The night before, I was alone in my hotel room. I . . . got drunk and flipped through channels and spent a lonely evening. I'd taken off my Hugo Boss suit and hung it on a suit caddie." He saw the vacant look on Quan's face. "This is a twenty-five-hundred-dollar suit, which is . . . a lot of yuan. Anyway, I suddenly had to vomit. I tried to get to the bathroom, but I didn't make it. I threw up on the suit. I had to call for a 2:00 A.M. dry cleaning. I told you this wasn't a good story."

"I never judge a story until it is finished," Quan said.

"I wowed them at the seminar. I really made them think I was some-thing. One guy had seen a feature article on me in *Kiplinger's* and actually asked me to autograph his program. Can you believe that? Anyway, a couple of big shots took me out to dinner, and I came back to the room again, feeling great. Except now that I was alone, the feeling wore off—like it always does—and then I felt empty again. I started drinking, then went down to the hotel bar. I sat there, hoping some woman would come over and flirt with me—so I could think I was a man, I guess. Well, sure enough, one woman did. She'd been at my seminar. I bought her a few drinks, and she cozied up to me. And then, right when I was about to get what I told myself I wanted, all I could think about was the guilt and the risk of disease and, worst of all, having to lie in the same bed with some strange woman, hoping all night she'd leave. So I made up an excuse and went back to the room and channel-surfed through all those aging baby-boomer commercials about laxatives and pain medications and Viagra."

"What is Viagra?"

"Never mind."

"What is the moral of Ben Fielding's story?"

"Does there have to be a moral?"

"To the wise, all that happens contains a moral."

"Maybe I'm not so wise, but . . . here I am, getting drunk, barfing on my suit, then acting like I've got it together, teaching a success seminar, with a room full of young guys taking notes on me the way I take notes on the guys I think of as successful. Then I try to pick up a woman, thinking that's what I wanted, then realizing I didn't want her once she wanted me. Or pretended to want me. Whatever. The moral? Nothing is what it seems to be. Even when you get what you want, it's never what you really want. Know what I mean?"

"Say more," Quan said.

Ben shrugged. "What do you want me to say? I've failed at being a husband and a father. I've failed at being a Christian. That night in Cincinnati I sort of faced up to it—Ben Fielding is a one-trick pony. Business is my thing. Put me in a boardroom or a sales meeting, and I'm floating on air. Put me with my family and I'm a loser. Leave me to myself and I'm miserable. But then, to top it off, I come over to China, wealthy and successful, and at first I feel sorry for my old roommate when I find out he's a poor locksmith's assistant and all his dreams have turned to ashes. See, Quan, I own the house you dreamed of—a couple of them, to be honest. Compared to me, you have nothing. But then I look at Ming and Shen and how they adore you, and I'm jealous. You're in jail, they're beating you up, and somehow I find myself wishing I had what you have. Compared to you, I'm the one who has nothing."

Quan nodded.

"Well, that's the ugly truth. Your old roommate is a flashy success at business and a miserable failure at everything that matters. And when I saw my best friend doing forced labor for a Chinese factory I helped build, I had to ask myself how successful I've even been in business."

"Li Quan is your best friend?"

"Well, not for the last twenty years, but before that, sure. And now, I sort of feel that way again. Anyway, that Cincinnati thing is my pathetic little story, the dirty little secret about Ben Fielding."

"Why did you tell this to me?"

"Because you made me. And maybe because . . . there's no one else I could tell."

"I am honored you would tell me your story. But there is someone else you should tell."

"Let me guess. Yesu."

"Ben Fielding is a good guesser."

"Do you remember when we discussed my goals, and you asked, 'What does it profit a man to gain the whole world and lose his soul?'"

"I remember."

"Be honest with me, Quan. Do you think I'm lost? I mean, if I died today, would I go to hell?"

Quan looked at Ben, searching his eyes. After a ten-second pause he said, "I have considered your question. I am not sure I know the answer. I once believed you were a Christian. And I still believe those in the Father's hand are held there by his grace. Yet I also have met many who think they are Christians, but I fear they are not. I saw this much in America. It seemed that being a Christian meant doing certain good things and abstaining from certain bad ones. I think many have been assured they are Christians who are not. This is one of Mogui's strategies."

"Do you think I'm a Christian?"

"You were raised in Christian home. You went to Christian meetings. You even invited your roommate to the campus ministry, and I will always be grateful. But could you do those things without being a Christian? Yes. I am not your soul's judge. But Yesu said his followers would be known by their fruit."

Ben nodded, bracing himself.

"I ask you, Ben—have you been bearing the fruit of Yesu? I do not think anyone could better answer that question about Li Quan than Ming or Shen or Zhou Jin. So, I ask you—what would Pam and Melissa and Kim say if asked, 'Is Ben Fielding a true Christian?' What would your secretary and employees and business associates say?"

Ben saw a string of faces, especially Pam's, Kim's, Melissa's, and Doug's.

They would say no.

The guard grabbed Li Quan's shoulder, but for once he held his ground. He stretched out his stick and drew the mark of the fish in the sand.

"Merry Christmas, Ben," Quan said, smiling broadly.

The guard shoved him. Quan fell. The guard kicked him, then quickly looked up at Ben, as if realizing he needed to restrain himself while being watched. Ben clamped his fingers on the fence, catching part of the barbed wire and immediately drawing blood. He wanted to go after the guard, but knew he couldn't. He watched Quan being pushed toward the cell blocks. Quan turned around again. He grinned ear to ear. Before he was back at the cell block doorway, Li Quan was singing that song about the fatherland. Three prisoners working the grounds joined in the same song. They sang louder and louder, smiles larger and larger. Three guards looked at each other, uncertain what to do. One of the guards, the tall one, opened his mouth and sang, "Heaven is my fatherland. Heaven is my home."

Ben saw the string of blood on his finger, wiped it on his coat, then put it to his mouth. He stood there watching and listening and yearning. Hearing these prisoners singing, he felt for a moment he was in the presence of Joy itself, as if it was almost within his reach. Almost.

Quan whispered into the darkness words hidden in his heart. "'I know that my Redeemer lives and that in the end he will stand upon the earth. And after my skin has been destroyed, yet in my flesh I will see God. I myself will see him with my own eyes—I, and not another. How my heart yearns within me!'"

The guard peered into Quan's cell through the little barred window, which was two handbreadths across. Long used to the darkness, Quan could see the contempt in his eyes.

"Stop smiling!" he yelled.

"I am not smiling," Quan said.

"Yes, you are!" shouted the guard. He rattled the door, but moved on to the next cell.

Suddenly, Li Quan stood and pressed his face against the bars. "Guard!" Quan called. When he didn't come, he called louder. "Su Gan!"

The guard came back and rattled the door violently. "Who told you my name? Be silent or I will come in and make you silent!"

"Su Gan, sir, please, I have a request for you."

"Unless you can pay me, I care nothing for your requests."

"Can I do some labor for you?"

Quan saw in the jailer's eyes surprise mixed with contempt.

"This prison is so filthy," Quan said. "There is waste everywhere. The rats and roaches feed on it. You are not a prisoner, but you must feel like you are. Su Gan has to breathe this foul air, to walk carefully because of what oozes out of the cells. Li Quan can help you. Let me go into the cells one by one and clean up this filthy place. Give me water and a brush and soap, and I will show you what I can do! My father, Li Tong, was a street sweeper, a great cleaner of the ground. The finest in China. And I am my father's son!"

38

*L*I YUE!"

Ming warmly welcomed the young man at the door. He wore glasses and dressed like a student. Pudgy faced, he had wide features and penetrating brown eyes. He looked familiar. *No wonder,* Ben thought. He looked like Shen would look in another fifteen years.

"Yue is Li Quan's favorite nephew!" Ming squealed with delight. "This is Ben Fielding, Quan's college roommate from America."

"Harvard," the young man said. "I am honored to meet you. Also, happy New Year."

"And a happy early Chinese New Year to you," Ben said. "You speak good English." The words generated a boyish grin from Yue.

"I will make green tea," Ming said. "Li Yue will tell Ben Fielding about himself."

Yue sat on the floor next to the high-backed chair. "I have attended seminary. I also visit nearby colleges and speak with students."

"Why?"

"To tell students about Yesu. To challenge them to investigate his claims. The Communist Party has been successful in stopping political dissent but has not been able to stop the movement of the Holy Spirit at universities. I dare not say much more. But I can tell you, God is at work."

"What's the seminary like?"

Yue shrugged. "Much of it is boring, because it is Party propaganda and not the Word of Yesu. Still, there is a professor who believes the Bible. He took some of us aside in the evenings to teach us."

"Only one teacher believes the Bible? Who is he?"

"No need to say. The Three-Self Church bishop has attacked orthodox theology. Only truth is dangerous, so if churches are liberal they are of no danger to the Party. In fact, they can be used to support it. The seminaries are strategic."

"How many seminaries are there?"

"There were eighteen, now twenty-one. Nanjing Seminary is the largest. One hundred seventy students—but for every ten who apply, nine are turned away. Mao closed Nanjing Seminary and turned its stone buildings into army barracks. It reopened under Deng's open-door policy. China Christian Council, which is like the Three-Self Church, runs Nanjing. Three students there were expelled. The seminary president publicly denounced them when they refused to sing Communist songs at a school ceremony because they believed Christian hymns should be sung. Faculty members who believe Shengjing, and some who had taught at house churches, were fired. Many senior staff and graduates were retired or expelled by the president. He is the Party's puppet."

"I've been told the seminaries are proof of China's religious freedom."

"What has happened at Nanjing Seminary does not seem like freedom. The bishop has called for 'theological adaptation to socialism.' Classes on Romans and Revelation and apologetics were all replaced by new courses on the teachings of Deng, Three-Self education, and military training. Things like this happened at my seminary too. This is why, five weeks ago, I dropped out. I have been going to underground seminary."

"Where?"

"No need to say. It was started by an eighty-two-year-old house church pastor. He has been threatened with imprisonment if he keeps seminary open. But prison is not much threat to a man who has already spent thirty-four years there. I help arrange other meetings, a different sort of seminary. That is why I am here."

"What kind of meetings do you mean?"

He stared. Then he and Ben said at the same time, "No need to say."

Ben stood in the chilly winter air. As usual, he waited nervously, trying to keep warm and to will Li Quan out of the black hole. Someone was being led out of the building now, a frail, older man with a pronounced limp and yellow skin, as if he had jaundice or hepatitis.

Ben watched the man, who for some reason was walking toward him. He felt his heart freeze. "Quan?" He tried to disguise his horror. They touched right index fingers through the fence. "You smell like . . . soap."

"Yes." Quan beamed, his face and voice surprisingly animated. "This is better than I smelled last time, yes? I have wonderful news! You must tell my family and house church. God has answered prayer. He has given me a ministry!"

"What?"

"I go from cell to cell, bringing Yesu's message."

"But I thought you were in an isolated cell."

"God opened the door. I go to the other men. Most have never had anyone else come into their cell except to beat them. I help and serve them as I clean their cells. I bring them the love of Yesu. Twelve men I have visited. When I left their cells, six I did not leave alone."

"What do you mean?"

"When I left, Yesu was with them. Three were already believers, one of them a pastor. He had known my father, Li Tong! Three more bowed their knees to Yesu, who promises never to leave or forsake them. When I walk by their cells on the way to clean others, I sing to them, 'Heaven is my fatherland.' When I finish cleaning all the cells I will start over. Then I can teach Shengjing to each of them. I will teach as I wash."

"The guards let you do this?"

"The smell that used to cling to the guards is now almost gone. Their shoes are not ruined. The prisoners are excited to no longer be alone. Excited to realize that even if they die here, they will have eternal life. Excited that God has not forgotten them, that this world is not their home, that they will find release."

"Sounds more like a revival meeting than a prison."

"Those in prison are not so distracted as those outside. They think about death more. They ask, 'Is this the day?' They do not put so much hope in their plans and successes in this world. I tell them about Yesu and his heaven, and they listen eagerly, much more intently than most free men I speak to in the locksmith's shop. Please, tell Ming and Shen and Zhou Jin about Li Quan's ministry."

"I'll tell them on one condition—there's a question you have to answer first."

"They called me a master carpenter," Li Wen said. "Compared to you I am but a novice."

They worked together, master and apprentice, building and fashioning, using a simple wood chisel and a plane, doing with their hands what no machinery could.

"Your hands are so skilled and powerful," Li Wen said. "Yet so delicate."

"I have much experience building. And these hands are familiar with wood."

"Anything I ever built in the Shadowlands was nothing compared to this."

"What you built had value, for you built it for me, and with me. But what Li Wen will build in the future shall be greater still. I am the source of your gifts and skills. It was I who built your heart and trained your hands in the dark world."

"You are the master builder."

"I am the builder of simple furniture and wooden plows. I am the builder of men and worlds. And I am the builder of the place made for you." His eyes looked over the horizon, to a part of this vast country Li Wen had not yet seen.

"Thank you for asking me to build this with you, for helping me learn by watching the skill of your hands."

The Carpenter put his hand on the head of his apprentice. "To build something with you, Li Wen, is for me a great pleasure."

"What is your important question, Ben?"

"You have to tell me about that chair!"

"What chair?" Li Quan asked, unable to keep the corners of his mouth from twitching.

"You know what chair. The mahogany chair, the empty one, with the high back. Ming and Shen say you have to tell me. I can't get a word out of them."

"Li Wen built the chair. He was a master craftsman, known throughout the province. It took him more than a year. He built it first in honor of his father, Li Manchu. But then it became for him the chair of Yesu. When others claimed to rule the world, it reminded him who was the true King."

"That's why it's almost like a throne?"

"A very modest throne. But yes. There is only one who is worthy to sit in it. That same one is always present in the house of Li. My father learned that as a child. I should have, too, but I was very slow to learn. Shen understands already."

"He's had a good teacher."

"Not good enough, I fear, though Ming has made up for my shortcomings. The chair is a remembrance of the Li family line of believers, going back to Li Manchu. But most important, this chair is a remembrance of Yesu's promise to always be with his children. At every meal we have, we remember he is with us. When we sit in the evening, when we go to sleep at night, we remember he is there, watching over us. No matter what."

"Has no one ever sat in the chair?"

"My father said his father, Li Wen, taught that Yesu was truly in the chair, that though he was everywhere and the chair was but a symbol, it was a very important symbol. As Li Wen did not let anyone sit in it, neither would Li Tong. He said if we sat in the chair we would forget its meaning. Whenever we had too many guests, the chair sat vacant while my father or I sat on the floor. I resented him for expecting me to sit on the ground rather than on a good chair. I was a young fool."

"Better a young fool than an old fool," Ben said.

"Yes." Quan smiled. "This would make a good Chinese proverb. There is hope for Ben Fielding. Tell me, old friend—how was Christmas?"

"I got oranges for Ming and Shen. And bananas and grapes."

"Ben Fielding is a worker of miracles," Quan said. Tears formed quickly and dripped freely down his cheeks. "They must have been very happy." He looked skyward. "Thank you for this kindness, Yesu."

Ben pushed his hand harder into the wire fence and wrapped his fingers around Quan's. Just then the guard came and herded him away to the black hole. Li Quan walked back to his desolate cell, singing. Ben Fielding, realizing he had never thanked God for a piece of fruit, walked back to his beautiful vehicle, despairing.

As Li Wen rubbed the wood grain with his hands, the King stood back and said, "There—it is finished." He smoothed his hand over the chair's arms and stood back, smiling. "This chair is made for Li Wen. Sit."

"No. I cannot. It is much too beautiful. I am not worthy."

"I decide who receives my gifts. Sit down."

Li Wen sat down. The chair was perfect, contoured to the exact specifications of his form. It was like sitting on air. He felt like he could remain in this chair for days on end. The craftsmanship was perfect. In ten thousand years this chair would be as stable as it was now.

"You can take it with you to my new earth. It will sit in the great house of Li."

"Thank you, my Master. Li Wen is most unworthy."

"Don't you think I know who's unworthy and who isn't?" the King asked, laughing. "Li Wen once built a chair for me. I do not forget such things. I am pleased now to have built one for him. And, remember, you assisted me in building it."

"But this chair is far beyond anything Li Wen could ever build."

"What you do for me has never equaled what I do for you, has it?"

"No. Never."

"So let us not imagine it should be different now."

The Carpenter stepped behind the chair and put his hands on Li Wen's shoulders. He massaged his neck with hands that at first seemed strong and rough, but then gentle and soft.

"Your gifts and skills are greater than you realize, Li Wen. I should know. I have plans for how you will use these skills in my new world, to do things you never dreamed of."

"How long will it be until then, my King?"

"Not long, my friend," he said, squeezing his neck firmly. "Not long."

39

"AUNTIE MING, Zhou Jin says I can trust Ben Fielding. Is this true?"

Ming nodded, though not as quickly as Ben would have liked.

Li Yue looked at Ben. "Do you remember the seminary I mentioned?"

"Nanjing?"

"No, the different kind of seminary, the one I am helping set up. As we speak, that seminary is being prepared. Some have been traveling days to get here." He nodded at Ben. "You will accompany me."

"What for? Do you need a ride?"

"No, we will walk. Not far. But it has been shown to us that after attending house church and standing beside the family of Li Quan, Ben Fielding should come and see for himself what there is to learn in our special seminary. Perhaps you will find answers to your questions."

"What questions?"

"The questions all men ask deep within their souls. It has been decided. You will join us." Quan's nephew, though young and slight, was as stubborn as his uncle.

"When?"

"Tomorrow night."

"But where do you meet?"

"No need to say. It is a school with places and times of meeting always changing. Uncle Li Quan has attended both as student and teacher. It is the closest he has come to being a professor."

"Where do the people come from?"

"Everywhere. Some are walking sixty kilometers, others riding bicycles two hundred kilometers. Some we will not know until they arrive. There will be a visiting teacher tomorrow night. Even when such a man has preached to exhaustion, the students, who are mostly farmers and factory laborers, are unwilling to let him rest. They urge him to continue teaching God's Word."

"Who is this visiting teacher?"

"He is from America."

"No kidding? What's his name?"

"No need to say. You will find out tomorrow night."

"It is part of my reeducation," Quan said, as Ben stared at the marks on his face. "But it seems not to be working. I am not their best student."

"Could you complain a little, so I can feel better about myself?"

"It is not so bad. I have two little roommates. I named them Yin and Yang."

"What?"

"They are cockroaches." He smiled.

"Are you alright, Quan?"

"I am not losing my mind. In jail a man learns to appreciate little things. Kongzi said, 'Everything has beauty, but not everyone sees it.' When you are deprived of much, you learn to see beauty in little. Kongzi was wrong about some things, but right about this."

"Who's Kongzi?"

"You have not heard of Confucius?"

"Of course. I forgot his Chinese name."

Quan smiled. "No problema."

"Yin and Yang, huh?"

"They are not the first unusual roommates Li Quan has had."

"Very funny." Ben relaxed slightly. "How do you keep your sanity?"

"I play Beethoven, Mozart, and Schubert. One night I played the entire score of the Messiah."

"You have access to a piano?"

"I did not say that. My father taught me the mind is free even when the body is chained. That is how I sit in Bible class every day, with Zhu Yesu as my teacher and Shengjing as my textbook."

"You have a Bible?"

"I have one in my heart."

"Are you . . . lonely?"

"For Ming and Shen and our house church? Yes. And for my friend,

Ben Fielding? Yes, though I thank God for the miracle of your visits. But Yesu is with me. And I have met many brothers from other areas. I have washed the floors and feet of fifteen prisoners now. I have learned men's names and told them to other men. I have asked if I may clean the upstairs cell block, that I may serve even more. I am behind in my work now because of . . . what they have done to me recently. But I have met a doctor arrested for 'disturbing the social order' because he kept telling his patients about the love of Yesu. And also three pastors."

"Three?"

"All of them are house church leaders in this province. One of the pastors has baptized over two thousand new believers. He works in an area where people are so poor they have only one set of clothing apiece. He baptizes only in the warm season, or they will freeze. Two men were discovered at an illegal seminary meeting in a house cave."

"Speaking of which . . . Li Yue has informed me I'll be attending a seminary tonight."

"They invited you? That is most unusual."

"I wouldn't call it an invitation. More of a demand."

Quan smiled broadly, and Ben saw that one tooth was missing and another was bent. "Their risk is much greater than yours. It is time for you to leave China anyway—it will not be so bad if the authorities send you home. But Chinese Christians don't get kicked out. We get kicked in. Most of the brothers caught in underground seminary have been in prison at least a few months. One has been here six years. Many have been tortured. They tell stories of martyrs in their areas, stories never reported in newspapers."

"Like what?"

"There have been mutilations and crucifixions. Other shameful things—in one city the flesh of Christians has been eaten."

"No way! I can't believe that."

"One of the pastors insists it is true. Believe what you want, Ben Fielding. But this much I know—Mogui hates the weak, the innocent, and all God's children. By striking out at them, he takes revenge on Yesu. Do you imagine it is a human power behind the one-child policy, enforced abortion, sterilization decrees, and the imprisonment and torture of believers?" Quan winced and put his hand to the side of his head.

"What have they done to you?"

"Wang Mingdao is the father of the house church movement. He said, 'Days of great testing lie ahead. The same water that floats a boat may also overturn it.'"

"Quan, tell me what they did to you."

"It is not important."

"It's important to me."

"The brothers wish not pity but prayer. And Bibles, that the thirsty may be able to drink."

"You need a lot more than prayer and Bibles."

"I am not so sure."

"You need to get out of here."

"To say yes to Yesu is to say yes to suffering. Besides, a man must climb mountains to see lowlands."

"What more can I do for you, Quan?"

"Ask my Ming and Shen and Li Yue and Zhou Jin to pray for Dewei, Dingbang, Hop, Jun, and Ho in their cells. They are all now my brothers. And are they yours, Ben Fielding?"

Ben pretended not to hear the question as he pulled out his pad and wrote down the names. "Isn't it hard for you to trust a God who makes his servants suffer?" he asked.

"Zhu Yesu is a ferocious lion. His claws are sharp. The fact that the Lion became a sacrificial lamb does not mean he ceases to be the Lion. He is not a tame lion, Ben. His ways are above ours. The gods of our imagination never surprise us. Yesu does. For he is far greater than what we imagine—that is why he can fill the hole in our hearts that man-made gods cannot."

"The lion on your table—is it a symbol of Yesu?"

"You are figuring out many things. My American roommate is not so dumb as he looks. Only kidding! The lion is a common Chinese figure, so the PSB does not know that when we look at the lion, we think of him. The lion's hand is upon a ball. That ball is the earth. The world is in the Lion's paw. Not even the dragon can take it from him."

"But if he's a lion, how do you know he won't . . . eat you?"

Quan thought for a moment. "I would rather be eaten by him than be fed by anyone else."

Ben stared at him, unsure what to say.

"Suffering reminds us we are in a spiritual war. We know who we are fighting for. We know who the enemy is. Even in our cells we pray for believers outside China, especially in America. In your affluence and freedom perhaps you forget you are at war."

"I'll get you your freedom."

"Someone else has already done that. The Lion."

"I'm talking about real freedom."

"Yesu said, 'You shall know the truth, and the truth will set you free.'

Shengjing says, 'If the Son sets you free, you will be free indeed.' That is real freedom. One man stands inside prison and is free. Another man stands outside prison and remains in bondage. Is this not true, Ben Fielding?"

Su Gan unlocked the cell to let Quan in, then locked it again behind him. Li Quan saw no one but sensed a presence in the darkest corner, from which the stench seemed worst.

On his hands and knees, dipping a large sponge into the bucket of soapy water, Quan introduced himself to the occupant. As he started scrubbing the cement floor, the man moved a little closer, and a beam of light shone on his face. Quan cringed, hoping the man didn't notice. He was pale and twisted and shriveled, barely recognizable as a human being. His face looked like the mask Quan's father had worn after many years in prison.

"How long have you been here?" Quan asked.

The man said nothing, then cleared his throat, as if trying to remember how to speak. "I . . . do not know."

Quan realized he'd never once heard the man's voice, not so much as a scream. He had no name for this man. He'd never prayed for him.

"Have you been alone?"

"For two years was with others, in upper cell block. But fell out of favor. I am a political dissident," he said wearily. "A guard heard me speak against Party. Tortured me. Put me here. That was . . . perhaps three years ago? I do not know."

"What is your name?"

He paused as if trying to remember. "Wan. My name is . . . Wan Hai."

"I am Li Quan." He reached out his hand. The man recoiled into the darkness. Quan kept his hand out, and Wan Hai inched back, then slowly extended what appeared to be a stick. His arm. Quan delicately gripped the frail crusty hand.

"Li Quan is honored to meet Wan Hai. And when he is done cleaning his floor, he would request to wash the feet of honorable Wan Hai. Then Li Quan will tell him stories, true stories, about a King who came to wash the feet of men."

40

$\mathcal{T}$HE NIGHT WAS MOONLESS, the stars brilliant. Just a few wispy clouds hung eerily, trying but failing to obscure the great points of light.

Ben walked through the grove following Li Yue, who pointed a flashlight. Ben kept tripping over rocks and fallen limbs. He started sinking into a mudhole. He cursed twice and hoped Yue didn't know those English words. He had Quan's English Bible in his left hand, since Li Yue insisted he bring it. He wished he had his own flashlight instead.

Suddenly Li Yue stopped in his tracks, turning off his light. To their left, someone stepped out from behind a tree. Ben pivoted, raising his hands.

"Ni hao," someone whispered. Li Yue embraced him.

This man also had a flashlight. A kilometer later someone else joined them, making three lights in the darkness. Ben was the only one without his own light, forced to walk in the light of others. The way was clearer now, easier to walk. Ben could see the mudholes, rocks, and branches, and avoid them. Their destination wasn't yet in sight, but traveling in the group made it much easier.

"Stop," one of the nameless travelers said with an old man's voice. "Turn off the lights of men." The flashlights all went off. "Wait and close eyes a few moments."

What's going on?

"Now open eyes and look up."

Ben looked up at a black sky swollen with stars. It was the most beautiful sky he'd ever seen. The stars seemed like pinpoints, brilliant blue and red and white, as if behind the black veil there was a great blast furnace on the verge of exploding through the pinpoints and consuming the earth in its heat and light. Ben felt like these points of light were arrows aimed at him. He longed to be pierced by them, yet was on guard to prevent that very thing.

"Behold," the old man said, "the face of God."

Pushan was blocked by the hill they'd traveled over. Ben couldn't see light from a single house.

"The face of God is easily blocked by the lights of men," the old man said. "It is there for us every cloudless night. Yet how seldom we look at it."

After they stood several minutes, Li Yue said, "We must go now."

"Always, the young must go now," the old man muttered.

Li Yue led the way another two kilometers to a small house built against a huge rock. Candlelight was barely discernible behind drawn shades on the only visible window. Yue led the way around the far side, where Ben saw a dozen bicycles. They walked inside the house, hearing warm welcomes.

The house was much bigger than it appeared from the outside. To the right, where Ben expected to see stone, was a room that was entered through the mouth of a cave. The house had been built right up to it. In the candlelight Ben could see withered greens, suggesting this space had been used to store vegetables. Ben had to stoop low to make his way in. The air was musty, with a moist, organic feel.

An old man with a long white chin beard edged him forward. Ben saw candlelight at the far end, then smelled and sensed in the shadows other people. His eyes searched the room. Wherever there was sufficient light he saw smiling faces. Three men stood, reaching out their hands to him. They wore jackets and shirts and trousers, old shoes with no socks. Work clothes. The old man led him to sit near a naked lightbulb, which hung from a hoe leaned against the stone wall.

They began singing a song with strange words, more like a story script than lyrics:

> *From the time the early church appeared on the day of Pentecost,*
> *the followers of the Lord all willingly sacrificed themselves.*
> *Tens of thousands have sacrificed their lives that the gospel might*
> *prosper.*
> *As such they have obtained the crown of life.*

Yue came to sit by Ben, squeezing between him and another man. Ben was pressed on both sides and from behind. Yue whispered, "This song is

called 'To Be a Martyr for the Lord.' It's very popular in house churches."
Ben listened as the song continued:

> *Those apostles who loved the Lord to the end*
> > *Willingly followed the Lord down the path of suffering.*
> *John was exiled to the lonely isle of Patmos.*
> > *Stephen was crushed to death with stones by the crowd.*
> *Matthew was cut to death in Persia by the people.*
> > *Mark died as his two legs were pulled apart by horses.*
> *Doctor Luke was cruelly hanged.*
> > *Peter, Philip, and Simon were crucified on the cross.*
> *Bartholomew was skinned alive by the heathen.*
> > *Thomas died in India as five horses pulled apart his body.*
> *The apostle James was beheaded by King Herod.*
> > *Little James was cut up by a sharp saw.*
> *James the brother of the Lord was stoned to death.*
> > *Judas was bound to a pillar and died by arrows.*
> *Matthias had his head cut off in Jerusalem.*
> > *Paul was a martyr under Emperor Nero.*

The song had a catchy beat, but Ben found the words bizarre and frightening. He wondered how people could sing them with such enthusiasm.

> *I am willing to take up the cross and go forward,*
> > *To follow the apostles down the road of sacrifice.*
> *That tens of thousands of precious souls can be saved,*
> > *I am willing to leave all and be a martyr for the Lord.*

Voices intensified as they sang the chorus:

> *To be a martyr for the Lord,*
> > *To be a martyr for the Lord,*
> *I am willing to die gloriously for the Lord.*

When the song was finally over, Yue said, "House caves are wonderful.
We can sing and pray as loud and long as we want. No one can hear us."

The old man whispered something to Yue, who in turn said to Ben,
"They have been praying three hours before we arrived."

"So the meeting must be nearly done?"

"No. Just starting. Chinese believers have motto: 'Little prayer, little
power. No prayer, no power.'"

Yue pointed to a few sacks. "Each brings a small bag containing food, to contribute for the two or three days they are here. Some have Bibles; some do not. Several lead a number of congregations. They are farmers, fishermen, teachers, millworkers, carpenters. Laborers of all kinds. There is a short break now. We need not whisper."

Ben looked at them sitting shoulder to shoulder, knees pressed into the backs of those sitting in front of them. He saw one man smiling broadly at him. Zhou Jin, Quan's pastor! Ben returned his smile.

The old man whispered eagerly to Yue, but Ben couldn't hear him. "He says six people are not here. They must have thought they were being followed. At least two of the pastors served as decoys."

"Decoys?"

"When we want to meet in one place, a few hours before it is time to leave, they go elsewhere and are followed by the PSB. This leaves the others more free to travel."

Zhou Jin now moved close to Ben, squeezing against him on the other side while someone else filled in his space. He pointed to a man wearing a stocking cap and whispered, "That is Chiu Yongxing. He walked a hundred and forty kilometers."

Ben did the math—over eighty miles.

"He may have been followed at first, but after thirty kilometers it is usually safe. They tire of following. He avoided police checkpoints along main roads."

"How long did it take him?"

"Five days."

Yue pointed to another man, about fifty, clothes worn but eyes and smile bright, though his teeth were a brownish yellow. "I am told this pastor lost his way. But when he arrived he was beaming. He said that as he sat at the fire last night, a man appeared to him out of the air."

"What?"

"The man said he must change his direction. He told him exactly how to get here. And then he disappeared."

Ben tried not to look as skeptical as he felt. "Do you always meet here?"

"No. If the gathering is large, sometimes in a field. We may climb the side of a mountain. One of our favorite spots is an orchard far from roads and prying eyes. This is best in winter."

"Why?"

"When it is very cold PSB does not follow us, and infiltrators usually do not come. One must want to come in order to endure such cold."

Another old man stood up. Li Yue whispered to Ben, "Meeting is starting again. He is a pastor also, from . . . sorry, no need to say."

The slightly built, hunched-over man stood behind a roughly hewn table with a single glass of water on it. Suddenly his face looked furious. He picked up the glass and stared at it, squeezing hard, shaking it and spilling water. He gripped it so hard Ben thought it would break. The veins in his temples bulged.

Is he having a seizure? Has he lost his mind?

He threw the glass to the ground three feet in front of Ben, then stomped on it, breaking it into pieces. Ben jumped to his feet and moved back, then realized he was the only one standing except the angry man. All others watched intently. A look of glee on his face, the man crushed more glass under his heel, marching around in a circle, celebrating. He looked around smugly.

Now the man peered down in the dust and saw something. He stooped to pick it up. It was a shard of glass. Then he found another shard, and another, and slivers here and there. He stomped on them again, creating more glass. He walked across the cave, then looked on the bottom of his sandals and picked off glass from them. The more he stomped on glass, the farther it spread. Now he tried frantically to reassemble the glass, as if piecing it together so he could hold it in his hand again. But it was impossible. Finally, he threw the pieces to the ground again in disgust, held up his hands in frustration, pushed people out of his way, and stalked out of the cave into the front room.

Ben stared in disbelief.

What have I gotten myself into?

Blessed are you who are poor, for yours is the kingdom of God. Blessed are you who hunger now, for you will be satisfied. Blessed are you who weep now, for you will laugh. Blessed are you when men hate you, when they exclude you and insult you and reject your name as evil, because of the Son of Man. Rejoice in that day and leap for joy, because great is your reward in heaven.

As he viewed his son languishing in prison, Li Tong recited the words, whispering their comfort, hoping somehow Quan might sense them.

His companion placed his hand on the man's shoulders. "And what of your faith, Li Tong, now that you have received your great reward—or rather, the beginnings of it?"

"I wish I had seen then with greater clarity. I did find peace. At times I rejoiced. But I never remember leaping for joy."

"But now you leap for joy, don't you?"

"Every day. Earth was going out in the cold and cutting the wood and shoveling the coal. Heaven is sitting in front of the fire with family and friends, basking in the warmth, and laughing and dreaming of tomorrow without fearing what it will bring."

Li Tong reached out to his companion's hands, lifting them up and inspecting them. "But know that I will never forget the price paid for my joy."

While Ben sat there still stunned, there were many smiles, affirming grunts, and a smattering of applause. Three younger men did their best to pick up shards of glass, then put them carefully in a silk scarf. Now the old pastor reentered the cave, smiling and nodding.

Ben leaned over to Li Yue. "What just happened?"

While they sang another song, Li Yue put his lips to Ben's ear and whispered. "Many years ago Ni Tuosheng—Watchman Nee—was asked to speak at a gathering. He knew in the crowd there were many authorities wanting to arrest him as soon as he spoke about Yesu or church. When he stood, there was a glass of water by him. Suddenly he threw it down, then crushed it with his heel. But the more violently he crushed it, the more the glass spread. Everywhere he put his foot down, glass spread farther. Then he sat down. The unbelievers thought he had gone mad. But the believers understood. It was a sermon without words. They did not arrest him—how can you arrest a man for preaching when he has said nothing?"

"But what did it mean?"

"In attempting to destroy the church, the government has spread it. Instead of holding the church safely in its hand, the state has lost control of it, for the church multiplies under Communism even as Israel multiplied under Pharaoh's tyranny. China's government is desperate to regain control over the church. But the more they stalk and stomp, the more they spread the church with their own heels. They lock men in prisons, and they take the gospel there. They send women to correction farms in the country, and they take the gospel there. The glass will not be controlled. It spreads everywhere. The same state that persecutes the church is an instrument in God's hands to make the church grow."

"Quite an illustration."

"Uncle Quan used to often use it."

"Used to?"

"Auntie Ming told him to please stop—he was breaking all their glasses!"

"We are ready to be taught Shengjing," said the bearded man. "Let the teacher open to us the Word of Yesu."

The room filled with murmurings. Ben looked around, searching in the darkness for the visiting American. "Where is the teacher?" he whispered to Li Yue.

"He is here."

"Where?"

"He is about to step forward."

"Who is he?"

"His name is . . . Ben Fielding."

41

SU GAN, knuckles bloody, struck Quan's face again.

"Write a confession!"

"Why do you need me to write one when you can write your own and say I wrote it?"

He hit him again. "Confess!"

"What shall I confess?"

"Treachery. Betrayal. All your crimes against the state."

"But I have done nothing wrong—I mean, not those crimes you accuse me of. I have done many wrongs of my own. Those I have confessed to my God." Quan's eyes were dark with grief. "What can I write?"

Su Gan struck him again and handed him the pencil and a pad of paper. "Illegal meetings. Illegal propaganda. Proselytizing children."

Quan grasped the pencil, his head throbbing and vision partly blurred. The words started coming out on the paper. He wrote faster and faster. Su Gan stepped backward, watching quietly. He began to smile.

After ten minutes, Li Quan finished writing. He handed the confession to Su Gan. The guard took it, opened the door, then marched to the warden's office.

The all-seeing eyes, a moment ago deep pools of grace and long-suffering, looked upon Su Gan and metamorphosed into something explosive and terrifying. The One who seconds earlier seemed poised to reach out and touch and heal now seemed more likely to reach out and grab a sword and bring it down upon the earth, slicing it in two. His love for the persecuted seemed inseparable from his wrath toward their persecutors.

As surely as the moist eyes of compassion had looked on Li Quan, so now the hot volcanic eyes stared down on Su Gan. He gazed over all the silent planet, the globe once green and blue that now looked ashen gray. Charis looked like it was about to breathe fire, and earth looked like dry paper about to burst into flames. Li Manchu, Li Wen, and Li Tong held their breath, wondering if the moment had come.

Then the King's eyes softened again. Blue and green returned to the earth. The planet that had seemed on the verge of destruction remained intact.

For now.

"God has sent you from America to speak to us. We are ready."

"But . . . I'm not . . . you don't understand. There's no way I can—"

Li Yue raised Ben to his feet.

"Is this some kind of trick? What do I have to say to these people?" He spoke to Yue in English, hoping no one else understood. They seemed not to. In the silent pause, each person in the cave looked at him . . . waiting . . . expecting.

Suddenly, as if on cue from hidden direction, each head bowed, and several prayed fervently. A billowing wave passed through Ben. Should he try to do this impossible thing?

"Welcome," someone cried out. "Teach us the words of God."

"What am I supposed to teach?" Ben asked Yue. "The only subject I know is business."

"Yesu has brought you to teach us. Not about business, but God's Word."

Li Yue turned to the group and spoke Chinese. "What would you like the American Ben Fielding to teach?" An animated discussion followed, some of which Ben couldn't understand. The pastor who had walked five days seemed to have some strong opinions, as did Zhou Jin.

"They do not care about business," Yue finally said. "They want you to teach the Bible. They are now deciding which book."

"Why are the old men doing all the talking?"

"Because they are *Lao Da*, First Brothers. Well versed in Shengjing. They have earned the right to decide. Many have spent long years in prison."

"Teach us," a Lao Da said, "book of John."

Ben flipped through Quan's English Bible, not remembering if John was at the beginning, middle, or end. Finally, he turned to the table of contents. There it was. He quickly turned to page 927. "I guess I can just read it."

"Yes, read each verse to us and then teach us what it means," Yue said. "For us to understand, you must understand. Simply read it out loud until you do."

"But . . . where do I start?"

"At the beginning."

Smiling faces leaned forward in anticipation, nearly a third of them with their own Bibles, and the others looking on. Ben glanced at Zhou Jin, the eloquent old pastor whose teaching he had sat under for several Sundays. Why wasn't he doing the speaking?

"Speak Mandarin or English," Yue said. "I can translate." Ben traded Bibles with Yue, then began reading in Mandarin. He struggled, still unfamiliar with some of the distinctively biblical vocabulary.

> From the first he was the Word, and the Word was in relation with God and was God. This Word was from the first in relation with God. All things came into existence through him, and without him nothing was. What came into existence in him was life, and the life was the light of men. And the light goes on shining in the dark; it is not overcome by the dark.

Li Yue led in prayer, asking God to empower Ben Fielding to open his Word. Ben looked up into the eyes of the twenty-one men and five women in this cave. He noticed for the first time a man in front, with an eager face, who had a long scar across his brow.

As he read, they nodded solemnly. Ben could see that the words meant far more to them than to him. He continued reading until he reached verse 18. He stopped because the Mandarin Bible had a section heading there.

Ben spoke English. "Well, I suppose this is talking about how . . . the Word was in relation with God and that it was . . . well, that it was . . . God, I guess, or something like that. And . . . that everything, or mostly everything anyway, came into existence through it . . . or him, or whatever. Maybe it all happened at the big bang or something. Anyway, you know what I'm saying?"

One look at Li Yue indicated he did not. Ben had turned to Yue for translation. What he got instead was a look of complete bewilderment.

Yue attempted a Mandarin translation that was also halting, but Ben noticed it came out much better than his original. Hearing Yue's improved version, he hoped that he'd bail him out so Ben wouldn't come across as idiotic as he felt. Ben attempted to read, then rephrase and comment on each verse. In his desperation, he started praying he would remember things he'd heard long ago, in college Bible studies and in church. He struggled to rephrase what the words themselves seemed to indicate.

Ben tried speaking Chinese again, but realized quickly that when he spoke English and Li Yue translated, they responded much better. When commenting, he returned to English, which was less of a strain and allowed him to think of what to say next while Yue translated. Backtracking a bit, he continued to read the actual verses directly from the Chinese Bible.

"'And so the Word became flesh and took a place among us for a time; and we saw his glory—such glory as is given to an only son by his father—saw it to be true and full of grace.'"

The murmurings were powerful. The men and women looked at Ben as if he were a profound teacher.

But all I'm doing is reading! Then it hit him. *It's the book that touches them, not my comments.*

When he resumed his commentary, they quieted down. At that moment it sunk in. *The Word is Yesu. Christ is the Word.* Ben was reading about Jesus. *That's who this Word is—Jesus!*

Learning from Yue's commentary, Ben began to see Jesus throughout the verses. By the time he got to chapter 2, Yue's translation was getting closer to what Ben was actually saying, because what Ben was saying was truer to the book. His words seemed redundant, but he saw that each person received each statement about Jesus with both solemnity and joy.

Ben read from chapter 3:

> For God had such love for the world that he gave his only Son, so that whoever has faith in him may not come to destruction but have eternal life. God did not send his Son into the world to be judge of the world; he sent him so that the world might have salvation through him. . . . And this is the test by which men are judged: the light has come into the world and men have more love for the dark than for the light, because their acts are evil. The light is hated by everyone whose acts are evil and he does not come to the light for fear that his acts will be seen. But he whose life is true comes to the light. . . .

Ben read and reread each verse, trying to convey the meaning. He continued through chapters 4 and 5.

Near the end of chapter 5 Ben read, "'How is it possible for you to believe while you accept praise from one another and make no effort to obtain the praise which comes from the only God?'"

Suddenly, Ben felt beads of sweat on his forehead. He was dizzy. He looked at his watch. It was eleven-thirty. He'd been speaking over three hours. "I need to sit down."

"Yes. But continue teaching," said a Lao Da.

One of the women brought him an old wicker chair, bumping it into heads along the way. Another brought him water. After the first sip he only pretended to drink. He assumed the water was unboiled and knew his American stomach couldn't tolerate it.

Sitting down, Ben read through chapter 6:

> The bread of God is the bread which comes down out of heaven and gives life to the world. "Ah, Lord, they said, give us that bread for ever!" And this was the answer of Jesus: "I am the bread of life. He who comes to me will never be in need of food, and he who has faith in me will never be in need of drink."

Ben departed from reading the text to ask a question. "Have you ever been really hungry?" They nodded. Moments later a woman brought him a hard yellow corn bun and, beside it, rice with warm broth poured on it. They all laughed. She passed around food to the others also.

Though some ate nothing, others had bowls of their own, and chopsticks flew as he spoke. When Yue translated, Ben took quick bites. The food helped, but his lips were parched. The cup was right in front of him, but he didn't dare drink tainted water.

Ben began to lose his focus. But he continued to read and reread into chapter 7.

> On the last day, the great day of the feast, Jesus got up and said in a loud voice, "If any man is in need of drink, let him come to me and I will give it to him. He who has faith in me, out of his body, as the Writings have said, will come rivers of living water."

"Have you ever been really thirsty?" Ben asked, licking his lips. Everyone nodded and grunted confirmation. "Perhaps only those who have thirsted deeply can appreciate these words." Ben felt his head bob to the left.

"The teacher must rest," Yue announced, standing up.

One of the women came forward with something in her hand. Bottled water! It must have been bought from the market. She opened the bottle for him. Hearing the sound of freshness, he grabbed it eagerly, put it to his mouth, tipped back his head, and swallowed. It was cool but, most importantly, it was wet. He couldn't remember anything tasting better. Oblivious to everyone watching him, he let his weary head tilt and the water fall into his mouth. A little splashed out from his lips and fell onto his shirt. A moment later, the bottle was empty.

This generated bursts of laughter and much nodding and whispering.

Yue said to Ben, "You ask *them* a question. You may eat or rest while they answer."

Ben asked in Mandarin, "Why do you come so far and stay up so late at this seminary?"

"Most of us with theological training are very old," said a Lao Da. "Without proper Bible instruction, heresy is big problem. Three-Self seminaries not many enough or good enough. House church leaders cannot go. Church grows too fast. Cannot keep up with the harvest."

"New believers lack discernment," said the powerfully built and deep-voiced man with the long scar above his brow. "They embrace strange teachings. Young leaders must be taught to recognize heresy."

"What kind of heresy?" Ben asked.

The Lao Da looked at each other as if wondering where to begin.

One little man, missing most of his teeth, spoke up. "A man who was disobeying Yesu fell into an old well while walking through a deserted field. He landed upside down, stuck in the well. It was not big enough to turn around in, so he started praying: 'Lord, if you get me out of here, I will follow you forever.' He called out for help, but he knew it was useless. The blood continued to rush to his head. Eventually he was too weak to cry out. Suddenly he heard voices. He felt a rope around his legs. Soon they pulled him out, and he breathed fresh air."

"That's wonderful," Ben said.

"What is not so wonderful is this—he now leads a cult of more than ten thousand who believe the only way to pray is while standing on your head."

"You're kidding."

"Very serious," said another Lao Da. "What the Communists cannot do to the church, heresy can. Most trouble comes not from atheists who say there is no God, but from those who adopt strange ideas because of no training in Shengjing. There are millions of new believers without Shengjing. Some are led by persons calling themselves christs or prophets. Some teach that believers must divorce nonbelieving spouses. Some say conversion must be evidenced by three days and nights of crying aloud to God."

"In my village," said one man, "two women have attempted to sacrifice their sons, imitating story of Abraham and Isaac. They had no other Bible portions."

"All this makes government distrust house churches," Li Yue said. "Yet government causes the heresy by keeping Shengjing from us, pushing us underground, forcing us either not to be taught Shengjing or to risk our freedom to meet like this."

"Perhaps this will change," said another man. "I have heard government is starting to permit radio broadcasts that teach Bible, so that if people must believe Shengjing, at least they will not fall into errors that endanger others."

"I am Pastor Fu Chi," said the powerfully built man with the scar on his brow. "I am from An Ning village across the mountain. I have met your friend Li Quan. A fine brother."

Ben nodded, surprised to feel a sudden wetness in his eyes. He looked at the man's scar again. "Wait. Are you the one spoken of by Wang Shaoming?"

"Yesu's mountain warrior? That is what we call Wang Shaoming," Fu Chi said, smiling. Several others grunted affirmation. "I came over the mountain to seek more training in Shengjing. Four weeks ago, my son was arrested for distributing gospel literature given him by Shaoming. I will not return to my village until I find what has happened to my only son."

"I understand," Ben said.

"But you asked a question," Fu Chi said in his rich, low voice, "and here is my answer. People are more hungry for spiritual food than for rice and bread. Without having the skills to discern the truth, they can easily be drawn into groups with false teachings. One man from a nearby village told me, 'I must hear the voice, I must hear the voice. . . .' His church elders had given him until the twenty-second of the month to hear the voice of God. If he did not hear the voice, he would be eternally damned. No wonder he was distraught, for it was nearly midnight of the twenty-first! Later, we learned he had committed suicide."

Fu Chi hung his head. "He belonged to one of the audible-voice cults. Its founder was given a single page of Scripture. The fragment was from Acts 9, the story of Paul's conversion on the road to Damascus. With no other passages to look at, the pastor concluded, 'This is how we know we are saved—when Jesus speaks audibly to us.'"

"You see why we need your help," said another Lao Da. "We need theological training. Persecution is not the worst problem we face. Heresy is. Zeal without knowledge. It is a crisis."

"The evil one is a deceiver, a liar," said Fu Chi. "If he cannot keep people from following Yesu, he will do all he can to twist their service. Our country is so big, the people so poor. Too poor to travel to discipleship classes. People in countryside have barely finished grammar school. In some rural provinces illiteracy is still eighty percent. New converts come from shamanism. Witchcraft and sorcery are common. Without good Bible teaching, how can we expect them to leave these things behind?"

They talked about this for thirty minutes. Ben was so fascinated by their stories that he had to remind himself to start eating again. Now they spoke of informants and infiltrators in the churches.

"Sometimes," Fu Chi said, unconsciously rubbing his long scar, "we must take extreme measures to be sure to weed out infiltrators."

"But sometimes," Zhou Jin said, looking right at Fu Chi, "the measures taken are too extreme."

"You are finished resting?" a woman said to Ben. "We ask you questions now. You are a pastor in America?"

"No."

"Elder? Deacon?"

"No."

"How you serve your church?"

"Well, I . . . uh . . . "

"You good teacher. You teach in your church?"

"No."

"Do you assist needy on behalf of church?"

"Well, not exactly."

"How do you serve your church, then?"

"Let our friend rest a few more minutes," Li Yue said. "He is weary. They do not teach so long in American churches. He must gather strength to stand again and teach words of Yesu."

"We're not done yet?" Ben asked.

After they sang and prayed half an hour, Ben read again until his head was bobbing. Li Yue insisted the meeting end for the night. He prayed a final blessing. It was nearly 3:00 A.M.

"Done now," Yue said to Ben. "Some will sleep outside. You are the teacher, so you sleep on bed. In the morning, we will have breakfast. Then you teach."

"Again?"

"They will leave only after you have finished the book of John."

"But we're only on chapter 9. How many chapters are there?"

"Twenty-one."

Ben stared blankly, unable to subtract nine from twenty-one.

"You are fortunate," Li Yue said, smiling. "I have seen them confiscate a Bible teacher's luggage to keep him from leaving town. They are eager to be taught."

Ben stumbled toward the bed that had been cleared for him. He was sure that once asleep, he'd never wake up again. But if he did, he would need to pick up the pace of his teaching. Ben Fielding put his ragged head down on the bed, with no pillow. Before he could decide if it was comfortable, before he could find just the right position, he fell sound asleep.

42

QUAN'S HEAD THROBBED. He'd had no water for a day and a half. He looked forward to Ben's next visit. Surely he would come soon. He prayed this time he might find the right words to say, words which Yesu might use to touch the heart of his old friend. He also asked himself a question: "Is this the day?"

Quan recited a psalm: "'As the deer pants for streams of water, so I long for you, O God.'" Then he spoke the words of Yesu: "'If anyone is thirsty, let him come to me and drink.'"

Li Quan could almost feel water in his mouth.

For a moment, he could see the wall at the other end of his six-foot cell. Somehow, from somewhere, a diffused light had filled the room. He felt as if words were being spoken to him. And though he could not make them out, he could see their light and sense their comfort. His thirst was still real. But he could almost taste the cool water of a hidden stream. Almost.

The Watchers searched the earth, their eyes probing every tent, cave, hole, and dungeon. The King looked at the continents, his eyes searching from place to place. He would pause periodically, watch, and nod.

In the Netherlands a small church gathered on its knees to pray for the persecuted. In Australia a church took a special offering to assist a ministry getting Bibles into closed countries. In Korea a church made plans to cross the border. In Singapore a man left his family to board a plane for a remote destination. The King's eyes rested now on a fifth-grade Sunday school class in America, as the children collected money.

"This is all I earned last summer mowing lawns," said a boy.

"This is the money I was saving for a bicycle," a little girl said, smiling.

Another boy proudly handed his teacher an envelope. She opened it, then looked at him. "Where did this come from?"

"I told Dad and Mom we'd been talking about persecuted Christians and how to help them. I told them how we were all making a sacrifice to collect money to help. My parents said they wanted to help, too. So I said we didn't have to go to Disneyland. Maybe we could just go to the beach for the weekend. That's what we did. We had a great time. This is all the money we would have spent, you know, for planes and hotels and admissions and everything."

The King watched, nodding and smiling. He whispered something. The King's whisper was so powerful all heaven heard it.

"Thank you," he said to the children in the Sunday school class. He turned to the men, women, and angels of the watching heavens. "Whatever you did for one of the least of these brothers of mine, you did it for me."

The King turned to Writer. "It is engraved in my mind. I will never forget it. But write it down, that all Charis will never forget either."

He looked back to the dark planet, to the people on their knees, the man on the airplane from Singapore, the church taking the offering, the children in the Sunday school class.

"Never will I forget what you have done for me—never will anyone forget. Your reward shall be great!"

The next thing Ben knew, something warm touched the tip of his nose. The morning light stung his eyes through the window, illuminating the bowl of sticky rice held by a Chinese woman. Her face brought back the memories of teaching Shengjing verse by verse inside a cave. Had it been a dream? No. The faces and smells were too real, as were the buzz and blur of bodies in the room around him now.

Within thirty minutes of waking, teacup in one hand and Bible on his lap, Ben sat in the wicker chair and slowly read John 10 aloud. He read and reread each verse over and over until he sensed that both he and everyone understood. Occasionally, he asked questions. Had any of them tended sheep? Two said they had. Or he might ask them to explain what it meant for Yesu to be a shepherd and for men to be his sheep. Their answers were insightful. Ben listened like he'd never listened before. In listening to their wisdom he learned things he'd never thought about. And as they spoke he sensed an urging, a nudging, as if some wonderful yet frightening moment was approaching. It was like watching summer clouds build on a hot afternoon, thunderheads gathering before a storm.

Two hours later, he read, "'Let not your heart be troubled: have faith in God and have faith in me. In my Father's house are rooms enough; if it was not so, would I have said that I am going to make ready a place for you? And if I go and make ready a place for you, I will come back again and will take you to be with me, so that you may be where I am.'"

"I guess this is talking about . . . heaven, isn't it?"

Fifty minutes later, he began the fifteenth chapter.

I am the true vine and my Father is the gardener. He takes away every branch in me which has no fruit, and every branch which has fruit he makes clean, so that it may have more fruit. . . . Be in me at all times as I am in you. As the branch is not able to give fruit of itself, if it is not still on the vine, so you are not able to do so if you are not in me. I am the vine, you are the branches: he who is in me at all times as I am in him, gives much fruit, because without me you are able to do nothing. If a man does not keep himself in me, he becomes dead and is cut off like a dry branch; such branches are taken up and put in the fire and burned.

Ben stared at the words. He said to the group, "I see the food is ready. We will eat now, and then I will explain these verses." Though he was truly hungry, Ben just wanted to buy time. If he was going to explain those verses, perhaps he could use the break to try to figure out what they meant.

Where was Ben? Had he gone back to America? Quan wanted to talk to him about his spiritual need. He had prayed Ben would come this morning. Why had God not answered his prayer?

Despair dropped upon Quan like a weight from the sky. Sleepless all night, in terrible pain, he was filled with dread and loathing of himself, fear for Shen and Ming, and despair for the soul of Ben Fielding. He writhed and trembled in the darkness, weeping in despair. "Help me, Yesu."

Then, standing, staggering across his cell, he cried out in a loud voice,

"Get away from me, Mogui! Li Quan is not yours to destroy. He belongs to another—the One who crushed your head. I call upon the blood of Yesu to take your claws off the soul of Li Quan." He picked up the chair, as if using it to ward off a great beast. "You have no power over me, Satan. Your battle is with my King. Him you cannot defeat!"

Li Quan fell to the ground like a rag doll, one hand still gripping the chair. In that instant, the invisible hand of another gave him the gift of sleep.

After a long afternoon and a short dinner, Ben stood and picked up where they'd left off, in the middle of John 19, two chapters from the end.

> "Here is your king," Pilate said to the Jews. Then they gave a loud cry, "Away with him! Away with him! To the cross!" Pilate said to them, "Am I to put your King to death on the cross?" The chief priests said in answer, "We have no king but Caesar." Finally Pilate handed him over to them to be crucified.

Since Ben had read the words in Mandarin, Li Yue didn't need to translate. But Ben stopped anyway. The words caught in his throat. He sat down.

Li Yue spoke for a few minutes, saying, "Only Yesu is Caesar." Then he taught his way into chapter 20, which told of Christ appearing after his resurrection. Finally, Ben indicated he was ready to continue. He stood up and read:

> Then he said to Thomas, "Put out your finger, and see my hands; and put your hand here into my side: and be no longer in doubt but have belief." And Thomas said in answer, "My Lord and my God!" Jesus said to him, "Because you have seen me you believe: a blessing will be on those who believe though they have not seen me!" A number of other signs Jesus did before his disciples which are not recorded in this book: But these are recorded, so that you may have faith that Jesus is the Christ, the Son of God, and so that, having this faith you may have life in his name.

Ben felt a great weight upon his shoulders and an aching emptiness inside his chest. He gestured for Li Yue to take his place again. He leaned against the chair. As he walked out he mumbled to the group, "I do not feel well. Li Yue will finish."

Ben pressed through the thick, humid air of the intimate gathering, then walked out the door under the night sky. Another moonless night. He breathed deeply.

He walked away from the house, approaching a lone ginkgo tree towering so high it seemed to penetrate the sky. He gazed at the stars and said many things to their Maker. He spoke of the terrible things he had done, dishonesties and abandonments and betrayals—things which up until recently he thought he'd had such good reasons for doing. He mentioned by name Pam, Melissa, Kimmy, and Doug among those he'd hurt. Ben Fielding fell to his knees, taking no thought for the appearance of his clothes.

"It is hard for me to believe in you, Jesus. Yet I do believe what is written. It has the ring of truth. You are the one I've run from. You are what I have longed for all these years. Maybe I never believed, even back in college when I thought I did. You're the King, not me. I'm tired of trying to run my life. I'm not qualified. I've messed up everything. I do believe now that Jesus is the Christ, the Son of God. I ask for the life you promised. I ask for your Holy Spirit inside me. Please wash me from my sins. Please fill the hole in my heart, Jesus. Please be to me what I have always longed for. I can't make it on my own. I need you."

In a dark cell fifteen kilometers away, a lonely prisoner prayed for the soul of Ben Fielding. Inside the house church twenty meters away, as the teaching continued, many were praying that the teacher from America would be healed. Outside, under the night sky—under the face of God—their prayers were being answered.

In another place, great cheering and rejoicing erupted. Shouts and laughter and celebration filled the air. Ben, still on his knees, looked up, thinking for a moment he heard something in the breeze, something from just over the hillside. For the first time he could remember, he felt as if he wasn't alone.

43

$\mathcal{Q}$UAN ENTERED THE CELL that housed the raspy baritone voice he'd vaguely recognized but hadn't been able to identify. He'd named him Silas and prayed for him daily.

Quan was stunned at what he saw. A body that looked as if it had once been powerful lay broken. His left leg and right arm had been shattered and not set. There was a huge gash across his forehead, infected and seeping. Quan did all he could to help him, wishing he'd had medical training.

He held Silas in his arms. He gave him the bottle of water Ben Fielding had gotten to him, at what price Quan didn't know.

"Drink more," he said to the man.

The man did so gratefully. Finally, he asked Quan, "Do you not recognize me?"

Quan stared at him. At first the wound reminded him of the long gash of Scarbrow. But it was more than that—yes, he saw the face of the young lieutenant in the house church raid. "Are you the son of Fu Chi?"

He nodded. "Fu Liko, only son of Fu Chi, pastor of An Ning village. Perhaps I will have a scar to match my father's."

Quan held him close and sang to him gently. Then he spoke words written on his heart, which no man could take from him: "'They will neither harm nor destroy on all my holy mountain, for the earth will be full of the knowledge of the Lord as the waters cover the sea.

"'In that day the Root of Jesse will stand as a banner for the peoples; the nations will rally to him, and his place of rest will be glorious.'"

"I ask you again to forgive me," Fu Liko whispered. "I regret what we did that morning. I am sorry especially to have frightened your son. He is a brave boy. I have a daughter his age."

"You need not ask twice for forgiveness," Li Quan said. "Our God hears and forgives the first time."

"I never made it back to my village. I have not seen my daughter for three months. Perhaps I will not see her again in this world."

Quan whispered to Fu Liko, *"Zhen jin bu ba huo lian."*

The young man nodded. "Real gold fears no fire."

Quan supported his brother's head, resting it against his chest. Softly he sang, "Heaven is my fatherland . . ." and stroked the hair of Scarbrow's only son.

A small man with coal-black skin stood before a huge assembly that stretched farther than Li Tong's perfect eyes could see.

"We have beheld the continents of the dark planet. We have witnessed the suffering of our brothers and sisters. We remember our afflictions, rejoicing that we have been forever delivered from them. But our brethren have not yet been delivered. I will read the words of Elyon. Listen now to the plea of the suffering. We pray on their behalf the inspired words:

> O Lord, how long will you look on? Rescue my life from their ravages, my precious life from these lions. I will give you thanks in the great assembly; among throngs of people I will praise you. Let not those gloat over me who are my enemies without cause; let not those who hate me without reason maliciously wink the eye. They devise false accusations against those who live quietly in the land. O Lord, you have seen this; be not silent. Do not be far from me, O Lord. Awake, and rise to my defense! Contend for me, my God and Lord."

With one voice a multitude of witnesses shouted, "O Lord, you have seen this; be not silent. Do not be far from them, O Lord."

The ground under Li Tong shook, and now he added his own voice to that of the throng. They turned toward the throne and met the eyes of him who sat upon it: "Awake, and rise to their defense! Contend for them, our God and Lord!"

"The warden will see Li Quan," the guard said, opening the door.

"You called me by my name, Su Gan. Have I become a person to you?"

Su Gan said nothing but gave Quan a halfhearted shove.

As they walked, Quan said, "I have told you before of the love of Yesu. Have you surrendered to him yet?"

The guard shoved him again, more lightly than before.

"You have told me many times to stop smiling, even when I wasn't. Why do you say that to me?"

"Because . . . your eyes seem always to smile."

They entered the warden's large office. Quan had never been there. Two guards he recognized stood there with three men he did not know, two of them in suits and ties.

The warden trembled, his face red. He stood behind his desk. "You call this a confession? How dare you write such things?"

Quan did not answer.

"Speak up or I will kill you where you stand!"

Quan breathed deeply. "You can kill me only if Yesu allows it, but you cannot kill his church. The early Christians said, 'The blood of the martyrs is the seed of the church.' When each martyr dies, a thousand Christians rise to stand in his place."

The warden, eyes dark and murky, stepped in front of his desk, walked within five feet of Li Quan, then whipped his head side to side menacingly, like a rabid dog.

"Listen to the confession of Li Quan!" The warden held up the letter to the light and read:

> Yesu created all men and women. They chose their own way and became sinners, falling away from their Creator. But he loves them so much he became one of them, and died on the cross for their sins. He invites each man or woman to confess their sins and accept his gift of salvation. All who do not do this go to eternal hell, sins unforgiven. All who accept God's gift in Yesu become part of his church. They will live with him forever in heaven. Bow your knees before him today, before it is too late.

The warden jerked his head so furiously, a fleck of spittle flew from the corner of his mouth. He threw the paper to the floor and stomped on it. Quan braced himself, certain he'd be struck.

But suddenly the warden froze. A stone silence fell upon the room. The warden tried to speak, but his tongue was stuck to the base of his mouth. It could not move. He choked, trying to swallow, then fell to the floor.

Su Gan ran to him and pulled him up. They staggered to his chair behind the desk. Su Gan brought him a glass of water. The warden drank, then tried to put the glass down on the desk, but it fell to the floor and broke. The warden stood and staggered again, accidentally stepping on the glass. Frustrated, he stomped on it, breaking it into little pieces that scattered across the floor, one large sliver sliding right up to Li Quan.

Still no words were spoken. The last words the warden had read—the words of Li Quan, the scrubber of prison floors—permeated the room like a rare flower's fragrance . . . or like an executioner's sword.

The great general approached the throne's right hand. He walked upon the transparent brown marble overlooking the earth's continents. He took care not to step upon the long red carpet with gold lines, for it was a path reserved strictly for others.

He knelt to the front right of his Commander's throne, with the continent of Archland, on earth called South America, directly under him.

"Welcome, Michael," said the King. "What do you hear from your comrades, and what do you see of Adam's race?"

"Your soldiers' request remains the same. That you give them leave to destroy your enemies and raise your royal standards in their blood. Your servants wish to invade the dark planet and fight the holy war at last. They do not want to witness the shedding of one more drop of innocent blood. They long to bury forever the twisted ones who insult their King and try to usurp that which belongs to you alone."

The King nodded. "Yes, I see them pacing like caged lions, looking down, eager to unleash my judgment. They wish to punch a wide hole into the dark planet and destroy all the enemies of Charis."

"Yes, my Lord. But is not this yearning from you? We are not the inventors of righteousness. Is not the destruction of evil and the establishment of justice what you yourself have ordained?"

"Yes," he nodded. "In the right time."

"But when, if I may ask, Lord, will the time be right? Your servants wonder why you do not end it all now."

"And you wonder the same, Michael, faithful warrior." The King stood and walked, Michael following one full stride behind him on his right side. "The moment I bring justice and relieve all suffering is the moment earth's inhabitants' eternal destiny is sealed. Not one more shall be joined to me then. To 'end it all,' as you say, will also mean to end the offer of grace—a grace I delight to offer, a violent grace that cost me dearly."

"We do not want the wicked to go unpunished."

"They will not."

"We do not want the righteous to go unrewarded."

"They will not."

"We want the wicked image-bearers to face their punishment."

"And so they will—all who reject my offer."

"We want your servants to be comforted."

"I comfort them every hour. And the day of eternal comfort will surely come, enfolding them like a warm blanket."

"Your servants wish also to take away the cause of your grief. For we see how you suffer the pains inflicted on your bride."

The King nodded. "Their passions are right and pure. I have borne my heartache as a choice. It too shall be relieved when the last of my suffering children is delivered. But not until then. I know the hour. It is not for you or them to know. Your legions mean well, Michael. But there is much about my grace that even now they do not understand."

"Yes, my Lord," Michael said.

"And what does my family say? What are the words of Elyon's children and Yesu's bride?"

"You know, Lord," Michael said. "They cry out to you, day and night. They plead for your intervention, for your return. I hear many ask, 'Where is he? Does he not care? Why does he allow us to suffer?'"

The King sighed. "Too quickly do they summon providence to the court of reason. The night will last only so long before it is swallowed whole by the morning. The longer their night lasts, the more they dream of the dawn." He looked at Michael. "This I whisper to my servants in their sleep."

The archangel nodded.

"They don't understand that I am not only at work here, preparing a place for them, but I am at work there, preparing them for that place." He looked away, then back at Michael. "It is not only men and warriors who wonder why I wait, Michael. Speak."

"How can I help but wonder why you hold back your hand of judgment and rescue?"

"My purpose is not clear to you?"

"No, my King. I am sorry. It is not." He dropped his left knee to the ground and stared at the brown floor, a bloody earth spread out beneath him.

"That's alright, faithful servant." The King put his hand on the general's great shoulder. "For my purpose is clear to me. It is the counsel of the Three I heed. None other."

Yesu looked down on the company of men suffering across the dark planet. The King lifted up his scarred hands, grotesque wounds, and turned them to the continents below. He whispered into the silent winds of cosmic space, "See, I have carved you into the palms of my hands."

44

*T*HE SUN SHONE unusually bright, but it was a frigid morning. Ben shivered as he paced back and forth. He'd been waiting at least half an hour.

The moment he saw his friend, his heart sank. Quan's body was hunched over. He looked four inches shorter. When he came close to the fence, the smell was overwhelming. Ben restrained himself from stepping away. He'd planned to tell Quan immediately about the seminary and his conversion, but not now.

"What did they do?"

"They chained my ankles and wrists together. The chain is very short. I have been bent for . . . five days."

"Five days?"

"I am not sure. Perhaps four. Or six. I am glad you came. They unshackled me and even fed me."

Ben reached out to touch the left side of Quan's face, which had an open sore only partially covered by a strip of blue cloth from his sleeve. His shirt was unbuttoned at the bottom, and the breeze showed terrible red marks that looked like burns.

"I did not expect they would let you see me again," Quan said. "Not like this."

Quan's instincts were right. Ben had been told he couldn't see Quan. He'd paid two hundred U.S. dollars to change their minds.

"What happened?"

"It is nothing bad."

"It's terrible."

"I am fortunate. Many are worse off."

"Who did this?"

"Tai Hong."

"How?"

Quan said a Mandarin word Ben had never heard.

"What's that?"

"I think you would call it a cattle prod."

Ben stared in disbelief. He wanted to scream, wanted to hire an army of mercenaries to storm this prison and burn it to the ground.

"I care about you, Quan, but this isn't just about you. These are human rights violations. The world needs to know."

"Chinese believers do not care about our rights as much as some of our Western brothers do. What consumes us is our responsibility to serve Yesu. But do not misunderstand. The efforts of our brothers for us mean much, as yours mean to me. But their prayers mean even more. So do their efforts to get us Bibles and theological training. God has given you much knowledge, and he has given us much zeal. The church in China needs both."

It seemed to Ben that a pale leathery mask had been put over his friend's real face. He could hardly bear to look at it, but he forced himself. He saw Quan's face suddenly break into a smile.

"I must tell you the wonderful news," Quan said, standing on tiptoe, reminding Ben of Li Shen. In that instant, he'd been transformed from an old man to a little boy. "There is a man named Wan Hai. A political dissident who has been here perhaps five years, two by himself. Twice I have cleaned his cell. Twice I have told him of the love of Yesu. The second time, just before they chained me, he confessed his sins and embraced Yesu. I am sorry for his suffering. And yet, if he were still a free man with an easy life, I do not think Wan Hai would have become a follower of Yesu. Temporary suffering is a small price to pay for eternal happiness."

Ben stared at his friend. "Quan, that's wonderful. But what's happening to you can't continue. You look like . . . crud."

Quan laughed. "I do not know how I look. There are no mirrors. From what you say, I should be thankful not to see a mirror, to spare myself of seeing . . . crud. But this much I know. A guard named Su Gan told me that my eyes smile."

Ben looked at him. "Yes, I believe they do." The men touched their fingers through the fence.

"I have some good news, too," Ben said. "Remember I was going to the underground seminary? Well, they asked me to teach—forced me, almost."

"To *teach*?"

"I couldn't believe it either. Somebody got mixed up, I guess. They told your nephew I was supposed to be the teacher. Given what he knew about me, he couldn't understand why, but he just did what he was told. We never figured out how they could make that mistake."

"Perhaps it was not a mistake. Or perhaps God was behind the mistake, with a hidden purpose."

"Maybe not so hidden. When I was speaking the words of Shengjing, something happened to me."

"What?"

"I started believing them."

At that moment, the guard walked toward Quan. "Wait. I have to tell you. I've become . . . a follower of Jesus. And this time I mean it!"

As the guard pulled on his arm, Quan turned his head around, smiling broadly, showing his missing teeth. He shouted, "Praise to Yesu!" then started singing. The guard slapped him. He sang louder.

The last thing Ben saw before Li Quan disappeared were his friend's tears. He knew they hadn't been caused by the slap.

"Prisoners complain we do not let them outside," the fat guard announced an hour after Ben's visit. "Today we have heard your complaints. We will put you outside."

Several murmured approval, but Li Quan knew better. The sun was bright, but it was bitterly cold. The guards led them out into a courtyard between cell blocks, not visible from the fences. They ordered them to take off their clothes and lie down on the ground. Stakes with chains attached to them were driven into the ground; then manacles were put onto the prisoners' wrists and ankles. The guards went inside. Some of them were laughing.

Quan's bare skin was already pierced by the cold. The worst part was being unable to rub his hands on his body, to move around and circulate his blood. The sun that looked like it should warm him was a fraud. The cold wind on his skin felt like he was being flayed alive. He couldn't discern the difference between freezing and burning. He wondered if hell would be like this, only without the light. He thanked Yesu that though he deserved hell he would never go there, because his King had gone to hell for him.

After four hours, his whole body went numb, and the brightness of the sun upon his closed eyes stung him. Quan's cracked lips longed for water.

He recited Shengjing in his mind. *"As the deer pants for streams of water, so my soul pants for you, O God. My soul thirsts for God, for the living God."*

At four o'clock, after five hours outside, Quan felt a shadow on his face. He opened his eyes. Two of the guards stood over him. One held out a blanket and put it over him. The other stooped over and held a cup of water close to his lips. Quan tilted his head up, trying to position himself. Then, slowly, the guard poured it out on the ground only inches from his lips. The other pulled the blanket off him. The two men laughed, then left to torment another prisoner.

Quan kept telling himself that no matter how bad this felt, the cross of Yesu Jidu had been much worse. Infinitely worse. And the one who went there for him had chosen to. No one forced him. No one could.

Delirious, half dreaming, Quan saw himself on the Florida beach he'd visited once while in college. For a moment he was warm. He saw himself biting into fruit, and felt himself swallowing its juices. For a fleeting instant, it tasted wonderful. Then the thirst returned, along with the cold.

"Hold on, beloved. It will not always be winter. The spring will come. The hard ground will thaw, and the sound of it will shake the foundations of the world."

While Writer scribbled furiously, the King stood, looked, and pointed, his eyes red with fury at the persecutors of Li Quan and his companions.

Reader said, "For the eyes of the Lord are on the righteous and his ears are attentive to their prayer, but the face of the Lord is against those who do evil."

The King cried, "Your deeds are being written, sons of dust. Every one of them. And you shall pay for every pain inflicted on those who are mine." He looked at the men, then trembled, veins showing on his face. "What you do to one of the least of these, my brothers and sisters, you are doing to me. I do not forget."

Those close to the throne backed away from the awful fury they felt as he looked down at hundreds of places across the dark planet. The penetrating eyes saw all deeds in the dark as well as those in the light. The King saw everything. And he forgot nothing.

"I can't come home yet, Martin. Quan's still in jail, he's being mistreated, and his wife and son are in trouble."

"What's wrong with you, Ben? Have you lost track of time? It's mid-January, for crying out loud. These people can take care of themselves. You're with Getz International, not Amnesty International!"

"They need me."

"*We* need you. And in case you've forgotten, we pay your salary!"

"This isn't a luxury vacation. It was your suggestion I stay with my old roommate in the first place."

"You think I don't regret that? I've regretted it every day for the last two months! I should have sent Jeffrey. This never would have happened. You've been gone twice as long as we agreed."

"We've had this discussion, Martin. I haven't taken a full vacation for five years. I've accumulated three months, easily. Not to mention sick leave."

"Are you sick?"

"Yeah, I am sick. I'm sick of a lot of things. But look on the bright side, Martin. Remember your ad slogan, 'Getz knows China—we've lived there.' Well, the longer I'm here, the more you can play that up!"

"Believe me, I've tried to console myself with that. But come on, Ben. I feel like I hardly know you anymore. What's going on?"

"What's going on is, I have a friend who's in big trouble—his rights are being trampled on."

"You can't solve the world's problems. Getz is doing twenty-eight million dollars a year in China, with potential to triple in the next five years. Remember the guy who gave me those figures? His name is Ben Fielding, and I'd like that guy to come back to earth. I won't hint anymore, Ben. The board has made it clear that if you sacrifice Getz for your personal agenda, you'll lose more than becoming CEO. You'll lose your job."

"I'm on my own, using earned vacation. I'm not representing the company."

"You'd better believe it. I was glad to hear Chi took back the Mitsubishi. I told him that, Ben. I don't want you in a company car. I don't want you passing out any more business cards when you go traipsing around like you're some private investigator or political lobbyist or something. I'd rather you not even mention Getz International. In fact, why don't you toss those business cards, will you? You've been going around like Don Quixote, jousting with windmills. You're embarrassing me, Ben. You've lost it. What do you have to say for yourself?"

"Well . . . I think I need to tell you something, Martin."

"I'm listening."

"I've . . ."

"Yes?"

"I've become a Christian."

There was a long silence.

"Oh . . . man. You've got to be kidding. Oh, that's *really* what I needed to hear, Ben. That's great. That's just *great.*"

45

$\mathcal{W}$HAT HAPPENED to your face?" Ben asked Quan.

"A little burned from sun and wind, that's all."

"They let you out in the sun?"

"Yes."

"Well, that's good. But I hope you stayed warm. Your skin looks so dry."

"It is much better now."

"But your lips are cracked and they've been bleeding. What—"

"It is better now, Ben Fielding. Do you have news from my family?"

"They miss you terribly. They send their love. But they're doing well. Shen's a pro with the Frisbee now. Ming's told me some great stories about my old roommate. Lots of visitors come by, women to help Ming, men offering to help me take care of the place. I've gotten to know most of your house church."

Quan smiled.

"I keep trying to get you out of here, and I keep hitting brick walls."

"China has many brick walls."

"When I see what you've been going through, I think about my brother-in-law. He attends a big church in California. For years he told Pam and me, 'If you serve God, you'll be healthy and prosperous.'"

"In China it is the opposite. You may be healthy and prosperous before you are a Christian. But once you start serving God, seldom will you stay that way."

"Well, maybe a gospel that's true in California but not in China isn't the true gospel."

"My friend has made a proverb. Very wise."

"You have to have hope, Quan. Don't you think things will get better?"

"They will. But in this world? That, we cannot know. Our hope is in another world. I wish you could hear the prayers in those cells I clean. The brothers are not just praying that China would be opened. We are praying that heaven would be opened in China!" He stretched his fingers through the fence. "God is accomplishing his purpose. He is above the jailers, the PSB, the mayor, and the Party. He uses them as tools in his hand. Just as he used Mao Zedong."

"Mao? God used *Mao*? Come on, Quan. When people look for evidence that there's no God, they point to Mao, Hitler, Stalin, Pol Pot, all of the mass murderers."

"Yet Mao was a tool in the hands of Yesu, to build his church."

Ben stared at Quan, incredulous.

"Mao was a mantis trying to stop a chariot," Quan said. "When the chariot driver decided it was time to move, he ran over Mao. The chairman was disposable. He tried to strangle the church. Mao died, but the church came alive. It rides in the chariot over his grave."

"Look, I'm a Christian now, Quan, and I'm really trying to understand. But . . . I just don't get what you're saying."

"Think, Ben Fielding. When Mao came to power there were fewer than a million Christians in China, and those were divided. Many leaders were seduced by Western modernism, no longer believing God's Word. The church needed inside cleansing, and outside there was little interest in Yesu. But then came Mao. My parents told me how they put loudspeakers in the lampposts and trees, and every morning they awoke to 'East Is Red,' a song about Mao being 'the great savior of the people.' Mao was a usurper, a pretender, a small man who did a large evil. His broken promises left a huge void. Many now realize Shengjing is the truth the red book claimed to be. And Yesu is the Savior Mao claimed to be."

"Still, the tens of millions of people who died . . . "

"My own father died under Mao's boot. Yet Li Tong used to say, 'Mao Zedong is China's greatest evangelist.' He created a vacuum only Zhu Yesu could fill. Mao expelled all the missionaries and persecuted the church. But a half million Christians multiplied to perhaps eighty or a hundred million today."

"But at what cost, Quan?"

"Who are we to speak of cost? God hated what Mao did, but he used it. We do not understand providence. But the Chinese say, 'A good fortune may forebode a bad luck, which may in turn disguise a good fortune.' God works beneath the surface and around the corner and above the roof. We have a saying: 'No man should judge a painting when he can only see the back of the canvas.'"

"Isn't it obvious things are out of control when you have madmen and dictators murdering people?"

"Out of whose control? Ben Fielding's? Li Quan's? Of course. But Yesu does not cower before strutting dictators. He does not bow before petty warlords like Mao and Stalin and Hitler. Mao is responsible for his evil. But Shengjing says, 'The king's heart is in the hand of the Lord; he directs it like a watercourse wherever he pleases.' Mao could not thwart God. In a hundred ways he prepared the way for the spread of the gospel like no missionary could."

"How? What do you mean?" Even as Ben asked, he saw a weary Li Quan energized, a history professor eager to teach and enlighten his student.

"When Mao came to power there was no road system. Missionaries who worked inland traveled for seven months. They lived on the backs of mules for the final weeks of their journey. When Mao built the roads, the church could reach to the same countryside in less than a week, and now on trains or buses, not mules."

"He built roads for his purposes, not the church's."

"That is what he thought. When he assumed power, China was divided by three hundred languages and a thousand dialects. But Mao signed a decree making Mandarin the official language. He required all business and education and public conversation to be in Mandarin. He ordered that the forty-seven thousand pictorial characters be simplified so his red book could be small and easy to carry. They were reduced to fifteen hundred. Suddenly God's Word could be translated much more easily, and the whole nation could be reached with one translation. You have heard of Wycliffe Bible Translators? They could not have done what Mao Zedong did for the church. Only six percent of the nation could read, so he ordered literacy training and now nearly ninety percent can read— nearly all who live in the cities. And are they reading his red book? No— they are reading the words of Yesu! That is, whenever we can get it into their hands."

"You really believe God was behind all this?"

"Of course. Mao intended it for evil, but God intended it for good. Mao set himself up as a god, but he was but an errand boy for the true God. As surely as God used Pharaoh to lead his people out of Egypt and into the Promised Land, he used Chairman Mao to establish the church in China."

Quan waved his hands like a professor intent on making his students understand. "Many Christians graduated with honors from their universities, yet when the government found they were attending house churches, they were punished. The authorities assigned them to the worst jobs—often in rural areas of provinces far from their homes. They were forced to do menial labor. Christian high school students were not permitted to attend college or the university. They were assigned to heavy labor in remote provinces, far from friends and families. Yet God was at work. First, he taught them humility. But then he used them as missionaries. No Christians had ever visited the remote villages where students were sent. When they went, they took the gospel. The spiritual harvest has been great. The gospel spread rapidly from one village to another. The many thousands of churches that began then are still here today, and they have spawned many more. Do you not see, Ben Fielding? Yesu defeats the purposes of Mogui. The dragon is but a dog on the Lion's leash."

"That's a picture with too many animals," Ben said, eyes closed.

"The Lion used the dragon to thwart his own desires. Instead of killing the church, he spread it."

"Like a man stepping on a glass and spreading it across the room under his feet," Ben said.

"Yes. Why, this is the very illustration used by—"

"Watchman Nee," Ben said. "Who else?"

Quan stopped speaking, clearly surprised. Ben smiled smugly, savoring the moment.

"Mao proclaimed a false gospel, and left behind a national longing for the true gospel. And still God works his plan even in acts of human evil—such as Six Four. Before then, it was very hard to talk to university students about Yesu. But their hopes for political reform were dashed, and ever since, many have looked for spiritual reform. They will listen to Yesu. As for Li Quan, I have been honored to bring Yesu's message to the locksmith's shop and now this prison."

"Why did God let Mao get away with all the suffering he inflicted? I'm not trying to be a skeptic anymore. It's an honest question."

Quan wrinkled his brow. "What makes you think he got away with it?"

"Well . . . didn't he?"

Quan studied Ben's face. "You told me you visited the Chairman's memorial in Tiananmen Square. What did you see there?"

"Well, if I hadn't been given the VIP treatment and escorted to the front, I never would have seen anything. There were thousands of Chinese in line. Everyone I saw inside held their children's hands and looked like they were mourning Mao."

"What was the room like? And the body?"

"What's that got to do with anything? Well, the building's big, but the room is small and dark. The body's in a glass case, lighted from above. I was surprised by how small the body looked. It was like a wax figure, not like a man, with the Chinese flag covering most of it."

"King Herod eaten by worms."

"Huh?"

"An angel of the Lord struck down King Herod because he did not give glory to God. Shengjing says he was consumed by worms and died, while the Word of God grew and multiplied. So it is here. Mao died. He wilted like a leaf. The Yesu he hated lives. And the church and Scriptures he tried to destroy live also."

"But Mao's party members go to their nice homes and drink champagne while you waste away in here. You don't look so good, Quan. But, frankly, they look like they're doing just fine."

"Ben Fielding speaks of looks. Man looks on the outside, but God looks on the heart. Man looks at the seen. God looks at what to us is unseen. The guard is about to come for me—it may appear he is free and I am not. But things are not as they appear. You say that evildoers are doing fine? If a man jumped off a building and you saw him out a window as he fell, he might appear to be doing fine. But very soon his condition will change, will it not? God is judge, Ben. If people turn to Yesu, they can be forgiven for evil. But never do they get away with evil. Death is not a wall; it is a doorway. We live on one side of death. There is another side."

Where is my palace? Where are my servants? Does no one know who I am?

The vast, cold darkness cut into his face. It felt like intense frostbite, burning his skin.

I was the most powerful man in Zhongguo. I created the People's Republic. I was the revered father of my country. They worshiped me. I was god! He waited, listening to the silence. *Cannot anyone hear me?*

His voice disappeared into the great dark void. It did not echo, for there was nothing for it to echo off. It was immediately absorbed into infinite nothingness. His words went no farther than his blistered lips.

A parade of untold millions marched inside his mind's eye. His sentence was to relive the suffering of each of his victims. He had been here over twenty-five years. Every minute of those years he had relived the sufferings he inflicted on others. Every torture his regime inflicted he now received, one after the next after the next. Eventually, perhaps, they would start over, so the millions he had already endured were but the first installment. The pain was unbearable, yet he had no choice but to bear it. There was no escape into unconsciousness—no drug to take, no sleeping pill, no alcohol. That which he had laid upon others was now laid upon him—endlessly, relentlessly.

He longed to pluck out his eyes, to keep from seeing what he saw, to puncture his eardrums to keep from hearing the wailing misery, to pull out his tongue to keep from tasting the awfulness he had legislated. But he had no ability to destroy himself. He had no control now over his destiny, no power over himself or others. There was no one he could command to fix the situation, no one to prepare him an eight-course meal to assuage the eternal hunger, no one to serve him mao-tai. No one with whom to plot and scheme, no one to do his work, no one to punish for their errors. No one to salute him, cower at his voice, or bow heads in his presence.

Where is everyone?

Misery loves company, and he had long sought the consolation of others. But all others were still on earth, secure in heaven, or confined to their own private hells at distances immeasurable.

The aloneness was stifling. He could hear nothing but his victims' cries, feel nothing but their pain, see nothing but their blood, taste nothing but their vomit, sense nothing but their torture. He had only himself. He could not enjoy his own company, for he saw himself as he really was. It was an ugly sight, revolting beyond comprehension.

He felt a burning. A fury welled up inside him. Anger and bitterness, unfocused hostility, frustration leading him to lash out. But there was no one to lash out at. No incompetent aide, no dissident, no Christian pastor, no helpless peasant. No one to beat or shoot or hang or starve. No one to cower in fear at the power of the great chairman, architect of the Republic. No one to shine his shoes or rub lotion upon his burning feet.

Grief and rage warred within him. His hell was a growing cancer, gnawing at him, eating away at him, devouring him. He was like a bush that burned yet was not consumed, so the burning could never stop.

He had come to death entirely unprepared—and now it was too late to prepare. If the torture was not enough, a sickening feeling of foreboding had gripped him from his first moments here. He had hoped it would subside, that he would get used to it. He hadn't. It only got worse.

He could see now through all his rationalizations. His arguments against belief in a Creator had never been intellectual ones, as he had claimed. By rejecting a Creator he thought he could rid himself of a Judge. But it had not worked. His atheism had been the opiate of his soul and the executioner of uncalculated millions. But now his comforting atheism could no longer exist, even for a fleeting moment, for he had been forever stripped of the power to deny reality.

He had lived his short todays as if there were no long tomorrow. He had believed the lie that all were accountable to him and he was accountable to none. He had believed the lie that death would slip him into eternal unconsciousness. He knew now—how well he knew—the curse of always being awake, ever alert, unable to allay his suffering with a moment's sleep or distraction.

The winds of hell blew upon him. On them floated sounds of laughter and joy from a place far distant. These voices were torture. Many he recognized as belonging to Christians he had persecuted, worshipers of the Carpenter he had murdered. He relived what he had done to them, this time on the other end of the cattle prod. By the time he had died, while he and all he stood for were in decline, they and all they embraced were in ascent. They had beaten him. Their King had dethroned him even in the other life—how much more in this one.

As they celebrated in their far-off realm, at first he had imagined they were cursing him, celebrating his demise. He thought of them as his eternal enemies who would forever speak of what a great foe he had been to them. But he had come to realize something far worse. They did not curse him. They did not relive his great campaigns against him. No. They simply did not think of him at all. He was unimportant. Insignificant. In the eternal scheme of things, he did not matter.

Not matter? How dare they ignore me! Don't they know who I am?

He had said, "I want there to be no God; I want nothing to do with him." His atheist's prayer had been answered. The everywhere-present God had chosen to withdraw his presence from this single place, turning it into a cosmic desert. This was a ghetto of massive proportions, yet so small it could slip through a single crack in the tiles of heaven. It was located in some distant and empty place, never to be feared or even stumbled upon by the citizens of Charis. His life, with all his supposed accomplishments, was but a puff of smoke, dissipating into nothingness.

Stop what you're doing and listen to me! Stop or I will . . . I will . . .

No power to give meaning to a threat. No reason to be listened to. And no one to hear him.

Thirst without water to quench it. Hunger without food to satisfy it.

Loneliness without company to alleviate it. There was no God here. He'd gotten his wish. On earth he'd managed to reject God while still enjoying his blessings and provisions. But it was excruciatingly clear now that God was the author of good. Therefore the absence of God meant the absence of good. He could not have it both ways, not here. No God, no good. Forever.

He had wanted a world where no one else was in charge, where no order was forced upon him. He had finally gotten it. He had secretly wondered if there was something beyond death, but if he went to hell, he'd fully expected to rule there. Yet here there was no king, for there were no subjects. Only one prisoner—himself—in eternal solitary confinement.

He missed the sound of laughter. There was no laughter here, nor could there be, for laughter cannot exist without joy or hope. An awful realization gripped him. There was no history here. No story line. No opening scene, no developing plot, no climax, no resolution. No character development. No travel, no movement. Only a setting of constant nothingness, going nowhere. Excruciating, eternal boredom. Nothing to distract him from the torment of the eternal now.

He had charmed his friends and cheated his enemies, but death he could not cheat, hell he could not charm. This nameless, ever-shriveling man writhed in terror. Faced with his own deeds, punished by them, he was receiving in himself the due penalty for what he had done. He longed for a visit from an emissary. He craved a well-wishing message from a foreign dignitary, delivered by a courier, a request for an audience in his illustrious presence. But no. He knew now none would ever come, or even want to. He could not return to Beijing—and knew Beijing itself would soon be gone, a flower withered in a summer's wind. Perhaps it was gone already.

No one to fear him. No one to revere him. No one to hear him. No one to think about him.

He who had claimed to be savior was forever without a Savior. Ignored and insignificant. Empty and embittered and regretful. Without a following. Without a heart. Without a hope.

Forever, time without end.

46

*B*EN, MING, AND SHEN all sat on the floor, writing with pens on the same piece of tan cloth. Ben looked at the Bible, wrote a few words, then kept looking back to be sure he had it right. Shen copied words also. Ben noticed Ming wrote swiftly yet carefully, but rarely had to look at Shengjing to know what she would write next.

The warden woke up sweating, clutching his throat, hearing a voice.

"Lan An—why do you persecute me?"

Where was the voice coming from?

"Stop hurting my children."

Lan An looked around him, waving his hands to ward off the darkness. Or to ward off the light. He fell on his knees in terror, weeping.

Li Quan sat on the bank of the Wenrong, Shen playing by the rocks, Ming at his side unwrapping a packed lunch. Ben Fielding sat nearby, with a fishing line in the water beside Quan's. Ming put ice on his burning forehead.

It was easy to imagine in the dark silence of the cell, easy to travel inside his head. Quan thanked God for his imagination, for all the books he'd read, for the stories he knew that ran through his mind when he was too weary to whisper them. The best stories had satisfied him, yet made him all the more thirsty. In this cell, stripped of comfort and ease, unable to do what he would like, he was free from distraction. He had only his mind, and what he had put into it. Quan thanked Yesu for every hour spent meditating on his Word, which constituted the reservoir from which he now drew daily. Even with the raging fire on his skin, somehow the cell became a sanctuary, a secret meeting place with his Beloved. A place where the emptiness could be filled and, when it leaked out, filled again and again.

"Then I said, 'He set my feet on solid ground and steadied me as I walked along. He has given me a new song to sing, a hymn of praise to our God.'" Though another had written the words, Quan spoke them as his own.

The cell door unlocked. Quan braced himself. In walked someone he had never seen in his cell. The warden? Was he dreaming? No. Lan An started to sit in the empty chair, but at the last moment decided to stand. He paced the small cell. "After I read your confession, something gripped my throat," the warden said. "It kept me from speaking. Do you know what it was?"

Quan nodded. "It was the hand of God."

"There is no God."

"If you believe that, why did you come to ask me?"

"I tell you, there is no God!"

"You repeat what you have been taught. Is everything you have been taught true?"

"I don't know."

"You are an educated man," Quan said. "A university graduate?"

"Shanghai Jiao Tong University." His back straightened as he said it.

"Then answer this question from another university graduate. Of all there is to know in the universe, how much do you know?"

"I am not sure."

"Then guess. Do you know thirty percent of all there is to know? Ten percent? Five?"

"Of *all* there is to know? Less than one percent."

"Yes. Much less than one percent. Now I ask you another question. Think carefully before you answer. In that greater than ninety-nine percent of all there is in the universe but which you know nothing of, is it possible God exists?"

He thought for twenty seconds, then said, "I suppose it is possible."

"Good. Then Mogui has not blinded you completely. Now it is time for Li Quan to tell you about this God. Who he is, what he demands . . . and what he offers."

On January 22, Ben came to the prison gate with a bag in his hand. The outer-perimeter guard approached him, dollar signs in his eyes.

Ben handed him the bag. The guard took out a tan Prince T-shirt with the image of a blue tennis racquet and yellow ball. He opened the neck to examine the tags. Ben swallowed hard. The man pointed to the tag.

"Extra large? Prisoner is not extra large."

"He likes his shirts big," Ben said.

"You would have to make it worthwhile for me to do this."

"Thirty dollars?"

"Before, you gave me one hundred American dollars to bring in clothes for him."

"Alright. I'll go fifty."

"One hundred," the guard said, handing the bag to Ben.

"Okay." Ben opened his wallet and gave him five twenty-dollar bills, along with the T-shirt. "But get him these two water bottles, will you? And see to it that we get a little more time to talk, okay?" The guard nodded. Ben walked to his visiting place at the fence, kicking himself for being a poor businessman by offering the hundred dollars last time.

After five minutes, Quan came out, looking closely at Ben. "My friend does not appear to have been sleeping well. As a polite American might say, you look like crud."

Ben laughed.

"Thank you for the shirt," Quan said. "I will enjoy it very much." He looked at Ben. "Are you paying bribes to visit me?"

Ben shrugged. "No matter how many phone calls and visits I make, I can't get you out."

"You must pray and be patient and not try to do so much that you oppose the hidden purposes of God."

"Yeah? Well, if I could pull it off, I'd storm this place with a bunch of Western TV cameras and expose all this corruption."

"I predict many broken cameras and broken bones, and no film leaving China. Old saying: You must cross the river before you tell the crocodile he has bad breath."

"Yeah, well I know another Chinese proverb: Man who waits for roast duck to fly into mouth must wait very long time."

Quan laughed weakly. "Ben Fielding is right. Sometimes we must not just wait, but take action!"

———————————————

"There are many wise sayings among my people."

"Yes, Li Tong. And who do you think gave them these insights?"

"You. Who else?"

The Carpenter smiled.

"One moment after men die," Li Tong said, "they know exactly how they should have lived. But then it is too late to go back and live their lives over again. Too late for the unbeliever, in the jaws of hell. But also too late for the believer, who cannot relive his life, remake his choices, this time following his King more faithfully."

"But I gave you my Word so that you did not have to wait until you died to know how you should have lived." He put his hand in the middle of Tong's back as they walked through a beautiful grove of carefully sculpted ginkgo trees, their fan-shaped leaves a rich green, swaying in a gentle breeze.

"You served me faithfully, Li Tong. Not perfectly. But faithfully. Your reward shall be great."

"My father taught me, 'Never postpone obedience to Yesu.'"

"This father of yours was wise," said someone approaching them from behind.

"Perhaps because *his* father taught *him* well," came another voice.

"Li Manchu and Li Wen," the King said, laughing. "Welcome, my friends." He put his hands on their heads and mussed their hair. "Soon there will be so many of the Li clan that I will have to add on rooms for them." All four of them laughed and embraced.

When the laughter subsided, Li Tong looked into the King's eyes and interceded for his son Li Quan, whom he could see through the portal talking with Ben Fielding outside his cell. Li Wen and Li Manchu spoke on his behalf as well. Then the King himself raised his head and prayed, calling upon his Father to work in the life of his sons Li Quan and Ben Fielding.

———————————————

"Before they take me back, I must ask you to get a message to Li Yue or Zhou Jin. They will know how to get it to the people across the mountains. It is a message for a pastor named Fu Chi."

"Fu Chi? The one with the long scar?"

"How did you know?"

"He was at the seminary in the cave. He said his son was in jail. He was looking for him. Is he here?"

"The first message from Fu Liko is for his father, Fu Chi. The second message is for Fu Liko's young bride and baby daughter. It is very important that you get these messages to them."

"I'll try." Ben took his notepad and pen from his inside jacket pocket.

"Write them carefully. The message for Fu Chi is 'I will see you again soon.'"

"He's getting out?"

"He is already out."

"I don't understand. If he's out, why can't he go home and give them the message himself?"

"He is already home."

"You've lost me, Quan."

"Fu Liko died two nights ago. Just before this, I was allowed into his cell to clean it. He knew he was about to die. He said to tell his wife and daughter three things. His daughter is just a child, so his wife must teach her these things as she gets older. I have repeated them so I would not forget. Write, Ben Fielding."

"I'm ready."

"These are the three messages of Fu Liko: Never forget Yesu is King. Never forget your home is in another world. Never forget your father will be waiting to see you again."

"I'll do everything I can to get the message to them."

"Write these words on your heart, Ben Fielding, not just on paper. For they are not only for the family of Fu Liko—they are also for me and for you."

47

*T*HE DELIVERY BOY handed the sealed envelope to Minghua. He insisted she sign for it, then quickly disappeared on his bicycle.

Minghua opened and stared at the letter.

"What is it, Ming?" Ben asked.

She handed him the notice. He read it aloud.

"'Under article seventeen of the Pushan code of justice, those who have violated ordinances making them a threat to the state shall forfeit their right to ownership of properties, which can be assumed or disposed of by the city. Because of crimes committed by Li Quan, he has forfeited the right to ownership as of the date of his imprisonment. Any residents of this house are notified that they must evacuate premises within ten days, when disposition of house and property will be assumed by Pushan Housing Authority, under command of Pushan Public Security Bureau.'"

"They are taking our house," Minghua said weakly. "Quan said it might happen someday. But . . . where will we go?" She stood, looking around the room, then began arranging things on her dresser. She went to a drawer and pulled out a sack. She put a saltshaker into it, then an unopened bottle of sauce.

"Ming—wait. You still have ten days. I'll call Johnny, our company lawyer. We'll try to fight this thing."

Ming looked at Ben. "How does the mouse fight the tiger?"

Reader spoke the Word into the portal, as if sending the message through the air to the people he and Writer watched below:

> Commit everything you do to the Lord. Trust him, and he will help you. He will make your innocence as clear as the dawn, and the justice of your cause will shine like the noonday sun. Be still in the presence of the Lord, and wait patiently for him to act. Don't worry about evil people who prosper or fret about their wicked schemes. Stop your anger! Turn from your rage! Do not envy others— it only leads to harm.
>
> For the wicked will be destroyed, but those who trust in the Lord will possess the land. In a little while, the wicked will disappear. Though you look for them, they will be gone. Those who are gentle and lowly will possess the land; they will live in prosperous security.
>
> The wicked plot against the godly; they snarl at them in defiance. But the Lord just laughs, for he sees their day of judgment coming. The wicked draw their swords and string their bows to kill the poor and the oppressed, to slaughter those who do right. But they will be stabbed through the heart with their own swords, and their bows will be broken.
>
> Day by day the Lord takes care of the innocent, and they will receive a reward that lasts forever. But the wicked will perish. The Lord's enemies are like flowers in a field—they will disappear like smoke.

Li Quan sat in Wan Hai's cell, washing his feet. When he finished, he took off his T-shirt, turned it inside out, and positioned it in a dry spot where the most light possible fell upon it. The words seemed to come off the cloth with a light of their own.

Quan pointed to the beautiful handwriting. "This is God's Word, copied by she who I am honored to call my wife, Chan Ming. This is Philippians, chapter 2. Written by the great apostle Paul. I taught you about his conversion on the road."

"Road to Damascus," Wan Hai said, sounding like an eager child.

"Yes. Wan Hai is good student. This letter was written by Paul when he was in jail."

"In jail?"

"Yes. He was in jail many times. God makes good use of people in jail.

He wants to make good use of Li Quan and Wan Hai also. Now, we will begin in verse 1."

After half an hour the guard had still not removed Quan from the cell. Su Gan was sick, and the tall, thin guard was his substitute. He stood outside the hallway, listening to every word. Li Quan occasionally asked Wan Hai a question, and he would whisper an answer.

"Now it is time for Wan Hai to read the verses." Quan moved the T-shirt, trying to find light. Suddenly, a light shone down upon it. They looked up at the window. The smiling guard held the flashlight. Both prisoners nodded to him.

Wan Hai began to read:

> Your attitude should be the same that Yesu had. Though he was God, he did not demand and cling to his rights as God. He made himself nothing; he took the humble position of a slave and appeared in human form. And in human form he obediently humbled himself even further by dying a criminal's death on a cross. Because of this, God raised him up to the heights of heaven and gave him a name that is above every other name, so that at the name of Yesu every knee will bow, in heaven and on earth and under the earth, and every tongue will confess that Yesu Jidu is Lord, to the glory of God the Father.

The men were quiet, pondering the words. What could any of them say that would be as powerful as the words themselves?

Twenty minutes later Quan pointed to a part of the shirt where the writing looked different. "This portion of the chapter was copied by Li Shen, my only son. He is eight years old."

"His handwriting is very good," Wan Hai said.

"Yes. And he is already a student of Shengjing."

They talked and discussed for another hour. Wan Hai would ask questions and Li Quan would quote Shengjing in answer to them. The guard would attend to other duties, then return and listen again.

"So Paul has said his life is to be poured out like a drink offering, but he will rejoice even in his imprisonment, and he will seek to bring joy to others. The one who dwelt in Paul in that Roman prison is the one who dwells in Li Quan and Wan Hai here in Pushan Facility Six, is he not?"

Wan Hai nodded.

"He gave his joy to Paul. Would he withhold it from Quan or Wan Hai?"

"No."

"And now we come to the final portion of the chapter." He turned the T-shirt to the side.

"What is that?" Wan Hai asked. "Those funny-looking marks?"

"That is English," Li Quan said.

Wan Hai scrunched his face. "It is very strange. It makes no sense. How can they read it?"

"No, it is not so good as Chinese. But it will serve to remind me of the right words," Quan said. "This was written by my friend Ben Fielding. He understands Mandarin, but does not write it well. So he used English. It is Ben Fielding who brought these Scriptures to us in the prison. Now, listen to what the apostle says . . . "

Wan Hai leaned forward, a thirsty man lapping up every word.

"He is a fine teacher," Li Tong said to his companion. "You have gifted him."

"Yes," said the One who had stepped down from his throne to walk with his friend in his favorite garden. "In all of Pushan there is no better teacher than Professor Li Quan."

"My source visited the prison," Johnny said. "Your friend's not doing well."

"I know that. I'm paying the guards to see him once a week, sometimes twice. The price has gone up. I've had my bank wire in money three times now. They're beating Quan, Johnny. They've even tortured him."

"I can't believe they've let you keep seeing him. Foreigners aren't allowed that kind of access. We're always given the orchestrated tour, to show us everything's okay, to make sure we don't see the dark side, nothing that could be bad PR for the regime. You know the drill, Ben. Image is everything. I'm telling you, I'm not a religious man, but it's a miracle you've been able to see your friend in this condition."

"Maybe it *is* a miracle," Ben said. "Maybe there're a lot of miracles going on around us that we don't even recognize."

"Well, I don't know about that. But watch your back, Ben. You've seen too much. I'm not trying to be melodramatic, but frankly, I've wondered . . ."

"What?"

"Just be careful, okay? I mean, visitors do die on foreign soil. Accidents. Medical problems. Whatever."

Ben tensed. "You've been reading too many lawyer novels, Johnny. What else did your contact say about Quan?"

"Apparently one of the guards had mercy and gave him a chair."

"Yeah? That's good."

"No. He says every day when the guard comes by and looks in, your friend is sitting on the floor."

"Yeah?"

"And he's talking to the chair."

Ben laughed.

"I mean it, Ben. He's not *sitting* on the chair. He's *talking* to it!"

Ben laughed again.

"I'm starting to wonder about you, Ben. Maybe Martin's right. Maybe your friend isn't the only one who's going nuts."

The King searched the silent planet, eyes burning for his needy children.

"He awaits the last martyr," Li Manchu said.

"Perhaps he's looking at him now," Li Wen said.

"It might be Li Quan," Li Tong said.

"Or perhaps Li Shen."

"Maybe even Ben Fielding."

"Will my son be a martyr?" Li Tong asked.

"Will he be the last martyr?" asked Li Manchu.

"Only One knows the answer," Li Tong said. "He whose eyes are a consuming fire."

"Martin? What's going on?"

"You're killing me, Ben. We've had two complaints lodged against you since we spoke last week. I got a phone call from some official I could hardly understand, somebody high up in PSB or the Party, I can't even tell you for sure. All I know is, if he took an English class he should demand his money back. Anyway, they're outraged at the hornet's nest you've been stirring up. They say if not for their high regard for Getz International you'd have been deported weeks ago. They're not confrontational—for them to call means they're taking this very seriously. It was an extremely unpleasant phone call, at least the part I could understand."

"You said there was a second complaint?"

"Zhang, at The Ling Group. He reminded me we're not the only semi-conductor or microchip company on the planet. He started listing off our competitors. Ben, I'm telling you, if they pull the rug out from under us, Getz could go down. Travis and his supporters on the board keep reminding me this is exactly the kind of situation they cautioned against. We're leveraged. We're depending on the China accounts. The forced-labor issue has been dealt with. You need to let it go. It's ancient history."

"How do we know that? They won't even give me access to employee files at our own factory. Why do you think that is?"

"You don't have the emotional distance to look at this objectively."

"You're right about that. I've run out of emotional distance. What I've got are firsthand observations."

"It's their culture. Don't presume to tell them what to do."

"If this was about whether or not I like to eat duck's feet, I'd overlook it in a heartbeat. But this isn't a cultural issue. It's a moral issue. There's a big difference."

"Just back off, Ben. You owe me that much. I've been your biggest cheerleader at GI. And lately, believe me, you've needed one. This is an internal affair. Theirs, not ours. Let them handle it!"

"Like the concentration camps were Germany's internal affair? Like the gulags were Moscow's internal affair?"

"Listen to yourself! You're losing it. You're talking Nazis and the KGB! Is this part of your new religion kick? I'm a churchgoing man myself, but you've gone off the deep end. Get a grip!"

"Martin, look, I just need—"

"It's over, Ben. I hoped I wouldn't have to pull the plug, but you've forced my hand. I've been way more patient than I should have been. But this is it. You have to let this go or I have to let *you* go! You understand what I'm saying? Get your stuff together and come home. That's not a request. I want you back in one week. That's January 31. No later. Leave in the next couple of days, and you can make it home for the Super Bowl. I'm sending Jeffrey to clean up your messes. Don't make his job any harder than you already have. Got it?"

A bicycler dropped by a sealed envelope with the name "Ben Fielding." The kid handed it to Ben, and he handed him some yuan. The boy smiled and rode off, looking at the treasure in his hand.

It's not FedEx, but it gets the job done.

Ben opened the envelope and read. "Ben Fielding is hereby expelled from China for engaging in activities incompatible with a visa. He must report to the Pushan PSB and leave China no later than February 2."

Wow. They gave me a couple more days than Martin did.

Quan's house was nearly empty. Ming and Shen were gone, setting up new living quarters in their half of Zhou Jin's tiny place. Ben sat on his bed, the only one of the three still there. He was about to make the final drop-off to Zhou Jin's. Only the bed, the mahogany chair, and a few odds and ends remained.

A cockroach skittered across his bed.

"You didn't get the eviction notice, huh, buddy? Well, I guess you'll be getting some new roommates. I'll miss you."

I'm talking to a cockroach. It could be worse. At least I haven't named him.

The draft was worse without furniture and bodies. Despite his jacket and the blanket covering his feet, Ben trembled.

After a few minutes he got up, crossed the room, and knelt in front of the empty chair. He wept. He opened his Bible in front of him and reread a line from First Peter he'd underlined, one that Ming had showed him that morning. "'Give all your worries and cares to God, for he cares about what happens to you.'"

Having done everything he could think of and still not getting the desired results, Ben laid his head on the soft untouched material of the chair. He felt comforted.

Well, I guess if I'm not in control, the next best thing is knowing you are. Come to think of it, that's a whole lot better, isn't it?

He laughed. Then he spoke some more to the Owner of the chair.

48

 $\mathcal{A}$ S QUAN STOOD SHIVERING on the other side, Ben threw the blanket, tied in a bundle, over the fence. Mercifully, the Christian guard had escorted Quan and looked the other way. The air was so cold it stung Ben's face.

"How are you?" Ben asked.

"I have been serving much fish," Quan said.

"Ming has a message for you." Ben handed him the piece of paper. Quan read it, keeping it blocked by his body from the sight of the three guards.

"What does she say?" Ben asked.

Quan blushed. He showed it to Ben, who read it aloud: "'I love you, Li Quan. Thank you for never giving me broken pottery and always giving me jade.'"

"But I have never given her jade. I can't afford it."

"You know what she means, don't you?"

Quan nodded, then smiled.

"I've failed you," Ben said. "I don't know how to tell you this."

"Have they hurt Ming or Shen?"

"No. But they're confiscating your home. Because of the illegal meetings and Bibles. We tried to block it with legal measures, but nothing worked. I have no clout here. No reputable law firm will help. Johnny says it's like throwing darts in the dark. We don't know what we're doing. I moved everything out of your house yesterday. I'm staying in a hotel now."

"Where will they live?"

"With Zhou Jin's family."

"That is good." Quan looked at his shoes. "It was never our home."

"What do you mean?"

"The house we lived in was not our home. No more than this jail is my home. Minghua knows that. Shen knows—or he will soon learn. Our home is somewhere else. I pray for Ming and Shen. Prison walls cannot stop my prayers."

"I'm sorry I couldn't keep it from happening."

"We are only men, Ben Fielding. We cannot make the earth turn. Our Father turns it without our assistance. And he does have his jokes of providence, jokes we do not figure out until much later, if ever at all. Bringing us together at Harvard was one of those, I think. And now, all these years later, he has brought us together again for his purposes. When I came to America, if not for my roommate taking me to those meetings, I might never have become Yesu's follower."

"And when I came to China, if not for my roommate taking me to those meetings, I might never have become Yesu's follower. Yes, I see. A joke of providence."

"Have you been reading Shengjing?"

"Every day. Zhou Jin and Li Yue have been a great help."

"Have you been praying to Yesu?"

"Every hour. Li Yue and I have met for prayer several times."

"Then Ben Fielding could not have brought me better news. This is far better than telling me I will be released."

He looked at Li Quan and knew he meant it. Ben took off his gloves and tugged at his frozen eyelashes. "My boss pulled the plug on me. I have to be home in six days. I also got an eviction notice from the PSB. I can't tell if it's an official deportation, but I'm not going to fight it. I'm surprised it didn't happen a long time ago."

"Yes. It is time for you to leave."

"Last night when I prayed, I was on my knees, with my head resting on the empty chair. I hope that was alright."

"He whose chair it is was pleased, I am sure. When you placed your head upon that chair, you put it on the lap of Yesu."

"I've been wanting to ask you something—when your parents' house burned to the ground, where was the chair?"

"In the same room where nearly everything else was destroyed. But the chair survived. It had the scent of the fire, but that was all. It is our family's greatest earthly treasure. Perhaps it is our only treasure besides the Word of God itself. No offense is meant to the leather coats you brought us. Or the Frisbee."

"I wish I didn't have to leave you here."

"My father used to tell me that a good follower of Yesu is like the ox—ready either for the plow or the altar, for service or for sacrifice. I do not know what lies ahead on this earth. I do know something greater awaits us beyond it. That is what I choose to live for. You are free to go, Ben Fielding. It is your time. I will pray for you."

"I will pray for you, too. This time I really will." Ben looked at Quan. "When you pray for me, what do you ask?"

"That you will face persecution."

"What?"

"And that through it you will grow. That you will learn to stand strong. That you will know you are in a war, and that you will put on your armor and learn to use the sword of the Spirit, God's Word."

"So, while I'm praying you will suffer less, you're praying that I will suffer more?"

"We both should pray that the other will live in a way pleasing to Yesu. I do not wish to see my friend suffer. But I believe it may be the only way for you to learn how to serve. In house churches we have little to hope in but our God. In America, you have much to hope in besides God. None but he can bear the weight of your hope. But that is often forgotten. The test of prosperity is not easily passed."

"I'm hoping to get to see you again before I leave. If I don't, then this is our good-bye."

"I will look for you one last time. Now I must ask you to give a message to Li Shen."

"Of course."

"Tell him, 'Do not be ashamed of your father's chains.'"

"He's not ashamed of you, Quan."

"He is a better son than I was. When I was young, I was ashamed of my father." Quan choked out the words and bowed his head.

"Ming misses her little grasshopper," Ben said.

Quan blushed. "Greet her for me. Convey my love." He stopped when he heard his voice break.

"She's a remarkable woman," Ben said.

"She is the finest woman I have ever known," Quan said. "She holds up more than her half of our little sky."

"Your sky is bigger than you think, my friend," Ben said. "Far bigger than all the skies I ever dreamed of."

"Until now?" Quan asked.

"Until now," Ben said.

Quan reached out three fingers through the chain links and touched them to his friend's head. He prayed aloud, with a passion that surged through Ben like an electric current.

"Okay, Ben, stop for a second. Are you alright?" Pam Fielding asked.

"Yes. Yes, I'm alright. For the first time in years, I'm alright."

"Have you been drinking?"

"Boiled water and green tea, that's all."

"This isn't some kind of joke or something?"

"No, Pam. I'm okay, and I'm not drinking." Ben paused for a second to gather himself. "I'm telling you that I've repented. I've surrendered my life to Jesus. He's my Lord and Savior. I don't know how else to tell you. It happened a couple of weeks ago. It was an underground sem—never mind. I'll tell you about it when I get home. I mean, if you want to hear the story."

"*Want* to hear the story? Yeah, actually, I'd be extremely interested—I mean, if this is the real thing, if you're serious. Okay, okay, let me get this straight, make sure I'm not dreaming," Pam said. Ben pictured her sitting up in bed and rubbing her face, still trying to wake up. "This is my ex-husband, Ben, whose voice I haven't heard for four months except on an answering machine. He wakes me up at 4:00 A.M., calling from China. He asks me to pray for Quan, who's in jail, and then to call around and see if I can find a dozen Chinese Bibles that someone can come by the house and pick up from me?"

"Uh, yeah. I guess that just about covers it."

Pam laughed. Her laugh still made him smile.

"Well, *sure*, Ben. Why not? Anything else I can do for you?"

"Yeah. Say hi to Melissa and Kim for me."

"I'll do better than that. Kimmy's standing right here—wondering if there was an emergency. Guess I was a little loud. Did I mention it's 4:00 A.M.?" She giggled and passed the phone, covering it and saying something to Kim he couldn't make out.

"Daddy? When are you coming home?"

"Within a week. How are you, baby?"

"Pretty good. Thanks for the Christmas card and the gifts you sent. We've really missed you."

"I miss you too, Kimmy. So much. There's a lot happening here. Mom will tell you some. But . . . will you pray for me?"

"*Pray* for you?" He heard more background whispering. "Of course I'll pray for you, Daddy. I don't think you've ever asked me that before."

"Well, I need it this time. My friend Li Quan is in jail."

"Why?"

"Because he . . . because he's a Christian."

"Wow."

"Yeah. Wow. Your mom will fill you in. I miss you, honey. I really do."

"I miss you too, Daddy. And I *will* pray for you, okay? Mom and I will pray together for you, right now."

"Hey, Jeffrey. You're coming to Shanghai, right? I'll see you at that meeting in the Bancorp Building, with The Ling Group. Yeah, I'll sort of pass the baton to you and fill you in on what's been happening. I mean, the Getz stuff. Not my personal business with my friend, the stuff Martin's upset with me about. Sorry if I've made things a little awkward for you, but you're good at unruffling feathers. I know it'll work out. But listen, Jeff, I need you to do me a favor. Could you swing by Pam's before you leave?"

"Pam? Your ex? I didn't think you two—"

"We're still friends. She's going to have a box ready to send to me."

"What kind of box?"

"It'll be kind of heavy. It's books."

"She's sending you books? But you're about to come home."

"It's for friends over here. They need stuff to read."

"O . . . kay."

"It's a goodwill thing. I've met a lot of Chinese, and they've been real helpful to me. Just wanted to give them some tokens of my appreciation."

"How about some nice little pens or those plastic Getz coffee mugs? They aren't so heavy."

"No. I need the books."

"I'm already stretching it on the luggage."

"You remember last year when I dragged you out of that bar in Hong Kong?"

"Okay, okay. Sheesh. A box of books it is."

Li Tong escorted the recent arrival, who was fascinated by the Watchers. "Reader always speaks. But Writer can answer your questions."

"Who are you?" Fu Liko asked Writer.

"I am the eyes of Elyon, the Witness to the works of men. I search the dark world for Elyon's oppressed children. I record their deeds of faithfulness, for the day of judgment and reward. Michael consults my records to deploy soldiers on their behalf. I also keep a record of all offenses against them . . . each shall surely be repaid."

"What have you been watching?" Fu Liko asked.

Writer delayed his answer, writing furiously as other images filled the portal. Finally he resumed speaking, never taking his eyes off the portal. "Places you knew as Indonesia, Myanmar, Laos, Cuba, Colombia, Morocco, Egypt, Nigeria, Saudi Arabia, Sri Lanka, Bangladesh, Vietnam, North Korea, Iran, Pakistan. And, of course, China. Others also."

"There's a reddish color on each of those countries. I didn't notice until you pointed them out."

"It is the blood of the martyrs, always visible from here. Heaven's eyes are unceasingly attentive to whatever Yesu's eyes are fixed upon. And his eyes are always on his suffering servants."

"Always?"

"Always."

When Fu Liko looked, all he could see was a blur of images. "I do not yet know how to see as you do. What are you looking at now?"

"Brothers in Laos are told they must sign a document renouncing their faith, or village officials will force them to leave their homes, crops, and jobs. Provincial governors, police chiefs, and village leaders work together to harass the followers of Elyon. Government leaders denounce Christians in newspapers, calling them subversive and a threat to national unity. Police shut down churches. They try to force them to pay money to Buddhist priests. Some are offered bribes to provide the names of Christians."

"What else do you see?"

"I see a girl in Pakistan, baptized three hours ago. Five minutes ago her throat was slit because her baptism is apostasy to Islam. I think she is about to join us. I see a girl raped in Morocco. They try to force her to memorize the Qur'an. She stays true to her Lord. At this moment in Indonesia two young boys are being burned and tortured. Their persecutors offer relief only if they will deny their Lord. They refuse." He kept writing tirelessly as he spoke.

Fu Liko turned to Li Tong. "But how can we see all this? I thought in heaven all sights and memories would only serve to make us happy."

"You imagined the happiness of heaven is based on ignorance of events on earth? No. It is a question of perspective, not ignorance. The King says he suffers with his children. Even here, pain can be felt."

"But doesn't Shengjing promise to wipe away all tears?"

"That promise is for after he defeats sin and ends suffering and sets up his kingdom. That time has not yet come."

"What is that country there? It's one of the reddest."

"We knew it as Sudan. Millions of suffering Christians live there. Many have been stolen and taken as slaves to the Muslim north. They are sexually abused and beaten. Their church buildings are burned to the ground. The government bombs them. Women are raped. Children are tortured. They try to force conversion to Islam. It is . . . unthinkable."

"I never expected to learn of such things here. I knew we were suffering in China, but I did not understand how many others suffered also. Had I known, I would have prayed for them."

Writer pointed to another atrocity, then put pen to paper to record it at lightning speed. Reader spoke: "Do they think the King is blind? Do they imagine he does not care what they do to his children? With one hand he will rescue and comfort his children; with the other he will bring down his sword upon their oppressors."

"When?" Fu Liko whispered to Li Tong.

"I do not know. But I think very soon."

"The warden gave me a nice bowl of rice and chicken," Quan said to Ben. "His wife fixed it for me."

"Why?"

"I think he is . . . interested in Li Quan now. He listens to my words and asks me many questions. And now it is time for Ben Fielding to listen to me. I wish to thank you for taking care of my family. And for attempting to get me out of jail. And for giving me the Shengjing T-shirt and water bottles and bringing me messages from home."

"You're welcome. But listen, Quan. The Christian guard told me when PSB heard about our visits they were furious. Apparently the assistant warden and three of the guards have been splitting the money, and someone found out." Ben raised his hand. "I know you didn't want me to pay, but I did. Anyway, I told them I'd be gone tomorrow and nobody would know if they let me in for one last visit." He didn't mention he'd waved three hundred-dollar bills in front of them to change their minds. "I still don't feel right about leaving you like this."

"You have your own family to look after."

"But I'm divorced. They don't live with me. And they don't really need me. . . ."

"Do not listen to Mogui. They *do* need you, Ben Fielding. Much more than you understand. The church here will take care of Ming and Shen. Who will take care of your family?"

"They have plenty. By your standards they want for nothing."

"They want for a husband and father to love and lead them. Should God take you from them, as he has taken me from Ming and Shen, that would be for him to decide. But it is not for you."

"Yeah, I've been thinking about that. A lot. I want things to be different. But I'm not sure I'm ready, Quan. Even though things are a mess here, I can sense God's presence. I'm afraid when I leave I could lose perspective again."

"I remember a rally when we were in college," Quan said. "It was not far from Harvard Yard. The evangelist asked all the people to bow their heads, close their eyes, and then raise their hands if they wished to follow Christ. What I remember is how he assured people that 'no one will see you if you raise your hand; this is a decision between you and God alone.' At the time I thought nothing of this. But I have thought since, that he who truly follows Yesu must acknowledge him in public. Even in China, we may meet secretly, but when the time is right we take the risks of making it known that we are his followers. Is it that way in America?"

"I'm no expert at being a Christian, but I don't think so. I know there are lots of Christian teachers and social workers and counselors and even businessmen who are afraid they'll get in trouble for being outspoken Christians. Sometimes they're right. There can be a big price. You can even . . . lose your job."

"Lose your job for speaking out as a Christian? In America? Have things changed that much?"

"Yeah, they have. I may as well confess it—your old roommate fired a Christian for speaking out too much in the office."

"I am sure you will do what is right to correct your past failures," Quan said. "Wang Mingdao was once asked if he had a message for Western Christians. He said, 'Remember the most common cause of stumbling is the fear of man.' It is God we must fear, not men. You must learn to stand boldly for your Lord, regardless of what men may think of you."

"I've seen a lot of that boldness here."

"While scrubbing their floors, I have discussed with two pastors their belief that God is raising up China as the missions base to reach every country in the world. We are not just beneficiaries of other people's obedience to the great commission. We intend to take the gospel of Yesu farther and more aggressively even than did Hudson Taylor and the missionaries who brought it to us."

"Maybe you should take it to America."

"Yes. And perhaps Ben Fielding will be one of our first missionaries."

"I've been wondering if I should resign from Getz. Maybe do some consulting or start my own company."

"Or perhaps you should do what might be more difficult—stay and stand firm as a follower of Zhu Yesu, and do what he wants in your business. If they fire you, that is their choice. And is it not time for you to go back to the business students you teach at the university and tell them what is happening in China—the good and the bad?"

"They might not let me come back."

"That is their choice. Your duty is to do what you can. God can close the doors without your help. And what about all the Chinese coming to study in America, like your roommate? Who knows their language and country better than Ben Fielding? You could open your home to them, open your heart, reach them for Zhu Yesu. Tell them about your old roommate."

"I'm not worthy to do that, Quan. I have so far to go."

"Yes, you are unworthy, as I am unworthy. But you must not neglect your calling. Did you know that in 1262 Kublai Khan asked for one hundred Christian scholars to be sent to China? His request was never fulfilled. China could have been reached with the gospel, but it was not. Now Chinese students come to study in your country, your city. You can certainly influence them."

"You were always the scholar, not me."

"I am but a locksmith's assistant, the son of a street sweeper, and now the scrubber of prison floors."

"But," Ben said, reaching his fingers through the fence, as Quan lowered his head so Ben could touch it, "all the hosts of heaven and earth will pause to say of Li Quan, 'Here lived a great locksmith's assistant, a great scrubber of prison floors, who did his job well.'"

The tall guard came over. He put his hand on Quan's shoulder.

"Is our time already up, brother?" Quan asked.

"Can we have ten more minutes?" Ben asked.

The guard nodded.

"When I go home, Quan, what do you want me to tell people?"

"Tell them if they wish to help, send us Bibles. And pray for us. Pray that those witnessing our suffering will see that Zhu Yesu must be real in order to sustain us. Pray that the rotten prison food will actually taste good to us. He has performed this miracle for me many times. Pray that the rags we prisoners wear in winter will keep us warm. Pray that the beatings and torture will not weaken us, but strengthen us in our faith. And that the enemy will not overcome us and our families with despair and discouragement. Pray that the prisons all across China will become centers of revival, and that Christians in registered churches will be bold, and that house churches will be invisible to the police but visible to everyone else. Pray that our sons and daughters will not be ashamed of their fathers and mothers in prison."

Ben jotted down notes on his pad.

"You have come to know God in China, Ben, and you have learned much. When you go back, remember that your American God is as big as your Chinese God."

"What do you mean?"

"While you've been here, you have realized you have very little power. The wheels of progress do not turn easily in China. You do not have the power to accomplish much of what you want. But this will change when you go home. You will think you can do things on your own. You will be tempted to pray less, to ask less, and to trust less. So, remember that God is the same there as he is here, and you must trust him as much there as you have learned to here."

"Quan . . . are you afraid?"

"I have been reciting a poem written in honor of a missionary martyr. It was widely printed throughout my country. My father had a copy in his Bible and under the desk in case his Bible was taken. I memorized it many years ago. I wrote it on my wall with the soap last week. When you are a great floor scrubber you have access to plenty of soap! It was first written in English, so I memorized it in English. May I recite it to you?"

Ben nodded.

> Afraid? Of what?
>   To feel the spirit's glad release?
> To pass from pain to perfect peace,
>   The strife and strain of life to cease?
> Afraid—of that?
>   Afraid? Of what?

Li Quan stopped. He turned his head suddenly.

"What's wrong?" Ben asked.

"For a moment . . . I didn't hear my voice. I thought . . . I heard another voice, perhaps two or three voices saying the words. I am sorry, Ben. Maybe my mind is becoming unclear."

"No problema. I'd trade my mind at its best for your mind at its worst. Why don't you rest for a while and—"

"I will continue." Quan thought a moment, looked up, then said:

354

Afraid? Of what?
Afraid to see the Savior's face
To hear his welcome, and to trace
The glory gleam from wounds of grace?
Afraid—of that?
Afraid? Of what?
A flash, a crash, a pierced heart;
Darkness, light, O Heaven's art!
A wound of his a counterpart!
Afraid—of that?
Afraid? Of what?
To do by death what life could not—
Baptize with blood a stony plot,
Till souls shall blossom from the spot?
Afraid—of that?

"You sound like you think you're going to die," Ben said.

"Of course I am going to die, Ben Fielding. As are you. The only question is 'Is *this* the day I die?' If it is, we should both be ready, should we not?"

"Yes."

"Please take a message to Ming and Shen. Tell them I love them and I will see them again. Give them this verse from Galatians: 'Don't get tired of doing what is good. Don't get discouraged and give up, for we will reap a harvest of blessing at the appropriate time.' Tell them the most important words are *dao le shihou*—'when the time arrives.'"

One moment Li Quan looked solemn, and the next, a smile crept across his face.

"What is it?" Ben asked.

"Do you remember how I always wanted to write a book?"

"Of course. You were going to be Professor Li Quan, author of many books."

"A locksmith's assistant does not become a writer. Yet I am writing a book on the walls of my cell."

"How?"

"After I work all day cleaning the other cells, I use a thin piece of soap to write my outline on my wall. When I am satisfied, I memorize it before sleeping. Then I recite it in the morning and begin writing again. Of course, there is no one who actually reads my book. I do not expect it to be published! Still, this is perhaps another joke of providence. *Dao le shihou*—the time has arrived for Li Quan to write a book!"

49

THE CHILD HUNG on to his mother as they lay back in their bed.

"What is wrong with my Li Shen?" his mother asked softly. She wiped his tears.

"What are they doing to Baba?"

"I do not know. But I know Yesu is with him."

"I don't want them to hurt him."

"Neither do I."

"I want my Baba to come home."

"Soon he will be home, safely home," Ming said. "I sense it. But until then he wants his Ming and his Shen to draw their strength from Yesu."

Shen drew near and cried upon his mother's neck. Their tears trickled down, mingling together.

They watched the King, surrounded by a great crowd of angels bringing their concerns before him. While few of them were permitted this close to his throne, these had special access—not because of who they were but whom they represented.

Li Manchu, Li Wen, and Li Tong came close. Because of their relation to the King, their blood was royal and their access unrestricted. The King drew them into the surface of his vast mind, that they could see what he saw— children abandoned and living on streets, abducted, beaten, molested, cut to pieces by men dressed in white, exterminated by human pesticides.

"See that you do not look down on one of these little ones," the King said, projecting his voice toward the dark world so loudly it was heard on earth as thunder. "For I tell you that their angels in heaven always behold the face of my Father."

The King pointed to a church custodian yelling at children unauthorized to play on the swings and chasing them away. "Let the little children come to me and do not hinder them, for the kingdom of heaven belongs to such as these."

The King spoke to people out for Sunday dinner after church, who turned away from the street children. "Your Father in heaven is not willing that any of these little ones should be lost."

Then he watched a man and a woman taking children off the streets, bringing them into a building, giving them a warm meal and a cot and safe refuge, and telling them about their Master. On the other side of the planet, in Africa, he watched his people caring for children born with AIDS, many of them orphans now, or soon to be.

The King nodded his approval. "Whoever welcomes one of these little children in my name welcomes me."

He watched his people give the children a warm bath, read stories to them, hug them, and laugh with them. He smiled broadly. "Thank you," the King whispered, "for doing this to me."

He looked now at men plotting and stalking and taking pictures of children, doing to them the unthinkable. He looked at men herding frightened little girls together and selling them to foreigners. He looked at the men in white coats, driving beautiful cars purchased by the blood of children. He looked at those who inflicted the suffering. His eyes smoldered.

"I made these children. I took them into my arms, put my hands on them, and blessed them. And yet you scorn them, use them for your gain, treat them as disposable. It would be better for you to have a millstone tied around your neck and be thrown into the sea than to face what I will surely do to you."

He looked now at others who turned their heads from the children, too busy to share a meal, a blanket, or a paycheck. They did little or nothing to help the children, and he regarded their failure to help as the inflicting of harm. "To you who look the other way, saying my children are not your concern: Repent! For it is I you have turned away from. I will not forget."

He gazed at another group of people, those watching out for and reaching out to and helping the children. He said simply, "Well done. Your reward shall be great."

The King watched the children again, though the men knew he had never stopped watching them. For a moment he smiled, then laughed; then suddenly he saw something else. Tears flowed from his eyes; then they burned with a blistering heat.

"Many on earth look away from the children," said Li Tong to Fu Liko. "But the eyes of heaven never look away from them. Never."

Sunday morning Quan recited Shengjing and wrote it on the wall with his sliver of soap, raising both hands as he wrote, since his wrists were manacled together. He wrote what he knew to be the words of Paul, written before he was beheaded by Nero: "The Lord stood at my side and gave me strength, so that through me the message might be fully proclaimed. . . . And I was delivered from the lion's mouth. The Lord will rescue me from every evil attack and will bring me safely to his heavenly kingdom. To him be glory for ever and ever. Amen."

Quan read the words, recited them, prayed them. He also prayed for the house church—for his and tens of thousands of others spread across his great country.

He heard the key turn in his lock. He expected food, but what he saw was Tai Hong. Quan shuffled backward.

"You distributed illegal Bibles. Others helped you. I want names from you. Names of Chinese and names of foreigners. If you give me those names, I will get you out of prison. If you do not, I will hurt you."

"I cannot betray my brothers."

"Then deny the Christ you profess to believe in. If you do that, I will go easy on you."

"I cannot deny my Lord."

"A Chinese citizen's loyalty is to the state!"

"My loyalty is to Yesu, Lord of heaven, Lord of China."

Tai Hong slapped Quan with an open hand and cried out from the sting of his own blow. Angrily, he pulled a flashlight from his belt. He hit the side of Quan's head with it, breaking the hard plastic molding. Now Hong held his hand, feeling even more pain.

Quan dragged himself to his feet. Hong raised the flashlight in the air, poised to strike again. Then he threw it against the wall. He drew a large pistol and pointed it at Quan, finger on the trigger. Then he shifted it in his hand, raised it high, and swung down the pistol's butt against Quan's head. It landed with a crunch. Quan's skull gave way.

"This is the day," said one father.

"Die well, my son," said the Other.

50

$\mathcal{T}$HE KING looked down at the earth and pointed his finger. "Why are you persecuting me?" His cry was heard to the ends of the cosmos. Only on earth did some not hear.

Running from outside the temple toward the sound, Michael stopped in his tracks. He watched wide-eyed as the King reached his right hand toward the sword that lay beside his throne. He grasped the sword's hilt and raised it two feet off the ground. Michael held his breath.

"The world is not worthy of them!" the King shouted. The sword shook in his hand. Then he slowly lowered it back to the floor.

Michael cried out toward the throne, "How long will the enemy mock you, mighty King? Will your foes revile your name forever? Why do you hold back your right hand? Take it from the folds of your garment and destroy them now!"

The King did not even look at Michael, a being who commanded the attention of every creature. The King looked instead at one man in one prison far away, yet not so far that he could not reach him. He opened toward him his swordless and wounded right hand.

"I await you, loyal servant. In my presence is fullness of joy. At my right hand are pleasures forever more. I am the happiness you have always hungered for, the pleasure you have thirsted after, the peace you have sought in long shadowy nights. The darkness is nearly done. Be faithful unto death, and I will give you the crown of life."

Accompanied by the tall thin guard, the warden, Lan An, rushed into Li Quan's cell. He saw the chief of police wiping off the butt of his sidearm with a white handkerchief, now soaked red. The warden got on his knees and checked Quan's pulse. He put his head to the prisoner's chest, pressing his ear against it.

"Get out of my prison," the warden shouted at Tai Hong as he leaped to his feet.

"I am the chief of police!" Tai Hong said.

"And I am the warden of Pushan Facility Six! This is not your jail."

The thin guard asked Tai Hong, "Why do you persecute Yesu?"

"This man is not Yesu. He is but a smelly prisoner."

"He is Yesu's prisoner." The guard braced himself, knowing it was time to take a stand. "To strike him is to strike Yesu."

"I will turn you in for what you have done," the warden screamed at Tai Hong. "Get out! You have no power over me!"

It was a dark Sunday morning, but the murky sky was steadily clearing. The pain had diminished. In fact, it seemed gone entirely, though he waited for it to come back with a vengeance. But something was happening, something thrilling, unlike anything he'd ever experienced, even in a dream.

He felt like a man with a dry throat, overcome with thirst, now on his hands and knees beginning to drink at the Source of a Stream he'd thought a mirage. But it was *real*, and now he was drinking greedily from it.

As Quan lay in the dust, he felt a strong hand grab his. He anticipated the struggle of standing, but there was no struggle. He stood effortlessly. He felt disoriented, as if on that roller coaster he'd ridden with Ben so many years ago in Atlantic City. He saw Tai Hong walk toward him and braced himself.

Tai walked through him. Quan turned around and saw his back. *Impossible.*

He looked on the ground and saw a crumpled body, wrists clamped with dirty gray manacles. The blue shirt, rolled up to the elbows, was filthy, bloody, torn. The pants were stained and worn. No socks. The face had raw wounds on the side. It dawned on him only gradually that he was looking at himself. Or what was left of him. Or rather . . . what he had left.

In a moment of mind-boggling clarity, Li Quan realized he had just eased out of his body as a man might ease out of his work shoes.

Led by the tall being holding his hand, he saw a man he'd seen only his first day in prison. It was the doctor, rushing to a phone. To his surprise, Quan could hear both ends of the conversation.

"He died only minutes ago. Is it too late? Can they still use him?"

"His heart is not beating?"

"No."

"By the time we could get him here, the liver would be no good. We have had this discussion before. You must call in advance, give us a head start."

The doctor cursed. "Tell that to Tai Hong."

"It is a terrible waste. A perfectly good liver, kidneys, heart—and more yuan than we've ever been offered. You must look for another prisoner about to die. But remember, the liver is needed soon. The mayor is anxious. His son is near death."

"We do not have to wait," the doctor said. "With a little help, another prisoner could die very quickly. I will reevaluate blood types and age and other factors. Next time it will work."

"See to it. Do not delay. But say nothing in front of Lan An. Something is happening to the warden. I do not want him to know."

Quan realized the men thought no one could hear them. Yet all the while an unseen universe eavesdropped. There was no such thing as a private moment.

Quan felt the hand on his arm again and only now did he turn to examine his companion. He was a powerful, longhaired dark man dressed in white. He had the strength and size of a great warrior. His rock-hard features made Quan shiver involuntarily. Quan turned his eyes from the warrior to himself. He appeared to be wearing his own tattered brown pants and shoes, the same ones as on the lifeless man in his cell. It was as if there were two identical men, one on the ground and one standing, as if there were a temporal overlap between death and the afterlife.

"Is that really me? Am I dead?"

"No, you are alive. The body on the floor is dead. Your kind must go through death's door to enter life."

"Then this is the day," Quan said, pondering the implications. "But who are you?"

"I am Jadorel. I have been with you since the day your father died. I was near you even before, when you were very young."

"Li Tong died over twenty-five years ago. I have never seen you."

"There is much you have never seen."

"Yet somehow you're familiar."

"Perhaps you have seen me, but you did not know it." His marbly face showed the slightest twitch at the corners of his mouth. He reached his hand out and touched Quan's skull, where the blow from the sidearm had landed.

Quan instinctively winced, anticipating the pain. But he felt only a gentle touch.

"You will never hurt again," Jadorel said. He looked at Quan's puzzled face. "You have many questions. There are many answers. It is time for your exodus, Li Quan of Hangzhou. Others await you in the great country, the world for which you were made."

"Jadorel," Quan said, as an inner light turned on. "It was you all along, wasn't it?"

"Yes," he said. "At times you sensed Elyon's Spirit himself within you. At other times, outside yourself but nearby, as in your jail cell, you sensed a presence standing guard. That was me, Jadorel, soldier of King Yesu. I was dispatched by Michael himself."

Jadorel took Quan's hand and led him straight for the cell wall. Quan stuck out his right hand, bracing himself for impact. But as Jadorel had done, Quan continued walking and went right through the wall, seeing gray stone on all sides of him, then the outer prison office, then another wall, then the brush beyond the compound, then the chain-link fence, which they walked right through. Now they seemed to be walking on air and, though their pace hadn't increased, they turned a corner in space and suddenly appeared at . . . the house of Zhou Jin. Through the walls Quan saw a woman inside.

"Minghua! I must go to her."

"She cannot hear you—just as you could not hear me until now."

"Yet somehow I knew you were there. Can she sense me?"

"Perhaps."

Quan walked through the wall and reached out his hand to touch his wife's forehead. It passed through her head, effortlessly, naturally, as a fish swimming through water.

Minghua smiled. Then her face changed. Suddenly she fell to her knees. "Be with Quan, Yesu. Protect him. Comfort him."

"I am here, Ming, my beloved. And I am well!"

A sleepy-faced boy got up from his bed.

"Come pray with me, Shen. Pray for your father."

"Is something wrong, Mama?" he asked, yawning.

"Quiet. Do not wake Zhou Jin. I think something is happening to your father. Pray for him."

Shen bent down in front of the empty chair, now in the corner of Zhou Jin's house, resting his head upon the felt cushion. *"Ganxie ni* for my baba, Li Quan. I am very proud of him."

"He is *proud* of me?" Quan said.

"He should be," Jadorel said. "Others are also proud."

Quan reached out to pat Shen on the head and, as before, his hand passed through him. As it did, he sensed the boy's thoughts, a cauldron of anxiety, yet somehow set on a foundation of peace.

"He is worried."

"Yes. But he believes what his parents taught him. He believes that the King's hand reaches into every corner of that world. No worry can stand in the face of that belief."

"I'm dead? You're sure? It's so much like . . . being alive. But a lot better!"

"You have walked out of the Shadowlands as a man walks out of a room. You are now in the universe next door, what we call 'the real world.' The Shadowlands are real, yes, but they are so pale and gray and vague, disconnected from the pulsating life of the rest of Elyon's cosmos. Those confined there cannot sense what lies beyond. Yet what lies beyond is nearly everything."

"I want to stay with them."

"No, you do not, because you know it is not the King's desire for you or for them."

"Yes. But may I say good-bye?"

Jadorel nodded. Quan knelt beside Ming. Since he couldn't rest his hands on her head, he held them inside her head, marveling he could do so.

"Farewell, Minghua. Thank you, beloved, for holding up your half of the sky . . . and much of mine as well. Come quickly." He walked over to Shen, passing his hand through his skin and placing it upon the boy's heart.

"Good-bye, Shen. Take care of your mother. Your father, Li Quan, is proud of you also. You were willing to die for Zhu Yesu. Now live for him. That may prove more difficult. Come quickly. But, perhaps, not too quickly. I will pray for you, my only son."

Quan looked at Jadorel. "I can still pray for him, can't I?"

"Of course," Jadorel said, looking as if he couldn't understand the question. "You talked to the King on earth. When you are in his country you will talk to him not less but more. But you are lingering too long on the path between worlds. It is time for Li Quan to come home, to the place he has never been but always longed for."

Quan backed away from Ming and Shen, then turned around, following Jadorel. Now they were walking upward, as if on an invisible staircase. His head began to spin. He wobbled, unaccustomed to walking on air. The next thing he knew, Jadorel picked him up in his massive arms, carrying him effortlessly, as if he had no weight.

"I am sorry I cannot walk better," Quan said.

"Do not apologize," Jadorel replied. "This is the first time you have ever died."

Quan saw many beings now. They seemed to be ascending through a passageway by which many warriors of Jadorel's race came and went. Suddenly Quan heard shrieks outside. He saw flying beasts cutting through the air and smashing themselves against the invisible barriers of the passageway, momentarily leaving on it a slimy mucus. Quan felt no fear, only fascination. The monsters looked remarkably like Jadorel himself, but their features were so twisted and their mannerisms so beastly, they appeared more like animals than intelligent beings. Yet Quan saw the intelligence in their eyes, an ancient brooding intelligence far surpassing his own.

"They were there all along too, weren't they?"

Quan thought he saw pain in Jadorel's eyes. The warrior said, "I fought them on behalf of the King . . . and you."

They passed through the between-world and came to what appeared to be a portal, with faces looking out at them. Quan heard voices, some Chinese, some English, and at least a dozen other languages that he was somehow able to understand.

"He's coming," shouted someone on the other side. "Li Quan is coming, and Jadorel carries him!"

They kept walking right through the transparent film, as if breaking through an amniotic sac, falling out into another world. Li Quan felt as if all his life he had been in the pains of labor and now at last he was being born.

Monday morning, Ben lay in bed half asleep in his Pushan hotel, the Zuanshi. The ringing telephone rattled him. He fumbled to find it.

"Ben?"

"Johnny? So it's your turn to wake me up? Don't you know Getz's prodigal son is coming home in a few days?"

"I just got a call from our contact in Shanghai—the one who gets his tips from his source at the prison."

"Yeah?"

"I don't know how to tell you this, Ben, and I'm hoping the info's wrong. We can't be sure."

"Sure about what?"

"It's Li Quan. They say he's . . . dead."

51

$\mathcal{A}$S HE WAS ONCE born from a secret intimate warmth into a world of cold confusion and blaring noise and painful artificial lights, Li Quan was now born out of cramped shadowy quarters into a wide-open realm of gentle warmth and natural light. His first instinct was to say to himself, "At last, the real world!"

The bright but comfortable light gave way to distinct faces. He saw Han Meizhen, whom his mother called Third Sister. He heard a familiar laugh, then turned to see his cousin Li Qiang, whom he'd often played with until Qiang died mysteriously when they were ten years old. He looked different, but his eyes were exactly the same, and the flood of memories of everything they'd done together rushed upon Quan in that single moment. Qiang grabbed his hand. It felt so warm, so fleshy, so human. Somehow Quan had expected heaven to be full of disembodied spirits floating in the clouds. He smiled broadly. This was so much better!

He turned his head and beheld a woman with the biggest smile he'd ever seen, a dimple-stretching smile of contagious delight. He froze at the sight of her. He heard her giggle, then watched tears of delight erupt from her dark almond eyes.

"Honorable mother!"

"Beloved son!"

They embraced. Though his mother had often hugged him, it seemed to Quan their embrace now was longer than any they'd shared on earth. Or was it that he sensed within her such a deep reservoir of loving memo-

369

ries and prayers that he could not imagine so much could be exchanged in a short embrace?

"I have so much to tell you, Mother. For one, a woman who saw you in her dreams."

"Lin Chaoxing, wife of Lin Shan, the police chief?" She smiled at his surprise. "I have much to tell you, my son! And to show you." She smiled broadly, teeth perfect. "I have picked out special places I know my son will love!"

Wading through the crowd of greeters and backslappers, Quan enjoyed many surprise reunions. But when he saw in front of him three men standing together, he stopped in his tracks. The first, the tallest, he did not recognize but felt he should. The man stepped forward, reached out, and put his hand on Quan's head. The moment the man touched him, he knew.

"Li Manchu? My revered great-grandfather."

"Do not revere me. But please, do embrace me!"

After they hugged, the second man, whom Quan had not seen since he was a boy, stepped forward and also touched his head.

"Li Wen. I am honored to see you again, Grandfather." They too embraced.

There was no mistaking the third man. His eyes were even brighter than on earth, eyes Quan had last seen behind a death mask. The living, fiery eyes of his father. But the smile now was much broader, more like his mother's, and his teeth white and straight.

"Li Quan," he said, eyes moist. "Welcome home, my son." They hugged and wept, both of them, chest to chest. Together they sobbed, the heavings of one absorbed into the other.

"I am so ashamed, Father," Quan whispered. "I have wanted so long to tell you I am sorry."

"I have heard you say it many times. Once would have been enough. I have watched you, Li Quan. Your father is very proud of you. Your shame will be cleansed from you forever, once your old clothes are removed and your new ones put on."

Until then Quan had forgotten his clothes still bore dirt and blood from the other world.

"We have much to talk about," Li Tong said. "I have much to show you. But first, the three of us have been granted the honor of leading you before the Audience of One, the King of all Charis."

Li Tong pointed to a great palace. Quan had not yet noticed it, having fixed his eyes on people. Now he beheld the gardens and countryside and the magnificent structures spanning the horizon. The four men walked together toward it. Or was it a temple?

"Before you is the path that leads to the throne. We will take you to the outer area. Then only you and Jadorel shall go farther. We will see you at the celebration." Quan watched his father, grandfather, and great-grandfather all three bow their heads together.

By Jadorel's side, Quan walked the marble pathway toward the great palace. Quan turned to him suddenly. "It was you at the earthquake, wasn't it? The man who helped me, who paid my tuition. It was you."

The corners of Jadorel's mouth bent upward, awkwardly, as if unaccustomed to smiling. "We will speak later of those times," he said. "I too have stories to tell you, things you will look back upon with wonder."

The wooden doors to the palace must have been thirty feet high. A great doorkeeper, taller than Jadorel, looked at Quan and nodded. He stepped aside, and the massive doors swung open. At that moment Quan saw at the far end One sitting on a throne. Li Quan fell to his knees. Jadorel did the same.

"Come in, faithful servants!" The voice rang with power and delight.

They rose, and Jadorel pushed Li Quan in front of him. "You must lead the way. This is your appointment. As is my place, I will follow behind and to your left."

Quan gaped at the long bloodred carpet, over a meter across with gold stripes on each side. About every twenty feet an inlaid gold crown of thorns decorated the carpet. Some of the thorns seemed to actually come out of the carpet, but they did not hurt the feet. Quan stepped forward, Jadorel mirroring his movement like a reflection, behind him and to the left, his feet never touching the carpet.

As he walked, Quan realized for the first time that the manacle was still chained to his right hand. Strangely, he'd not felt its weight or sensed its presence until now. He pulled at it self-consciously, then looked at his stained blue shirt and pants and soiled shoes. He felt out of place. He wished he'd had opportunity to bathe and come neatly dressed.

As he got closer to the throne, he saw it was beautiful but not as large and regal as he had imagined. It was a chair, obviously made by the hands of a great woodworker. In fact, it reminded him very much of the high-backed chair his grandfather had made, which sat empty at the table all those years and now sat empty in the house of Zhou Jin.

As Quan walked up the carpet, people crowded toward the sides. Many were Chinese, but there were faces of every color. He recognized some of them. Zhang On, an old friend of his father's. Han Ho, who had come to Zhu Yesu in the locksmith's shop, praying with Li Quan and Zhou Jin.

Han Ho spoke to Quan: "Xiexie." His smile was all the thanks Quan needed.

Now Quan saw a smooth, smiling face, which he'd last seen in his arms in the prison cell.

"Fu Liko!" he exclaimed, apparently loudly, because everyone laughed. He reached out his finger and touched the man's forehead. "Is this where the wound was?"

"I believe so. But—" Fu Liko ran his fingers over his own face and smiled—"I am not sure!"

Quan turned his eyes back to the carpeted walkway. About twenty meters from the throne he could see that beneath the transparent brown tiles were the continents of the earth, spread flat, perhaps so every event could be witnessed. Nothing could escape the attention of heaven.

As he came within ten meters, the One on the throne sprang up from it like a great lion and ran down the steps to Li Quan. Overcome with emotion, Quan fell to his knees before the Lion. He felt the manacle drop from his wrist and fall to his right, before the feet of the King. He saw that the moment the chains touched the floor, they were no longer a dirty gray. They'd been transformed into shining gold.

Li Quan breathed deeply, inhaling a wonderful fragrance, feeling the King's thick beard, and nestling his head in it as if it were a lion's mane. When the King reached out his hands to Quan's face, Quan saw the scars. The King brushed his hand over the old scars on Quan's ear and neck. The moment the King's scars touched his, he felt his disappear. Somehow his scars seemed to be drawn in, absorbed into the King's. As a result, Quan thought, the King's scars seemed a little bigger.

Then the King touched the matted, blood-dried hair on the left side of Quan's head. Quan felt something come into his skull, like a dry liquid. Though when Jadorel had touched him he had felt no pain, only now did he sense he'd been fully healed. This was more than just the absence of pain. This was the presence of an intense vitality.

After embracing him tightly again, the King slipped something into Quan's hands. It was heavy. He stared at it. A crown? Surely not for Li Quan, who had dishonored his father. Surely not for Li Quan, whose shame had been whispered in the dark silence of so many nights.

He held the crown up to the King. "I am not worthy to wear your crown," he whispered.

"What you say is half true. But those who realize their unworthiness and trust in my worthiness, I consider worthy. It is for me to say, is it not? And I say Li Quan will wear the crown I have made for him!"

The King put the crown on him. Quan let it rest on his head, sobbing with a joy uncontainable.

"I am sorry for being so dirty. I wish I could have cleaned myself."

The King put his mouth close to Quan's ear and whispered, "No problema." Quan looked at him to be sure it was alright to laugh. When he saw Yesu's smile, he unloosed his laughter. The King laughed long and hard with him, and all those standing there smiled and wondered about the private joke.

"As for your cleaning," the King said, "it falls upon me. Charis belongs not to those cleaned by their own hands, but to those cleaned by mine." Quan looked at the King's hands and saw not only the scars but the roughness and darkness of his palms, which looked as if they'd once gotten so dirty that the stain had never come out in ten thousand washings.

"I have made you clean. I will do so once more, for the last time. Then it will never be necessary again. I have a new name for you, which only you and I shall know." He whispered it into Li Quan's ear. Quan's eyes lit up. "You will rule at my side—over a land I have delegated to you. But this we will discuss later. Now there are other matters. Jadorel has brought your robe."

Quan turned and looked at the angel, who stood stiffly, with a white robe draped over his arms. The great being watched in silent awe, as if he could not grasp the loving familiarity, the intimacy of the exchange between the King and his human subject.

The King pulled Quan upward. They looked at each other face-to-face. There was a poignant pause. Quan sensed anticipation in the great gathering of witnesses around him.

Suddenly the King lifted him off the ground, held him out with arms straight, and cried out in a voice that did not hurt Quan's ears but, he was sure, could be heard a million light-years away.

"Well done, my good and faithful servant!" His voice roared like a lion's, and his sweet, hot breath blew upon Quan's face. "You were once Li Quan of Hangzhou. You are now Li Quan of Charis, the great city, capital of the eternal country without borders. You have been faithful over a little, and I will put you over much. Enter into the joy of your Lord!"

While Li Quan tried to assimilate the King's words, thunderclaps exploded. It took a moment to realize it was applause. He now saw many coming through the side doors of the palace. The guards stepped aside, permitting them this irregularity, this violation of palace protocol, since they were the King's own children. They rushed forward at Quan and the King, running across the red carpet that angels dared not touch.

Quan saw his great-grandfather, his grandfather, and his father stop together and applaud him, like those in the front row of a cloud of witnesses, who could vouch for a life well lived. He saw Jadorel, standing at the King's right hand, also applauding slowly and deliberately, making a powerful sound.

And then he saw something remarkable, something he had never imagined. Li Quan saw the King's hands clap against each other. The sound was so great it pushed him backward. It was the sound above all sounds, the sound for which his ears had been made and to which his hearing was now tuned. Never until this moment had Li Quan of Hangzhou, the lowly locksmith's assistant, heard the applause of heaven.

Ben held Ming until she fell to her knees, weeping. He sat on Shen's bed beside the child, who'd been awake for less than two minutes. Hearing Ben Fielding's words about his father, Li Shen's expression turned from confusion to disbelief to an attempt at stoicism. Now a slow, impending anguish overtook his face like a tide encroaching on new sand. He trembled, his pudgy face quivered, then slowly his high-pitched voice let out a great wail.

52

A MULTITUDE OF VOICES merged into a single hum of excitement. An intimacy pervaded this huge group, a closeness Li Quan had never known among large numbers, though he'd caught glimpses of it in the house church. He heard all the voices in different languages and enjoyed the distinctive tone of each. He heard several Chinese dialects, Swahili, Norwegian, Aboriginal languages, Hmong, Tagalog, Persian, Greek, Hebrew, Arabic. Strangely, he recognized them for exactly what they were, and hearing each caused him to visualize the distinguishing features of the cultures, even those he'd been unfamiliar with. People from every nation, tribe, people, and language were here, living together under one flag, one King.

Sometimes, without warning, the multitudes would turn toward the throne and break into singing. The power surge at these moments at first bowled Quan over, but now he was learning to catch the waves of praise, riding them ever closer to the Throne-dweller.

When a song finished, the King stepped off the throne and walked down to Li Quan. He put his arm around Quan; then they walked side by side.

"What do you think of your new home? I have made it for you. Parts of it I am still making with the building materials my children on earth send ahead to me. And of course, it will be a far greater place when I relocate it to the new earth. But already there is much to show you, Li Quan. More, in fact, than you will ever see!"

Quan gazed across the horizon, overwhelmed with hundreds of colors he'd never seen or, if he'd seen them, his eyes had been incapable of distinguishing their subtleties. He gasped at what he saw, so enthralled in it all he didn't hear himself gasp. He had never been so lost in something, so unaware of himself, so immersed in delight. The pure air of heaven filled his lungs. He saw horses and deer and dogs and cats and rabbits and squirrels and badgers and hedgehogs. Until now he'd never thought of animals celebrating or lost in joy, but that's exactly the impression he got when seeing them run and frolic and play with each other and with people. He saw trees that cast light instead of shadows. Some of them hung heavy with citrus fruits, picked and eaten freely by passersby.

Li Quan remembered his favorite fishing spot and climbing hill, and the flowers of the meadow where he and Ming had picnicked on their honeymoon. The best parts of that other world, he realized, had been but sneak previews of this one.

Compared to what he now beheld, the world he'd come from was a land of shadows, colorless and two-dimensional. This place was fresh and captivating, resonating with color and beauty. He could not only see and hear it, but feel and smell and taste it. Every hillside, every mountain, every waterfall, every frolicking animal in the fields seemed to beckon him to come join them, to come from the outside and plunge into the inside. This whole world had the feel of cool water on a blistering August afternoon. The light beckoned him to dive in with abandon, to come join the great adventure.

"I know what this is," Quan said.

"Tell me," said the Carpenter.

"It's the substance that casts all those shadows in the other world. The circles there are copies of the spheres here. The squares there are copies of the cubes here. The triangles there are copies of the pyramids here. Earth was a flatland. This is . . . well, the inside is bigger than the outside, isn't it? How many dimensions are there?"

"Far more than you have seen yet," the King said, laughing.

"This is the Place that defines and gives meaning to all places," Li Quan said. "I never imagined it would be like this."

"No more," the King said, "than an unborn child imagines the wonders that lie beyond the womb, the only world he has ever known." He grabbed Quan's hands with his. Quan felt roughness and the violence of the great scars.

He gazed at those hands. They were the hands of a Carpenter who cut wood and made things, including universes and angels and men. These same hands, Li Quan pondered, had once hauled heavy lumber up a long, lonely hill. These same hands and feet were once nailed to that lumber in the Shadowlands, in the most terrible moment from the dawn of time. Terrible and wonderful, for it was the Wound that healed all wounds. The hands and feet of the only innocent man became forever scarred so that guilty people would not have to bear the scars they deserved. He saw the pain in those hands. It was an ancient pain that was the doorway to eternal pleasures. Quan didn't know what to say. What response could be adequate?

"I did it for you," said the King. "And I would do it again. But I am grateful it is not necessary. It is finished. Paid in full. All that remains, before the great adventure begins, is to turn the fallen world right side up and make it the glorious place I have planned it to be."

Quan pointed to the Shadowlands. "Once here, no one could bear to go back to such a place."

"One would leave this place for that one only for a critical mission," the King said. "And only if there was no other way to accomplish it."

"I want to lose myself in you and in this world of yours, like one drop in the great river that becomes the vast waterfall."

"You will. All your life you have longed for a person and a place. I am that person. This is that place. You will lose yourself in me and it and, in so losing yourself, you will for the first time find yourself."

"I feel like I'm drinking from the Source of the Stream. Does this mean I will feel no more longing?"

"You will have the sweet longing of desire that can be fulfilled and shall be, again and again and again. Charis is not the absence of longing but its fulfillment. Heaven is not the absence of itches; it is the satisfying scratch for every itch. As for the accommodations, I think you'll agree this is better than any house you dreamed of in the other world!"

Quan laughed at this understatement, and the King laughed with him.

"When you longed for a great house in that world," the King said, "you were longing for my house. You just didn't know it. My children there never dream too big, you know. They dream too small. Like Ben Fielding once did, they set their sights far too low. They choose to play in the mud on a cold rainy day when I offer them open green meadows in the sun, clear flowing streams, majestic mountains, and endless beaches and blue skies that stretch to the stars themselves, stars that are gateways to innumerable worlds beyond. The sons of Adam try so hard to be satisfied with so little—which keeps them from ever being satisfied at all."

"Ben Fielding has changed, hasn't he?"

"Yes. I have changed him. Li Quan will have a front-row seat in seeing how far the changes go."

The new arrival was bursting with a thousand questions, and an unprecedented ability to articulate them. He felt if he started asking, he'd never stop.

The King smiled and raised his hand. "You have much to learn—and you will relish each moment of learning. You are inside—but you shall move farther and farther in, where your universe will expand farther and farther out. But this is yet to come. It is time for me now to wash you in warm water, dress you in your robe, and ready you for the celebration."

"Celebration?"

"I have scheduled a party in honor of my faithful servant, Li Quan."

Quan stared at him, stupefied.

"Oh, yes. I have invited thousands—everyone who touched your life and whose life you touched for eternity. Some you did not know; many you will have forgotten. But I never forget. Your mother and grand-mother insisted on arranging the meal. I knew enough not to argue with them!" He laughed, and the laughter was so palpable that it seemed to be a physical presence underneath Quan, lifting him up. "Do not tell them I let on to you, but they will be serving you fish. You will like the taste—the streams are clear and the fish are delicious!"

"Fish?"

"If you'd like, Li Quan, I will take you fishing. I have always been fond of carpenters and fishermen. And after you have rested and seen your new home, I have much for you to do. You will go to the great hall of literature. There is a book you started writing. I want you to finish it."

"A book?"

"Yes. But now you will not have to write it with soap. The book you started in the dark world survived the transition to this one. The rest of the story needs to be told, and many need to read it. You can interview the Boxer martyrs now. And there are an unlimited number of fascinating subjects for your future books. Now you can write it with clarity you caught only glimpses of in the Shadowlands. Now you see with bright discerning eyes invigorated by the pure air of Charis. Yes, I meant for you to write books, not in that world but this one. What you write here will bring insight and delight to you and all who read it. And it will bring pleasure to me. Besides, it will be of use when it comes time for you to teach your classes."

"Teach classes?"

"Charis is a place of learning and discovery, with minds hungry for ever-growing knowledge and insight. My creation cries out to be explored. You will always learn more about me and my world. I am inexhaustible, you know. Eventually you will teach others." He gazed at

378

Quan's dumbstruck expression. "Yes, it is true. In the University of Charis, I have made a faculty position just for Professor Li Quan!"

Ben stood in Zhou Jin's house, saying good-bye to the last guests. It had been a heartbreaking but triumphant funeral.

A woman in a faded black tunic and gray baggy pants rose to greet him. Her eyes were bright and vibrant, her hair shiny with black and silver in a bowl cut. Her warm smile reminded him of his mother. Her face seemed to shine, her eyes ablaze. Where . . . ? Of course—he had seen her his first Sunday in church, in the front corner of the room.

"This is Sun Fen," Ming said to Ben.

"Your name is familiar," Ben said to the woman.

"Did they tell you what Yesu did for Sun Fen?"

"I don't recall exactly."

"I was blind, and Yesu made me see."

"*You* were the blind woman?"

"Yes. He did a great miracle."

"You were really blind? You're sure?" As soon as he said it, he realized how silly it sounded.

"Yes. When you are blind for thirty-six years, you are very sure about it." She smiled and looked at Ming, whose little hand stifled a giggle, then back at Ben.

"But the greater miracle is that my heart was blind and now can see. I rejoice not just that I can see but that he has written my name in heaven. For there my bridegroom says I will see his face. The man who was to marry me decided not to when I became blind. I have never married. But I have a husband."

Fen looked at Ming again, and they giggled together.

"The One whose embrace I long to feel, whose face I long to see." And there it was again. The woman's face was shining.

After the last guest left, Ben walked outside with Minghua.

"My flight goes out in the morning. I need to pack and get a few hours' sleep before the drive to Shanghai."

"Will you come back to us, Ben Fielding?"

"I'm sure I will."

"For business?"

"Probably. But I'd like to come see you and Shen."

"Perhaps bring wife or daughters?"

"We'll see. I hope so. I've even thought of . . . walking with Wang Shaoming to the mountain villages."

Ming smiled. "That would be high calling." She gazed up at him. "Very kind of Ben Fielding to take care of his friend's wife and son."

"It's you who've taken care of me." Ben looked her in the eyes, searching for words. "Keep holding up the sky, Minghua."

"There is only One who holds up the sky. And he has not yet let it fall." She stood on tiptoe and kissed Ben on the cheek.

"Thank you, Ben Fielding, for giving me jade. Please give warm embrace to Pam Fielding, Kim, and Melissa from Chan Minghua, wife of Li Quan."

Quan and Jadorel walked side by side from the welcoming celebration, an event so wondrous Quan couldn't wait to reflect on every detail later. He rejoiced that he could, for, amazingly, there wasn't a single face or name or detail he'd forgotten. It was as if his brain's hard drive had multiplied a hundred times and he could retrieve whatever data he wanted to.

"I must say farewell," Jadorel said to Quan.

"What? You just returned from duty."

"Your work in the Shadowlands is done. Mine is not."

"Another assignment so soon?"

"Yes. A young man needs me now."

"Who?"

"His name is Li Shen."

"Shen? You're going to Shen?"

"I will serve him faithfully as I served his father Quan, his grandfather Tong, his great-grandfather Wen, and his great-great-grandfather Manchu."

"You were their guardians as well?"

"Yes."

"But doesn't Shen already have a guardian?"

"Perhaps he is special. Perhaps that is why the King believes he needs another."

"I . . . do not know how to thank you."

"Your faithfulness to Elyon is my thanks. It is when the children of dust do not serve him that the guardian's task is thankless."

He raised his sword in the air, cried out something in a language Quan could not understand, and disappeared. A few moments later, looking through the portal, Li Quan saw Jadorel appear beside Li Shen. The boy sat by himself in the corner, his father's Bible open in front of him. He was neatly copying into a notebook the book of Revelation. Quan could clearly see what he wrote:

> For the accuser of our brothers, who accuses them before our God day and night, has been hurled down. They overcame him by the blood of the Lamb and by the word of their testimony; they did not love their lives so much as to shrink from death. Therefore rejoice, you heavens and you who dwell in them! But woe to the earth and the sea, because the devil has gone down to you! He is filled with fury, because he knows that his time is short.

Quan felt Li Tong's hand on his shoulder. "We will watch him, just as we watched you. And we will pray the King will be glorified in the life of another Li. Ours is a proud heritage, my son. We are not worthy. But King Yesu is."

Li Quan noticed something ten feet away from Shen. He caught his breath, for he'd not seen it until now. There was someone else watching Shen, someone sitting in an old wooden chair. Someone with scarred hands. He who alone could be in two worlds at once.

Li Tong guided Quan away from the portal. "The martyrs assemble whenever a new one comes home. The welcoming has been arranged. You will meet men and women and children from many nations. It is the greatest of honors."

Quan looked again at Li Shen, who walked now to another ginkgo tree, flashlight in his hand, Jadorel beside him. Shen broke a little limb from the tree and drew in the sand, shining his light on the image.

"He draws the fish," said Li Quan.

"Perhaps he will be the one," said his father. "We have always wondered."

"Which one do you mean?"

"The last martyr. The one whose death will mark the King's invasion of the dark world. The one whose exodus from the Shadowlands will at last usher in the eternal kingdom of light."

53

So that's my story," Ben said to Doug, who stared at him from the couch in his living room, still stunned Ben had dropped by to see him, and even more by what he had to say.

"Wow."

"That's all you can say?"

"That pretty much covers it," Doug said. "Wow."

"When you spoke up like you did, it made me feel guilty for turning away from Christ. I resented you. Please forgive me."

"God forgave me, Ben, and what I've done to him is far worse than anything you've done to me. Who would I be to withhold forgiveness?"

"Well, that was the first reason for coming to see you. The second is, I want to rehire you."

"You're kidding."

"With full back pay for the time you were away—about four months, I guess, because I've been gone nearly that whole time."

"Is this a joke?"

"Do I look like I'm joking?"

"Mr. Getz approves?"

"He gave me full discretion. We were wrong. No. *I* was wrong. I was serving myself when I should have been serving God. An old friend reminded me of that."

"Well, I've been working part-time, haven't found the right place yet," Doug said. "I'll give it serious thought. Meanwhile, I want to invite you to church. Pam's always there, you know. Kim, too. I haven't seen Melissa for a while. But anyway, why don't you come with me Sunday?"

———————————

Li Quan's fathers, all three of them, introduced him to brothers and sisters from Indonesia, Libya, Vietnam, and Iran.

"I am Mehdi Dibaj. Welcome."

A man with deep black skin and a huge grin greeted him. "Benjamini Youhanna. Once ambassador to Sudan, now on home assignment!"

Three light-skinned males approached him. "I am Graham Staines. These are my sons, Philip and Timothy. Your father told us all about you."

Another stepped forward. "I am Juan Coy. Once of Colombia. Now of Charis!"

Quan wanted to talk at length with each martyr he met, but Li Tong eagerly grabbed his arm. "Now is a time to meet many whom you can seek out later. I wish to introduce you to five who have become my good friends—they arrived in Charis not long before I did."

Quan looked at the five men, one of whom reminded him of Ben. "These are my brothers," said Li Tong. "Nate, Pete, Ed, Roger, and Jim."

"We are honored to meet Li Quan," said one of them. "You have given what you could not keep to gain what you cannot lose. And what you have gained is immeasurable." The men embraced Quan, shared stories, and laughed together.

It was now Li Manchu who took Quan's arm and spun him around the other direction. "This is a special guest invited to join the fellowship of martyrs on this occasion. He is the man who did surgery upon my eyes when I was a small child. It was he who led me to Yesu when I was a child."

"Hudson Taylor?" Quan asked.

"Yes," the man said. "No relation to Elizabeth." He smiled, then looked at Quan earnestly. "I have watched you, interceded for you. It is a great privilege to meet Li Quan face-to-face."

Li Quan was speechless. Then he felt a hand on his shoulder again. It was Li Tong, standing next to a little man with a bright face. "This is my only son, Li Quan. And this, Quan, is the first of our kind. Our brother Stephen."

———————————

"You rehired Doug?" Martin said. "Fine. I don't care, Ben. What I do care about is doing business in China."

"I'm not suggesting we stop doing business. Not at all. I'm just suggesting we use our presence there, use the relationships we've developed and make clear we're not going to look the other way on human rights issues. We can tell them we want to be present at employee interviews ourselves. I've got a plan to make sure there aren't political and religious prisoners in any factory we own or have contracts with."

"Tread carefully, Ben. You're on the bubble. The time you spent in China hurt you. I'm not sure you'll ever recover. You've lost a lot of credibility. You were in the driver's seat, writing your own ticket—you could have run the whole show in three years. But now the board's asking a lot of questions. Travis and others are just waiting for the other shoe to drop. Jeffrey's in Shanghai cleaning up your mess with Won Chi and smoothing things over with the authorities. Some on the board think Jeffrey's the smart choice for CEO; they say I should be grooming him, that we can't count on you like we used to. We have to think of the company. We have to know who we can trust to act in the best interests of Getz International."

"I think doing the right thing is ultimately in everybody's best interests."

"An interesting theory. But who decides what's right and wrong? Look, Ben, I'm still sick about what happened to your friend. But you've got to move on, leave it behind. If you don't, you're kissing CEO good-bye."

Ben sighed. "Maybe some things are more important than my being CEO."

Martin looked at him as if he couldn't believe what he was hearing. "Is this one of those body-snatcher deals? What have you done with the real Ben Fielding?"

Ben laughed. "I guess hearing myself say it, I'm as surprised as you are. But I mean it."

"I hate to have to say it, Ben, but we're all watching you."

"You're not my only audience," Ben said. "God is watching me. And he sees everything, including a lot that you don't."

"Yeah? Well, we're the ones who pay your salary."

"Real gold fears no fire," Ben said.

"What?"

"Something Li Quan used to say."

Ben walked out of Martin's office and into his own. He took the high-backed chair from behind his desk and wheeled it over by the visitors' couch. He went to storage and found an old chair, a smaller one, then moved it behind his desk.

He went back to the couch, staring at the high-backed chair he'd sat in the last five years. He got on his knees and spoke to the empty chair's occupant.

"King Elyon has taken hold of him," said Li Tong.

"Yes," said Li Quan. "Yes."

"Perhaps one day he will do more for Yesu than any of us," said Li Wen.

"Let us hope so," said Li Manchu.

Quan sensed another presence behind him. He felt the unmistakable hand, the strong soothing grip, upon his neck.

"I have great plans for Ben Fielding. Watch and witness."

When they stood to sing, Ben thought he heard a gasp behind him. He looked back one row, across the aisle. His eyes met Kim's. Then he saw Pam next to her. While Kim's face was morphing from shock to delight, Pam's was still frozen in shock.

Pretty soon Kim was giggling; then Pam got sucked in too. Ben noticed the smiles of several others around them at the outburst, as well as the cold stares of one disapproving woman.

The song ended, and the pastor stood up to preach. "My message title is 'Worshiping a God Who Doesn't Do What We Want Him To.' Please turn in your Bibles to the book of Habakkuk."

Ben looked down at Quan's English Bible. Ming and Shen didn't read English well enough to get much from it, and she'd insisted he take it. He did, on the condition that he would figure out how to get her as many Mandarin Bibles as he could.

"What did he call that book?" Ben whispered to Doug.

"Habakkuk. Here, let me help you." Doug flipped the pages for him.

"I know right where to find the book of John," Ben whispered back.

As soon as the service was over, Kim wove through the crowd to her father. She threw her arms around him. "Daddy! How long have you been back?"

"Just a few days."

"I'm glad you came to church."

"Me too, Kimmy. Me too."

Pam walked up cautiously, joining them. They chitchatted a few minutes; then Ben said to Pam and Kim, "Can I take you to lunch?"

Pam said, "Well, Sandy's expecting me over at her place and—"

"Of course she'll have lunch with you, Daddy. I'll call Sandy and explain. I'm meeting Melissa at Taco Bell. Later!" Kim turned back around, all smiles, and said to Ben, "I'll take you up on lunch myself, later. Or how about Tuesday dinner?"

"Uh, sure. Tuesday evening's great."

"Don't you have to check your schedule?" Pam whispered.

"No." He said to Kim, "I'll call you and let you know when I'll pick you up Tuesday." She waved energetically and disappeared into the crowd.

Ben and Pam went to her car and stood by it, talking for a half hour. "I want to meet this Ming," Pam said.

"You'd love her. And she'd love you."

"Oh?"

"Yeah. You're both . . . well, you're a lot alike."

"Thank you."

"In fact, she asked me to give you a hug from her."

"Well, what are you waiting for?"

He put his arms around her awkwardly, but when he felt her embrace, he squeezed her and didn't want the hug to end. He forced himself to step back.

"What happened to you over there, Ben?"

"I saw things. For the first time. Things I can't explain. Things a lot bigger than me."

"Bigger than *you?* Wow."

"Okay, okay." He laughed. "I've changed, Pam. I've become a follower of Jesus. Really."

"What does that mean to you, to be his follower?"

"I've been asking myself, if Quan was willing to die for Christ, am I willing to risk people disapproving of me at work? Willing to risk my job? My popularity? Maybe someday my freedom? Or even my life?"

"Heavy questions."

"Yeah. But the right answers are getting clearer all the time."

Neither spoke for ten seconds, until Pam broke the silence. "I'm hungry. How about we go get Chinese?"

Li Quan had enjoyed every moment in this place. He'd found the unknown beauty that had always called to him. He'd wanted to get behind the beauty, to get underneath it and nestle in it as a blanket. He'd wanted to become part of the beauty and the joy, inseparable from it. He didn't want to stand outside and look in at it. He wanted to be inside. Now, at last, he was.

The fire of Joy that had broken out on the wet logs of the Shadowlands now roared wildly in the dry tinder of Charis. Its flames rose to unrestrained heights, and just when he thought they could go no higher there came the next discovery, the next person to meet, the newest delight that poured fuel on that raging fire of Joy.

The thing Quan couldn't believe was that everyone kept assuring him this was just heaven's lobby, the waiting room, and what was still to come was the main venue, the real place. Once they had resurrection bodies and dwelt on the new earth, Li Tong kept insisting, everything would be far better. But how could anything be better than what already exceeded the best he'd ever imagined?

He saw something in the distance. "What is that great building beyond the Hall of Martyrs?" Quan asked.

"It is the Hall of Justice," his father said. "Solomon built his hall of justice, but he did not know it was only a small-scaled model of this, the real one."

"What will happen there?"

"The King will judge the nations. His justice will awaken. And it will not sleep until all good is rewarded and all evil is destroyed."

"How long will it be until then?" Li Quan asked.

Li Tong looked at the King sitting on his throne. "His sword is still in its sheath, but even now his thumb is stroking the edge of its hilt."

"Yeah, hi. This is Ben Fielding from Getz International. I've taught some business classes there at the university. . . . Right. Anyway, I just returned from four months in China. I do a lot of business there. And I know the language pretty well. I know you've got a lot of Chinese students. . . . That many? Wow. Anyway, I'm sure a lot of them get over here, and they're pretty disoriented—culture shock and all. I just wanted to volunteer to show some of them around. Maybe offer them some help adjusting. Does that make sense? . . . No kidding? Yeah, that sounds great. I'll be there."

Ben put down the phone, smiling. He looked at the message from his secretary, Jen, and dialed the number.

"Chew Gan? Yes, this is Ben Fielding at Getz International. Ni hao. Very good, xiexie. Did you know I was in China four months? . . . Yeah, just got back. It was an amazing trip. Listen, how long will you be in Portland? Are you free for lunch Thursday? I thought maybe we could talk. I have a book I'd like to give you too. I'll explain. You know Couch Street Fish House over on Third Avenue, where we met last summer? . . . Right. That's it. 11:45? Excellent. See you Thursday."

"And now, I have a promise to fulfill," his father said to Quan.

"What promise?"

"Li Tong once promised Li Quan he would take him to the Great Wall. I referred to what we called the Great Wall—though it is not so great, for soon it will no longer have one stone upon another. Where I take you now is the Wall of Remembrance and Honor, which the King says he will relocate from here to the new earth. This wall is dedicated to the martyrs. The name of every martyr of every place and time is upon it. Everyone you met at the gathering has their name engraved upon it. The King inscribes every name himself, using the point of a nail. The first name is Stephen's. My name is on it. So is Li Manchu's and Li Wen's. So is yours. Perhaps one day Li Shen's will be. Only Yesu knows."

After walking and talking a long while, they came to the structure.

"It is magnificent," Quan said. "I have never seen such stone, such craftsmanship." It towered above them, curving outward so that names were above them as well as in front. His father put his arm around Quan, and they began to view name after name on the wall. When Li Tong would touch a name, they would immediately see the person as he or she lived upon the earth and served Yesu. Quan and his father walked a great distance, weaving in and out of beautifully curved portions of the wall that served as a walkway through history. Quan was amazed at how many names were on the wall, some of them living in places he'd never heard of. For a student of history, this was . . . well, heaven.

"No story is forgotten here," said Li Tong. "Yesu has made this living memorial. By his decree, the stories of faithfulness on earth will forever be recounted around the fires and dinner tables of Charis. We have seen today only a fraction of the great stories. We will come back as often as you like."

"I would like that, honorable father. Very much."

Li Tong pointed to a freshly engraved name: Li Quan.

"My name upon the Wall of Remembrance and Honor," whispered Li Quan, voice trembling. "The Wall of the Martyrs."

"Yes," said Li Tong, "but here we call it by the name Yesu has given it. He calls it 'The Great Wall.'"

Epilogue

"HOW LONG, O Lord?" the voices of millions cried out.

"Because of the oppression of the weak and the groaning of the needy, I will now arise," said the King. "I will rescue them."

The King stood in front of his throne. His eyes—and all those across the heavens—were fixed now on a young locksmith from Pushan, who languished in prison, dying of tuberculosis, coughing up blood. As Li Shen's life faded, the King gripped the hilt of the sword, then unsheathed it. He lifted it up, stretching out his arm. He whistled to a white stallion, a creature unlike any other. It flew to him, dancing and snorting, rising up on its back legs, eager to run to battle. The King, shining with the brilliance of a thousand quasars, mounted his great steed.

All heaven watched the young man breathe his last at the feet of his tormentors. At that moment the Warrior-King, eyes wet and white-hot, cried out with a voice that shook heaven and earth: *"No longer!"*

Michael threw his arm forward, the hosts of heaven shouted, and millions of horses gathered, mounted by warriors of every tribe, nation, and tongue. Eternity's door swung open on its hinges. Out of one realm and into another rode an army like there had never been.

"The time has come," roared the King. "Rescue my people! Destroy my enemies!" The Morning Star, who had once come as Lamb, now returned as Lion, with ten thousand galaxies forming the train of his imperial robe.

A mighty army appeared from the distant reaches of the cosmos, progressing across billions of stars and planets. Vast hordes of warriors moved past Orion's nebula in an explosion of colors. The army advanced toward earth in rumbling cadence. Without saddle or bridle, they rode great white Thoroughbreds, proud stallions that seemed to know their mission as well as they knew their riders. Some of the mounts pulled chariots of fire, streaking like meteors across the sky.

A legion of angels gathered in formation in back of and to the sides of the Commander. Not far behind him were twelve men and, following them, a great company of martyrs, warriors whose hands moved to the hilts of their swords, the fire of righteousness in their eyes exploding into infernos.

Among them rode a man of brilliance and burning intensity, mounted tall and proud upon a great horse. The warrior's name was Li Quan. Four more men named Li kept pace, two on each side of him, including one who had joined them but moments before. The newcomer, riding wide-eyed and trying to assimilate what had happened to him, began to understand that he had been transported from a filthy jail in Pushan to the back of a great stallion beside his dead father, who in fact was more alive than he'd ever known him.

Streams of red-hot molten rock spewed from mountains across the broken planet. A bright red river of heat and light burned through trees and stone, consuming all in its path. Earthquakes and tidal waves and floods assaulted the cities. A tormented earth exacted revenge on the fallen stewards who had caused its ruin. The world heaved and moaned in destruction—or was it rebirth?

"Deliver us!" cried scattered bands of fugitives, strangers, and pilgrims—those whose home had never been on earth, those of whom the world was not worthy.

On the dark planet, kingdoms of men dissolved into ruin. Like a scythe clearing a path, earthquakes brought down rows of skyscrapers. Stock exchanges crumbled. Businesses burned. All whose hope and refuge was earth . . . in an instant became homeless.

Then I saw heaven opened, and a white horse was standing there. And the one sitting on the horse was named Faithful and True. For he judges fairly and then goes to war. His eyes were bright like flames of fire, and on his head were many crowns. A name was written on him, and only he knew what it meant. He was clothed with a robe dipped in blood, and his title was the Word of God. The armies of heaven, dressed in pure white linen, followed him on white horses. From his mouth came a sharp sword, and with it he struck down the nations. He ruled them with an iron rod, and he trod the winepress of the fierce wrath of almighty God. On his robe and thigh was written this title: King of kings and Lord of lords.

The sun became as dark as black cloth, and the moon became as red as blood. Then the stars of the sky fell to the earth like green figs falling from trees shaken by mighty winds. And the sky was rolled up like a scroll and taken away. And all of the mountains and all of the islands disappeared. Then the kings of the earth, the rulers, the generals, the wealthy people, the people with great power, and every slave and every free person—all hid themselves in the caves and among the rocks of the mountains. And they cried to the mountains and the rocks, "Fall on us and hide us from the face of the one who sits on the throne and from the wrath of the Lamb."

Michael pointed to the earth, to the god Mammon and his consort, Babylon, and cried out, "Her sins are piled as high as heaven, and God is ready to judge her for her evil deeds. Do to her as she has done to your people. Give her a double penalty for all her evil deeds. She brewed a cup of terror for others, so give her twice as much as she gave out. She has lived in luxury and pleasure, so match it now with torments and sorrows. She boasts, 'I am queen on my throne. I am no helpless widow. I will not experience sorrow.' Therefore, the sorrows of death and mourning and famine will overtake her in a single day. She will be utterly consumed by fire, for the Lord God who judges her is mighty."

The rulers of the world who took part in her immoral acts and enjoyed her great luxury mourned for her as they saw the smoke rising from her charred remains. They stood at a distance, terrified by her great torment. They cried out, "How terrible, how terrible for Babylon, that great city! In a single moment God's judgment came upon her."

They wept and mourned over the destruction . . . for they had become inseparable from the gods they worshiped.

Now but a hundred feet above scorched earth, Reader, riding a great horse behind Michael, cried out, "In your cities was found the blood of prophets and of the saints, the young and the old, the tiny and the grown. Elyon has beheld the blood of all who have been murdered on the earth." He turned to the multitude of riders behind him and said, "But you, O heaven, rejoice over her fate. And you also rejoice, O holy people of God and apostles and prophets! For at last God has judged her on your behalf."

Even as Reader spoke, a great beast mobilized the kings of the earth, and their armies gathered together to make war against the Rider and his army. All eyes that could bear to look fixed upon the Man on the great white steed, the Man with the face of the lion, eyebrows singed by the awful heat of his anger. But their eyes could not stay upon him, for he caused their hearts to melt like ice under the noonday sun.

The battle cry of a hundred million warriors erupted from one end of the heavens to the other. There was war on that narrow isthmus between heaven and hell, a planet called Earth. The air was filled with the din of combat—the wails of oppressors being slain and the joyous celebrations of the oppressed, rejoicing that at long last their liberators had arrived.

Some of the warriors sang as they slew, swinging swords to hew the oppressors with one arm and, with the other, pulling victims up onto their horses.

The long arm of the King moved with swiftness and power. The hope of reward that kept the sufferers sane was vindicated at last. No child of heaven was touched by the sword this day, for the universe could not tolerate the shedding of one more drop of righteous blood.

Heaven released fury. Earth bled fear. It was the old world's last night.

At the Lion's nod, Michael raised his mighty sword and brought it down upon the great dragon. His muscles bulging at the strain, Michael picked up his evil twin and cast the writhing beast into a great pit. The mauler of men, the hunter of women, the predator of children, the persecutor of the righteous shrieked in terror. The vast army of heaven's warriors cheered.

The battalions of Charis gazed upon the decimated face of the earth, the scorched soil of the old world. Nothing had survived the fires of this holocaust of things. Nothing but the King's Word, his people, and the deeds of gold and silver and precious stones they had done for him during the long night since Eden's twilight.

Soldiers dropped their weapons, the crippled tossed their crutches and ran, the blind opened their eyes and saw. They pointed and shouted and danced, throwing their arms around each other, for each knew that any now left on earth were under the King's blood and could be fully trusted. The King gathered children upon his lap. He wiped away their tears.

Then spoke the powerful voice of Reader, "Praise our God, all you his servants, you who fear him, both small and great!"

The sound of a great multitude, like the roar of rushing waters and loud peals of thunder, shouted, "Hallelujah! For our Lord God Almighty reigns. Let us rejoice and be glad and give him glory! For the wedding of the Lamb has come, and his bride has made herself ready. She wears the fine linen, bright and clean, of the righteous acts of the saints, empowered by the King."

Michael wiped blood from his sword and carefully placed it back in its scabbard. He called to Writer in a thunderous voice, heard above the rejoicing multitudes, "Write it down—blessed are those who are invited to the wedding supper of the Lamb!"

All eyes turned to the King. The entire universe fell silent, anticipating his words.

"I will turn the wasteland into a garden," the King announced. "I will bring here the home I have made for you, my bride. There will be a new world, a life-filled blue-green world, greater than all that has ever been. The Shadowlands are mine again, and I shall transform them. My kingdom has come. My will shall be done. Winter is over. Spring is here at last!"

A great roar rose from the vast crowd. The King raised his hands. Upon seeing those scars, the cheering crowds remembered the unthinkable cost of this great celebration.

Warriors slapped each other on the back. The delivered hugged their deliverers, enjoying a great reunion with those once parted from them. In the milling crowd two men came face-to-face. Their eyes locked on each other. Li Quan and Ben Fielding embraced.

The multitudes innumerable began to sing the song for which they had been made, a song that echoed off a trillion planets and reverberated in a quadrillion places in every nook and cranny of the creation's expanse. Audience and orchestra and choir all blended into one great symphony, one grand cantata of rhapsodic melodies and powerful sustaining harmonies. All were participants. Only one was an audience, the Audience of One. The smile of the King's approval swept through the choir like fire across dry wheat fields.

When the song was complete, the Audience of One stood and raised his great arms, then clapped his scarred hands together in thunderous applause, shaking ground and sky, jarring every corner of the cosmos. His applause went on and on, unstopping and unstoppable.

Among the great throngs of worshipers of Yesu, standing side by side, were the families of Li Quan and Ben Fielding, women and children seeing each other for the first time, but not the last.

Every one of them realized something with undiminished clarity in that instant. They wondered why they had not seen it all along. What they knew in that moment, in every fiber of their beings, was that this Person and this Place were all they had ever longed for . . . and ever would.

$\mathcal{N}$ote to $\mathcal{R}$eaders

$\mathcal{T}$HE AUTHOR and inside-cover artist have designated all royalties from this book to the persecuted church. Funds will bring relief, aid, and encouragement to the families of martyrs and suffering Christians. They also will extend Christ's love by spreading the gospel and providing Bibles to countries where Christians are persecuted.

Randy Alcorn, Ron DiCianni, and Tyndale House Publishers encourage readers to learn more about the persecuted church around the world. We can minister to our brothers and sisters in Christ through our prayers, financial support, and other tangible ways. For up-to-date information, including a list of worthy organizations serving the persecuted church, see www.epm.org/safelyhome. This site will link you to various ministries and current prayer requests for suffering believers, as well as the National Day of Prayer for the persecuted church. It also features many Scriptures on persecution and martyrdom.

If you don't have Internet access but desire this information, we'll be glad to send you a copy if you call or write Eternal Perspective Ministries, 2229 East Burnside #23, Gresham, OR 97030; ralcorn@epm.org; (503) 663-6481.

And the King will tell them, "I assure you, when you did it to one of the least of these my brothers and sisters, you were doing it to me!" (Matthew 25:40, NLT)

Note from the Artist

$\mathcal{W}$HEN RANDY and I set out to make a statement concerning the persecuted church, I had no idea this would emerge. What started as an attempt to educate, challenge, and motivate those who knew little about the plight of the persecuted has turned into a literary masterpiece that cannot—and by God's grace, will not—go ignored.

This is an important book, because the Word of God commands us to "remember those in prison . . . and those who are mistreated as if you yourselves were suffering."

What Randy has written is fiction, but not fantasy. From my work with Voice of the Martyrs, for whom *Safely Home* was painted, I heard first-hand of those who suffer. I knew Richard Wurmbrand, who spent fourteen years in a Romanian prison. I know Tom White, who spent two years in a Cuban prison, until Mother Teresa asked Fidel Castro for his release. I have heard people tell of their loved ones being tortured for their faith. Their response: it's the cost of discipleship! I don't pretend to understand how they can adopt that perspective, but it is not important that I understand. It's more important that I support them through it.

When Christ returns, I want to be able to look him in the eye and know that I had a hand in doing whatever I could to stand with his persecuted servants, wherever they are. May this novel be used powerfully toward that end.

Ron DiCianni

About the Author

$\mathcal{R}$ANDY ALCORN is the founder and director of Eternal Perspective Ministries (EPM), a nonprofit organization devoted to encouraging an eternal viewpoint and to drawing attention to people in special need of advocacy and help, including the poor, the persecuted, and the unborn.

A pastor for fourteen years before founding EPM, Randy is a popular teacher and conference speaker. He has spoken in many countries and has been interviewed on more than 350 radio and television programs. He has taught part-time on the faculties of Western Seminary and Multnomah Bible College. Randy lives in Gresham, Oregon, with his wife, Nanci. They have two grown daughters, Karina and Angela.

Randy produces the free quarterly issues-oriented magazine *Eternal Perspectives*. He's the author of thirteen other books, including *In Light of Eternity: Perspectives on Heaven; Money, Possessions, and Eternity; ProLife Answers to ProChoice Arguments; Sexual Temptation; Restoring Sexual Sanity; Is Rescuing Right?; Does the Birth Control Pill Cause Abortions?; Women Under Stress,* coauthored with his wife, Nanci; and *The Ishbane Conspiracy,* coauthored with his daughters, Angela and Karina. His four best-selling novels are *Deadline, Dominion, Edge of Eternity,* and *Lord Foulgrin's Letters.*

Randy's life emphasis is on (1) communicating the strategic importance of using our earthly time, money, possessions, and opportunities to invest in need-meeting ministries that will count for eternity; and (2) analyzing, teaching, and applying the moral, social, and relational implications of Christian truth in the current age.

Feedback on books and inquiries regarding publications and other matters can be directed to Eternal Perspective Ministries (EPM), 2229 East Burnside #23, Gresham, OR 97030; (503) 663-6481. EPM can also be reached at ralcorn@epm.org. For information on EPM or Randy Alcorn, and for resources on missions, persecuted church, pro-life issues, and matters of eternal perspective, see www.epm.org.